What people are saying about the
How to Ruin... books by Simone Elkeles

"Fresh, fun and fabulous! Guaranteed NOT
to ruin your summer vacation!"
—Mari Mancusi, author of *Boys that Bite*

"I highly recommend *How to Ruin a Summer Vacation*.
It reads easily, as if watching a good coming-of-age movie."
—*JVibe* magazine

"A fun read that also digs deeper into complex emotions."
— *Kliatt*

"Amy's thoughtfulness and depth raise this book above
most of the chick-lit genre."
—*VOYA*

"... the choice for teens who seek realistic YA fiction ..."
—*School Library Journal*

Ruined

SIMONE ELKELES

Ruined

Includes:

How to Ruin a Summer Vacation

How to Ruin My Teenage Life

How to Ruin Your Boyfriend's Reputation

flux™
Woodbury, Minnesota

First Edition
First Printing, 2010

Cover design by Lisa Novak
Cover photo © iStockphoto.com/Lóránd Gelner

Flux, an imprint of Llewellyn Worldwide Ltd.

How to Ruin a Summer Vacation
ISBN 978-0-7387-0961-1
Text copyright © 2006 by Simone Elkeles

How to Ruin My Teenage Life
ISBN 978-0-7387-1019-8
Text copyright © 2007 by Simone Elkeles

How to Ruin Your Boyfriend's Reputation
ISBN 978-0-7387-1879-8
Text copyright © 2009 by Simone Elkeles

How to Ruin a Summer Vacation was originally published by Flux in 2006.
How to Ruin My Teenage Life was originally published by Flux in 2007.
How to Ruin Your Boyfriend's Reputation was originally published by Flux in 2009.

ISBN 978-0-7387-2733-2

Flux
Llewellyn Worldwide Ltd.
2143 Wooddale Drive
Woodbury, MN 55125-2989
www.fluxnow.com

Printed in the United States of America

How to Ruin

a

Summer Vacation

1

---

*In a matter of seconds parents can
change the course of your life.*

How does a relatively smart sixteen-year-old girl get stuck
in a sucky situation she can't get out of? Well, as I sit at
Chicago's O'Hare International Airport on a Monday afternoon during the one hour and forty-five minute delay, I
think about the past twenty-four hours of my now messed-
up life.

I was sitting in my room yesterday when my biological
father, Ron, called. No, you don't get it . . . Ron *never* calls.
Well, unless it's my birthday, and that was eight months
ago.

You see, after their affair in college, my mom found
out she was pregnant. She comes from money, and Ron
. . . well, he doesn't. Mom, with her parents pushing her

along, told Ron it would be best if he didn't have a big part in our lives. Boy, were they wrong. But the worst part is he gave up without even trying.

I know he puts money into an account for me. He also comes by to take me out to dinner for my birthdays. But so what? I want a father who'll always be there for me.

He used to come around more, but I finally told him to leave me alone so my mom could find me a real dad. I didn't really mean it; I guess I was just trying to test him. He failed miserably.

Well, the guy phones this time and tells my mom he wants to take me to Israel. *Israel!* You know, that little country in the Middle East that causes so much controversy. You don't have to TiVo the news to know Israel is a hotbed of international hostility.

I know I'm off on a tangent, so let's get back to what happened. My mom hands me the phone without so much as an "it's your dad" or "it's the guy who I had a one-night stand with, but never married" to warn me it was *him*.

I still remember what he said. "Hi, Amy. It's Ron."

"Who?" I answer.

I'm not trying to be a smartass, it just doesn't register that the guy who gave me fifty percent of my genes is actually calling me.

"Ron . . . Ron Barak," he says a bit louder and slower as if I'm a complete imbecile.

I freeze and end up saying nothing. Believe it or not, sometimes saying nothing actually works in my favor. I've learned this from years of practice. It makes people nervous and, well, better them than me. I huff loudly to let him know I'm still on the line.

"Amy?"

"Yeah?"

"Um, I just wanted you to know *dat* your *grandmudder* is sick," he says in his Israeli accent.

A faceless image of a small white-haired old lady who smells like baby powder and mildew, and whose life's goal is baking chocolate chip cookies, briefly races across my mind.

"I didn't know I had a grandmother," I say, emphasizing the 'th' because Ron, like every other Israeli I've ever met, can't say the 'th'—that sound is not in their language.

My mom's mom died shortly after I was born so I was one of those kids without a grandma. A pang of sorrow and self-pity from never knowing I had a grandma and now knowing she's 'sick' makes me feel yucky. But I shove those feelings into the back of my head where they're safe.

Ron clears his throat. "She lives in Israel and, uh, I'm going for the summer. I'd like to take you with me."

Israel?

"I'm not Jewish," I blurt out.

A little sound, like one of pain, escapes from his mouth before he says, "You don't have to be Jewish to go to Israel, Amy."

And you don't have to be a rocket scientist to know Israel is smack dab in the middle of a war zone. *A war zone!*

"Thanks for the offer, but I'm going to tennis camp this summer. Tell *Grandma* I hope she gets over her illness. Bye," I say and hang up.

Wouldn't you know it, not more than four seconds go by before the phone rings again. I know it's Ron. A little ironic he's hardly called twice in a year and here he is calling twice in a matter of seconds.

My mom picks up the phone in the living room. I try to listen through my bedroom door. I can't hear much. Just mumble, mumble, mumble. After about forty long minutes she comes knocking at my door and tells me to pack for Israel.

"You're kidding, right?"

"Amy, you can't avoid him forever. It's not fair."

Not fair? I cross my arms in front of my chest. "Excuse me, what's not fair is that you two didn't even *try* and live like parents. Don't talk to me about fairness."

I know I'm sixteen and should be over it by now, but I'm not. I never said I was perfect.

"Life isn't simple, you'll realize that when you're older," she says. "We've all made mistakes in the past, but it's time to mend them. You're going. It's already settled."

Panic starts to set in and I decide to take the guilt trip route.

"I'll be killed. Unless that's what you ultimately want—"

"Amy, stop the dramatics. He's promised me he'll keep you safe. It'll be a great experience."

I try for another two hours to get out of it, I really do. I should have known trying to argue with my mom would get me nothing except a sore throat.

I decide to call my best friend, Jessica. Supportive, understanding Jessica. "Hey, Amy, what's up?" a cheery voice answers on the other end of the line. Gotta love caller ID.

"My parents decided to ruin my life," I tell her.

"What do you mean 'parents'? Ron called?"

"Oh, yeah, he called. And somehow he convinced my mom to cancel my summer plans so he could take me to Israel. Could you just die?"

"Um, you don't really want to hear my opinion, Amy. Trust me."

My eyebrows furrow as I slowly realize Jessica, my very dearest friend in the world, isn't going to back me up one hundred and ten percent.

"It's a *war zone!*" I say it slowly so she gets the full impact.

Is that a laugh I hear on the other end of the line?

"Are you kidding?" Jessica says. "Heck, my mom goes to Tel Aviv every year to go shopping. She says they have the clearest diamonds ever cut. You know the little black dress I *love?* She got it for me there. They have the *best* European styles and—"

"I need support here, Jess, not some crap about diamonds and clothes," I say, cutting off her 'Israel is all that' speech. Jeez!

"Sorry. You're right," she says.

"Don't you ever watch the news?"

"Sure, Israel has its share of problems. But my parents say a lot of what we see on TV is propaganda. Just don't hang out at bus stops or go to coffee shops. Ron will keep you safe."

"Ha," I say.

"Are you mad at me?" Jess asks. "I could lie and tell you your life is ruined beyond repair. Would that make you feel better?"

Jessica is the only person who can make fun of me and get away with it. "You're just a laugh a minute, Jess. You know I'd never get mad at you, you're my BFF."

Although what does it say about our friendship when my BFF has no problems sending me into a war zone?

Less than twenty-four hours later I'm sitting in the airport waiting for our El Al Israel Airlines flight to start boarding.

Looking around, I watch a guy in a dark suit as he crouches on the floor and examines the underside of each row of benches. If he finds a bomb, will he know how to disarm it?

I glance at my biological father, the almost non-existent man in my life, who's reading the newspaper. He tried talking to me on the way to the airport. I cut him off by putting on my headphones and listening to my iPod.

As if he knows I'm staring at him, he puts his paper down and turns my way. His hair is short. It's thick and dark, just like mine. I know if he'd grow it out it would be curly, too. As hard as it is, I straighten my curly hair every morning. I hate my hair.

My mom's eyes are green, mine are blue. People say my eyes are such a bright blue they glow. I consider my eyes my best feature.

Unfortunately, the main thing I inherited from Mom is a big chest. Besides changing my hair, I'd like to have smaller boobs. When I play tennis, they get in the way. Have you ever tried a two-handed backhand with mongo boobs? They seriously should have handicaps in tennis for people with big chests.

When I get older maybe I'll get a reduction. But Jessica said during a boob reduction the doctor removes your whole areola . . . you know, that pinky part in the middle of your boob, and then after they take out the excess boob they reattach the areola.

I don't think I'd like my pinky parts detached at all.

As I think about detached areolas, I realize Ron is still looking at me. Although from the expression on his face he probably thinks I'm disgusted with *him*. I can't possibly explain I'm thinking of what I'd actually look like with detached pinky parts.

Anyway, I'm still mad at him for bringing me on this stupid trip in the first place. Because of him, I had to drop out of tennis camp this summer. Which means I probably won't make it on the high school team when tryouts start in the fall. I totally want to make the varsity team.

To make matters worse, Mitch, my boyfriend, won't even know I'm gone. He went camping with his dad for a couple weeks on a 'cell phone free' vacation. It's still a new relationship. If we're not together the rest of the summer, he just might find someone else who will be there for him.

I don't even know why Ron wants me to go with him. He doesn't even like me. Mom probably wanted me out of the house so she could have privacy with her latest guy.

Her current boyfriend, Marc with a 'c', thinks he's *the one. As if.* Doesn't he realize once Mom meets someone bigger or better he's out of the picture?

"I'm going to the bathroom," I say to Ron.

I really don't have to go, but I take my purse and walk down the hallway. When I get out of Ron's line of vision, I take out my trusty cell phone and keep walking. Mom got me the cell "for emergencies only."

I'm definitely feeling an emergency coming on.

2

*Being on an airplane for twelve
hours should be outlawed.*

I walk farther down the hallway and dial Jessica's number.

"Please be home," I pray as I stop by a window and look out at airplanes parked at their gates.

I usually don't pray; it's not in my nature. But desperate times call for desperate measures and I'm nothing if not flexible. Well, sometimes.

"Amy?"

I feel better already hearing her voice.

"Yeah, it's me. My flight is delayed."

"Are you still freaking out?"

"Yes. Tell me again why I shouldn't be worried?"

"Amy, it won't be so bad. If there was anything I could do . . ."

It's time to tell Jess of my plan. I just thought of it.

"There *is* one thing . . ."

"What is it?"

"Come get me at the airport. International terminal. I'll be hiding by the, uh, Air Iberia arrivals. Wait for me there."

"Then what?"

"Then I'll somehow get to go to tennis camp and . . . oh, I don't know. Ron wants me to be a perfect daughter, but he's the crappiest dad ever—"

My cell phone is being snatched out of my hand, cutting my 'crappy dad' speech short. The snatcher, of course, is none other than the crapper himself.

"Hey, give that back!" I say.

"Hello? Who is dis?" Ron barks into my phone like an army commander with a speech impediment.

I can't hear Jessica. I hope she doesn't answer him.

"Jessica, she'll call you when she can," he says, then snaps the cover shut.

He didn't even give me a chance to tell her to call Mitch so he knows I'm gone for the summer.

"Why? Why are you ruining my summer and taking me to Israel?"

He clips *my* phone to *his* back pocket.

"Because I want you to meet your *grandmudder* before it's too late. That's why."

So this has nothing to do with Ron wanting to get to know me and spend time with me. No *from now on I want to be the father I always should have been* from him.

I shouldn't be disappointed, but I am.

"Boarding now for El Al flight 001 to Tel Aviv with a connection in Newark," a voice with an Israeli accent blasts through the loudspeaker. "Passengers in rows *turdy*-five to forty-five please have your boarding cards and passports out for the attendants."

"Tell you what," Ron says. "I'll give you back the phone if you'll cooperate and get on that plane. Deal?"

As if I have any other option.

"Fine," I say and hold out my hand. At least I'll have my little connection to sanity and independence.

He hands me the phone and I reluctantly follow him on the plane.

Ron and I are assigned to row sixty, the last row. I'm kind of glad nobody will be sitting behind me so I can rest comfortably on the twelve-hour flight to Tel Aviv.

Unless, of course, a bomb is planted on the plane or terrorists hijack it and we die before we even get to the *war zone*. As I think about terrorists on the plane, I look over at Ron.

"I heard there are air marshals on all El Al flights," I say as I shove my backpack under the seat in front of me. "Is it true?"

I don't know if I've ever actually started a conversation with Ron before, and he seems stunned. He looks around to see if I'm asking someone else the question before he answers.

"El Al has always had air marshals."

"How many?" Because if there's only one air marshall against five terrorists, the air marshall is toast.

"A lot. Don't worry, El Al's security is second to none."

"Uh huh," I say, not very convinced as I look to my left at a guy with a mono-brow who looks pretty suspicious. Mr. Mono-brow smiles at me. His smile fades as I realize Ron is glaring at him.

After so many years with Ron as a 'birthday only' figure in my life, I feel like he doesn't have any right to say he's my dad. When I was younger and he came to take me for my annual birthday outing, I worshipped the ground he walked on. He was like this superhero who granted my every wish and treated me like a "princess for a day."

But by the time I realized a father should actually be there for you *every* day, I started resenting him. Last year I actually blew him off. I snuck out of the house, left a note I'd gone out with friends, and came back after dark.

My mom isn't easy. She throws men away for sport. But from what I know of Ron, he was once a commando in the Israeli Defense Forces.

A commando who's too chickenshit to fight for marriage to a woman he impregnated isn't worth much in my book.

I won't be like my mother when I'm older. I won't be like Ron, either.

Before long, we land in Newark to pick up more passengers. I've never eaten sardines, but when people start piling in and filling each and every empty spot on the plane, the disgusting little fishes come to mind. It boggles my mind how many people pack the plane to fly to a place on the warning list for American citizens.

When we lift off, I push that little button to recline my seat because I'm starting to get tired.

Only since we have the back row, I realize pretty quickly the back row *doesn't recline*. Okay, now this isn't funny. It's not just a short flight to Orlando. This is a whopping twelve-hour flight to a place I don't want to go to in the first place to meet a sick grandmother I didn't know existed in the first place. (That's two first places, I know, but at this point nothing in my life that bugs me is second place . . . it *all* takes first place.)

As I try and force the chair to recline for the fifth time and the person in front of me reclines theirs so far back I hardly have room for my legs, this feeling in the pit of my stomach makes me want to cry. I can't help it. I hate this plane, I hate Mom for making me come on this stupid trip, and I hate Ron for just about everything else.

After a few hours I get up to go to the bathroom, this time for real. Unfortunately, at least one hundred people have already used the facilities and the floor is full of little pieces of unflushed toilet paper shreds. To top it off (in the first place) the floor is full of these little droplets. Are the droplets pee or water? My Dansko clogs are not used to being subjected to this kind of abuse.

I go back to my seat and to my astonishment I'm finally able to get into a comfortable, albeit upright, sleeping position. Sleep right now would be bliss. The captain turns off all the lights and I close my eyes.

Someone yells, and I'm jerked awake from dreamland. Right above me, like practically in my face, is a Hasidic

Jew. You know, one of those guys who wears a black hat and coat and has long, curly sideburns running down his face and neck. Jessica (she's Jewish) told me they're ultra, ultra religious and try to follow all of God's six hundred or so rules. I have enough trouble following my mom's rules, let alone six hundred of God's.

It takes me a minute to realize his eyes are closed and he's praying. But he's not praying in his seat, he's praying right over mine. He's bobbing up and down, his eyes are shut, and his face is in total concentration. In fact, as my eyes focus in the dark, I realize all of the Hasidic Jews have congregated at the back of the plane to pray.

But it doesn't sound like prayers at all, more like some chant mixed with mumbling. They might not even be praying. But then one of the guys, I guess he's the leader, says a couple of words loudly and they all respond and keep on doing their mumbling chant. Yeah, they're praying.

Do they all have to do it at the same time?

And what are those straps on the back of their hands and arms or the box strapped to their forehead?

Now that I watch them more intently, I admire the men for being so devoted to their religion they would pray instead of sleep. Don't get me wrong, I admire it, but I wouldn't do it.

I look over at Ron, sound asleep. He's a good-looking man, if you like the dark, brooding kind of guy. Which I don't. My mother is pastey white and has blond hair and green eyes. She was probably in her "opposite" stage when she and my dad got together that fateful night.

I wonder if Ron wishes I wasn't born. If he'd chosen to stay at his cousin's dorm room at the University of Illinois, instead of following my mom to her sorority house seventeen years ago, then he wouldn't be stuck with a kid who resented him.

His eyes suddenly open and I sit back in my chair, pretending to watch the television screen in front of me without the headphones on my ears. I have one good thing to say about El Al Israel Airline—it has personal television screens embedded into the backs of every single seat. A miracle in its own right.

"I think you'll like it there," Ron says. "Even though I've lived in America for seventeen years, Israel will always be a part of me."

"And . . . ?" I say.

He shifts in his seat and looks at me straight on. "And your *grandmudder* will want it to be a part of you, too. Don't disappoint her."

I blink and give him my famous sneer, the one where my top lip curls up just the right amount. "You've got to be kidding. Don't disappoint *her*? I didn't know she existed before yesterday. What about her disappointing *me*? If you haven't forgotten, she hasn't been the doting grandma."

Believe me, I know people who have doting grandmas. Jessica's Grandma Pearl spent four years knitting her a blanket. *Four years*! And she's got arthritis. I wonder what Grandma Pearl would think if she knew Jessica lost her virginity to Michael Greenberg under the blanket she spent four years knitting with her crooked fingers.

Ron sighs and turns his attention to his little personal television screen. I note he's not wearing the headphones, either.

I sit back. There's a long silence, so long I think if I look at him I'll find him sleeping again.

"What do I call her?" I ask, still staring at the screen in front of me.

"She'll like it if you call her *Safta*. It means grandma in Hebrew."

"*Safta*," I say quietly to myself, trying out how the word sounds coming out of my mouth. Glancing over at the Sperm Donor, I notice he's nodding. His chin is raised and he's giving me a little smile like he's proud. Ugh!

Looking forward, I turn my personal TV to the channel showing how much longer until we land in Israel. Four hours and fifty-five minutes.

By this time the Hasidic Jews have gone back to their seats. I close my eyes again, thankfully drifting off to sleep.

Before I know it, the flight attendant says something in Hebrew. I wait until the information is repeated in English.

"We're starting our descent into Tel Aviv, please put your seats in the upright position . . ."

News flash—my seat has been in the upright position for the whole twelve-hour flight!

3

I'm not rude,
I'm just a teen with attitude.

The immigration officer inside Ben Gurion Airport in Tel Aviv asks Ron (who has dual Israeli and American citizenship) who I am.

"My daughter," he replies.

"Is she registered as an Israeli citizen?" she asks.

Is the woman joking? Me? An Israeli citizen? But when I see the serious look on the immigration officer's face, I panic. I've heard of Middle East countries where American kids are taken and aren't allowed to leave. I don't want to be Israeli. I want to go home, like right now!

I turn around, heading back to the plane. Hopefully the captain will let me back on . . . I'll go in the belly of the aircraft, in someone's luggage, in a damn animal carrier. Just get me out of here!

I'm almost at the door. Freedom is in sight when I feel a hand on my shoulder.

"Amy," Ron's familiar brooding voice says from behind me.

I turn around and face him. "They won't let me go back home, will they? You've kidnapped me to this country that wants me to be a citizen. Oh, God. They make everyone, even girls, go into the army at eighteen, right? I've heard that, don't try and deny it."

I know I'm sounding like a crazy sixteen-year-old right now, my voice several octaves higher than usual. I can't help it and I keep rambling.

"You're going to make me stay here and be drafted into the army, aren't you?"

I can just see them making me trade in my Abercrombie & Fitch for fatigues. My heart is beating fast and little droplets of sweat are running down my face. I swear they're not tears, just droplets of sweat.

"Ron, to be honest I doubt I'm even your kid. Did you ever get a paternity test? Because I saw a picture of this one guy my mom dated in college who looks just like me."

Ron looks at the ceiling and lets out a breath. When he looks back at me, his brown eyes are darker than usual. His jaw is clenched tight.

"Calm down, Amy. You're causing a scene."

"Dude," I say really tough, getting a grip on my voice. Now I sound like Angelina Jolie, in that movie where she kicks everyone's ass that crosses her. "I haven't even *started* to cause a scene."

A soldier with a very, very large machine gun walks up to us. He has an almost shaved head and I can tell just by looking at him he has a twitchy trigger finger. Great, my life is over, I'm going to be stuck in this third world country for the rest of my days . . . which are probably numbered now.

"*Mah carrah?*" the soldier says to Ron in Hebrew. It sounds either like "Macarena?" or "Kill Amy?" to me.

"*Ha'kol b'seder,*" Ron responds.

I never thought I'd be sorry I don't know Hebrew. In school, I take *Español.*

My heart is still racing when I ask, "What are you saying? What's going on?" I'm afraid of the answer, but I'm trying to be brave so I can tell the American Secret Service agents all the information I obtained before I escaped. The American government will want to know what's going on here, I'm sure of it.

"You're *not* an Israeli citizen," Ron says. "And you're not about to be drafted into any army."

"Then what did that soldier say to you?"

"He asked me what was wrong and I told him everything's fine. That was it."

Likely story, I think. But I follow him back to the immigration lady, mostly because he has a grip on my arm like a vise.

He speaks to the lady in Hebrew this time, probably to make sure I don't understand him. For all I know he's negotiating a deal to have me sold into child slavery. Although I consider myself pretty up-to-date on current events and I've never actually heard of Israeli child slavery.

Before long, the lady stamps my passport (which Mom had me get for emergency purposes a year ago and dummy me agreed to it, thinking she was secretly planning to take me to Jamaica or the Bahamas) and we head to the baggage claim area. We only have to walk twelve steps before we're there.

"Come with me while I get a cart," Ron orders.

"I'll just wait here," I say, because I want him to know I refuse to take parental orders from him.

He crosses his arms across his chest. "Amy, with the drama you just created back there I'm not about to play the trusting *fadder* right now."

I'm on a roll and can't resist. "You haven't been good at playing the loving *fadder*, either," I say, the words rolling off my tongue as if someone else is making me say them. "What kind of *fadder* can you play, Ron? You know, so I can recognize it when I see it."

Ron doesn't show anger too often, but even in the small amount of time I've spent with him I know by the sounds he makes or the change in his breathing patterns when something gets in his craw.

"Don't think you're too old to get punished by me, young lady."

I have my famous sneer ready. "Get a clue, Daddy Dearest. Being here with you is punishment enough."

I'm not usually this rude, truly I'm not. But my resentment toward Ron and insecurity about his fatherly love makes me act bitchy. I'm not even aware of it half the time. I guess if I'm rude to him, I'm giving him a reason not to love me.

Breathing pattern change. "Wait. Here. Or. Else," he says.

He stalks off, but I can't just stand here. I scan the airport and my eyes focus on the one thing most teenagers can't resist.

A Coke machine. (Insert harp music here, because that's what's playing inside my head.)

I walk through the crowd as if in a trance. Cold Cokes are calling out to me, "Amy, Amy, Amy. I know you're hot and cranky. Amy, Amy, Amy. I know you're sweating like a disgusting pig. Amy, Amy, Amy. I'll solve all of your problems."

I touch the Coke machine and immediately feel refreshed. I get ready to put my money in the inviting slot and for the first time in twenty-four hours I feel a smile coming on. It's comforting to know even in the Middle East Coke is available. Then I look at the price. My Coke addiction is about to cost me a sizeable amount of cash.

My mouth goes wide and I give a little shriek. "Seven dollars and eighty cents? That's robbery!"

"That's the price in shekels," a mother with two children hanging on her says in an Israeli accent. "Seven shekels and eighty ah-goo-roat."

"Shekels? Ah-goo-roat?" I don't have shekels. And I sure as hell don't have ah-goo-roats. Or goats if that's what she'd said.

I only have American dollars, but I find a sign that indicates a bank is in the airport. I follow the sign, heading straight for the bank. It's at the other end of the terminal. If I hurry, Ron won't even notice I'm gone.

But as I get to the bank, there's a line. To top it off, the biggest group of slowpokes are in front of me. I should go back to the baggage claim area, but I don't want to lose my spot in line. If these people would just move a little faster, I'd have my shekels and ah-goo-roats for my Coke in no time.

When I look at my watch, I wonder how many minutes I've been waiting. Ten? Twenty? It's so easy to lose track.

Finally, I'm next. I take a twenty-dollar bill out of my wallet and hand it to the banker dude.

"Passport?" he says.

"I just want to exchange money," I clarify.

"Yes, I understand. I need your passport number for the exchange."

"My . . . dad has it," I say. Ron took it after it was stamped so it wouldn't get lost. "Can't you just give me shekels without it?"

"No. Next," he says, then hands me my twenty back and looks behind me for the next customer.

My mouth drops open. I wasted all this time for a Coke and I still can't get one. Unbelievable.

I head back to the baggage claim and spot Ron. He's talking to two soldiers and when he looks my way, my first instinct is to run in the opposite direction. I did nothing wrong. Yes, he told me to stay put, but I swear I thought I'd only be gone a minute.

Call it teenage intuition, but somehow I don't think Ron will listen to my explanation with an open mind. He tells the soldiers something and then walks over to me, deliberately slow. I think he's taking so long because he's very likely thinking of ways to kill and dismember me. Do they teach Dismemberment 101 in commando school?

Ron finally reaches me and I brace myself. Sounds like "arrr" and "yuh" come out of his mouth, but then he turns toward the baggage claim carousel with our luggage taking a ride on it. I notice our bags are the only ones left. He yanks them off and tosses them on a cart as if they weigh two pounds.

My suitcase was over the weight limit. I know this because he had to pay over a hundred dollars extra to get it on the plane. Note to self: Ron is very strong.

I just watch him, waiting for his wrath to come. Believe me, I know it's coming. What's scary is I expected it to have come already.

A predictable parent is good. On the other hand, an unpredictable parent is a teenager's worst nightmare.

Now Ron storms off through the area marked "exit" pushing the cart with our bags.

And I'm still standing here, my feet planted on the ground in this strange airport.

Right about now it occurs to me my dear old daddy just one-upped me.

Damn.

Normally I'd wait it out as long as I could and make *him* sweat. Let him think I may not follow him *ever*. But as I glance at the two soldiers who are now walking toward me, I turn and hightail my ass right through the exit.

Goodbye pride, hello Israel.

4

Change
makes me itch.

I spot Ron by the car rental counter. He's not even concerned about me or looking to see if I followed him. I stand next to him, but he doesn't acknowledge my presence.

I huff loudly.

He still doesn't look at me.

The lady at the counter hands him a key and tells him something in Hebrew. He smiles at her, says "*Todah*," and starts pushing the cart with our bags on it.

"I'm sorry," I say. "Now stop ignoring me."

He stops. "Does it ever occur to you that I worry about you?"

I could lie, but what good would it do?

"Frankly, no," I say.

He runs his hand through his hair. Why do guys do that when they're frustrated? Do they think it's macho? I know why girls don't do it. They'd mess up their hair they spent half an hour trying to tame, that's why. And also girls don't have to pretend to be macho.

"Come on," he says. "By the time we reach the *moshav* it'll be dark."

"*Moshav? What's a moshav?*" Is it "shopping mall" in Hebrew? I mean, from what Jessica was telling me Israeli stores have the latest fashions from Europe. That black dress Jessica has *is* really awesome. I know I'd be selling out if I go with the Sperm Donor to a mall, but I keep thinking about all the great stuff I could bring back home.

It's funny, when I think about the mall, I forget about the terrorist bombing that could happen there.

As we drive along the highway in our red rented Subaru, it's also easy to forget this is a war zone. It looks like a highway in the middle of New Mexico or something like that.

As we hit the Tel Aviv area, traffic jam city starts. I look out the window at the tall buildings.

Ron points to the right. "That's the Azrieli Tower. It's the tallest building in the Middle East," he says proudly.

It might as well have a bull's-eye on it. "What a great terrorist target," I mumble, but then realize Ron is looking at me sideways. "Well, it is." I hope it's well protected, because 9/11 changed just about every American I know. I look out the window as we're passing high tech buildings with names of American companies on them.

"Israel doesn't look anything like a third world country," I say.

"She's not a third world country."

She? Israel is a "she"? Well, *she's* pretty darn modern. In fact, the traffic looks just like we have back home.

Although I realize pretty quickly Israelis need to go to road rage school.

They're all yelling at each other out the windows and giving each other the finger when cut off. And I shriek when a bunch of people on those little motor scooters and motorcycles ride right in between the cars. They're not even weaving in the lanes; they're riding on the lines themselves!

"We've been in the car an hour. When are we gonna get there?" I say.

"In another hour or so."

"You never answered me. What's a *moshav?* Is it a mall?"

He laughs and I don't think a *moshav* is a mall anymore.

"Have you ever heard of a *kibbutz?*" he asks me.

"You mean community living where people share *everything?* Listen, if you're taking me to a sick commune—"

"Why do you always do that?"

"Do what?"

"Overreact."

"For your information, I do *not* overreact. Mom overreacts, especially when it comes to me coming home after my curfew. Oh, yeah, you wouldn't know anything about that because you're never there," I say sarcastically.

Silence.

"Then why don't you come live with me for a while," he challenges.

Me, live with him? "Do you have a girlfriend?" I ask. I want him to say no because I have plans for him and Mom. It'll be easier if he's not attached.

"No. Do you have a boyfriend?"

Now wait one second. When did it turn around to him asking me the questions? "Maybe."

"Amy, when are you going to learn to trust me? I'm not the enemy, you know."

"Then tell me what a *moshav* is."

"A *moshav* is a close-knit community. It's similar to a kibbutz, but everyone owns their own property and farmland. The money isn't shared or pooled together."

Still sounds like a commune to me.

"I hope we're not staying there for long," I say. "I need to take a shower at the hotel and unpack. I have stuff probably melting in this heat—"

"We're not staying at a hotel," he says.

Now I'm going to overreact.

"What?" I say really loudly.

"We'll be staying with your aunt, uncle, cousins, and *Safta*." He pauses. I know what's coming next, I do. But I'm not mentally prepared for it when he adds, "At the *moshav*."

"Let's set the record straight, Ron. I'm an all-American girl with red, white, and blue blood running through these veins. I do not stay at places called *moshavs*. Unless I've signed up for the Girl Scouts, which I didn't. I need amenities. Amenities! Do you know what those are?"

"Yes. But don't expect many where we're going. Last time I visited, only one family on the *moshav* had electricity and it wasn't mine."

I open the glove compartment.

"What are you doing?" Ron asks.

"Looking for a map so I know which direction to go when I escape from the *moshav*," I say.

He chuckles.

"Ha, ha, funny, funny. I bet you won't be laughing when you wake up one morning and find I've gone back to civilization."

Ron pats my knee with his hand. "I was just kidding, Amy. They have electricity."

Kidding? Ron was *kidding* with me?

"I knew you were joking. Do you actually think I'm that gullible?"

He doesn't answer, but I know he knows the truth by the quirky way his mouth is moving.

"Will you at least give me the keys to your car so I can drive myself to a mall?"

"Sorry. Driving age here is eighteen."

"What!"

"I'll take you wherever you want to go. Don't worry. Besides, if you get lost you won't know how to get back."

Good, I think to myself. Getting lost sounds like a great idea.

I sigh and look out the window. On one side of the car is the Mediterranean Sea and on the other side are mountains with houses built into them. If I was in a better mood

I might even think the scenery is beautiful, but I'm cranky and tired and my butt is numb.

I start doing my butt exercises. I was watching a late night talk show a couple of years ago when some action star, maybe Steven Seagal or Antonio Banderas, was talking about how they do butt exercises while in the car.

Just tighten, then release. Tighten. Release. Tighten. Release. I'm "feeling it burn," but after ten minutes my butt cheeks start to quiver on the tighten part and I stop.

By now we've taken a turn away from the sea and all around us are small trees in rows.

"What are those?" I ask.

"Olive trees."

"I hate olives."

"I love them."

Figures. "I hope you're not one of those pit-spitters."

"Huh?"

"You know, those people who spit out the pit right in front of other people at the table. That's totally gross."

He doesn't answer. I would bet my grandmother's underpants Ron is a pit-spitter.

"What kind of food do you like?" he asks. "I'm sure I can get it for you."

"Sushi."

"You mean raw fish?" he asks, wincing.

"Yep."

I used to hate it. When Mom first had me try it I gagged and spit it out (into my napkin, very discreetly I might add, unlike gross pit-spitters). Mom loves sushi. I guess it's like alcohol. You want to puke the first time you have it, but then it grows on you and you like it. It's probably why they say there's a thin line between love and hate. Now I don't just like sushi, I crave it. Ron obviously needs to be introduced to sushi with a professional sushi-eater like me.

We're now driving through the mountains on an extremely curvy road and I'm getting nauseous. The last time I noticed civilization was about fifteen minutes ago.

We wind our way down one mountain and stop at the road leading to another one. I read a sign with the words MOSHAV MENORA in English and some words in Hebrew on it.

Ron takes the road to Moshav Menora. Now the place looks like Switzerland, with grassy hills surrounding us on all sides.

He stops at a scenic rest stop built into the mountain.

"This is it?" I ask.

He turns to me and takes the key out of the ignition. "This is the Golan Heights, a very special and beautiful place. Let's go see the view."

"Do I have to?" I ask. "I got to pee."

"Can you hold it for a few minutes longer? I really need to talk with you before you meet my family."

This I have to hear. I open the car door and walk outside. We stroll in silence to the edge of the mountain. When I look over the edge, it reminds me of a scene from a postcard.

"They don't know about you," Ron blurts out.

Huh?

"Who doesn't know about me?"

"My *mudder*, my *brudder* and his wife . . ."

A pang of pain stabs my chest as if something pierced it. My heart starts beating fast and I'm breathing heavily. "Why?" I whisper, barely able to get the words out.

"It's complicated," he says, and then looks away from me. "You see, when I came to America I wanted to prove to everyone back here I could make it. You know, The American Dream."

"And you didn't expect me to come along and ruin your dream," I say.

"I met your mom the first weekend I was in the U.S. I was a cocky Israeli who just wanted to have a good time. A few months later I found out I was going to be a *fadder*."

I start walking away from him. What does he want me to do, apologize for being born?

"I hate you," I say as I head back to the car. I wipe the stupid tears I can't help from falling down my cheeks.

"Amy, please. For once let me set the record straight—"

"Just unlock the door." I hear the click and get inside the car. He's looking at me like he wants to explain more, but I don't want to hear it. "Let's go already!" I yell.

He gets back in the car and we ride up to the top of the mountain. I thought I was ready to meet Ron's family, but now all I want to do is crawl into a hole.

Because he's not just going to introduce me to his family, he's going to tell them for the first time he has an illegitimate daughter.

5

---

*If I close my eyes, will life stop
spinning out of control?*

We reach a gate and a guy with a large machine gun comes up
to our car. I've never even seen a machine gun before today
and cringe every time I think about what they're used for.

Ron says something in Hebrew. The guy smiles and
signals for the gate to open. We drive down a dirt road on
top of the mountain and pass six rows of houses. There
are about seven to ten houses down each road on either
side. Ron turns down one of them and parks in front of a
house.

"I'm not going in until you tell them who I am," I say.

I think he's going to argue and I ready myself for a
fight. But Ron just says, "Fair enough."

He gets out of the car and I stay put. I watch as he enters the small one-story house.

The windows are open in the car, but there's no breeze. And it's not only hot, I think the devil himself must live on this mountain because sweat is pouring down my face, neck, and chest. My Abercrombie & Fitch shirt has wet marks on it already from disgusting armpit sweat.

How can these people stand the heat? I look at my nail before biting on it. What is Ron saying to them? Is he sweating as much as I am? I hope so.

I step out of the car and lean against the side of it, listening for the scolding *Safta* should be giving Ron. Boy is he going to get it. If I were *Safta* I'd rip him a new one for denying her, well, me. But I don't hear yelling. In fact, I don't hear much coming from the house.

Instead, something hits my arm. Hard.

"Hey!" I yell and panic.

I'm not stupid, I know it's not a bullet. Not that I wouldn't be surprised if Ron's family decided "do away" with his illegitimate daughter once they heard the truth.

As I have that thought, I look down and see the offending object.

A soccer ball.

"*Tizreki le'kan*," a voice bellows from behind the car. As if I can understand. But I can't, so I ignore it. Besides, I already feel a bruise forming on my arm.

The sound of running footsteps echoes before I'm face to face with an Israeli boy about my age.

"*Shalom*," he says.

He's wearing jeans, has a dusty and ripped white T-shirt on, and is wearing Greek sandals. You know, the ones like the Greek philosophers wore. But that's not the worst part. The guy is wearing white socks along with the sandals. Socks with sandals! Seeing that makes me laugh so I look up at his face instead of his feet. I don't want to insult the guy.

"Hi," I say.

Does he speak English? I don't know so I just stand there in silence.

Two more boys run up to us. One starts to talk to the boy in Hebrew but becomes silent when he notices me.

"I America," I say slowly and loud like I'm talking to a chimpanzee. I'm hoping by some miracle they'll understand me.

They turn to each other with confused looks on their faces and I realize these next three months are going to be like living in a bubble. A bubble with people who don't understand a word I'm saying, except for the Sperm Donor. Could my summer vacation be ruined more?

The first boy steps closer to me. He has dark blond hair and a rugged, boyish grin. I know, I know, rugged and boyish don't really go together. But on this guy it does, trust me. "You speak English?" he asks with a heavy accent.

Huh? "Yes. Do you?"

"Yes. But what does 'I America' mean?"

"Nothing. Just forget it."

"You a friend us not?" he asks.

Huh? Obviously his English isn't good. Was he asking if I'm a friend or not? I'm almost afraid to say no. "Yes."

The second guy turns to me. "What's your name?"

"Amy."

"Hi Amy, I'm Doo-Doo," he says. Then he points to the other two guys. "And this is Moron and O'dead."

Now, I've never said these four words in a row before. In fact, I don't think they've ever come out of someone less than the age of sixty, but they come out of my mouth almost automatically.

"I beg your pardon?" I say. My eyes are squinting as if that would clear my ears so I could hear right.

They all look at me like *I'm* the one who's got the problem. I have this urge to burst out laughing. But I suppress it because they obviously don't get the joke. Which actually makes it all the more funny. Okay, so some parts of my trip are actually going to be amusing.

But my amusement fades as another guy comes up to us. He's got dark brown hair that matches his eyes. And he's tall, bronzed, and wearing no shirt. He has jeans hugging those slender hips of his, a washboard stomach, and by every measure he's just about the toughest looking teenager I've ever seen.

"*Americayit*," Moron says, pointing to me.

No-shirt guy says some stuff to Doo-Doo, Moron, and O'dead in Hebrew and ignores me completely. Which just proves one of my many theories . . . the gorgeous guys are always the biggest jerks. At least the other guys smiled and introduced themselves. No-shirt guy just barks some words at his friends, then walks away.

"How long are you visiting for?" Moron asks, eyeing the suitcases in the back seat.

For a helluva lot longer than I want to. "The whole summer."

"We're going to hang out at the beach tomorrow tonight. Do you want to join us?" Doo-Doo asks.

"Sure," I say.

I look over at the house and there's a crowd of four strangers plus Ron standing in the open doorway. They're all staring at me. How could I have forgotten why I was here in the first place?

Ron walks up to me. I want to ask, "How did it go?" but don't.

So now I find myself walking up this muddy pathway, to this small house that's going to be my residence for the next three months. As the cherry on top of the cake called my life, I'm going to live with family members who I've never met before and a biological father who I hardly know.

"Amy, this is my *brudder*, Chaim."

My uncle holds out his hand and shakes mine. He's a tall guy with a definite resemblance to Ron. They both have that same strong, muscular build.

The guy is smiling, but I can tell there's tension behind that façade. Anger, too, although I don't know if it's directed at me or SD (short for Sperm Donor, I'm too hot and sweaty to think of him as anything other than SD).

"Call me *Dod* or Uncle Chaim," he says.

As if I could even say that name. He pronounces the C-h like he's about to hack a loogie. I swear I can't do those back throat noises for the life of me without making a complete ass of myself. I'll just call him Uncle Chime and leave off the gurgling back-throat noise.

The lady beside Uncle Chime steps forward. I'm shocked when she pulls me to her and hugs me tightly. My first instinct is to push her away, but her embrace is so warm and loving. I find myself leaning into her arms. She releases me after a long time, puts her hands on my shoulders, and holds me at arm's length.

"Beautiful girl," she says with a deep Israeli accent.

She has these earrings with bells on them and no makeup on her face. My mom wouldn't be caught dead outside the house without makeup. Or earrings with bells dangling from them. The truth is, this woman is pretty without makeup and the bells just make her look angelic instead of stupid.

She lets go of me and says with a smile, "I'm your aunt Yikara. Just call me *Doda* Yucky, okay?"

"Ookaay," I say in a singsong voice to alert SD I'm not comfortable calling this lady Yucky.

"*Doda* is 'aunt' in Hebrew," SD explains as if that was the part of this whole exchange that needed explanation.

She just asked me to call her yucky!

There are two more people standing there. One is a small boy, probably around three years old, with blond curls spiraling out of his head like Medusa's snakes. He's wearing nothing but a pair of Power Ranger underpants.

"*Shalom, ani* Matan," he says in a cute little voice. I have no clue what he's saying, but he's so adorable and his curls bounce on his head as he speaks. I step toward him and shake his little hand affectionately.

The last one, a dirty blonde-haired teenager who is a bit taller than me, just stands there with her arms crossed over her chest. She's wearing the tightest jeans I've ever seen on a human being and a crop shirt showing most of her flat stomach. I don't need a sixth sense to know she's royally pissed-off.

"This is your cousin, O'snot."

This time my laugh just comes out without warning. Although when I come to my senses and realize nobody else is laughing, I stop pretty quick. Okay, now O'snot is not just pissed-off, she's got *my* famous, one-of-a-kind sneer down pat as if she'd invented it herself.

I don't hold out my hand in greeting because I'm pretty sure my snotty cousin will ignore it. So I just say, "Hi."

"Hi," she says through gritted teeth. Nice.

"Let's go inside so you can meet your *Safta*," Uncle Chime says.

I'm getting a little piece of satisfaction when I notice Ron's armpits are wet through his shirt. My armpit wet spots are the size of grapefruits, but Ron's are the size of small watermelons. He's more nervous than I am for me to meet my grandmother.

Ha!

6

You can run from some problems,
but then you get caught up in others.

I enter the house slowly and peer inside. A kitchen is right in front of me. I follow Ron to the left and find a woman sitting on a rocking chair next to a window. She has white hair massively peppered with dark strands.

She looks at me with bright blue eyes that almost glow. Our gazes meet and I feel like I'm looking in the mirror at my own eyes. I'm so overwhelmed it almost chokes me. Is the air getting thicker?

I start breathing heavier, trying to get air into my constricting lungs.

My Grandma.

My sick Grandma.

She looks small and weak. Is she dying?

Turning to the rest of the family, I realize they're all staring at me. It makes me feel like I'm being judged on some reality show they're watching. An over-excited television announcer's voice in my head says, *Will Amy make a mistake and screw up this first meeting? Watch next week's episode of Illegitimate Children and find out if her sick grandmother accepts or rejects her in front of thirty million viewers . . .*

Before I even realize it, I turn and run out of the house before anyone can see the tears welling in my eyes. I run and run and run until my legs want to give out. I'm passing rows of houses, haystacks, horses, cows, and sheep as if I'm on some kind of farm set in Hollywood.

When I stop running and start walking, I think *Safta* must think I'm some stupid idiot. I meant to hug her, I really did. But not in front the rest of the family. I feel like they're analyzing my every move.

I keep walking, pissed at SD for making my first meeting with *Safta* a spectacle. A small wire fence is in front of me, and as I attempt to step over it, a voice stops me.

"You can't go there."

I freeze and turn to the harsh voice. It's no-shirt guy standing in front of a pile of hay about three stories tall. A sheen of sweat on his chest sparkles in the sunshine, but I'm trying not to pay attention to it. Instead, I think about something gross. Like how he must smell like sheep and sweat and how he's in desperate need of a shower. But, for that matter, so am I. I wipe the tears falling down my cheek with my fingertips.

"Isn't this a free country?" I say with attitude.

The last thing I need is for some hard-ass teenager to think I'm weak.

He turns around and flings a whole bale of hay into the sheep pens.

"The sign says a minefield is behind the fence. If you want to take your chances, I won't stop you," no-shirt-cute-jerk says as he enters the sheep enclosure.

At this point I'm still straddling the fence. Damn. This IS a war zone. I eye my foot on the other side of the wire, feeling lucky it's still there and not blown off. I slowly lift it and bring it back to the side of the wire without mine-fields.

"You don't know where you are, do you?" he asks gruffly as he gets another bale of hay.

"Sure I do," I say. "I'm on top of a mountain in the middle of Israel." Duh.

"Actually, you're in the northern part of Israel, not in the middle. In the Golan Heights."

"So?"

"Americans," he mumbles, then slowly shakes his head in disgust.

"Okay, what's so special about the Golan Heights?"

"Let's just say Syria is about ten miles that way," he says, pointing. "For a Jewish girl, you don't know much about the Jewish homeland."

Yeah, but I'm not Jewish. I don't tell him this, he'll probably go off on me about it. I'm glad when he turns away and walks back into the sheep enclosure.

"Arg!"

I jump at the sound at my feet. A mangy, dirt-encrusted puppy, who I think at one time was white, is furiously wagging his tail at me. Once we make eye contact, he rolls onto his back and puts his paws in the air.

"I'm sorry," I say to the mutt. "I'm not a dog person."

Go find some other sucker to rub their hands on that filthy, flea-ridden tummy of yours. I'm not a cat person, either. In fact, I'm not an animal person at all. And being surrounded by a farmload of the things is making me itch.

I start to walk away. Unfortunately, the mutt follows.

"Arg!" the thing says again.

I keep walking.

"Don't you know dogs say 'ruff,' not 'arg'?" I ask it. "What are you trying to be, a pirate?"

The dog answers with another, "Arg!" this time screechier than the last as if he's trying to annoy me on purpose. Hey, the way my day has been going, I wouldn't doubt it.

"Ruff! Ruff! Ruff!"

You'd think the mutt was joking with me, wouldn't you? But as I turn to the rough, deep barking sound I realize pretty quickly the mutt has friends. A lot of them.

In the first place, I was wrong about it being dirt-encrusted. These five dogs are caked in mud and definitely dirtier than the mutt-puppy. Also (in the first place) they're very, very big.

And they're running right toward me barking up a storm as if I'd kidnapped their child.

Panic isn't the word to describe how I feel right now. As my life flashes before my eyes, I briefly weigh my two options. I could either head toward the wire and run into the minefields or jump into the sheep pens.

I don't have time to waste so I just run as fast as my sweaty, tired, sorry legs can carry me. As I move, I'm not even conscious about which option I've chosen.

I run faster and faster, barely aware of the high-pitched "arg" sound at my feet and the hefty "ruffs" not far behind. Just a little farther, I say to my clouded mind. I think I'm screaming and yelling obscenities, but I can't be sure because I'm too busy worrying about what my legs are doing and can't be bothered with censoring my mouth, too.

It seems like a long time, but when I reach the enclosure my pace doesn't falter. Mr. Haraldson, my gym teacher, would be proud of my leap. I was nowhere near getting the presidential award in physical fitness last year, but I'm probably making a world-record jump right now.

I don't really aim where I'm going; it's all just a blur. And when I land, I close my eyes. I hope I don't squash a sheep during my crash landing.

But instead of colliding with a sheep, something hard and solid breaks my fall.

I'm afraid to open my eyes, so I can't see, but my sense of smell is heightened. I know this because the scent of boy sweat surrounds me.

It's not grody body odor, just this musky guy aroma that makes me inhale deeper.

Okay, now I realize what I'm doing, where I am, and who I'm smelling—like he's a damn rose petal—but it's really just a boy. I open my eyes wide.

Don't ask me how I came to be straddling no-shirt-cute-jerk. His hands are on me. To be specific, one of them is on the small of my back and the other one is on my hip. And I get caught staring into mocha eyes that could definitely put someone in a trance.

I'm about to push away from him, but I hear the sound of someone walking along the grass beside the sheep's pen. I look over at who it is. I'm acutely aware the position I'm currently in looks really promiscuous and will probably get me in a ton of trouble.

When I finally lean away from him, it opens my view to whoever has witnessed my debacle. I realize it's the last person I wanted to see.

O'snot.

And when I see her lips in a tight line and her hands accusingly on her hips I come to the only conclusion one can muster.

No-shirt-cute-jerk is my cousin O'snot's boyfriend.

O'shit.

7

---

*I'll never get used to
being humiliated.*

"I swear, Ron, it's not my fault."

"Those words come off your lips pretty often, Amy," he says to me. "Now explain again why you ran away before you even met *Safta* and then, within a matter of fifteen minutes, end up on top of a boy. In the middle of a pile of hay, no less."

I dig some dirt out of my fingernail while the Sperm Donor has this very serious talk.

"Actually, to be technical, I fell on him," I say. I finger a piece of my hair that's been caked with mud. "I really don't recall exactly how I ended up straddling him."

We're sitting on the front lawn of my grandmother/uncle/aunt/cousin's house. Ron does that thing with his hand through his hair again.

And then unending silence. Should I explain what happened? I'm not afraid to admit I want to be in control of my life.

Don't ask me why, I just blurt out, "I felt like everybody was watching and analyzing me and it sucked so I ran."

"Did you kiss Avi?"

"Who's Avi?"

SD gives me the you've-got-to-be-kidding look.

I stand up.

"No! Why? Did Cousin Snotty say I did? Listen, there were vicious dogs chasing me—"

He looks down at the mutt who hasn't figured out my feet aren't his personal playground.

"Like that one?" he says.

I shake the thing off my leg. "No. Yes. Well, they looked like him, but were a lot bigger. And so I ran and sort of fell on Snotty's boyfriend."

"Her name is O. S. N. A. T. Osnat. It's a beautiful name."

"Not where I come from."

"Just . . . just give her a chance. Don't judge her before you get to know her."

I want to argue, to tell SD Snotty hated *me* before she knew me, but I'm keeping silent. Right now I'll attribute my lack of ability to argue to sleep deprivation because usually I'm ready for a good knockdown-dragout verbal war.

"Fine," I say.

"And stop calling her Snotty."

Geez, you give the guy a little and like a vacuum cleaner he wants to take up all the dirt, not just the little pieces of lint.

"Fine. Where's *Safta*? I'm ready to meet her now if there aren't any spectators around."

"She's resting in her room. No spectators, I promise."

This would be about the time I have the urge to hug the SD. But it would feel weird because I haven't hugged him in years.

SD stands and I follow him into the house. Once we enter, the smell of fresh baked bread wafting from the kitchen makes my stomach growl.

"Come eat," *Doda* Yucky says. She's lost a bit of her cheery disposition. Is it because she thinks I kissed O.S.N.A.T's boyfriend?

"Thanks, but I'm not hungry." I'm too nervous to eat. Ron leads me to a small room at the back of the house and I peek in the door.

Safta is lying down on her bed. When she sees me enter, she sits up.

I swallow hard and close the door behind me. The room is small, the floor is made of tile, and the walls are stark white cement. The drapes are closed, so it's a little dark. But that's the way I want it now, because I don't want the world peeking into my conversation.

"Hi, *Safta*. I'm Amy," I say. My voice cracks while I'm saying it and I feel a little foolish.

She nods and pats the side of the bed. "Come over here, Amy. Sit with me."

I take small, slow steps to her bed. When I reach it, I carefully sit on the edge. To my surprise, she takes my hand in hers.

"Are you really sick?" I ask tentatively.

"I'll be fine. You know doctors, they like to make a big fuss about nothing."

"Ron thinks you're real sick," I say, and then want to suck those words right back in my mouth.

She shakes her head. "Your father needs to have his *cup* examined. That means 'head' in Yiddish. Imagine, keeping my granddaughter from me for sixteen years."

"Yeah," I say, urging her on. I like *Safta* immediately.

"What's your mother like?" she asks, changing the subject.

How do I describe Mom?

"She's pretty, for a mom," I say. "And she has a job that pays her a lot of money. She doesn't have a lot of friends, though, 'cause she's always working."

I watch as *Safta* takes this all in.

"And tell me about yourself."

"I do okay in school, I guess. My best friend's name is Jessica . . . she's Jewish," I add to make some connection to *Safta* on the religious end. "And I like to play tennis, ski, and shop."

She nods her head. "I'm going to like getting to know you, Amy. You sound like a very energetic, interesting girl."

"I should add I don't have the most positive attitude," I say while biting my bottom lip nervously. I mean, the lady'll figure it out sooner or later so I might as well give it to her straight up front.

"Maybe your trip here will change that."

I highly doubt it but I say, "I guess so," just to make her think this trip might miraculously change my outlook on life.

"I was like you when I was your age," she says.

"Why? Were you illegitimate, too?"

"No," she says, still holding my hand. "But my family fell on some tough times and we didn't have a home for a few years."

"Where did you live?"

"On the beach. It was a long time ago. Life changes when you least expect it."

As this information sinks into my brain, *Safta* tells me to go relax and unpack. And she smiles at me as if she's been my grandmother forever.

I can't keep blaming her for not being there for me the past sixteen years. The poor woman didn't even know I existed.

"Where's my suitcase?" I ask Ron after my enlightening talk with *Safta*.

"It's in O'snot's room," he says.

I didn't just hear right. I couldn't have. "You're kiddin' me, right?"

"There's only a few rooms here," SD explains. "You'll be sleeping in O'snot's room. I'm getting the sofa."

"What about the little guy?"

"Matan? He sleeps on a bed in his parents' room."

I'm about to suggest I sleep on the floor, but I see three ants crawling across the tile. Gross. And when I look over at *Doda* Yucky, she has this pathetic look on her face as if she'll win the lottery if my happy meter reaches a certain level.

I give her a little smile and it apparently worked because she heads back to the kitchen humming a cheerful tune.

But seriously, if there's one thing an American teenage girl needs, it's privacy. Can I tell O'snot to leave the room? It is, in fact, HER room so I think not. Thank goodness I'm not a twin. There are these twins at my school, Marlene and Darlene, and they have to not only share a room with each other, but their older sister, Charlene too. Don't ask.

SD leads me to a bedroom in the back of the house. I walk in the room and Snotty is putting on makeup while sitting on her bed. She knows I'm there, but she hasn't acknowledged me.

The Sperm Donor stands beside me. "Do you need help?"

"No, I'm fine," I say back to him.

He takes this as his cue to leave. I would have liked him to stay. Only to pose as a buffer between me and Snotty.

"Listen, I'm sorry about your boyfriend," I say.

She looks up and I see she's overdone the makeup on her eyes. It's as if she's outlined her eyes in black charcoal and now my cousin looks like she's in her twenties instead of a teenager. How old is she, anyway? She could use a few tips on makeup application.

One of my mom's clients is a cosmetic company. They actually used me in one of the shoots for their teen line. I learned a lot about how makeup should enhance your best features and not look all gloppy and dark (like Snotty). After my picture appeared in most of the teen magazines, my group of friends kind of dubbed me the guru of makeup.

I go over to my suitcase on the bed I suppose is mine for the next three months and pick out some clothes to change into that aren't caked with mud and straw.

"Avi isn't my boyfriend."

I'm not sure if it's Snotty talking, or my imagination playing with me.

I face my cousin. "What?"

She points her charcoal eye-circle bull's-eyes in my direction. "I don't have a boyfriend."

I take a pair of red shorts out of my suitcase. The word BITCH is printed across the butt in big white letters. Jessica got me the shorts for my birthday as a joke along with an anklet that wasn't a joke. I never thought I'd ever wear the shorts but then again, I never thought I'd find myself on a farm on top of a mountain in the middle of a war zone.

But, to be perfectly honest with myself, Israel doesn't actually feel or look like a war zone. Well, except for the heavily armed guards at the airport and the minefield I stepped on.

I look down at my shorts. I didn't think anyone here would be able to speak English so I packed them. I'm tempted to offer them to Snotty but instead ask, "Does Avi have a girlfriend?"

Okay, now if I wouldn't gag from the grossness of it, I'd insert my foot into my mouth. I don't care whether the guy has a girlfriend or not, but here I am asking Snotty about him.

Sometimes my mouth gets me going in a direction I have no intention of heading.

What's worse is my cousin ignores my question. So even if I didn't mean to ask the question, I'm more curious than ever to know the answer. But I'd never give her the satisfaction of asking her about Avi twice. She's already been spreading false rumors I've been mashing with the guy. It would suck if she really thought I cared what his girlfriend status was.

I set my clothes out on the bed, and head for the ONE bathroom in the whole house. I'm trying not to think about living for the next three months in a house with seven people and one bathroom. Scary, isn't it? At home we have three bathrooms . . . and it's only me and mom living there (along with Marc with a "c" when he stays over).

I have this friend, Emily. She's obsessed with smelling EVERYTHING. Like, when she eats she smells each bite before she puts the food into her mouth. I hate having meals with her because every time I hear her sniff-eat-sniff-eat-sniff-eat I get extremely irritated. Nobody really likes me when I'm irritated, except maybe Jessica.

As I enter the bathroom, my gag meter indicates low readings of any smells other than the ones emanating from my own body. Man, Emily would have a field day with me.

I am SO looking forward to getting clean. Thinking about how long it's been since I took a shower is making me dizzy.

I close the door to the bathroom and look on the handle for a lock. But the problem is there isn't one. Just a hole, as if there was a lock at one point in time.

This isn't funny. There are seven people living in this house and no lock on the bathroom door. And the damn door has a peephole where a lock should be.

I need to get into bed fast so this day can be over. I don't want to undress in front of a peephole so I step into the tub, close the curtain, and take my clothes off. I figure out how to turn on the water.

Thankfully a spray of hot water comes hard and fast. I can't stop the moan from escaping my mouth. Hot showers rock. I'm so tired I can hardly stand so I quickly wash myself.

After the shower I head back to Snotty's room, wondering why I didn't bring a change of clothes with me to the bathroom-that-doesn't-lock. I sure as hell don't want to change in front of Snotty. As I'm thinking about where to change into pjs, I wrap the towel tightly around myself.

I don't want to make eye contact with her, 'cause I want to avoid having to make any positive facial gestures, like smiling. I don't have any positive facial gestures left, at least not any today. In fact, all my positive gestures are probably used up for tomorrow, too.

So I look down at the floor as I enter the room, close the door, and head straight for my suitcase. I know Snotty is still in the room, I can hear her breathing. I pull a tank top and underwear out of my suitcase. I can go back to the bathroom and feel like a big dork that I'm embarrassed to change in front of her or I can just suck it up and change right here with my back turned.

I drop the towel and put my underwear on. Then I put on the BITCH shorts. When I reach for my white tank top, the door opens. I quickly cover my large breasts with my tank and get ready to yell at the intruder. The intruder, I assume, is none other than SD. "Do you mind?" I say.

But the person who walks into the room is not SD. It's Snotty. Which means there's someone else on her bed. I whip my head around and find Avi sitting there.

"Aaaahhhhhh!" I scream at the top of my lungs.

Avi just had a very big peep show starring yours truly.

Unfortunately my scream only alerts SD and Uncle Chime, who come barging into the room. SD's eyes dart back and forth between Avi and the half-dressed me with the BITCH shorts on.

"What's going on in here?" SD barks, accusing me with his eyes.

Avi actually saw me undressed . . . my butt, my boobs, my cellulite thighs. My tongue is in shock, just like the rest of me. Even if I could talk, I wouldn't even know what to say.

Except I smell a rat.

I look at Snotty, who has this very subtle self-satisfied smirk on her face. She's the rat, no question about it.

Uncle Chime is eyeing Ron accusingly. I know I didn't do anything, but I feel like a *ho* nonetheless.

Out of the corner of my eye I notice Avi standing up. He says something in Hebrew to SD I can't understand.

Ron says something angrily back to him.

Snotty starts arguing with Ron.

Uncle Chime stands as straight as a soldier, blocking the door, his hands on his hips.

And I'm just standing here, half naked. I push past Uncle Chime and run to the bathroom. After I put on my tank, I still hear loud arguing coming from Snotty's room.

I sit on the edge of the bathtub until the arguing stops.

If this is my initiation to Israel, I'm scared to find out what the next three months here are going to be like.

8

You can attract bees with honey,
but why would you want to?

The jet lag excuse works like a dream on the Sperm Donor my second day in Israel, with the added benefit that I've been able to sleep most of the day.

But now it's the late afternoon and I'm fully rested. After grabbing a bite to eat, I put on my jogging outfit, grab my iPod, and head outside. As I venture down the street, I spot *Safta* sitting outside on a lounge chair on the edge of the mountain.

When she notices me, she waves me over.

I jog down the dirt road and stand next to her. Peering down the mountain, at the lake far below, and at the other mountains in the distance takes my breath away. "Chicago is as flat as . . ." I'm about to say "Snotty," but I don't.

Instead, I say, "We don't have any mountains where I live. I guess that's why they make skyscrapers, they're like Chicago's mountains."

"I've never been to Chicago," *Safta* says.

"Well, you'll have to come visit me. I can take you to the Sears Tower. You can see, like, four states from the top floor. It's totally cool. And we have Lake Michigan. It's so wide you can't even see across it."

I get excited thinking about taking her around Chicago when she comes to visit me. She will love Millennium Park, where she can watch people and have lunch on the grass smack dab in the middle of the city.

And I bet she'll love the Art Institute of Chicago and Museum of Science and Industry. The museum has awesome exhibits. My favorite is the dead baby exhibit.

It's really called the Neonatal exhibit, but I say just tell it like it is. It's a bunch of real, dead babies of every stage, all encased in formaldehyde or some other liquid. They have about thirty embryos and fetuses that are one week old on up to a full term baby. They even show identical twin embryos. It's the coolest thing I've ever seen.

Yeah, it would be neat to have *Safta* come visit.

I sigh, getting caught up in the moment. "I feel like I could scan the whole country from up here." Then I think about the malls, miles and miles from here. "But it's so far from everything."

"You're a city girl, eh?"

"Through and through. Give me a Kate Spade purse and a pair of Lucky jeans and I'm a happy girl."

She laughs, the soft, warm sound filling the air.

"I love it here. Away from the noise, away from crowds. It's the perfect place on earth for an old woman like me. Besides, at my age I don't need a Kate Spade purse or Lucky jeans."

"I'm sure you were one hot mama when you were a teenager," I say, then want to take those words right back. Talking to her like she's one of my friends is a stupid thing to do.

"I married your grandfather when I was eighteen years old."

"Was it love at first sight?"

"No. I couldn't stand the sight of him. Until one day he bought me flowers."

Flowers? That's the oldest trick in the book. "So he brought you some roses and you fell in love?" It's a cute story, if a little boring.

Safta pats my hand. "No, *motek*. He bought me the whole flower shop. And the poor man was allergic to pollen."

"Wow." I'd be sold if a guy bought me my own Abercrombie and Fitch store. Now, that would be true love.

Safta starts to get up, and I grab her elbow to help her. Even though she told me she's fine, I have a feeling I'm not getting the whole story.

"I'm going to lie down," she says once she stands. "Go explore the moshav, your father should be back with dinner soon." I watch as she walks back down the dirt path toward the house.

Taking a deep breath, I head toward the entrance to the moshav. The winding road will be a great place for me to take a jog.

As I reach the security booth, a guy sticks his head out of the window.

"I'm going for a run," I say.

He nods his head and opens the gate.

When I start to jog, the fresh air in my lungs energizes me. The mountainous view is like out of a movie, and the music in my ears reminds me of home. I'm in heaven as my stride matches the rhythm of the song I'm listening to.

If only Mitch could see me now, jogging down a mountain. He's a nature nut. My best friend Jessica is, too. She'd probably be jealous of me.

While I'm thinking of Mitch and Jess, I whiz past some white boxes. Only after I pass them do I realize what they are.

Beehives.

What the hell are beehives doing on the side of the road?

I think I'm safe, until I see one of the stinging suckers has followed me. "Go away," I say, running faster. The bee flies faster, and he's doing circles around me.

I stop and stand as still as those guards in London who stand at the palace, hoping that will make him go away. But it doesn't, it only attracts another bee. And another. And another.

It feels like time has stopped, except my iPod is still playing music in my ear.

"Help!" I scream, and take off again. I'm waving my arms around like a madwoman, trying to get the bees off of me. Gross, I think one just got caught in my hair!

I'm running.

And waving my arms.

And shaking my head.

When I spot a car coming up the road, I'm hopeful it's Ron. But I'm shaking my head around so hard that I don't see who it is. The car passes me, but then I hear tires screech.

I run toward the car, until I realize who's getting out of the driver's side.

Avi.

The last possible person in the world I want to see.

"Get in," he says, opening up the passenger side.

I have two options: get in the car with a jerk who saw me buck naked or get stung by seven bees.

Call me crazy, call me stupid. But I choose option number two. "Go to hell," I say, and keep running down the mountain.

About three-quarters of the way down, the bees finally leave me alone. By some miracle, I've managed to avoid getting stung.

But now I'm stuck at the bottom of the mountain. And I don't want to go back up and pass the beehives again.

I have a brilliant idea. I'll wait for the Sperm Donor. *Safta* said he'll be coming back soon.

So I wait. And wait.

Forty-five minutes later, I'm still waiting.

I swear, this vacation is a total disaster. If I were home, I'd be playing tennis and hanging out with friends.

An hour goes by before I spot a car coming up the road. I recognize Doo-Doo. I wave my arms in the air like an air traffic control guy to make him stop. There's a girl in the car with him. The girl sticks her head out the window. "Do you need a ride?"

"Uh, yeah."

"Get inside."

Doo-Doo introduces me to the girl as I hop in the back seat. Her name is Ofra, and she also lives on the moshav. I lean back and enjoy the air conditioning blasting in the car.

"O'dead says you're going to come to the beach with us tonight." Ofra turns around and faces me from the front seat. "It's a special occasion."

"Your birthday?" I guess.

"No. Moron is going to the army."

That's something to celebrate?

Ofra looks excited when she says, "You have to bring something of yours to give him, then offer a piece of advice. It's the *moshav* ritual."

Ritual?

I think I'm allergic to rituals.

9

Before you speak up, make sure you know what you're saying.

The beach we go to is sandy, and borders a huge lake they tell me is called the Kineret. It's all seven of us tonight: me, Ofra, Snotty, Avi, Moron, Doo-Doo, and O'dead. The guys have made a huge bonfire, and we're sitting around it.

Avi leads Moron to a chair he's placed in the sand. Then he pulls out a shirt from a bag with Hebrew letters ironed on it. When he holds it up, everyone laughs.

Except me, of course, because I have no clue what's written on the shirt.

"What does it say?" I ask Ofra.

"Where's the bathroom?" she says.

"I don't know," I say. "I guess you're going to have to wait or pee in the sand."

They all laugh harder. And I realize they're laughing at me. "What?" I say.

Ofra pats my back. "I wasn't asking you where the bathroom is, I was telling you that's what the shirt says."

Oh, man.

"Avi, speak in English so Amy can understand," Ofra says.

He stands there, totally intimidating. "*Beseder*," he says begrudgingly. "My friend Moron here has gotten us lost on many occasions. His sense of direction is legendary, to say the least. So with this shirt, he might not be able to find his way home, but he'll be able to find his way to the nearest *sheruteem*." Then he looks at me and says, "That means bathroom."

Everyone else chuckles and claps.

"And my piece of advice is . . . don't flirt with any of the female instructors. They all have access to weapons bigger than yours."

This amuses everyone. I assume Moron has a reputation for flirting with girls.

After Avi sits down, Ofra and Snotty go up to Moron and give him a wrapped present. He opens it and holds a pair of boxer shorts up to us.

The front is just plain white, but ironed to the back is a map of Israel. "This way," Snotty says, "when you get lost you can always find your way back home."

"Yeah, but he's got to get naked to see the map," Doo-Doo says, laughing.

I laugh, too. Imagining Moron stuck in the middle of the desert, lost, wearing a shirt that says *Where's the bathroom* while he's naked from the waist down as he examines the map on his boxers, is pretty hysterical.

Ofra sits on one of Moron's legs, and Snotty sits on the other. "Our piece of advice is . . . let us shave your head instead of the army hairdresser."

I watch as Ofra pulls a cordless razor out of a bag. Moron gives a nervous smile to the rest of us. To be honest, he has a great head of hair. It's sandy brown, almost reaches his shoulders, and is really thick. Is he gonna let them shave it off?

Ofra turns on the razor, then she and Snotty stand up and go behind him.

"Take your shirt off," Doo-Doo suggests.

Moron pulls his shirt over his head, then raises his eyebrows. "Be gentle with me, girls," he teases.

"Keep your pants on," Ofra jokes and everyone, including me, laughs.

Snotty makes the first stripe down the middle of Moron's head as he squints his eyes shut.

O'dead takes a picture just as Snotty finishes one line. Then Ofra takes the razor and makes another stripe. They're all having a good time. Even, dare I admit it, me.

"Give Amy a turn," Doo-Doo suggests, then gives me a little push of encouragement.

I shake my head. "I'm not great with a razor," I say. Especially electric ones next to people's scalps.

Ofra and Snotty finish shaving Moron's head. They're having fun making designs with his hair as they do the job.

After they're done, O'dead stands next to Moron. "We've been friends since we were three, and I know how scared you are of the dark." O'dead pulls out a small flashlight. "So now, when they stick you in the Negev desert, you won't have anything to fear."

"Except the deadly snakes," Doo-Doo chimes in, making everyone laugh again.

"As long as I have females in my unit," Moron says, "I won't need any light, if you know what I mean."

"Which brings me to *my* gift," Doo-Doo says, then pulls out a small, pink, stuffed teddy bear. "This is for you to sleep with when you're alone at night and need something to hug."

"Our piece of advice is . . . when you sleep with your gun, make sure the safety is on."

Moron nods his head. "Great advice, guys."

"Now it's Amy's turn," Ofra says.

I look over at Snotty. The girl won't even acknowledge me. Then I turn to Ofra. "Go ahead," she says, urging me with her hand to get up.

Tentatively, I walk over to Moron and hold out a piece of material. "It's a bandana," I explain. "With a peace sign on it."

He takes the material from my hand and studies it. "*Todah*, thank you."

"They told me I should give you a piece of advice, too," I say. Then I clear my throat. Everyone is looking at me, even Snotty. And it makes me feel all sweaty inside. Talk about pressure.

"My piece of advice is . . ."

I swear, I had something to say, but forgot it. I'm on the spot here and my mind draws a blank. Shit. I look at the horizon, where the sun is falling into the water. The first thing that comes into my mind and out of my mouth is, "don't swim on a full stomach."

Oh my God. I can't believe I just said that. The guy is going to the desert for basic training. What are the chances that he's going to be swimming in the middle of the desert during military training?

My advice is met with silence.

"That was very . . . deep, Amy," Snotty says, clearly making fun of me.

I hear Doo-Doo ask O'dead, "Is she joking?"

If I knew how to get back to the moshav, I'd run there right now without turning back. But I can't, so I sit back down and try and shrink as much as I can into the sand.

"Well, I guess I should say something," Moron says, then stands. "Thank you for this great party, the gifts, and advice. Your friendship means a lot to me. Now, I know you're supposed to throw me into the Kineret, but you better not even try it."

"You have to get wet," Avi says matter-of-factly, gesturing toward the lake.

Doo-Doo and O'dead are ready to back Avi as he chases Moron around the beach.

I'm shocked when they tackle him and throw him into the water, making a huge splash. Moron is soaking wet, but he's not pissed. I would be if my friends tossed me, clothes and all, into a lake. But he's laughing right along with the rest of them.

Ofra goes to help Moron out of the water, until he grabs her arm and pulls her in with him.

Snotty joins the group. I watch as she puts her arms around Avi, and they both splash in the water together.

Hel-*lo*. Don't these people know it's usually the custom to swim with bathing suits, not fully clothed? Of course I'm not jealous they're in the water, laughing and having fun. I am absolutely content to stand here all alone.

"Amy, join us!" Moron calls out to me.

"Yeah," Ofra says. "The water's great."

I'm a land person, and don't particularly love water. "No, thanks," I say.

The first one out of the lake is my cousin. She stands straight in front of the bonfire, warming herself. I try to avoid making eye contact with her—I'm afraid if I do my mouth might get me in trouble.

But maybe I should try, like Ron said, to get to know her. Even though she's been rude, it could be because she doesn't know what a great and fun person I am. I guess I really haven't given her much of a chance. I'll attempt to soften her up a bit first. "Osnat, I really enjoyed meeting your friends," I say, thinking of how Ron said her name is spelled.

I swear, I deserve a medal for being so nice. She's probably going to say how much she's glad I opened up the lines of communication. Maybe by the end of the summer she'll be like the sister I never had.

My wayward thoughts are squashed as I watch her turn to me with a toss of her hair and say, "Just remember, Amy. They're my friends, not yours."

And just like that she goes back to being Snotty.

10

Sometimes we have to prove to others
we're strong even when we're not.

I've been in Israel for three weeks now.

Thankfully, I'm able to avoid Snotty and Avi. That means I'm spending a lot of time in the house with *Safta*, which is just fine with me.

She relayed stories about when she was a kid here in Israel and more about my grandfather, who died before I was born. She also told me about her parents, who escaped from Germany during World War II. Learning about my extended family has opened my eyes to another world.

As I wake up one morning to Ron's cheery, "Rise and shine, sleepyhead," I just want to go back to sleep.

What time is it anyway?

SD's words are buzzing around in my head like one of those bees that wouldn't leave me alone. I glance at my watch.

"Six thirty!" I say with a groggy voice. "Please have a very good reason why you're waking me before the sun shines through that window."

Now I know I'm being crabby, but I'm just not a morning person. Never have been, never will be. In my opinion, six thirty isn't even morning; it's still the middle of the night.

"Amy, we've been here a while now and I've left you alone. If you keep sleeping all day, you'll never get over your jet lag. Besides, work needs to be done around here and everyone pitches in. I want you to at least act like you're my daughter and help out."

I sit up and say, "Listen, I'm still tired and cranky. Just come back in, let's say, a couple of hours and we can discuss whatever you want."

"You're always tired and cranky and you need to get out of bed so Yucky can wash the sheets. There's probably mushrooms growing on them."

"Very funny."

"I've promised to help your uncle sell some of the sheep these next few weeks. After that, I want to show you my country."

"Yeah, let's do that. In a couple of weeks," I say just so he'll leave me alone.

I lie back down and pull the covers over my head. A little more sleep is what I need, not to work on my summer vacation or go sightsee. I'll have to convince the

Sperm Donor just because I happen to be on this stupid trip doesn't mean I have to do anything on it.

I let out a breath when I hear him leave the room. Looking over at Snotty's bed, I see it's empty. She's probably over at Avi's house.

Not that I'm jealous, 'cause I'm not. I just don't know why he's friends with her. She might be pretty, but she's mean.

Or maybe she's just mean to me. Which makes me hate her even more.

I close my eyes and try to think about good things, like going back home.

Nothing really makes me happy now. Is that what being sixteen is all about? If so, I can understand why teenagers express themselves in so many different ways. It's not as if we're stupid, we're just trying to figure out where we fit.

Me? I don't seem to fit anywhere these days. I'm like a square peg trying to fit into a round society. Now that I think about it more, I'm not square or round. More like an octagon. And I don't fit anywhere now. I thought I did, but my nice, super-dictated world has complicated all that. I wonder how Mitch is doing without me. Does he miss me?

I fall asleep again and when I wake up my stomach growls so I head to the kitchen. Everyone is gone and the house is quiet.

I glance over at *Safta*, who's sitting in a velour chair reading some book.

"*Boker tov*, Amy," she says in this dignified voice as I reach into the refrigerator and scan the contents.

"I'm sorry," I say. "I don't know what that means."

I finally learned *shalom* means three things: hello, goodbye, and peace. My Hebrew knowledge is pathetic, at best.

"*Boker tov* means 'good morning.'"

"Oh. *Boker tov* to you, too."

Gram seems a little quiet this morning. I'll sit with her and chitchat while I eat breakfast, maybe that'll cheer her up. In fact, I'll prepare something special for her.

As I arrange a plate of fruit, I take my time and cut little pieces of banana and melon in these shapes Jessica's mom taught me. Jessica calls things people rave about "crowd pleasers." Little cut-up fruit in the shape of a clown face is a definite crowd pleaser.

I set the plate down in front of her on a side table. "*Todah*," she says.

"You're welcome." I look down at my masterpiece. "It's a clown face."

"Very creative. Do you like cooking?"

"Not really. Eating I like. We go to restaurants mostly back home."

"Your father doesn't cook for you?"

I know what you're thinking. This is a great opportunity for me to tell *Safta* how it really is back home. But as I look at the old lady's glowing blue eyes I feel protective of her. As much as I'd like my gram to be ashamed of the Sperm Donor, I just can't make myself upset her.

"Well, every Friday he makes this great lasagna," I say, my mouth moving without my brain thinking too long about it. "And his chicken picatta is out of this world. He even bakes blueberry muffins for me on Sunday mornings."

The ol' lady has this little twinkle in her eye that I can't decipher.

"Chicken picatta, huh?" she says.

Oh, shit. She's onto me. I probably should have left out the muffins or made it BBQ chicken instead of picatta. But I'm stickin' with my story for better or worse.

"Yep. I'm sure if you ask him he'll make you some," I say as I look down at my feet and notice my toenail polish is chipped.

I hear the door open and *Doda* Yucky comes floating into the house. "Amy, *Safta* is starting her chemotherapy treatment in an hour," she says. We both help my grandma up. "Everyone is with the *sheeps*," *Doda* Yucky says. "They're waiting for you."

I am bowled over by a terrible sense of worry about *Safta*. Chemotherapy? Oh no . . . that means cancer.

"Can I go with you?" I ask. "I can read to you if you'd like."

Safta pats the back of my hand lightly. "Don't worry, I'll be fine. Go with the young people and enjoy your stay here. You don't want to be hanging around a hospital all day. Okay?"

"Okay."

I want to go with her, to make sure the doctors know she's *my Safta* and she needs the best care possible. Do they know how important she is?

Doda Yucky shuffles *Safta* out the door and I'm alone again. I continue to avoid the *sheeps* today. Ron wants me to help, but what if he gives me a job I can't do?

I don't want to give him a reason to resent I'm his kid. And if the opposite happened, if he bragged to everyone how great I am, I don't want the truth to come out that I'm less than perfect.

Deep down, even though we have major issues to overcome, I want him to be proud of me. I know it's a dumb thought, but it's true.

I spend the next hour rearranging my side of the closet. My eye catches on the skimpy clothes on the other side. Snotty sure does like showing a lot of skin.

I walk outside and wouldn't you know the yelping pup is waiting for me at the door. Great, the only one who likes me here is a dog.

"Arg!"

"Dumb mutt," I mutter.

"Arg!"

I ignore the mop following me at my feet. My spirits lift a bit when in front of the house, right under a nice big tree, is a hammock. I maneuver myself into it and put my hands behind my head as a pillow.

"Arg!"

I look in between the holes in the hammock and notice the mutt under me.

"What do you want?" I ask it.

"Arg! Arg! Arg!"

I groan. Dogs aren't my thing. They're really not. But just to shut it up I get off the hammock and pick up the nuisance. I get back on the hammock with the thing in my arms. It has to lay on me because he'd fall through the holes otherwise. He finds a comfortable spot on my stomach and sighs contentedly.

Against my better judgment, I find myself petting him. Even though he probably has fleas and other insects living off his body, he's soft and fluffy, like a down comforter.

"I-me!"

I look down and spot a cherubic face smiling up at me. It's my little cousin, Matan. He can't say my name right, he just calls me I-me. I think it's cute so I don't correct him.

Mutt jumps off my lap and I sit up. I see Matan has collected flowers in his chubby hands, and they're for me. My frozen heart starts to melt as he hands me the yellow, purple, and white wildflowers (or weeds, however you choose to look at them).

His smile widens when I take the flowers from him, smell them, and say, "Mmmm."

It's amazing how little effort it takes to make a child happy. Unfortunately, they all grow up and become cynical sixteen-year-olds like me.

Picking Matan up, I set him on the hammock next to me. He laughs as I swing the thing back and forth. I take one of the flowers and push the stem into his hair, the flower sticking out of his long, curly locks.

"Pretty," I say, laughing.

I know he doesn't understand a word of English, but he laughs back, then takes a flower out of my hand and puts it into *my* hair. We do this for about ten minutes, until we're both full of colorful wildflowers sticking out of our hair.

He speaks Hebrew to me and I speak English back to him. It doesn't matter that we're both oblivious to what the other is saying, we're having fun. And fun is universal in any language.

A lady who I haven't seen before comes up to us and says something to Matan. He jumps off the hammock and runs to her.

"Yucky left him with me, but he wanted to come see you. I hope it was okay," she says.

"It's fine," I say. "What does the name Matan mean in Hebrew?"

She looks down at my little cousin. "It means 'gift,'" she explains before leading him away.

He turns back, runs to me, and gives me a big hug. "*Shalom*, I-me," he says, then bounds off.

I give a little wave. "*Shalom*, Matan."

When he looks back with his hair full of flowers and furiously waves back at me, I realize I've just made my second friend in Israel (Mutt being the first).

11

Don't trust males.
Human or otherwise.

Going into the house, I take out my nail polish and hold it up. Cotton Candy is the name of the color. It's a bright, shiny pink that sparkles in the sunlight. I think it'll look great when the hellish sun reflects off of it.

I decide to paint my nails outside in the sun after I take the old polish off. Sitting down on the concrete in front of the house, I open the bottle. I feel better. I guess doing something I'm used to doing back home helps.

The mutt lies down next to me, using me as his shady tree. I let him, just because he'll keep bugging me anyway. I paint my toenails until I hear a sound coming out of the mutt's butt that sounds surprisingly like a fart.

"Eww," I say.

The dog doesn't get up, he just looks at me like *I'm* bothering *him*.

"Listen, if you're going to hang around me there's a couple of rules. Rule number one: bark like a dog. Rule number two: take a bath before you rub up against me. Rule number three: I don't want a dog, so go find someone else to bug. Rule number four, five, and six: no dog farts. Got it?"

Wouldn't you know it the mutt gets his lazy ass up and walks away. Did I say something wrong? Maybe I should go play with him later. Just so there's no hard feelings.

I go back to painting my nails when I hear someone walk up to the house. I look over and it's Avi, the last guy in the universe I want to see. And he's staring at me.

I dip the brush in the nail polish.

"Why stare? You've already seen me without my clothes on," I say, trying not to look in his direction. It's pretty hard, because he looks like an Abercrombie model.

But then I remember he saw me naked and I want him to be anywhere but in my line of vision. I can't walk because my toenails are wet and I don't want to smudge them. Anyway, why should I be the one to move?

Mutt decides at that moment to come back. I expect him to come directly to me, but instead he hobbles over to Avi.

Traitor.

"I wouldn't touch that thing," I say. "He's dirtier than my Uncle Bob."

Uncle Bob works in a factory. He cleans up okay, but no matter how many times he washes his hands, there's always this black, gooey gunk stuck under his nails.

Avi bends down and pets the traitor, who wags his tail so vigorously you'd think it was a flag in some parade. Then he looks at me. Not the traitor, Avi.

"You're not much for helping, are you?" he says.

I don't even have to try and sneer, his comment makes my lip curl on its own.

"What*ever*," I say.

Then I go back to painting my toenails a second coat. But now I'm so pissed at what Avi said my hand starts shaking and I'm getting nail polish on my toe-skin. Each stroke now looks like a two-year-old kid had a field day with the brush on my toes.

The dog trots over to me and buries his wet nose under my arm.

"Go away," I say.

He won't leave, he just sits down in front of me. I look over at Avi again, who's still eyeing me. Why does he do that?

"Arg!"

"Traitor," I grumble through gritted teeth to the mutt.

"Arg!"

If I tell you what the mutt does next you're not going to believe me. He sticks that butt of his in the air, like he's trying to play with me or something. When I don't take the bait, he grabs my shoe with his teeth and runs away.

Now this isn't just any shoe, it's my one and only pair of Ferragamo jelly sandals.

"Give that back!" I yell. "Do you have any idea how much that cost?"

I try to grab for it, but the white devil-pup starts shaking it back and forth in its mouth like a chew toy.

"Stop it," I say in a loud, warning tone.

But he doesn't. He starts running away with it. I get up, trying not to ruin my still-wet toenails in the process. But it's no use. As I head toward the dog, it trots away in the opposite direction.

Now it's war.

Most of the time I go through life at a relatively slow pace, but that doesn't mean I can't haul ass every once in a while. The only problem is my boobs bob up and down when I run fast. But I try not to think of that. I'm concentrating on saving my Ferragamo sandal.

The mutt stops beside one of the houses and I pretend I'm not going to get it. I sneak behind a lemon tree with the hugest lemons I've ever seen. They're as big as a baby's head.

When I think he might forget I'm behind the tree, I sneak a look at him. His butt is in the air again and his tail is wagging a mile a minute. He's looking straight at me.

And my sandal is still in his mangy, slobbery mouth.

"You should get neutered," I say as I step from behind the tree. Maybe then he'd have some respect for Ferragamo.

"Grrrr."

"What, no 'arg'?" While I'm talking to him, I'm sneaking up to him. "Keep that tail wagging so I can have something to grab at when I catch you, you slimy mutt."

"Grrrr."

"You don't scare me," I continue, inching closer. I'm almost within reach.

"Grrrr."

My concentration is solely on the sandal until I step and feel something squishy squeeze in between my toes. I look down and realize I've just stepped on an old, rotten cucumber. But at second glance, I realize it's not a cucumber, it's a DEAD SNAKE. It's black, but shimmers a bright fluorescent green in the sunlight.

I've never been more grossed out as I am now, running toward my uncle and aunt's house. Obscenities, some I even make up, are streaming out of my mouth. I'm trying hard not to think about the snake-guts that must be in the crevices of my toes as I run as fast as my legs can carry me.

"Ho . . ." I say to Avi in-between gagging. Please dear God let me get the word out before gagging again. "Ho . . ." Gag. "Hose!" I point to my foot just in case he doesn't get it.

The jerk gives a short laugh (at my expense) and I follow him to the back of the house. When I see the hose, I run toward it as fast as my snake-encrusted feet can carry me.

Avi turns the handle and I quickly chance a glance at my gross foot. Little pieces of black, stringy guts are peeking out from in between my toes. My toenails are dry now, with pieces of grass or hay stuck to them permanently.

I'm still gagging, I can't help it. I think if I stop looking at my toes I can get through this. When the water starts spurting out of the hose, I take it from him and aim the water toward my foot. My gaze lands on Avi. "Thanks a lot for helping me get my sandal," I say sarcastically.

"Thanks a lot for helping with the *sheeps*," he counters.

"It's *sheep*, not *sheeps*. Whether you have one sheep or a million of 'em, it's still sheep."

He walks forward and pulls the hose out of my hand. I watch wide-eyed as he bends on one knee and lifts my gross foot and places it in his hand. Then, if you can believe it, he washes my foot thoroughly.

I'm about to lose my balance, I really am. And it's not because I want Avi to catch me or anything. I hate playing the damsel in distress every time he's around.

I'm lightheaded because it's ungodly hot outside and I just busted my ass to run after a Ferragamo-stealing mutt. To top it off, this boy who I'm determined to hate has one of my feet in his hands.

"You can stop gagging. Whatever you stepped in is gone."

"It was a snake!"

He shrugs. Like it's no biggie.

"You ever stepped on a snake?" I ask.

"I usually watch where I step."

I yank my foot out of his grasp. "Well, where I live there are no snakes. Dead or otherwise."

He stands, which is not so great because I was feeling superior when he was on his knee. But he's probably six feet tall and when he looks down at me I feel small. Instead of responding, he gently pulls a flower out of my hair. "Cute," he says, twirling the stem between his fingers.

Oy, I forgot Matan filled my hair with white, purple, and yellow wildflowers. I must look like a clown.

"Your father wanted me to tell you everyone's at my house eating what you call lunch. If you want to join them, follow me."

I step beside him as he's walking, but then I stop. "Why didn't he tell me himself?"

Avi shoots me a withering glance. "He also wanted me to apologize for watching you undress the first night you were here."

"Well?"

"Israelis don't apologize for what they're not sorry for."

Now I'm really getting riled up. "You're *not* going to apologize?"

He looks at me straight in the eye. "What I saw was beautiful and natural, so why should I say sorry?"

12

Boys are either jerks or clueless.
Take your pick.

"Ron, I need to call home and my cell phone won't work."

I've been in Israel almost six weeks and need to call home once again. First of all, Mitch is back from his camping trip and I need to talk to him. Second of all, I need to call Mom and Jessica.

Ron is sitting on the couch watching some news channel in Hebrew. Uncle Chime is with him, along with the corkscrew-haired Matan.

Matan is naked and he's been like that for the better part of my trip so far. Who am I to bring it up to them that their son isn't dressed and his pee-wee is dangling out for all the *moshav* to see. You'd think they would have noticed they're not living in a nudist colony.

"I think your mom was going out of town," Ron says, his face still turned toward the television.

"So I'll call a friend."

"What's the number," he says as he heads toward the phone in the kitchen.

Obviously, like everywhere else around here, there's no privacy.

I recite Mitch's number and then he hands me the phone. I pull up a chair in front of the refrigerator and park myself there for the call.

"Hello," a scratchy voice answers.

"Mitch?" I say.

"Yeah?"

"It's Amy."

"Huh?"

"You know, your girlfriend," I say, starting to get pissed.

"Hey, babe. Sorry I haven't called, I got back late last night. Do you know what time it is?" he says, his voice still ragged.

"I'm in Israel, Mitch. And no, I don't know what time it is in Chicago because *I'm halfway across the globe.*"

"Wait, you lost me. Israel?"

"Are you sleeping or listening to me? 'Cause I can only make one call here and I've chosen to call you. It's like jail."

I hear him yawn and I can tell he's attempting to sit up instead of lie in bed. Hopefully now he'll pay some attention to what I'm saying.

"Mitch?"

"Wait, I gotta pee."

I have an urge to bang my head against the wall.

"Can't it wait?"

"No."

I'm trying to disguise my annoyance in front of the rest of the family.

"Well, can you hurry it up a bit? This is long distance, you know."

"I'm tryin', babe."

In the background I hear a stream of pee hitting water and Mitch lets out a long, satisfying sigh. I don't know if I should feel flattered he feels comfortable enough to pee while he's on the phone with me, or grossed out.

"You done?" I ask after I hear a loud flush.

"Yeah," he says. "I'm back in my room."

"You didn't wash your hands."

I mean, if I heard him pee and flush I would have definitely heard the sound of him washing his hands.

"You just told me to hurry up. If I wash my hands I have to put the phone down. You wanna wait?"

"I guess not. Just remember to wash them when you get off with me," I say. "And then disinfect the phone with antibacterial spray."

"Leave it to you, Amy, to tell it like it is."

Unfortunately, Snotty opens the front door and walks in the house with Ofra. Avi, Doo-Doo, and Moron follow them into the house. Great. Just my luck. Now I have a bigger audience to eavesdrop on my conversation with my boyfriend.

Out of the corner of my eye I catch Avi looking at me, his jaw tense. I haven't talked to him since he *purposely* didn't apologize for watching me undress. I think we've been avoiding each other, actually. Which is just fine with me.

I turn my chair around so I'm facing the wall and say quietly into the phone, "You know what I like about you?"

"Shit," Mitch says, "I just stubbed my toe on my skateboard."

It's not the response I was aiming for.

"You okay?" I ask, trying not to lose my patience.

"I think I'm bleeding. Wait a minute."

As I wonder how much a phone call costs per minute from Israel to the United States, I twirl the cord around my finger.

It's hard while I'm waiting not to turn around to catch a glimpse of what the others are doing. They're talking loudly in Hebrew.

I can't stand it anymore. I take a glimpse at Avi. He's wearing a black T-shirt with some Hebrew lettering on it and faded jeans ripped in both knees. He's also wearing a silver-linked chain around his wrist.

Now, I've seen boys wear jewelry before and haven't thought it enhances masculinity in the least. But Avi wears the bracelet like it's a manly accessory. He makes the other guys look dorky for not having a silver link chain bracelet on their wrists.

When my gaze travels up, I feel like a Peeping Tom when I realize he's caught me checking him out. Lifting the bracelet hand, he gives me a mock salute.

I can feel my face turn red and my blood starts to pound loudly in my head. He's seen me check him out. I want to die now, especially when he then walks up to Snotty and grabs her hand. That hand holding Snotty's is the same one that held my snake-guts-covered foot two weeks ago.

"Okay, I'm back," Mitch says. "No blood, but it still hurts like a bitch."

I forgot I was even on hold and, to be honest, wasn't paying attention to what Mitch just said. Turning back around, I giggle softly into the phone. Avi is trying to concentrate on Snotty, but I know for a fact he's listening to my end of the conversation.

"What's so funny?" Mitch asks. "I'm hurting here and all you can do is laugh?"

Have you ever tried to make other people think you're having a good time when you're not? What sucks is when the person you're with doesn't get it. They need to play along, but you can't tell them for fear of being discovered. *Play along with me, Mitch.*

"I can't wait to go camping with you," I say.

Let Snotty and all of them realize I have someone back home waiting for me. For some reason I'll feel like less of a loser here for hanging out by myself every day.

"What's wrong with you?" he says. "You hate camping."

"Of course I do," I say, then giggle again.

Giggling doesn't come naturally to me, but I do a pretty good job of making it sound authentic. I think.

Although my boyfriend now thinks I'm a freakoid.

"What about our tickets to the BoDeans concert at Ravinia for next weekend?" he says. "I spent fourteen bucks on those tickets, along with the extra thirty I spent on the Renaissance Faire tickets. You said you'd go with me."

Thankfully, the group heads outside. I let out a breath because I can finally be myself again.

I turn back around in the chair and stare at a flying spider-like thingy near the ceiling.

"Yeah, well that was before I got sucked into going to a country infested with Ferragamo-stealing mutts and flying spiders."

"Huh?"

"Forget it. I wish I could be there with you, really I do."

God, I hope he doesn't ask Roxanne Jeffries to go out with him. She's his next-door neighbor and has been flirting with him all year. He even told me she undresses with the curtains wide open.

"Say, I've got an awesome idea. Take Jessica. She's not doing anything this summer except working at a day camp for kids. She'll go with you." And she'll keep an eye on you for me.

"Don't you think it'd be weird if I go out with your best friend?"

"It's not like it'd be romantic or anything."

Jessica doesn't even think Mitch is cute. She's told me he reminds her of a poodle on Prozac. Everyone's entitled to an opinion. Mom always says, "Opinions are like assholes, everybody's got one and everyone thinks everyone else's stinks." It's true.

"I guess I could call her," he finally says.

"Tell her I miss her."

"Sure. When are you coming back?"

If I can manipulate Ron, very soon. "Before school starts, but who knows." We both go to Chicago Academy, a private high school.

He yawns. "Have fun."

As if. "You, too. Don't miss me too much."

He gives a short laugh before saying, "Bye, Amy."

I think I hear the phone click before I answer, "Bye."

13

A star is just a star.
Or is it?

It's nine o'clock the next morning and I'm bored, as usual.
I eat breakfast, alone again, as I watch *Safta* sit in her chair.
Snotty came home late last night, her friends all laughing
and making noise at two o'clock in the morning. I hate to
admit it, but I'm sorry I stayed home. With the exception
of Snotty and Avi, hanging with the group is kind of fun.

"Your *aba* wants you to go to the *sheeps*. He's waiting
for you," *Safta* says.

"I don't want to."

I know I sound like a little kid, but why go into detail
and hurt the ol' woman.

"He misses you."

What? He wouldn't miss me even if I disappeared from this earth.

"I don't think so," I say as I stuff hummus into a pita and take a bite.

"He loves his homeland and wants to share it with you."

I have a mouth full of hummus as I blurt out, "Why doesn't he move back here if he loves it so much?"

"I bet you know the answer to that question, Amy. He stays away because of you. You're his family. His future. His blood. Wherever you are is his home now."

I kneel beside her while I listen to her voice. It's soothing, and when she talks it almost sounds like a lullaby. I'm loud. My mom is loud. I talk loud. I walk loud. I'm just a loud person. But this old lady is like cotton, everything about her is soft and quiet. She leans over and takes something out of her pocket.

"Hold out your hand," she says.

I hold my hand out. She drops something into it and gently closes my fingers over my palm.

"What is it?" I ask.

"Look at it."

I open my fist and look at a small gold and diamond Jewish star glittering in the center of my palm. It's attached to a thin gold necklace. The star is smaller than a nickel, just big enough to know what it is, but small enough to be almost . . . private.

I don't know what to say to her. Being Jewish isn't a part of me. Mom doesn't believe in religion so I've never been to church except for my cousin's wedding. I've never been to a synagogue, either, except for Jessica's bat mitzvah.

"I'd like you to have it," *Safta* says. "It's called the *Magen David*, the star of David."

Man, I want it. I don't know why I want it, but I do. I'm not Jewish and would feel like a huge faker if I did take it. I mean, I could never wear it or anything. It's just so shiny and glittery and it actually means something important to *Safta*.

"I can't take this," I say. When I note the disappointment in the eyes that are an exact replica of mine I add, "It's too beautiful."

"You have something else to say, don't you?"

How does she know?

I stand up and say, "I'm not Jewish."

I can't look at her. If I do, I might see she's upset because a non-Jewish girl is her granddaughter. I don't know how Israelis feel about non-Jews. For some reason I don't want to know if she resents me. 'Cause I like *Safta*. A lot.

"Look at me, my sweet Amy."

Me? Sweet? I raise my eyes and look straight at her.

She's smiling, the wrinkles around her eyes making deep creases as she takes my hand in hers, the one still holding the necklace with the small Jewish star pendant.

"Being Jewish is more in your heart than in your mind. For some, being Jewish is strictly following the laws and customs of our ancestors. For others, it's being part of a community. Religion is very personal. It will always be there for you if you want or need it. You can choose to embrace it or decide your life doesn't need it. Nobody can force religion on you or it's not real."

Looking down at the necklace in my hand, I say, "Can I keep it? Just for a little while. I'll give it back, I promise."

She pats the top of my head. "I used to wonder why my son stayed away from Israel for so long, but I see the way he looks at you. He wants to protect you, keep you from hurt or harm while trying to respect that inner fire you possess. It is genuine and pure. Take the necklace," she says, then hesitates before adding, "for as long as you want it."

Staring at this woman, who has eyes that mirror mine and who says words that turn my world upside down, disturbs my inner being. I clutch the necklace in my hand. Then I turn around and head for the refrigerator, looking for some water. Even though it's right in front of my face as I open the door, my limbs feel paralyzed.

I close the fridge and turn to *Safta* as I walk toward the door.

"I think I'll take a walk," I say.

I take one more look at the necklace before gently placing it in my back pocket.

I find myself walking toward the sheep. When I get close to the pens, the Ferragamo-stealing mutt bounds toward me. Its filthy tail is wagging furiously, fanning his behind. Remembering my toes filled with snake-guts, I walk right past the dog and ignore its pathetic attempts at making up with me.

"Arg!"

I look down at the thing. "Arg, yourself. Where's my sandal?"

"Arg!" Wag. "Arg!" Wag.

He trots off toward a hilly area beyond the pens and I think of how lucky that dog is to be free to do as he pleases. Even steal other people's shoes without repercussions.

I walk farther into the pens, the sound of baying sheep and electric razors leading me in the right direction. Spotting Ron, I head toward him. I convince myself that as long as I just hang out here, there's no reason Ron will think I'm incompetent and regret I'm his daughter.

"Amy, honey, over here!"

My eyes wander to the direction of Ron's voice. He's never called me honey before and it kind of startles me. What does that mean, anyway? Honey. It's sweet, but it's also sticky and doesn't come off your hands easily. Annoyingly sweet. Is that me? Not on your life.

He's leaning down, and his knees are locking a sheep down while he's shearing its wooly hair off. The sheep doesn't seem to mind, but I do.

"Ron, that's inhumane," I say.

He finishes running the razor through the sheep's fur while the fluff falls beside him. He finally releases the poor, naked animal and looks up at me.

"You have a better way?" he asks.

It's then I realize Ron isn't the only one shearing the sheep. O'dead is next to Ron, Doo-Doo is next to O'dead, Uncle Chime is next to Doo-Doo, and Avi is next to my uncle. They're all exhausted, I can tell by the way they're breathing heavily and their shirts are wet with sweat. Not just their armpits and chests, their entire shirts are soaked through.

And they're all staring at me. Except O'dead. He's staring at Snotty, across in another pen. Hmmm.

The razor sounds stop and I feel like the world has, too. I think of something quick to say.

It comes to me like lightning and I blurt out, "Why don't you just leave the fur on?" Duh. It sounds so simple I give a short laugh.

Chuckles from my right side alert me to my cousin and Ofra. Snotty's wearing a tight black shirt and her dark makeup is running down her cheeks while feeding a lamb with a bottle. Hasn't she ever heard of waterproof mascara? Or the term *less is more?*

"They'll be too hot during summer months," Ron explains.

I sit down on one of the metal railings and watch. There are dogs in the middle of the pens, eating something red and gooey on the ground. My lips curl.

"What are the dogs eating?" I ask. Maybe I don't want to know, but my curiosity gets the best of me.

"One of the female sheep had a baby this morning."

"They're eating a lamb?"

"No, the placenta. It's very nutritious."

I gag. "Eww!" I say.

I shouldn't have asked. If I hadn't asked, I wouldn't know. GROSS! Baby sheep placenta. Blech! Stop thinking about it. Stop thinking about it.

But the more I will myself to stop thinking about it the more I can't look away. Kind of like those bloody crime scenes they show on television. You don't want to watch, but can't help it.

Out of the corner of my eye I see Mutt coming into the enclosure. He's small enough to go under the metal railings. When he looks at me, I squint at him.

"Do NOT eat sheep placenta," I tell him.

He nods at me, as if he understands what I just said. Then he tromps over to the placenta, starts to lick it, takes a part of the gooey, bloody thing in his mouth and tugs at it. I can't look any more.

If only Jessica were here, we could have a huge laugh at the whole grody situation. But she's not.

I walk over to where the newborn sheep are. A baby lamb stumbles over to me and I pet it with my hand.

"Hey sweetheart," I say.

"Baa," it whines back, which makes me smile.

I think it's the first time I've smiled since Matan put the flowers in my hair.

"Don't get too attached, he's going to be killed soon."

My heart sinks and my smile fades as quickly as it appeared. I turn to Snotty while I pick up the baby lamb.

"What?" I say.

"We have them slaughtered at three months old. That one's a boy so he'll be one of the first to go."

I look into the eyes of the small, helpless newborn and pull it closer to me protectively.

I'm a carnivore. Although meeting the animal I'm going to eat up close and personal makes me sick to my stomach. He's so cute. How can I even think about the poor guy being slaughtered? Maybe I won't cut out carbs after all.

Matan comes trotting up the lane with *Doda* Yucky behind him. He's naked, as usual. What's funny is I'm getting so used to seeing the kid naked that it doesn't even faze me.

He comes into the pen and runs around with the lambs. He's screeching in delight as he runs and tries to catch them.

After a minute the lambs start running after him. But it's not to play, I realize they think his little pee-wee is another baby bottle nipple. He's laughing and running away from the lambs that are trying to get milk out of his thingy like it's a game. Looking around, I notice *Doda* Yucky is laughing, as well as the rest of the people who have now stopped shearing the sheep.

I run over to Matan and pick his naked little body up to protect him from the perverted lambs.

After I carry him back to safety, I say very loudly to anyone who can hear me, "That. Is. *Not.* Okay."

Matan isn't fazed, neither is anyone else. They're still laughing. *Doda* Yucky talks to Uncle Chime before she and Matan trot happily back to the house, thank goodness.

The razors start up again, all the men except for Ron bending over the poor sheep. He says something to Uncle Chime in Hebrew before coming over to me.

"I have a job for you," he says.

14

*Determination and skill is half of
the job. Dumb luck is the other half.*

I follow him to the other end of the enclosure, which is
thankfully in the shade.

"When the *sheeps* are done being sheared, herd them
into this pen."

I look over at the skinny, bare-assed animal. Man, they
looked so fat, puffy, and large with all that fuzzy hair, it's
unbelievable how much smaller and vulnerable they look
after a shave. I can just sense their self-consciousness as a
shiver runs through my bones.

But I'm determined to help. I think. *Don't screw this
up, Amy.* My eyes wander to Snotty, feeding the baby animals with bottles of milk. That looks like fun. Why do
I get stuck with herding the bare-assed ones into a pen?

What if they start getting frisky with me? Worse, what if they start getting frisky with each other? Blech!

"You able to do it?" Ron asks.

"Of course," I say with more conviction than I feel. "Piece of cake," I add.

If I do this, maybe he'll be proud of me.

Uncle Chime lets one of the sheep go and it struggles to its feet. It's a male one, I can tell by the dangling thing in between its legs. And he's staring at me from the corner of the pen.

"Go on," I say.

But above the buzzing of the shearing I bet he can't hear me.

The sheep stares at me with his big, spooky, gray eyes. I wonder if he'll charge me. I move a step closer. He doesn't move.

"Go on," I say a bit louder this time.

Sincerely hoping nobody is watching me, I take another step toward the animal.

He backs up.

"This way, dummy," I say.

The thing won't listen to me. Damn. I look over at Ron, but thankfully he's not paying attention.

It's me against the sheep. Did I say the thing looked small and vulnerable after being shaved? I take that back. Before I step toward the menacing four-legged, bare-assed sheep with a dangling thing between its legs, out of the corner of my eye I see another sheep stand up. It heads next to the first one. Now I have two to deal with.

Avi stands up and heads over to get another fuzzy, fur-filled sheep to shear. As he does, our eyes meet. I still haven't forgiven him for the snake-guts incident. It's unbelievable he won't apologize for watching me while I was as naked as the sheep he's shearing. Kind of ironic, isn't it? I plead to him with my eyes, *Help me.*

He looks back at me with contempt. *Not on your life, Amy. You're on your own.* Jerk. Not that he actually voiced those words, but I know he was thinking it.

Screw him. I take another step toward the two sheep. Maybe if I channel their psyche they'll do what I want. I open my eyes wide and look at the bigger one intently. *Go inside the pen*, I urge with my mind. Focus, Amy, I tell myself. I put my fingertips on my temples in order to channel my thoughts to the damn four-legged creature who's looking at me like I'm a nutcase.

I feel a presence standing beside me. Turning abruptly, I almost knock into Avi. The confused expression on his face, with furrowed eyebrows and chocolate irises, tells me he thinks I'm a mashed potato (which, just in case you aren't familiar with the slang term, means a brainless human being).

"Yah!" he yells while stomping his foot on the ground. This coming from a guy who thinks *I'm* a mashed potato.

I turn back to the sheep, who have now just run into the adjacent pen at his command/stomp routine.

Avi's got this arrogant smirk on his face like he's done some massive accomplishment.

"I bet your boyfriend can't do that," he says.

How dare he bring Mitch into this . . . this . . . this . . . "I bet he wouldn't even want to," I say back.

For the rest of the afternoon, I copy the yell-stomp technique Avi showed me and I've become quite the herder.

At one point Ron even said, "Good job, honey." He'll never know how much those words meant to me.

Right after the adults leave the pens for the day, I watch as the teens gather together on bales of hay over ten feet tall.

I walk past them until Ofra yells down at me. "Amy, come up here."

Snotty glares at her, but Ofra ignores her.

"No, thanks," I say.

Avi is up there, sitting like he was born ten feet off the ground.

"She's scared to climb up here," he says. "She's got big words, but little courage."

Unbelievable. One minute he's trying to help me and the next he's being the biggest showoff and insulting me. It doesn't take more to get me climbing up the yellow, wiry straw.

When I get to the top, I don't know where to sit. I hang my feet over the edge of the hay and lean back. All eyes are on me. I turn to Avi and give him a little to stew about.

"Why do you hate me?" I ask.

I know this shouldn't be laundered in public like this, but I can't help it. I need to know, and I need to know now.

Avi doesn't answer and everyone else is looking away from him.

"Don't take it personally," Doo-Doo says. "He's been like this for a while."

"Why?" I direct my question to Doo-Doo, but I'm still looking at Avi.

Nobody says anything. The tension is as hot as the sun beating down on my back.

Avi barks out words in Hebrew I obviously can't possibly understand. My Hebrew vocabulary is limited to about five words. He knows this. Snotty knows this. Hell, they all know it.

Which makes me feel like one of those flying spider-looking things back at the house. Not a spider, not a fly. Just somewhere in-between.

They all start arguing. At once. Very loudly. It sounds like one big phlegm-fest because it seems as if every word in Hebrew has the 'ch' sound coming out of the middle of their throats.

It'd be nice to know what they're all talking about. Are they discussing why Avi hates me? It sure feels that way. But they're arguing.

It's obvious Avi and Snotty hate me, I'm so glad the other kids have been nice. O'dead leans his body closer to Snotty's each time he talks. Interesting observation I'll reserve for later. I wonder what it is about her that attracts all the guys? Anyone can have black makeup running down their face.

I stand, ready to climb down from this haystack. I feel so uncomfortable around Avi and Snotty.

"You want to come on a camping trip with us?" Doo-Doo asks.

My eyebrows furrow. Before I can answer, Avi interrupts me.

"*Mah-pee-tome!*" Avi says to Doo-Doo.

"*Llama-low?*" Doo-Doo says back to his friend.

"Hello? Why don't you speak English?" I finally say. "Don't you realize it's rude to talk privately while I'm right in front of you?"

Ofra leans back on her elbows and nods her head. "She has a point."

My eyes blink. I could almost kiss the girl on the lips for supporting me so much. Although I don't go that way. But if I did, I would.

Avi groans.

"I don't go camping," I say.

"You said you were going with your boyfriend. I heard you on the phone," Avi challenges.

Think quick, Amy. He's got your number.

"Yeah, well, I only go with him. Mitch has been a Boy Scout since he was, like, five years old or something."

Snotty hisses. "Amy, you make up stuff to try and look good. What's real with you and what's not? Avi's right about you."

Silence. Until I feel my patience snap inside my body.

I know I shouldn't start up with someone I have to share a room with. And I know it probably isn't the smartest thing to go off on my cousin in front of an audience. She probably won't understand what I'm going to say anyway because of the language barrier. But I can't help it, there's like an overload of adrenaline running through my brain.

Even as I tell myself to keep my mouth closed, I hear myself say, "Do you get off on being a royal bitch? 'Cause ever since I met you, you've treated me like a piece of shit." I'm on a roll and my mouth is working overtime. "I can't stand you, your short shirts, tight pants . . . or your sorry excuse for breasts! How's that for being real?"

I wave my finger at Avi. "And you, all you've got to offer is a bad attitude and a chip on your shoulder. I *will* go camping, just to piss . . . you . . . off! You don't like it, don't go. Then you can be an Israeli with a big mouth and little courage."

"You think you got courage?" Avi challenges me.

"Damn straight. I could push you off this thing without thinking twice."

He stands up, his mouth upturned in a smirk. "I dare you."

Okay, I think about it. But only once. Then I push his chest with all the strength I have.

He doesn't budge, the guy is like a rock.

When I hear his laugh, I turn around and jump down the piles of hay until I reach the ground. Wouldn't you know it a feeling of rationality comes over me right now. And I think:

I don't know why tears are rolling down my face.

I don't know why I just blew up at two people I'm going to have to see for the next month.

And I sure as hell don't know why I agreed to go on a camping trip in the middle of a war zone with people who hate me.

God, I'm in Israel, the Holy Land. Where are you?

15

When the pickins are slim,
you take what you can get.

That night after dinner, I'm watching television with *Doda* Yucky when Snotty's friends come barging in the door. Why don't people lock their doors around here?

Snotty and Ofra come out of the bedroom dressed in slinky, short, tight-fitting dresses. Avi, Doo-Doo, and O'dead are wearing jeans with long-sleeve T-shirts.

I don't ask where they're going tonight, because I don't care. I'm perfectly happy to sit in front of the television all day. I've been pleasantly surprised that there's a lot of American shows on TV in Israel. That's probably why Israelis know so much English.

Ron, who has been talking on the phone most of the evening, comes over to me. "The kids are going to a disco."

A disco? Discos went out in, like, the seventies. "Good for them," I say.

"Don't you want to go?"

"No."

"It might be fun to get off the *moshav*."

If he only knew what I said to O'snot earlier. I insulted her clothes *and* her boobs. I'm not about to admit those little facts to Ron.

"I'm going to ask them to take you," he says, and before I can stop him he stands up and walks over to Snotty. He says something in Hebrew to her.

She says something back.

At this point *Doda* Yucky interrupts her, her voice in a scolding tone. Then my aunt walks over to me and takes my hand. "O'snot wants to take you out with her friends."

Yeah, right. But the lady just fought on my behalf, and I don't have the heart to argue with her. Instead, I shoot a scalding look at Ron, the person who got me into this mess in the first place.

Ten minutes later I find myself in Avi's car, being driven down the mountain. Avi and Snotty ignore me, but I don't blame them. I hate them, they hate me. It's a mutual hate-hate relationship.

When we pull up to the "disco," I get out of the car and follow Snotty, Ofra, Doo-Doo, O'dead, and Avi to the entrance. It looks like a large warehouse. Loud music is blaring from the place and colorful, blinking lights are shining through large windows.

I halt as soon as I scan the long line of people waiting to get in. "Is it safe?" I ask.

"I promise there aren't any snakes inside for you to accidentally step on," Snotty says, then laughs at me.

My eyes flash in outrage as I focus on Avi. How could he have told Snotty about the snake-guts mishap? What a betrayal. Now I feel humiliated because of him.

"Come on," Ofra says, locking my arm with hers as she leads me to the line.

I toss my hair back and stand in line. When I reach the front, an army guard makes me open my purse and he checks the contents. I expect him to ask me for an ID, but he doesn't. I guess in Israel there are no age restrictions for dance clubs. When the army guy waves me on, I have to go through a metal detector in order to enter the 'disco.'

Boy, they're not taking any chances. If we had a soldier at the entrance to every town, shopping mall, and bar in the United States, we'd be out of soldiers. There wouldn't be anyone left to protect our country.

I walk in, and the floor is vibrating to the beat of the music because it's so loud. Snotty, Ofra, O'dead, and Doo-Doo go directly to the dance floor and start dancing. Avi is leaning against a railing, brooding as usual. But he's surrounded by girls while he's standing there so he doesn't look like a loner.

Me? Well, I'm standing here alone because I don't feel like dancing right now. It's wall-to-wall people, but I manage to squeeze through the crowd, heading for the bar. I need a Coke, or at least something in my hand so I'm not just standing around staring at people.

Luckily, I snag the only open barstool before anyone else can get their butt on it.

I take a moment to take it all in. The people at the disco are wearing very trendy outfits. They're also dancing, laughing, and drinking. The air smells like cigarette smoke; obviously there aren't smoking laws here.

I don't go to clubs back home because I'm only sixteen and they won't let me in until I'm twenty-one. But when I do, I'm going to have as much fun as these Israelis.

The bartender says something to me in Hebrew and places a beer mug in front of me with yellow liquid inside.

"I speak English," I say at the top of my lungs so he can hear me above the music.

He leans forward and says in my ear, "The guy over there bought you the drink."

He points to the other end of the bar, where a guy wearing a white button-down shirt with most of the buttons undone is sitting. Is he kidding? The guy looks as if he's about Avi's age, and has long hair. And it's not cool long hair, it looks like it's been greased back with too much hair gel. He's probably the *one* uncool guy in the whole place.

Great. I'm an uncool guy magnet.

To my horror, the guy is walking over to me as if he's some macho dude. He's wearing a huge grin on his face, which looks like it hasn't been shaved in a week.

I need help here.

Snotty and the gang are on the dance floor so they won't be much help. I search the room for Avi, who's obviously moved away from the railing. If I find him, I could pretend he's my date so this guy will leave me alone.

When my eyes finally settle on Avi, I realize he's not brooding anymore. He's dancing with some Hilary Duff look-alike.

To make matters worse, he's a good dancer. Not one of those guys who only moves from side to side. No, Avi moves like he's been born to dance with a girl in his arms.

I watch in disgust as he leans forward and says something into her ear, then they both laugh. For some reason I wish it wasn't so loud that he would have to be so close to her to talk. I don't care about him, I'm just pissed that he's having a good time and I'm not.

"*Allo, ay zeh cusit,*" Uncool Guy says once he's weaved his way through the crowd and is now standing in front of me.

"I speak English," I say, shrugging apologetically.

"My English not so good," he says. "You American?"

"Yes."

His eyes light up. "You want dance with me? My dancing better than my English."

I peer around him and take a peek at Avi, who is still dancing with his blond bimbo. Grabbing the guy's hand, I lead him to the middle of the dance floor.

I've taken classes at Julie's Dance Studio since I was four years old, so I'm not afraid to let loose. Listen, I wouldn't choose this guy to dance with, but at this point I can't be picky.

As I listen to the music, I pretend I'm dancing with my boyfriend. When the guy puts his hands around my waist, I want to think it's Mitch's hands holding me against him.

I close my eyes. The only problem is that in my imagination they're not Mitch's hands. They're Avi's. The guy I hate is haunting pure thoughts of me and my boyfriend.

Wait a minute. I think the guy I'm dancing with is feeling my back as if he's trying to locate the clasp on my bra. I open my eyes and whip around to face the *perv*. Lucky for me my bra fastens in the front.

I stop dancing. The perv leans forward to talk to me—it's too loud to hear unless the person is screaming in your ear. I think he's about to apologize, until I feel this slimy wet thing trying to climb into my ear canal.

What the hell *is* that?

When I realize Uncool Guy is trying to turn me on by sliding his Gene Simmons tongue around my ear and trying to shove it down my ear canal, I shriek and push him back. Anything to get his tongue as far away from my ear as possible.

Unfortunately, I've pushed him into some other people who were dancing. They're not too happy with me or the licker and push him back. This starts more pushing, and soon the place is out of control.

Oh, crap.

I'm lost in the crowd, unable to move because the crowd has turned into a mob. When someone grabs my hand and leads me out, I'm grateful.

Until I recognize Avi's bracelet attached to that hand.

I stumble outside with Avi and the rest of the mob. They've cleared out the club. When I see a police car with its lights flashing, I panic. Because someone over by the police car is talking to the soldiers and policemen while pointing at me.

"Shit. Amy, don't say anything," Avi says. "Let me talk."

When the soldiers and policeman come up to us, I zip my mouth shut.

"*Mah aseet*," the soldier says.

When Avi starts to talk, the guy puts up a hand and points to me.

I wanted to keep my mouth shut, I really did. My intentions were to stand here and stay silent. "I speak English," I blurt out.

"Did you start pushing people on the dance floor?" the soldier guy asks gruffly.

"Only because of the ear licker. I mean, at first he tried to feel me up but then, well, I thought he was going to apologize. Instead, my ear starts getting slimy and I realize he's not apologizing, he's giving my ear a tongue bath."

I know I'm rambling. I'm scared, and I know I deserve to be punished for causing a whole club to clear out because of me. A cold knot is forming in my stomach and I clutch Avi's hand.

Then, suddenly, out of the corner of my eye I catch a glimpse of the guy with the tongue. "There he is!" I yell.

The licker just backs up and disappears behind a car.

The soldier barks out orders at Avi and storms off.

"What did he say?"

"To take you home now or else he'll arrest you. Come on," he says.

"Do you have a Q-tip?" I ask him.

"Why?"

Duh! "So I can wipe that guy's germs out of my ear. I bet I already have an ear infection because of that dude."

He's walking so fast I can hardly keep up with him.

"You don't blame me for what happened back there, do you?"

When we reach Avi's car, he turns to me. "You were turning that guy on with your dancing. What did you expect?"

I meet his accusing eyes without flinching. "He knew I was American. Maybe Israelis like wet tongues in their ear, but in America—"

"He knew you were American?"

"Yeah. I told him when he bought me the beer."

"Beer? You were drinking alcohol with that guy? No wonder he thought you were easy."

"For your information, I am not easy."

"American girls have a reputation around here."

"Stop using me as proof of your stereotypes, Avi. It's not fair. Besides, you were shakin' it plenty tonight. You're just jealous because your blond bimbo didn't want to suck *your* ear off."

Snotty and friends are walking toward us. I cross my arms in front of my chest, waiting for them so we can go home.

"Someone started a fight inside the disco," Ofra says to me, offering her explanation of the commotion.

I bite my tongue and keep silent, but Avi glances sideways at me.

"You," Snotty says. "You started it, didn't you? I should have guessed. You can't do anything right."

"Leave her alone," Doo-Doo says. I want to kiss him right now for sticking up for me.

Feeling like I have support, I say to Snotty defiantly, "I can do anything you can do." And then, because adrenaline is flowing through my body I add, "And I can do it better."

The look on her face is priceless. She's thinking. I can almost hear her rusty, unused brain creaking as it's working. "Shear a sheep," she blurts out. "Tomorrow morning."

"No problem," I say with confidence, even though on the inside I'm shuddering at the thought of holding down a poor, defenseless sheep while I cut his fur off until he's naked.

But I'll do it, just to prove to everyone I don't screw everything up.

I just hope I don't make a fool out of myself.

16

> *I can do anything you can do,*
> *and I can do it better. I think.*

Just call me Amy the Sheep Shearer. That's what I've been trying to convince myself of all morning. After I found the note that Snotty wants to meet me after breakfast for our little challenge, that is.

Unfortunately, last night was not a nightmare. I really and truly challenged Snotty, and I hadn't even had any of that beer I was accused of consuming. Okay, I realize I'm the stupid one here, but I'm still determined to prove to her that I do not screw everything up.

I dress in jeans and a long-sleeve T-shirt for full protection. I don't have any protective goggles, so I put on my Coach sunglasses. Walking outside, I see Mutt bouncing toward me.

"You find my sandal yet?"

To answer me, he rolls onto his back. His tongue is hanging out of his mouth like a beggar.

"Don't grovel," I say. "It's not attractive."

I pick the mutt up and carry him with me. He might prove useful when I'm trying to corner the sheep. "Okay," I say. "Let's get a game plan. You make me look good, and I'll forget the sandal incident. Okay?"

Mutt's answer is a big fart.

This is not going to be my day.

When I reach the sheep pens, Ofra is the first person I see.

"You don't have to do this," she says.

Oh, yes I do. For me. For Mutt. For Americans all over the globe. Ofra's lack of confidence in me just furthers my resolve.

"That's okay. I want to do it," I assure her.

Doo-Doo comes over to me and gives me pointers. "Hold him down. Keep your eye on him. Don't drop the razor on your toe."

He's like a boxing coach, and in the ring is my opponent.

They've placed one sheep in the pen, along with a large razor hanging from the ceiling. Doo-Doo helps me strap the razor to my hand.

I survey my surroundings. Snotty is sitting on top of a railing with O'dead at her side. Ofra and Doo-Doo, my supporters, are beside me.

Avi is nowhere in sight. I'm surprised he didn't come to watch me get eaten alive by a sheep.

In the opposite pen is another sheep. Snotty's. I swear, it looks a lot smaller than mine.

Taking a deep breath, I enter the pen with the unsuspecting animal. He's even bigger than I thought. You'd think Snotty would have enough compassion to give me a lamb like the one in the nursery rhyme, but no.

This is definitely not Mary's little lamb. And its fleece is as dirty as Mutt's, not white as snow.

Snotty enters the other pen. She jumps right in, like she does this every day. Then she turns to me. "You're really going to go through with it?"

"Hell, yeah." I once saw a bumper sticker that showed a picture of an American flag and the caption below *These Colors Don't Run*. I'm not about to chicken out. Even though I really, really want to.

"Okay," she says, pure disbelief on her face. "On the count of three we'll start. Whoever finishes first, wins."

"Fair enough."

"One. Two. Three."

I put Mutt down and whisper, "Go do your thing."

Immediately, Mutt starts barking and the sheep scurries into the corner. I turn on the razor and head toward the menacing animal.

Until it looks at me with those big, gray eyes. I keep thinking that Ron told me it's too hot for them with their hair all bushy. I understand and sympathize. Okay, I'm trying to convince myself that I understand and sympathize.

It's not working.

I look down at Mutt, who's staring at me as if saying, *Do it!* He's right. There's no chickening out now. I have to face my fears and just do it. I hold up the razor like a sword and head into battle.

Except the stupid sheep runs away in fear. When it passes me, I hold out the razor like an idiot. Now the thing has a bald stripe down its back.

I try not to listen to or look at the progress in the other pen. I'm trying to concentrate solely on my mission. Mutt is barking up a storm, making the sheep nervous.

"Wrestle him to the ground and hold him there," I hear from my cheering section.

Should I break the news that I never had a brother to teach me to wrestle? Or a sister, for that matter.

"Mutt, you got to help me here."

Mutt is a great sheep herder. I realize this when the animal tries to move. Mutt expertly heads him off and gets him in the corner again.

With a swift move, I hold my weight against the wooly creature and start shearing. There's no rhyme or reason to it, I'm just so happy when the dirty, wooly fur starts flying off.

I hear lots of laughing, some cheering and various directions from Doo-Doo. I don't stop, I'm like a sheep shearing nut gone wild.

I step back and look at the poor animal. Okay, so I haven't done such a hot job. He has a Mohawk hairdo and his body looks like it's a road map. But I did it and I feel victorious.

Until I hear Ron's voice yell, "What the hell is going on here?"

17

*This roller coaster called life
is making me dizzy.*

"Amy, we need to talk."

I hate when parents think they can sit down and tell you what you've been doing wrong while they expect you to sit quiet and nod like a bobblehead figurine.

"What do you want?"

Right now I'm sitting outside the house petting Mutt. I'm proud of him, he's a great sheep herder. I can hear Uncle Chime yelling at Snotty inside the house. He didn't look too happy when Ron explained our little competition.

"I want to know what's going on with you," Ron says, sitting next to me.

"Nothing," I say.

He places one of his hands on my forearm. "Believe it or not, I want you to be happy. You don't have to shear sheep to prove anything to me."

I shrug his hand off me.

"If you want me to be happy, give me a ticket home right now. I don't belong here," I say. Then I add, "and I don't belong with you."

I don't know why I said it. I knew as the words left my lips it would hurt him. Maybe deep down I want to hurt him for not being there for me the past sixteen years of my life. I keep looking at Mutt and rubbing his tummy so I don't have to look at the disappointment of my life.

"Fine."

Wait. Did he just say "fine"? I think he did, but the word still doesn't register.

When I look up, Ron's back is to me. He's walking inside the house. My legs are a little numb from having the mutt on my lap for so long, but I scurry to get up and follow him.

When I enter the house, I walk up to him. He's rummaging through his suitcase.

"What did you say?" I ask.

He glances sideways at me before rummaging through his bag again. "I said 'fine,' Amy."

"Fine as in . . ."

"As in if you want me out of your life, if that will make you happy, then that's what I want for you." He takes papers out of his suitcase and holds them out to me. "Here's your ticket back to the States."

I hesitate for a moment. Then my hand reaches out and slips the paper out of his extended hand.

A wave of sorrow and confusion makes me freeze. Then I run out of the house and head to the place where *Safta* and I talked about her love for this place.

Sitting on the edge of the mountain, I think about everything here that I'll leave behind if I go home. Like Matan. Like my aunt and uncle, who I've just met. And Mutt.

But most of all, I want to be here for *Safta*. I love her, and can't just leave while I know she's going through chemo treatments.

I hug my knees to myself, thinking about this life here in Israel. It's a part of me, but not.

Walking back to the house, I look for Ron. I have to tell him I want to stay here for another reason, too: to find out where I fit into his life. When I see him talking on the phone, I sit on the kitchen chair, waiting.

Ron hands me the phone. "It's your mom. I called her."

"We need to talk, okay," I say to Ron before taking the phone out of his hand.

I watch as he nods, puts his hands in his pockets, and walks outside.

I put the receiver to my ear. "Hello?"

"Amy, are you okay? Ron just told me you want to come home."

"I did, but not anymore."

"You've changed your mind?"

"I guess," I say.

I hear her getting out of bed and closing a door. I bet she's locked herself in the bathroom because Marc with a "c" is in her bed and she doesn't want to wake the dork up.

After a minute she says to me in a very bubbly voice, "I have some great news."

"You broke up with Marc?" I say with a sigh of relief. "Finally."

"No, silly. Marc asked me to marry him last night. And I said yes."

"What!" I say as my heart sinks into my chest. This is not happening to me.

"It's so exciting," she says, oblivious to the fact that I'm totally freaking out here. "He had this special dinner planned. The ring was at the bottom of my champagne glass."

"He's a dork, Mom." Definitely NOT dad material. The ring at the bottom of the champagne glass is so cliché.

"He's one of the top real estate developers in the country. The new project on the Gold Coast, the most sought-after location in Chicago, is being done by his firm."

"So? We only have one parking spot for our condo. There's no room for his Mercedes," I say.

"I thought we'd look in the suburbs for a place. You know, something bigger . . . with a backyard and everything."

Huh? "As in you're moving to the 'burbs?"

"Isn't that wonderful!"

"Where does that leave me? Homeless?"

"Of course not, honey. Don't be ridiculous. Your home is with me and Marc."

Since when did "you and me" become "you, me, and Marc"?

Nice to know I'm important enough to consult with.

"Marc hates me, Mom." Right about now I feel as if everybody hates me.

"He does not. You haven't given him a fair chance."

I swallow hard and try not to cry.

"I know it's a shock to you, but I swear it's the best thing for us. We'll be a *family*."

I swear I'm going to hurl. A *family*? But Marc isn't my *family*.

"I thought you'd be happy. After you come back from Israel, you can help me plan for the wedding and look for a new house. We'll make a fresh start, the three of us."

I don't want a fresh start, I want an old start.

"I love you," she says.

If she loved me so much she would've thought before going ahead and screwing up my plans.

I have a huge lump in my throat when I say, "Congratulations. I love you, too."

"Bye, sweetheart. Call me next week, okay?" she says. "I just want us to be happy."

"Me, too," I say, then hang up. Happy is all in the eye of the beholder.

I march out of the house and spot Ron by an old, green tractor parked in the back of the house.

"You blew it!" I yell.

He has the audacity to look at me without saying anything.

I cross my arms in front of my chest. "Just keep standing there silent, Ron. You do that really well."

"What are you talking about?"

"I was just informed that Mom's dork boyfriend proposed to her. Couldn't *you* have proposed? It would have been nice to have my parents married; at the very least to say my parents were married at one point in time. But you were too selfish and worried about making sure you achieved the American Dream while basking in bachelorhood. You never fought for us. Worse, you never fought for me."

There, I finally said it. It may have taken me sixteen years and an attitude to cover up my insecurities, but I finally spilled the truth.

He blinks a couple of times, then says, "She's getting married?"

"I just said that, didn't I?"

He takes a deep breath, then sits on the bumper of the tractor. "Don't think I didn't fight, Amy. I asked her to marry me. And not just once. Before you were born and practically every time I saw her after your birth I got down on my knee. You were too busy running away from me to realize it."

"*If*, and I mean *if* you did propose, why didn't it happen? You were a commando, for God's sake. You're specially trained to get the mission accomplished."

He takes a long, deep breath. "She said she didn't want you growing up seeing a loveless marriage. She wanted to find a solid guy to be your *fadder*, not some Israeli immigrant. Every time I came to see you, I'd get a letter from her *fadder* threatening to tell the INS to cancel my visa. He accused me of getting her pregnant on purpose, to secure my American citizenship by marrying her. It wasn't true, but I feared never seeing you again. He was a powerful man, Amy."

He looks at me with a pained expression. "I don't expect you to understand."

"I do and I don't," I say, confused.

"When you told me to stop coming around, I didn't know what they'd told you about me. I just wanted a relationship with you, even if it was once a year."

"You're a real disappointment," I say.

I expect the you-must-respect-me-because-I'm-your-parent lecture, but instead Ron says, "You're right."

I'm shocked but say, "Damn straight I'm right. Maybe there's still a chance with Mom. You can call her and—"

"It's not going to change anything," he says, "and you know it. Deep down, you know she won't marry me."

"I feel so alone," I say, almost in a whisper.

"I love you," he says back. "It doesn't matter that you don't call me 'dad' or want to hug me. I've wanted that, but I want your friendship and trust even more."

This is a lot of information for me in one day. I need some time to digest it.

"I'm going to stay in Israel for the summer," I finally tell him. "Maybe we can, oh, I don't know."

The beginning of a smile tips the corners of his mouth.

With a shake of my head I say, "Don't get too excited, I'm still upset."

"I'm glad you're staying."

I turn around and head back into the house and into my bedroom.

Snotty is there.

Honestly, she's the last person I want to see. I remember I told her something about having small boobs or something like that, but it seems so long ago. I plop myself down on my bed.

"Are you packed?" she asks, bending over her backpack while putting things inside.

I lean back on my elbows. "For what?"

She turns around, those black-charcoal circles directed right at me. "Camping. You said you were going."

Laying back down on the bed, I say, "I lied."

"Just like an American."

"Excuse me? What's that supposed to mean?"

"Israelis say what we mean. You Americans just talk without meaning anything you say."

"We do not!" Geez, everyone is on my case lately. "For your information, I'm proud to be American. We may not always do or say the right thing, but what can you expect? Nobody wants to police the world, so they look to us to do it for them. We save everyone else's ass and then get blamed for it. Real fair, isn't it?"

Now I sound like an ambassador for the U.S.

Snotty lifts her backpack over her shoulder and walks out of the room.

"*Shalom*, Amy. We're leaving in ten minutes."

She leaves me with two choices: prove Snotty wrong and go on the camping trip to save face. Or stay on the moshav with nothing to do except herd bald sheep with Ron and Uncle Chime.

I walk into *Safta's* room and sit on the edge of her bed. My entire screwed-up life comes to a head and I'm completely confused.

"I need your advice."

She smiles warmly at me, like always. I am so happy to have her in my life, even if we did get a late start on getting to know each other.

"You see, it's like this," I say. I take a deep breath and let it all out as I talk. "My mom wants to marry her boyfriend, this guy I don't particularly like. Ron . . . you know, your son, has been a disappointment to me because to be honest he hasn't been a permanent fixture in my life. I resent them both, and I'm confused about who I am and where I fit in. And to top it off, O'snot is going on a trip with her friends, and I kind of want to get away and prove to her I'm capable, so I'm considering it."

Safta nods her head in thought, obviously understanding my predicament and giving it serious consideration.

"For a sixteen-year-old girl, you have a lot to deal with."

I let out another long breath. "Ain't that the truth."

"Maybe you need some time away. I think the camping trip is a good idea. Israel is a magical place, Amy. You just might find what you're looking for."

She's right. I need to get away from reality for a while. I kiss *Safta* on her cheek and head out of the room. But I stop at the door, turn around, and say, "I'm glad you're my *Safta*."

She tilts her head and smiles. "Me, too."

18

---

*Did you ever get the feeling you
were outnumbered?*

.

My heart is racing as I spot an empty backpack on the foot
of my bed. I must not have noticed it was there. It was
probably left for me. I hurry and stuff some clothes into
the bag and head outside.

When I get to the front of the house, all of the teenagers are climbing into the back of an open Jeep. It's like a
flatbed truck, but not. It has a cab part up front and in the
back is like a flatbed, but it has seats on both sides and rails
on top of the truck.

I catch sight of Snotty and she gives me this half-smile.
Yeah, yeah. I know. She realizes now she has the upper
hand because she kind of duped me into going on this trip.
Kind of. It was really my decision all along to come.

Ron comes up to me. "I don't want you going," he says. "You're too young and are going through a lot right now."

Realizing everyone is already in the car and just watching us have it out, I freeze. "Are you telling me I can't go?"

"I'm not saying that . . . exactly."

"I want to go."

Avi, who was in the driver's seat, gets out of the car and walks up to Ron. He takes Ron to the side of the house, away from my earshot. I wonder what he's saying. I wonder what they're both saying.

I watch as Ron and Avi shake hands after a few minutes. Then Avi walks up to me. I can tell he's not in a good mood.

"What?" I say.

"Avi assures me he'll look out for you," Ron says, then goes back into the house because *Doda* Yucky is calling him.

"I can take care of myself," I assure Avi when Ron is out of sight.

"Get in the car," Avi orders.

"I don't appreciate being ordered around by you."

"And I don't appreciate a spoiled American bitch delaying my vacation," he says low enough so only I can hear.

If my looks could kill, I'd be staring at a dead guy right about now. Spoiled American bitch my ass. I am *not* spoiled. I know this because I have two parents who want to destroy my life. I mean it. One took me on this trip so he could prove to me he's a great dad. But I bet after the trip he'll go back to his comfy bachelor life. My other parent wants to be rid of me for the summer so she can get engaged to a dork.

If I was spoiled, I'd be surrounded by people who love me. Like Jessica. Her parents spoil her rotten. And I mean rotten with a capital R. She not only has two brothers and a sister, she has two parents who *live* together. They *like* each other, so much so they even hold hands while watching TV. I've even seen them kiss. And this is *after* having four kids. And they're old, like in their forties or something.

To top it off, Jessica's mom makes these little fluffy low-carb cookies that just melt in your mouth. And you know why she makes 'em? I'll tell you why. For the sole reason she knows Jess likes them. Not only do I *not* get fluffy melt-in-your-mouth low-carb cookies, Mom won't even buy anything low-carb at the store. Why? Because my Mom doesn't believe in low-carb diets.

How dare Avi call me spoiled.

Avi walks back around the front of the car and I think he may just drive off without waiting for me. It's like a test.

I hate tests.

What's worse, I feel like this whole trip has been full of tests.

I reach into my pocket and feel the Jewish star *Safta* gave me. She told me the ancient Jewish warrior, Judah Maccabbee, put a six-point star on his war shield. The six points dig into my palm. I'm keeping it in my pocket wherever I go . . . like my very own shield.

When I hear the truck start up again, it doesn't take me long to throw my backpack into the flatbed and jump in.

Within minutes we're on a dirt road, the dust behind us proof of our journey. I have to hold on to the sides of the truck, the rocks in the road make the ride feel like a bumpy roller coaster.

And my boobs are bouncing around like crazy. As if they're not even attached to my body. I thought it was bad enough I had a backpack to be responsible for not flipping out of the truck. Now I have to make sure my boobs stay inside the truck, too.

At least, that's what it feels like. One's bouncing this way, one that way. Every time I cross my arms in front of my chest to keep them in one place, I lose my balance and bump into Doo-Doo (who's on one side of me) or Ofra, (who's on the other).

Can't Avi drive a little slower? It feels like this rocky dirt road has never been traveled before.

The sun is setting over the mountains. It's really pretty to see the reds, oranges, and yellows fade behind the mountains, outlining the landscape before finally disappearing for the night. It's getting darker as we drive, the light fading with each minute that passes. Before long, it's pitch black.

An hour later we finally stop. There's nothing around here, although I can see blinking lights from towns in the distance like twinkling stars in the night.

I forgot since I started this wild journey that I'm in Israel. Otherwise known as the war zone.

Nobody seems to mind as they pile out of the back of the truck. I scan the area as much as I can, which isn't much. I'm still in the truck when Avi comes around to the back of it.

Our eyes meet. "Are you coming out?" he asks.

I still have a bad feeling, as if there's something I'm not getting. And I'm still not over the fact that he called me a spoiled American bitch.

When I don't answer, he shrugs and starts to walk off. I can't see where he's going because it's so dark. But I know he's walking because I can hear the gravel crunch beneath his feet.

"Wait!" I say.

I hear the gravel stop. Then I hear him coming closer to the truck. He's staring at me, I can sense it.

"I, uh, need help getting out of the truck," I say lamely.

I feel his hand shoot out and reach for mine. I grab it and he leads me gently to the edge of the truck. Before I know it, he's released my grip and I feel both of his hands surround my waist as he lifts me from the truck and sets me safely on the ground.

We're both standing there, face to face as he keeps his hands on my waist and doesn't release me. His grasp almost feels like a caress and I don't want him to let me go. I feel safe when he's touching me, even though in the back of my head I can still hear him calling me a spoiled American bitch.

Just thinking of it makes me stiffen and I take a step back.

"Do you mind keeping your hands to yourself?" I find myself saying.

He drops his hands from my body and says, "Be careful for snakes."

"Snakes?"

As if I wasn't stiff enough at that moment. He walks away from me and I hear him give a short laugh. Snakes? Is he kidding?

"Don't worry," Doo-Doo says as he hands me a flashlight. "He's just trying to scare you."

"Well he's doing a good job of it," I mumble under my breath.

I watch as the girls sit down, close to where the guys are trying to start a fire. And I'm standing here by the Jeep.

I should have brought Mutt, he'd protect me from snakes and rude boys. Getting attached to the pup wasn't my idea, he just kind of got under my skin. Even though he is an annoying, Ferragamo-stealing beast.

19

I hate when others know more
about me than I do.

"Are you okay, Amy?" Ofra says. She's sitting with everybody next to the fire pit.

"Just super," I say.

I keep my backpack in the back of the Jeep and join the girls. They're talking in Hebrew. I'm used to that by now even though it still annoys me.

I have to sit there and smile when they smile, and like a dork I even let out a laugh when they laugh. I'm like a dumb mimic, because I don't even know what they're talking about!

For all I know they're saying, "Amy's got a booger sticking out of her nose." Then I go ahead and laugh right along with them, which makes it funnier to them but makes me and my hanging booger look like one big loser. When I think of this, every time they laugh I pretend to scratch my nose and feel for anything foreign hanging from my nostrils.

"So, tell me about American boys," Ofra says, and I could just kiss her for starting a conversation with me. "Are they as cute as I see on television? I like the boys on *The Young and the Restless*."

Believe it or not, I watch *The Young and the Restless*. Maybe I actually have something in common with an Israeli girl after all.

I give them all the scoop on the soaps. I can't believe they're so behind on the episodes here.

"You know so much," Ofra says.

I'm feeling a bit better now, thanks to Ofra. Even Snotty seems to be listening to me without my famous sneer on her face.

After about an hour of laughing and talking and drinking and eating, Ofra and I go off to find a place to pee. But since there are no toilets in the middle of nowhere, we have to squat. Luckily Ofra brought some toilet paper, or else I don't know what I'd do.

We walk away from the group to find a good place for squatting in private. We both have our flashlights on. I'm so afraid of stepping on a snake or other animal I keep the light moving from one side of me to the other.

Now that we're a little ways from the group, should I turn my flashlight off so Ofra doesn't have to see the show of me squatting?

Who cares? I hold the flashlight between my neck and my chin so I can see what I'm doing.

I realize pretty quickly I'm not a good squatter. Especially while trying to hold a flashlight under my chin. In fact, I'm horrible at it. Of course with a toilet I have no problems. Girls biologically weren't made to squat.

As I bend my knees as far as I can without falling, I try to relax. But I can feel the pee dripping right down my leg. So I quickly get into a crab position, with both my hands and feet on the ground. At least this way gravity can aid me in my endeavor.

Dare I look over at Ofra? Can she see me? I should turn off my flashlight, but that's impossible in the position I'm in. And I'm feeling a bit lightheaded. I know what you're thinking. That I'm probably going to fall right into the pee because I'm in a crab position and am feeling kind of off-balance.

But to my surprise, I'm able to keep my crab-pee position just fine. And when I'm done I wipe the best I can and put my shorts back on. I'm utterly proud of myself for this accomplishment. I can probably try out for that show Survivor now that I've peed without a proper toilet.

"Why does O'snot hate me?" I ask Ofra as we walk back to the campsite. I thought I didn't want to know, but I guess when it comes right down to it, I do.

She stops and looks at me thoughtfully. "It's a pride thing."

"Could you be a little more specific?"

"Well, Avi and O'snot have a history . . ."

"I knew it!" I say loudly.

"No, not like that. Well, it's like, uh . . ."

I'm standing patiently waiting for her to finish. Okay, not so patiently. But I don't think she realizes it.

Ofra starts biting a fingernail. "She'd kill me if I told you," she says.

"I'm going to kill you if you *don't* tell me."

"They've always been more than great friends. They've been like brother and sister. Avi used to date a lot of girls, but he hasn't in over a year."

"And . . ."

"Avi's going through a rough time right now. He's kind of been a jerk to everyone. O'snot thought if she and Avi were a couple, he'd get over whatever is eating him on the inside. He rejected her and I guess she's still upset about it."

"She hated me before she even met me."

"Well, she wasn't planning on sharing her room for the summer with an American either."

"What's wrong with being American? I thought the U.S. and Israel were allies."

"We are," she says as we start heading back to the campfire. "I guess we get a little pissed off that American kids don't have to join the army while we have to go as soon as we turn eighteen. Girls for two years, boys for three. Don't get me wrong, I want to go. But you American Jews sit in your nice houses on your nice pieces of land and party at your universities while we Jews in Israel put our lives on the line to prevent the destruction of our people and our tiny little piece of land."

"Really? It's that small?"

"The whole state of Israel is like the size of New Jersey."

"No kidding?"

"Nope."

Man, the way it sounds I'm starting to think American kids really do get the better end of the stick.

Ofra and I walk back to the campfire, where the rest of the group is setting out sleeping bags.

Now I panic.

I didn't plan for sleeping bags. Where are the tents? When people go camping back home there's tents. Or cabins. Or teepees.

"I didn't bring a sleeping bag," I say quietly to Ofra.

"That's okay," she says. "I'm sure Avi will share with you."

I blink, as if that would clear my hearing problem.

"Come on, Amy," Ofra says as she pushes my shoulder back. "You know Avi likes you."

Avi? *Likes* me? I don't think so.

"He *hates* me," I say.

I look over at the guy, and he's sitting on his sleeping bag Indian style, a guitar resting on his leg. "He called me a spoiled American bitch," I say to prove my point.

"Maybe he likes spoiled American bitches," she says before walking off to join Snotty, Doo-Doo, and O'dead.

"Right," I mumble back, although I know she can't hear me.

And for the first time since I came to Israel, I'm truly confused to the point where I'm getting this weird feeling inside my stomach every time I look at Avi.

Yes, he's hot as all get out.

Yes, he's about as masculine as a guy could get.

Yes, he's helped me with the snake-guts and herding the sheep.

But he's also arrogant, rude, and totally ignorant.

Could a guy like that actually be attracted to me?

On the other hand, could I actually be attracted to a guy like that?

20

Faking it . . .
It's another way of manipulating
people into doing what we want.

We're all sitting in front of the campfire, which is blazing now thanks to all three of the guys. And we're listening to Avi play his guitar. I have to admit, his voice is very soothing. Of course I don't have the foggiest idea what he's singing about because it's in Hebrew. Who knew the phlegm language could actually sound harmonious when put to music.

He's not looking at me as he's singing. O'dead and Snotty are singing along to the music, all very mellow now due to the mood of the night. Doo-Doo and Ofra are holding hands and are swaying to the sounds of the guitar.

Snotty and O'dead are sitting across from each other. He's staring at her googly-eyed while he's singing. She's oblivious.

When the song is over, I say to Avi, "That's a beautiful song. Did you write it?"

I can still hear the hum of the last note as Avi responds, "Yes."

"What's it about?" I ask.

His expression grows serious. "A guy who loses an important person in his life."

I automatically assume it's a girl and hate the wave of jealousy that comes over me. I don't respond. Silence fills the air. I think he hates me, but somehow I'm getting this weird feeling there's some sort of pain behind his words.

Thinking about what Ofra said, I can't help but wonder how I can figure out his true feelings for me. Not that I care what they are, but listen, an informed girl is a smart girl.

All indications up until now tell me he resents my presence in Israel and he thinks I'm spoiled (which I'm not).

Silence still hangs in the air. It's as if everyone is waiting for something to happen between me and Avi. Love or hate. Peace or war. I won't give them the satisfaction of knowing what I'm feeling. Heck, *I* don't even know what I'm feeling half the time or where my life is headed, thanks to my parents.

I've been trying to put out of my mind the fact that Mom wants to move to the suburbs. The next thing you know she'll be wanting babies with this guy. I may just be a sixteen-year-old kid, but I do know one thing: I am not, I repeat, I am NOT changing dirty diapers.

Just the thought of moving makes my stomach weak. Maybe Jessica's parents will let me move into their condo for junior and senior year. I could even pay them from the money Ron puts in the bank for me. Normally I wouldn't touch that money, but pride hasn't been a word in my vocabulary since coming to Israel. Why should anything be different when I go home?

While I've been daydreaming, I notice the rest of the group has started getting into their sleeping bags.

Only I don't have one. I scan the area. There's three guys and three girls now that Moron has left for his army service. I could sleep with Ofra, but she and Doo-Doo have found a spot off to the side and they've zippered their sleeping bags together. I didn't even know they were a couple until tonight.

Avi is putting his guitar back in its case. There's no way I'm going to ask Snotty if I can sleep with her, she was the person who manipulated me into coming on this little "survivor" vacation in the first place.

Avi knows I'm just standing here watching everyone. This sucks, because I want to make him squirm. Oh, great. Now he's walking up to me. Instead of waiting for him, a light bulb goes off in my brain.

Now I've got a plan. Okay, it's not well thought out and it does require some manipulation, but I think it will have the desired consequence.

I ignore Avi advancing on me and hurriedly crouch next to O'dead.

"O'dead," I say really sweetly. I imagine Avi watching my every move. His eyes are like lasers on the back of my head.

O'dead finally looks in my direction. "Huh?"

Now I'm doing this really big yawn with the arm stretch and everything. It looks authentic, I think. And it definitely gets everyone's attention, except Ofra and Doo-Doo. They're still making out and probably won't be coming up for air for a while.

"I'm really tired and I forgot to bring a sleeping bag," I say, making sure you-know-who hears. "Would you mind if I shared yours?"

O'dead right now looks like a mouse cornered by a cat. By the way, I'm the cat. Meow! O'dead looks from me to Avi.

I'm so tempted to look behind me to see Avi's expression. I'm also wondering what Snotty thinks; she seems to be oblivious to everything else around here.

Before the poor guy can answer me, I say, "Thanks," and go back to the car where there's some privacy to change into my PJs.

I have a huge grin on my face and I don't even know why. I know Avi was going to offer his sleeping bag to me, like he's playing the hero or something. Then he could have more ammunition that I'm a spoiled American bitch who's ruining his vacation. Screw that. I'm going to stay away from him as much as possible on this trip.

Starting with sleeping with O'dead.

Of course I'm not actually going to *sleep* with O'dead. Just sleep with him. Although as I think about how small the sleeping bag is, I'm probably not going to get much sleep tonight.

I can't believe it's getting so cold outside. It's so hot during the day I could fry an egg on a rock in seconds. But now, as I take my bra off underneath my T-shirt and hurriedly change into another shirt, I've got goose bumps all over my body. Brr! I wish I'd thought to bring sweats.

I bind my hair in a high ponytail, brush my teeth with bottled water from the back of the truck, and trot quickly back to O'dead's sleeping bag. I'm rubbing my forearms with my hands to keep warm, but it's no use.

"It's so cold," I say to nobody in particular.

Avi's the only one in his sleeping bag. The rest have gone off to who knows where.

I unzip the bag and examine the interior.

"What are you doing?" Avi asks.

"Checking for snakes," I say before making sure the bag is safe and start zippering it back up. "You know, you should do the same. I wouldn't want you to get bit or anything."

He sits up and regards me with those big, dark eyes. "I bet you'd like it if I got bit."

"No. What I'd like is if you'd leave me alone. You're eighteen. Don't you have to join the army or something?" I say as I settle into O'dead's sleeping bag.

I suddenly realize as I try to lay down I'm *sans* pillow. That means without. Avi throws his at me and it hits me in the face. I grimace, but take the soft thing as Avi turns around and lays down, his head resting on his bent arm. I should feel guilty about taking his pillow, but I don't.

"In two months," he murmurs.

I sit up. "What?"

He doesn't answer. Instead, he says, *"Lyla tov,* Amy."

I don't know much Hebrew, but I've been in Israel long enough to know *lyla tov* means "good night." He's trying to piss me off. I just know it.

I unzip the sleeping bag and stand up. Then I walk over to Avi and crouch next to him. His eyes are closed. Faker.

"Helloooo?"

He opens one eye. "What?"

I sigh loudly. "A second ago, you said two months. What's in two months, besides me leaving this awful place that's as hot as hell in the day, but as frosty as the North Pole now."

He doesn't move, just says with eyes closed as if he's talking in his sleep, "I start basic training for the IDF in September."

"What's the IDF?" I ask.

"Israeli Defense Forces."

Basic training in the Israeli Defense Forces? I feel a little bit bad for Avi he has to go join the army whether he wants to or not.

"I'm sorry," I say.

This time he opens both eyes. "For what? I'm proud to be able to protect my people, my country. What do you do to protect yours?"

What a bitter, bitter dude.

"I do enough," I say. "If Israel didn't piss off all its neighbors then maybe—"

He leans forward, his expression hard. "Don't you dare judge my country. Until you've walked in our shoes," he says, "you have no clue what it's like to be Israeli."

I'm trying not to be nervous, but the way he's talking makes me shake a little.

"Yeah, well, don't judge my country either," I say back.

I start to get up. He grabs my wrist and pulls me back down.

"That's the difference between us. I *am* my country. You're just a product of yours."

Yanking my arm away I say, "That's not the only difference, Avi. I'm going to college and will be successful after high school. And you, you'll probably just be a dumb Israeli sheep farmer the rest of your life."

Stomping back to O'dead's sleeping bag, I feel better thinking about how now I really proved to him I am a bitch.

I undo the sleeping bag once again to check for any fanged creatures who have decided to nest in the place I'm going to sleep. Luckily, there are none so I zip the thing back up and shimmy inside.

Looking back at Avi, I see his back is to me. Good.

Unfortunately, just as I'm getting comfortable O'dead and the gang come back. I'm trying to take up the least amount of space possible, but it's no use. This bag wasn't made for two people.

O'dead kneels down and climbs into the bag with me. I give him a small smile. I don't want him to think I'm not grateful he's agreed to share his warm sleeping bag with me. But I definitely don't want him to think I'm coming on to him either.

He might suspect I'm going to rip his clothes off or something. *As if.* I haven't even done more than kiss my own boyfriend. I'm what you call a sexually slow girl. Because I know what they teach in sex ed is actually true. There *are* real-life consequences to having sex before marriage.

Like AIDS.

Like other sexually transmitted diseases that last a lifetime.

Like an unwanted baby—like *me!*

There's no way in hell I'm going to risk bringing a baby into this world without being married to the man I love. Unlike both of my parents. I mean, what were they thinking? Don't get me wrong, I'm glad to be alive. But the crap I've had to go through my whole life, including this trip and my mom's brain fart by agreeing to marry Marc is ruining my life.

I mean, if we were a normal family I'd be in heaven—not Israel.

Great. Now I'm lying spoon-style with a guy I'm not even remotely interested in. In fact, I know he likes my cousin.

How do I get myself into these situations in the first place? This sleeping bag is way too small for the two of us. And I'm painfully aware my mongo boobs are pressed against O'dead's back.

Closing my eyes, I pray sleep will come fast. But now that I can't see, my other senses are heightened. Like the sound of the fire crackling, the crickets chirping. Like the masculine, musky scent of Avi lingering on his pillow. Like hoping my nipples aren't poking O'dead's back because it's so damn cold outside. It's all keeping me awake, which gives me a great idea.

I wait five minutes before I start snoring.

Of course I'm up, but I have to make it sound authentic. I make sure my mouth is close to O'dead's ear before I start. First, I make this long, slow snoring sound that doesn't really sound like a snore at all, but loud breathing.

Keeping my eyes closed, I breathe in loudly and exhale with the back of my tongue vibrating against the roof of my mouth.

O'dead shifts, probably attempting to wake me up. Only I'm not really sleeping so it doesn't work.

I snore a little louder, and this time add a little nose and extra back-throat noises with just the right touch.

I continue this for a few minutes, ignoring his fidgeting and restless moving around in the sleeping bag made for one-and-a-half. In fact, I should be up for an academy award for this performance. Some would say it's not nice to trick people. But listen, sleep is more important than anything. And if I don't get enough sleep, I'm going to be crabbier than I usually am come morning.

Heavy breath. Exhale loudly. Nose and back-throat combo. Exhale softer. Nose only. Exhale loudly. Heavy breath. Exhale normal.

I'm mixing up the order so it sounds authentic. Genius, right?

The finale is coming. I know it, but nobody else does.

Heavy breath. Exhale softly.

Here it comes . . .

Sleep apnea-type choke as loud as possible. Exhale normal. I know how to do this because Marc snores. Mom thinks I can't tell when he sleeps over because he leaves at five in the morning or something like that. The guy sounds louder than a train wreck. I wonder how Mom can stand it; it keeps *me* up half the night and my room is way down the hall.

I do another one of those obnoxious apnea-type snorts and sure enough O'dead starts wiggling out of the sleeping bag.

Mission accomplished.

I hear O'dead walk away and I squeeze one eye open to spy on him. I know he's going to ask Snotty to sleep in her sleeping bag. Ha! I am so sneaky.

But as my one eyeball scans the area inconspicuously, I get a weird feeling someone's watching me. Then I realize why I feel that way. Avi's looking straight at me, and he gives me this I-know-you're-a-faker look with those depthless, brown eyes of his.

He's getting to be a real pain in my ass.

I give him a harrumph, quickly shut my eye and go back to pretending I'm sleeping.

21

If humans were meant to be in water,
we would have been born with fins.

"Amy, wake up."

I squint to the sound of my cousin's voice and the early morning sun.

"I'm sleeping," I say, then shut my eyes and turn over.

"You can sleep later," Snotty says. "We're leaving in five minutes."

I moan, because as I stated earlier I'm not a morning person. Heck, sometimes I'm not even a day person. I turn back around and squint my eyes open again as I look at her.

"I thought this camping thing was supposed to be a vacation."

"Yeah. So?"

"Yeah, so . . . why wake up before you have to?" I say.

Snotty crouches down and whips the pillow out from under my head. Which, by the way, slams down on the rock beneath it.

"Ouch!" I yell. "Give that back!"

But she's not listening to me because my dear cousin's back is facing me as she walks away. With, I might add, my pillow under her smelly armpit.

Okay, so it's not exactly *my* pillow. But it was last night and it was really fluffy and soft and smelled really comforting. I know that's probably not possible. That's just how it felt to me.

Reluctantly, I get up and head over to the Jeep where the rest of the gang is hanging out.

"It's too early," I say in a moaning, groggy voice.

Nobody answers me, they're all packing up their stuff. And they're all dressed. What is it with these people, getting up and dressed at the crack of dawn?

"Ready to go," Avi says to me.

I open my arms wide, showing him my pajamas. "Do I look ready?"

"Maybe there's miscommunication. I didn't ask you if you were ready to go. I'm saying we're going. Now. It's not always about you, Amy."

I give him my famous sneer. "I do not always think it's about me," I say.

I watch as one of his eyebrows rises up in amused contempt. Then he has the audacity to fetch my backpack and shove it at me.

"I'd advise you to wear a bathing suit," he says.

"Why, where are we going?" I ask.

"Kayaking. Down the Jordan River."

When should I break the news to him I'm not going to kayak down the Jordan River, or any other river for that matter? I don't kayak. I don't canoe. I don't even swim well.

But just to show him I don't think it's all about me, I stalk off to change behind some bushes.

When I come back, everything is packed up and in the flatbed truck. O'dead is driving and next to him in the front is O'snot. Of course Ofra is cuddling up next to Doo-Doo. So that means I have to sit next to Avi.

Great, just what I need first thing in the morning. I park myself next to him and make sure I don't make eye contact. It's starting to get warm outside so I have shorts on and a bikini top.

But as we start moving, I realize my choice in tops is not the best. Damn, I forgot the rocky road we're driving on does not bode well for my boobs.

The bikini top I'm wearing is not a support bra, not even close. And when O'dead starts driving faster, I have no choice but to hold on to the railing. Which means my boobs are bouncing around like buoys on a windy day. Maybe I will have a boob reduction after all, detached pinky parts or not.

I guess Avi realizes I'm uncomfortable because he shifts closer to me and puts his arm around my shoulders. He holds me so strongly I don't have to hold on to anything and my boobs are shmushed so tightly they aren't moving, either.

I should pull away from him. I should slap him for holding me like I'm his. But I feel so . . . stable against him. Nothing's bouncing out of control and that's a good thing. So I stay where I am.

Until, minutes later, we finally turn onto a paved road. I yank myself out of his embrace and push my shoulders back in a dignified manner. Or as dignified as I can while wearing a bikini top.

Luckily, as I look at Ofra and Doo-Doo, they're too involved in gazing into each other's eyes to notice what's going on. Good.

Before long, we've turned into a large parking lot. Everyone gets out of the Jeep and heads to the entrance of the place. Except me.

"Come on," Snotty says as she puts on her backpack.

"I'm not going."

"Why?"

"I'll just wait until you get back."

"You'll be waiting a long time, Amy. Moron is meeting us at the end of the river. We're not coming back here for a couple of days."

My heart starts pounding fast.

"Did you say a couple of *days?*"

"Yeah. Don't be scared. Kayaking is fun."

I give a little huff as I think of white-water rapids and all the different ways I could die in the water.

"I'm not scared. I just . . . well, I don't like water all that much. Maybe there's a phone around here and I can . . ."

She puts her hands on her hips and interrupts me, saying, "You're scared, but you won't admit it. If you're such a baby, I'll ride with you."

I pick up my backpack and jump out of the truck, my feet landing on the gravel parking lot with a loud thud. I put on my sunglasses and look up at her. "You don't know anything."

"I know you think you're tough, but you're really not."

I start walking toward the entrance to the kayak place and say, "And I know O'dead likes you way more than a friend."

She runs to catch up with me. "What did you say?"

"O'dead likes you."

"Only as a friend."

I throw my backpack over my shoulder. "I see the way he looks at you. It's definitely more than friendship."

"Can you find out for sure?" she asks with hope in her voice.

I shrug. "You're Israeli," I say. "Why don't you go straight up to him and ask him? You keep reminding me how Israelis don't bullshit or beat around the bush."

"I . . . I can't."

I huff loudly, mocking her like she mocks me all the time. "Okay, I'll ask him for you." We start walking toward the river together. "By the way, I don't *think* I'm tough," I say. "I *am* tough."

22

> *Being a good kisser has a direct*
> *correlation to how much you like*
> *the person you're kissing.*

Walking with attitude over to the kayak place is hard while I have a sinking feeling in my stomach I'm not going to get out of this situation alive. But at least Snotty will come in my kayak; I see they're only made for two.

Listen, I know if I sink everyone will be happy, including my cousin. Too bad for her if I go down, she goes with me.

I watch carefully as Doo-Doo and Ofra get into the first kayak. It seems unstable, to say the least. The kayak is not one of those hard plastic-made ones, it's a blow-up rubber one. Whoever the hell thought of a blow-up kayak is one dumb sucker. Don't they know one sharp stick poking it or a hungry piranha and the kayak will pop?

"You okay?" Avi asks. I look at him and he's wearing a blue Nike bathing suit with a white stripe down the sides.

I give him a look. "Of course I'm okay," I say. "What would make you think I'm not okay?"

They're all looking at me like I'm a mashed potato.

"Get in," Snotty says as she tosses our backpacks into the kayak.

My eyes dart back and forth between her and the guy who's launching the inflatable kayaks. He looks like he'll push me in if I don't move faster.

"Do you need a life vest?" the guy asks me.

Yes. "No. But this kayak is running out of air," I say as I point to the floating thing. "I think it has a hole in it."

Kayak-Man has the audacity to actually snicker at me until Avi jerks the life vest out of the guy's hand and says to me, "Get in. I'll help you."

"O'snot's going with me," I counter. Then I look at Avi over the top of my sunglasses. "You're going with O'dead."

I say this then push my sunglasses back up.

Before I realize what he's doing, Avi picks me up and throws me like a bale of hay over his shoulder. Then he jumps right into the kayak. It's wobbly and I'm scared and I'm clawing at him and I'm yelling obscenities.

He sets me down on the bottom of the kayak and pushes off with one of the oars.

"Why did you do that?!" I scream, obviously having a very hard time controlling my fear.

He ignores me and keeps paddling our kayak down the river, letting O'dead and O'snot pass us.

"Put on the jacket. It's gonna get rough," he says after he's been paddling for a few minutes.

I thread my arms through the holes, but I can't click the belt shut.

"My boobs are too big for this thing," I say irritably. "It doesn't fit."

He steers the kayak to the side of the river and holds on to a branch to stop us from moving forward. "Lean toward me," Avi says.

I expect him to make some comment about my cleavage which now, thanks to the life jacket, resembles butt cheeks. But he doesn't. Instead, he leans forward and takes the straps, loosens them to make them longer, and fastens them.

When I realize we're not moving and are still against the bank of the river, I look up. Avi is still close to me, his face inches from mine.

Suddenly I start to feel something in the pit of my stomach. Like I'm going to be sick, but not.

He's watching me intensely and his nearness is making me dizzy. Then he leans closer and closer.

"What are you doing?" I ask.

He touches his fingers lightly to my cheek and all I can think about is the softness of his fingertips on my skin.

"I'm going to kiss you," he explains.

At first, I'm dumbfounded.

"I have a boyfriend," I blurt out softly.

"I know," he says as he rubs my lip gently with his thumb.

"And . . . and you're a jerk most of the time."

His lips are so close I can feel the heat of them.

"Amy?"

"Yeah," I say nervously.

"Stop talking so I can kiss you."

Before I can answer with some smart-ass remark, his lips are on mine. And when I say it's nothing like I've ever felt before, I mean it.

I have to be detailed here so you get the whole picture.

So one hand of his is on my face, cupping it gently as if it was porcelain and could break at the slightest touch. Then he slowly brushes his lips against mine, almost as if he's painting each part of my mouth with his.

It's wonderful. It's intoxicating. And it's totally intense to the point that my mind is reeling out of control. Mitch never kissed me like he would treasure and memorize my lips forever.

When he slowly pulls back and drops his fingers from my cheek, I say, "Why did you do that?"

His mouth twists into a wry smile. "Why did I kiss you or why did I stop kissing you?"

"The first one."

He settles on his seat in the kayak and leans back. I hear the birds chirping in the trees and the wind shaking the leaves. As if they're whispering about what just happened between me and Avi. I wonder what they're saying.

"You needed it," he finally says.

Somewhere in all of this my sunglasses have fallen off and are resting on the bottom of the kayak. I snatch them up and push them back on the bridge of my nose before he can tell what I'm truly feeling.

"Excuse me?" I say. I *needed* to be kissed? What the hell kind of comment is that?

He pushes the kayak away from the bank of the river, picks up an oar, and starts paddling. Then he hands me the other oar. What I really want to do is bang him over the head with the thing. Instead, I yank my oar from his grip and say dumbly, "You kissed me."

He shrugs and paddles some more, the muscles in his arms flexing each time he strokes against the small current. "Just forget about it."

As if I could. That wasn't just some little peck—that was like a slam dunk in the NBA playoffs. And it wasn't even a French kiss, but it was more intimate. I don't know exactly what I was feeling during it. My whole being, my whole spirit, was involved. Not just my lips. I know I'm sounding like a geek, even to myself. And before you think it, it wasn't the four-letter word called love.

"Amy?" he says.

"What?" I think he's going to apologize and tell me our kiss was a soul-searching experience and it's changed his life forever.

"Hold on."

"As in 'wait, I have something to tell you'?" I ask.

"As in 'hold on to the kayak, we're reaching the rapids.'"

23

If you start a fight,
I'll finish it.

If I tell you my life just flashed before my eyes, I'd be telling you the truth. Even Avi's kiss seems like a million years ago as I turn around and see the running waves, the bubbling water, and the white, foamy top to the rapids.

"I don't want to die!" I screech.

"You're not going to die," he says loudly above the sound of the massive rush of water. "Just stay on that side of the kayak so we don't tip over."

"I can't swim," I admit to him.

"You have a life jacket on. Just relax. If we tip you'll be safe."

"I'm scared." And all I want to do is have him hold me so I feel safe. I close my eyes tightly as I hold a deathgrip on the sides of the kayak.

"Don't worry, I'd never let anything happen to you. Just talk to me and it'll be over before you know it."

"What do you want me to talk about?" I say.

Does he want me to tell him where I want to be buried or who I'd like to say my eulogy after we DIE in this river? I think he might not be able to hear me because I know he's working hard by the way the kayak is maneuvering around the rapids.

"Tell me about your mom."

Not the best start to a conversation at this moment. I guess it's better than talking about my burial.

"She's going to marry her boyfriend."

"You don't like the guy?"

"Not really," I say emphatically.

"So move in with your *aba.*"

I open my eyes. "My *aba?*"

"You know . . . Ron. *Aba* is *father* in Hebrew."

"I know that. But I'm for sure *not* moving in with him."

"Doesn't he live in Chicago?"

"Yeah."

"So what's the problem?"

"The problem is that he's not my father. Biologically speaking, maybe. We have a lot to work out between us before he can be considered a real father."

"If you say so," he says matter-of-factly.

I'm suddenly aware we've passed the rapids and are now slowly gliding down the river.

"Don't tell me Moses survived going down this river in a basket as a newborn," I say.

He throws his head back and gives a hardy laugh, the first I've seen or heard from him.

"That would be the Nile River, Amy."

"Yeah, well I'll stick to bathtubs. They're much less dangerous."

We ride the rest of the way in silence and I rest my head on the rim of the kayak. I hope some sun rays will give me a golden tan and not burn my skin to a crisp. Believe it or not, I'm trying not to think about that comment Avi said to me after our kiss. But, in fact, I'm obsessing about it.

You needed it. Yeah, that's what he said. Can you believe it?

Maybe *he* needed it. Either way, it's not going to happen again. What would I say to Mitch? Maybe I shouldn't even tell him I kissed another guy. It's not like he's going to find out on his own or anything. And it didn't mean anything; it was just an innocent one-timer.

If food falling on the floor gets a five-second rule, shouldn't an innocent kiss get a one-timer rule? Of course it should, although I guess there is this itsy-bitsy-teensy-weensy part of my brain that's nagging me it wasn't an innocent kiss.

And I'm definitely ignoring the fact that there's this itsy-bitsy-teensy-weensy little part of me that wants to try it again. But not because I *need* it, that's for damn sure.

I sit up. Just as I'm about to ask Avi what he meant by his comment about the kiss, we catch up to the other two kayaks.

"What took you guys so long?" Snotty asks.

I instantaneously blush when everyone focuses on us. My eyes dart from Avi to the rest of the gang guiltily.

A sly smile crosses O'dead's face and he raises his eyebrows a few times.

Instead of admitting we kissed and thinking of ways to divert the attention of the others, I take my paddle (which up until now I haven't used) and whack it on the water to splash Snotty and O'dead.

Direct hit!

My cousin and O'dead are shocked, their clothes are soaked, and I feel triumphant. Ha! That'll teach them to butt into my business.

Snotty and O'dead try paddling closer to us and I frantically paddle away from them. Looking over at my kayak partner, I notice his paddle is not even in the water.

"Help me!" I scream while laughing.

"This is your fight, not mine," he says.

To answer him, I stick my paddle in the water and whack it in his direction. Avi is now dripping with Jordan River water.

I stick my tongue out at him, then say, "Now it is your fight."

Oh, I know what's coming next. I'm not stupid enough to think I'm going to stay dry for long. When Avi's paddle goes into the water and out of the corner of my eye I see

O'dead and Snotty's kayak come closer, I just keep whacking my paddle on the river like a madwoman.

Water from all sides is coming at me. Ofra and Doo-Doo must be joining the chaos. Not that I could actually see anything, because my eyes are shut tight. For all I know I could be whacking water all over myself along with everyone else.

Suddenly, it's quiet except for my paddle hitting the water. So I stop and open my eyes.

Of course when I do, I realize it's the oldest trick in the book. Because as soon as I open my eyes, water splashes on me with a vengeance by everyone else.

"Truce!" I scream, especially when I realize how much water has entered the bottom of our kayak. "We're going to sink!"

The splashing stops and I realize we're all laughing together. And it makes me feel like I'm really part of their little club of friends.

By the time Avi and I reach the landing spot, our kayak is miraculously still floating. And waiting for us is a soldier with a machine gun slung over his shoulder.

At first, I'm startled. Then I realize who the soldier is . . . it's Moron, Avi's friend from the moshav. And the bandana I gave him with the peace sign is wrapped around the butt of his gun.

Wow. My gift did mean something to him.

"Hi, Moron," I say when I get out of the kayak.

He smiles at me. "Hey, Amy."

I wish I could take a picture of him smiling like that in his uniform and gun with a peace sign on it. He looks so . . . nice and harmless, not like someone who would actually shoot that gun at people. I could see the caption now in some national magazine: Moron, Israeli soldier.

The way the media likes to twist things around, the caption would probably get read like this: Moron Israeli soldier. Like he's a complete idiot instead of realizing it's the guy's name.

Moron walks up to me and says, "I'll be your military escort for the rest of your trip."

Military escort? Why do we need a military escort?

"You're kidding, right?"

"No."

I don't want anyone to laugh at me so I don't ask the other questions running through my head. Listen, I'm just starting to feel comfortable with these people and I don't want to make myself an outcast again.

We take a minibus and drive for hours and hours. The landscape of this beautiful land is breathtaking . . . one minute we're driving through grassy mountains resembling the rolling hills in *The Sound of Music* and the next we're in the middle of a large, populated city. If that weren't enough contrast, in another hour we're smack dab in the middle of a desert without a tree or house in sight.

Out the window I see Bedouin Arabs herding their goats in the desert. It's as if I'm looking at hundreds of years in the past through a piece of glass.

A half hour later I see military tanks trekking on the desert floor, shooting.

"What are they doing with those tanks?" I ask nervously.

"Target practice," Avi says.

I hope their aim is accurate.

In less than two months Avi will be a soldier, too, learning to shoot a gun. And he's less than two years older than me.

It's the strangest thing. I'm actually getting used to seeing soldiers all around and guns and tanks daily . . . it boggles my mind how different life is here.

We stop off at a little store to get Cokes (thank the mighty lord) and snacks.

I watch through the store window as Avi goes out to the parking lot alone. I pay for my Kit Kat with the few shekels Snotty gave me and head after him.

"Okay, let's have it out," I say.

He turns to me as if surprised I'm cornering him. "What do you mean?"

"Duh! Why did you say back in the kayak you kissed me because I needed it? If that wasn't the biggest copout, I don't know what is."

"What's a copout?"

I roll my eyes. "You know, taking the easy way out instead of admitting you liked kissing me. Admit it, Avi."

"I told your *aba* I would take care of you on this trip and nothing would happen to you."

"Yeah, well you can throw that promise out the window."

"I'm sorry if I led you on, but it's not going to happen between us."

I'm tired of arguing. Instead, to prove my point I reach out and grab the back of his head and pull him toward me. Instantly, our lips touch and it's like I'm in that kayak with him once again. I close my eyes and wrap both arms around his neck, glad when his arms go around my waist and he pulls me closer. I don't care who's watching, I wouldn't change this for the world.

But suddenly he drops his hands from my waist and pulls away. Then I watch in horror as he swipes his mouth with the back of his hand, as if he wants to erase the kiss off his lips.

"I can't do this, Amy. Don't make it hard for me."

Tears are welling in my eyes and I'm not even trying to stop them or wipe them.

"Don't cry," he says, reaching out to wipe a tear streaming down my cheek. "You're a great girl—"

"Don't say that just to try and make me feel better. In fact, don't say anything to me. I get it, loud and clear."

I start to walk away from him and head to the minibus.

"Amy, let me explain," he says, catching me on my arm.

I stand there, waiting for words I'm not sure I want to hear. I look up at his face and for the first time I see something I've never seen before from him. Sorrow. It is so prevalent it makes me scared.

He squeezes his eyes shut for a second, as if the words coming out of his mouth will cause him pain just by saying them.

"My brother Micha died last year in a bombing."

He looks at me for my reaction, but I'm too stunned to say anything. Instead, I hug Avi tight, wishing I could take some of the pain away from him even though I know in my heart I can't.

"I'm so sorry," I whisper into his chest.

We stay that way for a long time. When he pulls back, I notice his eyes are bloodshot. He covers them with the palms of his hands.

"I hate being emotional," he says.

"I'm probably one of the most emotional people I know," I admit.

He gives me one of his rare smiles, then his expression turns serious.

"I like you, Amy. Probably more than I want to admit, even to myself. But I don't want to get serious with anyone right now. I have a nephew without a father and a sister-in-law who just sits at home grieving her dead husband. I'm going into the army next month. If something happens—"

"If I promise not to grieve for you if you die, will that make you feel better?" I say.

He shakes his head. "It's not funny, Amy. I'm going to be trained as a commando."

"Listen, I'm just talking about a summer fling, not some lifetime love affair." I'm not even thinking about Mitch right now. And I have a feeling Mitch isn't thinking about me, either. Avi and I have a connection I can't ignore.

"You're too emotional not to get involved. You could never have a summer fling. Not the way it's been between us, at least."

"Then what about we end it when this little adventure trip is over. If you want to be a coward for the rest of your life, go ahead. But if you want to have a great time with a kickass girl, you're going to have to face your fears." I want to say *please, please, please*, but I don't. Listen, a girl's got to have a little dignity left if she's rejected by the guy she likes.

"Who's the kickass girl?" he asks, pretending to look around for one.

Playfully I punch him in the stomach.

Nothing more is said about our non-relationship, but he kisses me and says, "You ready for this?"

I wink at him and say playfully, "Absolutely."

When he grabs my hand and leads me toward the rest of the gang, I'm not surprised their eyes are wide with shock. Listen, if I were in their shoes I'd think the world spun on its axis a bit too fast to see me and Avi trying out an actual relationship. Even if it's only a non-committed, short fling.

The only thing nagging me in the back of my head is . . . what are the sleeping arrangements going to be like tonight?

Avi is eighteen, and way more experienced than me.

Will he expect more than I'm willing to give?

24

Doing the wrong thing
sometimes feels so right.

Moron drives us to a hotel. To be honest, I don't know how he found the place. It's in the middle of the desert with nothing else for miles around, or at least that's what it seems like.

The whole ride to Beersheva, Avi and I were really close, almost as if an invisible wall has been lifted between us. I rest comfortably in his arms and even sleep on his lap during the ride. And you know what? He strokes my hair, as if he treasures it. It feels sooooo good, almost too good because I'm getting these tingling sensations all over my body from just thinking about him kissing me again.

But as we arrive at the hotel and head to the front desk in the lobby, I'm getting a bit nervous. Sleeping next to

O'dead was safe and uneventful. To be fair, we never actually slept together because of my fake snoring.

I look over at Avi. I know I couldn't pass the fake snoring past him; he knows when I'm faking. Besides, I wouldn't even want to be fake with him.

But I'm nervous as to what he expects from me. I don't want to be one of those girls who gets in trouble with a guy and then says, "Yes, I slept in the same bed with him, but I didn't expect it to get out of hand . . ." I'm always thinking, *You shouldn't have slept in the same bed with him in the first place, dummy.*

"What are the sleeping arrangements?" I ask Ofra.

"Who do you want to sleep with?" she asks with a hint of sarcasm in her voice.

Snotty dangles three keys in our faces and says, "The girls are sleeping with the girls and the guys with the guys."

I'm relieved the guys and girls are going to be sleeping in separate rooms. Somehow I have the feeling things could get out of hand with me and Avi. Our relationship is so explosive in other ways I'm sure it will be that way if we're alone together.

We settle ourselves into our rooms, take a short *siesta,* and head to the restaurant in the hotel for dinner in the evening.

After dinner, I make it my business to sit next to O'dead as we all sit in the lobby of the hotel.

"O'dead, will you help me with something?" I ask.

He shrugs. "Sure."

I give O'snot a wink and lead him to my hotel room. It's the one I'm sharing with Ofra and O'snot. When we get in the room I motion to the bed and say, "Sit down."

He shuffles his feet uncomfortably. "Amy, I'm not interested in you like that."

I lean against the wall. "Is there someone you *are* interested in? Like O'snot?"

His mouth goes wide. "How did you know?"

I roll my eyes. "It's obvious. And you need a little kick in the butt to make it happen between the two of you."

A knock on the door interrupts us. When I open it, it's Avi. And he's not looking too happy.

"What's going on here?" Avi asks.

I put my arm around Avi and kiss him on the lips to calm him down. "Are you jealous?"

He just stares into my eyes without saying anything.

"I'm trying to fix up O'dead and O'snot," I explain.

Avi's eyes dart from me to O'dead, whose nod confirms what I just said.

I say to O'dead, "O'snot wants to know how you feel, so go to her and spill your guts." When his eyebrows are furrowed I realize my slang English has confused him. "Go tell her how you feel. Now, before she finds some other guy."

He leaves the room quicker than I've ever seen him move before.

Avi grins.

"What?" I ask.

"You did a very nice thing, Amy. Totally selfless."

I turn away from him. "No I didn't. I was just getting sick and tired of watching him look at her like he'd die if she didn't pay attention to him." God forbid I should be seen as soft.

He comes up behind me and wraps his arms around my waist.

"You want to go for a walk?"

I nod.

He holds my hand as we exit the hotel and aimlessly trek down a gravel path. I get a sweet fluttering feeling in my heart just by being close to Avi.

"Tell me more about your brother."

Avi's pace slows and he takes a deep breath. "I don't talk about him much."

"Why?"

He hesitates before saying, "It hurts. Like deep inside here." He points to his heart. "I know, it's not very cool."

I squeeze his hand. "No, it is cool. I mean, it shows you loved him. But you have to talk about it. If you don't, part of your brother's spirit dies along with him."

He stops and thinks about this for a minute. Then he nods his head slowly. "He loved playing soccer. He was way better than me, but he let me win most of the time to boost my ego."

"Sounds like a cool brother to me. You're lucky."

"Yeah." He shakes his head and sighs. "I wish it was me who died instead."

"Is that why you're Mr. Angry all the time?"

"I don't know," he says. "I guess so."

"You can't change the past, Avi. Believe me, I've tried. But it doesn't work."

"This conversation is deep."

I laugh. "You're right."

"Let's talk about something else. Like how much you like me."

I want to say *I am totally into you*, but instead blurt out, "Ofra says you've dated a lot of girls. Is it true?"

This feeling in my heart scares me and maybe I want to push him away subconsciously. If I hear about his other girlfriends, it will be easier to protect myself because I'll distance myself emotionally from him.

"I've dated," he answers. "But not for a while. I was afraid in the kayak I'd be a bad kisser, it's been so long."

"Your kissing was just fine," I say. More than fine. We start climbing a rocky hill next to the hotel. "I want to know more about you," I say as he helps me reach a large rock that sits high on the hill.

Avi sits down overlooking the dark desert on one side and lights twinkling like diamonds from a town in the distance on the other. It's a very romantic setting and I wonder if Avi's taken other girls here. He guides me down and I sit in front of him, between his outstretched legs.

"What do you want to know?" he asks.

A lot, to be honest. But I say the most common question a girl asks a guy, hating I can't come up with something original or something sounding more mature.

"How many girls have you been with?"

"Been with?" he says from behind me. I feel his warm breath on the back of my head as he leans closer to me. I resist the urge to lean back into him and close my eyes. "Kissed?"

I don't want to think about other things he's done with girls so I say, "Yeah. Kissed."

"Including my mother?"

"No, smart-ass, not your mom. You know what I mean. A real kiss."

"A guy isn't supposed to talk about how many girls he's kissed. I'll tell you what. If you'll tell me, I'll tell you."

I give him a look as if I'll kill him if he doesn't spill the beans. "You first."

"I guess about eight," he finally admits.

"Eight!" I say, flabbergasted.

"Why?" he asks, and I can sense the alarm in his voice. "How many have you kissed? I bet it's a lot more by the way you kissed me in the kayak."

I smile at his compliment but say, "Less than you."

Try two, although the first one probably shouldn't count because that was during a camp overnighter and it happened accidentally in the dark.

You might wonder how I *accidentally* kissed someone. Well, I thought I was kissing this guy I liked during a "lights out mashing session" and it turned out to be the one guy who'd kissed about half the girls in the whole camp. I still remember the taste of soap in my mouth from trying to wash his germs out. You know what they say . . . it's like you've kissed whoever they've kissed. Blech!

Unfortunately when the lights came on during the "lights out mashing session" and I was lip-locked with Guy Wrong, Guy Right saw us and then ended up liking Jessica instead of me.

"Seven?"

"No, not seven, you ho," I say.

"You know what, don't tell me. I don't want you to think about other guys you've kissed. And I'm not what you call a ho. Besides, I just want you to concentrate your thoughts on me . . . on us."

"I thought you hated me."

"I wanted to push you away because I couldn't stop watching you." His voice is hoarse and full of emotion. "Sometimes I can't fall asleep at night. I get hot *tinking* about you," he says, his accent deeper than usual.

"You *tink* about me at night?" I ask and by mistake say tink instead of think. "Why?" *Please don't say my boobs.*

"First of all," he says as he fingers the curls at the end of my hair that have started to frizz in the desert heat, "you're beautiful. But the way you handle yourself in every situation with your own style mesmerizes me. You're animated, you're honest to a fault, you've got this feisty personality I just can't help but watch because I don't know what you're going to say or do next. You're very exciting. And to top it off, you have a big heart even though you don't open it up often."

I twist around to face him. "I've never had anyone describe me like that."

"When you tried to push me off the haystack back at the moshav, it totally shocked me."

"Yeah, except it didn't work. You're like one big mass of muscle."

He laughs. "Don't feed my ego. Now tell me what attracts you to me. Besides my big mass of muscle."

"Ha, ha. But seriously," I say, then take my finger and slowly draw a path from the corner of his eye, past the stubble on his chin and end up at his full lips. "Besides you being a gorgeous male specimen, I like the way you were always there for me when I did freak out. Even though you made it sound like a chore, you've helped me with every challenge I've had here. You let me fall on you when Mutt's friends were about to attack me," I say and kiss him gently on the mouth.

"You helped me herd the sheep," I continue, kissing him again, "and you were my hero by washing off the snake-guts."

Before I can kiss him again and continue telling him all of the incredible things I now see in him that I was blind to before, he crushes his lips to mine.

"Amy," he says against my lips. "I think we're about to get ourselves in trouble. How old are you again?"

"I'll be seventeen soon," I say breathlessly.

He says something in Hebrew I obviously can't understand. "We shouldn't be doing this."

"We're not doing anything except kissing."

"Yeah, but—"

"We can kiss, can't we?" I say as I graze my lips down his neck.

"Yeah," he says in a strained, low voice, "we can kiss."

I don't want him to think about my age right now. I want him to enjoy the time and the kissing. Especially the kissing. I press my open lips to his, because I can't imagine right now not touching my lips to his. He deepens the kiss and I follow, only barely aware we've changed positions and are now lying down side by side.

Okay, I've never in my sixteen (almost seventeen) years felt like this before. It's as if I've crossed the bridge from being a girl to a woman just by experiencing the strange, unfamiliar, steamy sensations deep in my body. My bodily reactions have intensified tenfold as my knight with an Israeli accent caresses my back. I feel like I'll die if we stop and I sense he feels the same.

"I'm going to remember tonight when I'm in basic training," he says as he nips my earlobe. "When they try and wear me out, I'll recall this moment and get through it."

My body feels like it's enduring sweet torture and I want to learn everything about Avi and his body right now. I grab his head to bring it closer to me and then I caress his body with my fingertips. Our lips and mouths are exploring each other's and our hands are doing the same.

When I touch his back, his muscles tense beneath my fingers. My hand moves around to the front of his shirt and I pull the material up to feel his smooth skin and hard six-pack against my hand. His heart is beating fast; I can feel it pumping in an erratic rhythm.

Moving my hand lower, I reach the waistband of his jeans and glide my index finger inside the band. Slowly, my fingers move downward.

Avi groans softly and gently takes my hand and guides it away.

"We can't . . ." he says.

"Why not?" I ask breathlessly, still reeling from our intense kisses. I feel drunk (although I've never been drunk, I can sure guess how it feels) and out of control.

"Besides the fact your *aba* would kill me?"

Great, my dad's not even here and still he's able to ruin my life.

"I don't care about what Ron thinks."

"You may not," he says as he sits up. "But I do. I don't want either of us to regret anything tomorrow."

I sit up, too. "I won't regret anything." Ever.

He kisses me on the top of my forehead. "Let me take you to your room. It's getting late."

25

---

*Approach me
at your own risk.*

"Boker tov," Avi says good morning to me in the breakfast buffet line the next morning. He leans forward to kiss me, but I pull away.

"What's wrong?" he asks.

Duh! He totally rejected me last night.

"Nothing."

I continue to place whatever is in front of me on my plate. I barely realize it's this creamy stuff with whole pieces of little sardiny-like fishes inside (with the silver scales attached, thank you very much). It is DEFINITELY not like sushi. It's gross, but now that I've put it on my plate, I'm going to have to stare at it while I eat.

Before I can add more to my plate, Avi grabs the dish out of my hand and puts it on the nearest table.

I put my hands on my hips. "Hey! That's my breakfast."

I realize I'm making a scene. I don't care.

He grabs my hand and leads me toward the exit. "It'll wait. We need to talk."

He leads me into the lobby and out the front doors. A blast of steamy, hot desert air smacks me in the face.

"Okay, talk. Before I melt, please."

He rubs his eyes in frustration. Next thing you know he'll be running his fingers through his hair.

He looks straight at me and says, "You think last night I stopped things from getting out of hand because I didn't want to be more intimate with you?"

"Bingo," I say sarcastically. "But I'm wiser this morning and won't throw myself on you anymore. Besides, it's not like we were going to have sex or anything."

"Where you and I go physically, our emotions are starting to follow. I can't deal with that."

"You're right. God forbid we should be emotional people. We should just call ourselves 'friends with benefits.' Or, better yet, why don't we just call this whole thing off so you can find another girl to be non-emotional with," I say as I head back inside before my armpits get damp through the shirt I'm wearing. In hindsight, I'm glad I decided to borrow Snotty's tank top.

"You are so stubborn," he says.

I turn around and face him before I reach the door. "I am not."

"Amy, you're the most stubborn person I've ever met. You play games in your mind and create drama that isn't there just to piss everyone off, including yourself."

I just stare incredulously at him.

He takes my hands in his. "Look at me." When I don't he says again, "Look at me."

I raise my eyes and look into his, which are wide and sincere.

"I wanted more last night," he says. "Don't lie to yourself and think I didn't. I beat myself up about a million times after I left you. Believe me, I *want* you to throw yourself at me. But this thing between us is more serious than we're admitting to each other. You're leaving in a couple of weeks whether I want you to or not. And I'm going into the army for three years."

I can't argue his points, so I just stand there staring into his brown eyes.

He lets go of my hands and says, "You want to call it off right now, just say the word."

Then he just stalks back into the hotel and leaves me here in the hot desert heat, sweaty armpits and all.

Damn. Why does Avi have to be so logical about everything? I hate being logical. But I'm too hot to have an attitude and realistically Avi is right. We're getting too attached already.

Slowly I walk back into the hotel and enter the restaurant. Avi is sitting down at a table, talking to his friends. There's an empty seat next to him with my plate on the table in front of it.

I know for a fact I don't want to end it with him right now. I want to keep this thing going for as long as possible.

Our eyes meet and he gives me a short smile. The problem is everyone else is looking at me, too. Okay, I guess I deserve it for causing a scene. I want to cringe in embarrassment, but I hold my head high and sit down next to him.

I avert my eyes from everyone around us, including Avi. But when he reaches for my hand under the table and gives it a squeeze, I squeeze back. *I can handle this relationship* I tell myself. Even with its ups and downs.

"Have you ever been to an alpaca farm?" Ofra asks me.

"What's an alpaca?" I ask.

"It looks kind of like a llama," Avi answers.

"Cool."

Ofra pats me on the back. "We're going right after breakfast so make sure you're ready."

By ten in the morning, we're parked at the entrance to the alpaca farm. Then we pay for bags of food to feed the tall, furry animals with long necks. I expect the alpacas to be in cages, but they're all running around. We actually walk into the large enclosure with them.

I regard the alpacas warily. They're all shades of brown, red, black, and tan. And their bottom teeth are so huge they look like alpaca hillbillies.

I watch avidly as Avi holds out a handful of food for a large speckled gray and black one. It eats it straight from his palm.

"Watch out," I warn. "He could bite your hand off with those massive buck teeth of his."

"They're harmless," he says. "They won't bite you. Try it."

I look at the brown bag of food I've just paid ten sheckels for. Ten sheckels for the risk of getting a huge buck alpaca tooth in your palm. No thank you very much. I walk up to a small baby alpaca and just pet it. Its fur is soft, but a bit wiry. And I laugh when she looks at me with her big gunmetal eyes and large underbite. My orthodontist, Dr. Robbins (otherwise known as Miracle Worker to his patients), could have a field day with this animal.

I feel like I can try and feed this one because it's small. And she looks at my brown bag the way I look when I see a good sushi restaurant. I reach in the bag and pull out some 'feed'. The little bugger can't even wait for me to situate the stuff in my hand before she noses it with her face and scoops it all up with her choppers.

"Hey, don't you have any manners?"

The alpaca starts chewing the food in a very unladylike manner; little pieces of food are falling out of her mouth with each chew.

"Watch out," Ofra says as she walks up behind me.

"For what?" I step back several steps, away from the animal. "Avi . . . Avi told me they're harmless."

"They are," Moron chimes in. "But they spit."

"Whad'ya mean, 'they spit'?" I say, moving farther back away from the buck-toothed spitter.

"Well," Snotty says. "It's more like a loud growling-like burp, then spit. At least they give you warning."

As if having the small alpaca after my brown bag wasn't enough, once they hear me close my bag the noise alerts about ten of the large ones and they come after me, too.

"I'm not an animal person," I say as I run toward Avi. "I'm not an animal person," I chant repeatedly until I reach him.

"They love you," Avi says. "Look, they're all following you."

I place the brown paper bag with the 'feed' (what exactly is inside this stuff to make it 'feed'?) into his hand and hide behind him.

The fearless Avi takes the whole bag and dumps it into one of his palms. As he feeds the things, I hear what Snotty was talking about . . . this loud growl-like burping sound. I crouch farther behind Avi in fear.

"Shit," I hear him say.

"What?" I can't see anything because I'm still behind him.

"It got me."

"Who got you?"

He turns around and I see, stuck in Avi's hair, a slob-ber-phlegm spot with little pieces of chewed-up 'feed' inside it.

"Ew, gross!" I say, stepping away from him.

"I got spit on trying to protect you from it."

"You're my hero, now get away from me. It's totally grossing me out," I say, then laugh at him.

"It wasn't that long ago I washed the snake off your foot. That was pretty nasty. Now give me a kiss," he says, moving toward me.

I hide behind a laughing Ofra. "I did *not* ask you to kiss me after the snake incident."

He stops. And looks so cute all 'feed' encrusted and vulnerable. I walk up to him, keep my distance, and pucker so it's just my lips touching his. Then I pull back. "Now you have to wash your hair." Then I add, "Twice."

26

---

*History is something that should be
remembered but never repeated.*

Our next stop (after Avi washed his hair in the sink back at
the alpaca farm) is a place called Mount Masada. I've never
heard of it and I wonder why a "mount" could be a place
people would want to go.

But as we drive (And I realize the vast majority of Israel
is a barren desert. I truly wonder why it is so sought after.)
and we come up to Mount Masada, I ask Avi, "Why are we
going to this place?"

"To show you a piece of the history of your people. I
think you'll like it."

My people? Who exactly are *my people?* I'm not sure
myself, even though the rest of the gang thinks I'm Jewish.
The fact is I've been brought up as nothing. Mom doesn't

believe in religion, just like she doesn't believe in low-carb diets.

We used to light a Christmas tree for the holidays until I realized at the age of seven Santa wasn't a real guy. They should honestly tell the older kids on the school bus not to tell the first graders the truth about the tooth fairy or Santa. You'd be surprised what kids learn on that yellow bus.

Well, after I found out Santa wasn't real, I told Mom I didn't need a tree anymore. The tree didn't symbolize Christianity or anything. It symbolized Santa. Since the reality of Santa was gone there was no reason for a tree anymore. That was the extent of my religious experience, which wasn't really religious in the first place.

I gaze at the reddish-colored massive thing called Mount Masada as I get out of the car. Everybody is taking their water bottles out of the car and I wonder why they aren't staring at the mountain.

"How old is it?" I ask no one in particular.

Moron, with his ever-present gun strapped to his shoulder, says, "The war here was in seventy-three."

I turn to him. "Nineteen seventy-three?" I guess.

"No. Earlier."

"Fourteen seventy-three?"

"No," Doo-Doo says. "Just plain seventy-three."

Just plain seventy-three? "You mean, like, almost two thousand years ago?"

"Yep."

I gaze again, this time more carefully, at this important mountain in the middle of the Israeli desert. I try to imagine a war here two thousand years ago between the Jews and their enemies.

"I wonder what it's like up there," I say.

"Well, you're about to find out," Avi says as he hands me a water bottle. "You'll need to drink regularly or you'll get dehydrated during the climb."

"You think I can climb this thing?" I ask.

"I know you can, Amy. Like your ancestors before you. See that winding snake path?"

"Do they call it a snake path because it's infested with snakes?" 'Cause I'm tough, but I've had all the snake experiences for one trip, thank you very much.

"It's called that because of its shape," he says, only temporarily reassuring me.

We walk closer to the bottom of the 'mount' and I can make out the narrow, winding path leading to the top. I watch as Doo-Doo, Snotty, Ofra, O'dead, and Moron start their ascent up the mountain. Off to my left I see a big cable coming from the top. I follow where it leads and the end is a cable car situated at the foot of the mountain.

"Why don't we take the cable car?"

Avi starts toward the supposedly non-infested 'snake' path. "Because then you'll miss the great sense of accomplishment of actually reaching the top on your own. I've done it many times and it's like nothing else."

I follow Avi to the start of the snake path. At first it's easy . . . if I just put one foot in front of the other I'll be at the top in no time at all.

But twenty minutes later, I'm panting and my thigh muscles are starting to quiver. I mean, Illinois doesn't have mountains, let alone hills, and I'm not used to it. I slow down, and Avi stays right with me. I know he could go way faster up the mountain.

"Go ahead," I say as we reach about midpoint of the thing. "If I don't die of heat exhaustion, I'm going to die of drowning in my own sweat."

He shakes his head.

"I mean it."

"I'm sure you do. Now get those feet moving so we can reach the top before sundown."

I do it, only because he grabs my hand and guides my limp body.

"Who were the Jews fighting here?" I ask. "The Palestinians?"

"No. The Romans."

Why would the Romans want to come here?

"Then why do the Jews hate all Palestinians?"

He stops and turns to me. "We do not hate all Palestinians."

I snort in disbelief. "I'll believe *that* when I see it on CNN," I tell him.

Finally, the top of Mount Masada is in sight and it's only taken me an hour to walk up the thing. I can't believe I've actually climbed it.

When I reach the top, the ancient ruins amaze me.

"So, the Jews won the battle with the Romans here?" I ask.

O'dead says, "Not really. Jews committed suicide here."

"Huh?" I say, shocked and a little creeped out.

Ofra steps in front of him. "Our ancestors climbed Masada and lived up here during the war. The Romans were at a loss, they couldn't safely climb the mountain without being attacked from the top of Masada."

Avi leads me to one of the ruins. "It is said nine hundred and sixty Jews lived here. They fought as long as they could, but knew it wouldn't be long before the Romans' weapons would be able to reach the top of it. If they were captured by the Romans, they would be killed or sold into slavery."

I look over at Moron, who's gazing down onto a colorful tile mosaic inside one of the homes built inside the mountain. It's absolutely beautiful and it touches my heart people lived on this mountain to save themselves and their families.

"So they committed suicide?" I ask.

Avi continues, "They agreed as Jews they should be servants to God and God alone. To be sold into slavery wasn't an option. They would rather die bravely as free people than become slaves at the hands of the Romans."

"They destroyed all of their possessions except their food supply so the Romans would know it was not starvation that led to their demise, but to show they preferred death over slavery."

My knees go weak from the story and I get chills all over my body. I can't believe how strong-willed the Jews were . . . and still are. I aimlessly walk on the flat-topped mountain and take in all of the half-walls made of stone my ancestors built.

Touching a brick with my fingers, I imagine the women and men two thousand years ago knowing their chances of survival were slim, but having enough courage to build beautiful homes for themselves that would last thousands of years.

As I scan the top of the mountain, I see a group of soldiers reach the top of Masada and congregate together. I notice little pockets on the sides of their army boots.

"What are those little pockets in their boots?" I ask Moron.

"Americans call the identification tags around a soldier's neck 'dog tags'?"

"Yes."

"Well, Israeli combat soldiers wear tags around their necks and one in each shoe. In case their body parts are separated during combat, they can be identified. It is Jewish custom that every person be buried with all body parts, so every effort is taken to make sure that happens for our soldiers."

Wow. What a somber thing to think about.

"What are they doing?" I ask him as I watch the soldiers gather together and recite some Hebrew words.

"They're taking an oath here 'Masada shall not fall again'," Moron explains. "This is a very spiritual place for all Jewish people."

As if the rock I was touching is hot, I pull my hand back. "Ohmygod," I say, and stumble backward.

"What?" Avi says, concerned.

"Nothing." I don't want to admit Masada is a spiritual place for me, too. And for the first time since coming to Israel I know why I'm here and it scares me.

I remember what *Safta* said. *Being Jewish is more in your heart than in your mind. Religion is very personal. It will always be there for you if you want or need it. You can choose to embrace it . . .*

My past might be shady and blurry, but my future is clearer thanks to this horrible, wonderful, shocking trip to a land so different, but so much a part of me nonetheless.

Looking down the mountain and trying to understand how the Jews . . . my ancestors . . . felt with the strong Roman warriors at the bottom, I realize this country has been a war zone since the beginning of time.

Why should the twenty-first century be different than the first?

27

Sometimes our enemies
are our closest friends.

"Where are you taking me?" I ask Avi.

As the others were eating breakfast our last morning in the south of Israel, he borrowed a car from the rental agency in the hotel and is taking me for a drive. He won't tell me where we're going, though, so I'm nervous.

"To meet a friend."

As we drive over the barren, dirt road, he looks at me with those dark, mysterious eyes.

"You scared?"

"Should I be?" I ask.

"No. You should never be scared with me."

Gee, most of the time I am scared to be with him. But mostly it's because I'm afraid of my own feelings, which are out of control when I'm with him.

I put my hands in my lap and stare out at the beautiful scenery. Who knew rocks and the desert landscape could be so beautiful and so different from the grassy mountains of the moshav.

We're listening to Israeli music on the radio, but I need to get rid of my nervous energy. I start my butt exercises. Tighten. Release. Tighten. Release.

"What are you doing?" Avi asks.

I look over at him and say casually, "Butt exercises."

He stares at me for a second, then bursts out laughing.

"It's not funny," I counter. "If you sit for a long time, your butt'll look like one great big blob of jelly."

"We wouldn't want that, would we?" he says.

I shake my finger at him. "Go ahead and make fun of me. You'll be sorry when you have the biggest butt on the moshav." I lean back in the car seat. "Before you make fun of me you should try it out first."

"You have a nice butt." Avi's lips twitch in amusement. "Okay, tell me how to do it."

"Not if you're going to make fun of me." I don't want to make a fool out of myself again.

"Come on," he urges me. "I won't make fun of you. I promise."

"Fine," I say.

I take a deep breath and realize I'm about to tell a very masculine boy how to do butt exercises. I want to cringe with embarrassment, but he actually looks serious.

I say quickly, "You just tighten your butt muscles like this and then release. The longer you hold the tightened part, the harder it gets."

I attempt to demonstrate the action and feel like a complete dork.

But then I look over at him and he's actually trying the exercise. I can tell by the concentrated look on his face.

"Do you ever vary it, tightening one cheek then the other?" he asks.

I try to suppress a giggle, but I can't. In fact, I can't stop laughing as I watch Avi trying to tighten each cheek in rhythm to the music playing on the radio. He's making fun of himself, emphasizing each movement of his butt along with the rhythm of the song.

I try it, too, and can't stop tightening to the beat of the music. It's contagious, and I'm having one of the best times of my life.

"I didn't know you could be so funny," I tell him, still trying to keep my giggles to a minimum, but having a hard time of it.

"Yeah, well, you caught me off guard."

"Be off guard more often," I say in a very flirty way and smile at him when he looks over at me.

He shakes his head and sighs in resignation. "You're going to get me in trouble with Ron. I told him I'd take care of you."

"You are."

I mean it. Avi was a royal pain in my butt (pardon the pun) when I first got to Israel. But now that he's opened up and let me into his personal life, I feel closer to him than I've felt to anyone in a long time. Even Mitch.

And I realize now Mitch and I are not compatible. In truth, he probably doesn't even know me. I keep a wall of my own up so I don't get hurt. I like Mitch. But I think if he knew me, I mean REALLY knew me, he wouldn't even consider being my boyfriend.

Why? Because I'm high maintenance, for one thing. And second of all I need a strong guy to take my crap and give it right back to me. I guess Avi's a little bit like Ron in that respect. Could it be I'm compatible with a guy who's a mirror image of the Sperm Donor?

We turn onto a small, paved road and drive for another fifteen minutes.

"Where are we?" I ask as he parks the car in front of a small house.

He opens his car door. "Here."

"Where's here?"

He smiles this great big smile, comes around to my side of the car, and opens my door. I know it's considered the gentlemanly thing to do, but let's be honest. I am no lady, and Avi . . . we'll, he's no gentleman. He's a rough, rugged Israeli who can whip bales of hay around effort-lessly. Just the way I like 'em.

I step out of the car and survey my surroundings. I was wrong before—at the moshav it's the North Pole compared to this place in the middle of the desert. I seriously think if I break an egg on the street, it'll be cooked from the hot sun in less than ten seconds.

There are houses in front of me, made of cement, and they're all the same. By that, I mean the houses are all white. No brick, no paint . . . just all white cement.

"Who lives here?" I ask quietly. It's like a little village in the middle of nowhere.

He walks toward the entrance to one of the primitive houses, and I follow dumbly.

"Palestinians," he answers.

WHAT!

Why would an Israeli take me to a Palestinian person's house? I want to ask questions, but I don't have enough time because the front door to the house starts to open.

A teenager, about our age, opens the door. His skin is darker than mine, about the same shade as Avi's. In fact, if Avi hadn't told me this guy was a Palestinian, I would have thought he was Israeli.

I know current events. You'd have to live in a cave not to know Palestinians and Israelis do not see eye to eye on anything. And that's putting it mildly.

But as I watch this Palestinian guy shake Avi's hand and pull him into a short embrace, once again what I know and who I know is tilted on its axis.

"Tarik, this my friend, Amy Barak. She's an American."

Nobody's ever called me Amy Barak before and I'm taken aback. I was born by the name of Amy Nelson because that was my mother's maiden name. Am I Amy Barak?

Some part of me, way deep down, likes the way it sounds. Or maybe I like the way it sounds coming out of Avi's full lips.

Either way, it doesn't matter. I'm nervous. I do everything in my power not to bite my nails or act as shocked as I feel on the inside.

But Tarik smiles, putting me a little at ease. And it's a real smile, not one of those fake ones people do just to be polite (like Marc does). No, this smile of Tarik's reaches his eyes.

"Come in!" Tarik says eagerly. "It's been a long time, friend," he says to Avi as he pats him on the shoulder.

"How's university hunting?" Avi asks him.

Tarik chuckles. "Not worth talking about. Although I did get a letter from UCLA and Northwestern. So tell me, Amy, what brings you here?" he adds as he leads us to a small room.

There are pillows in the middle of the floor and lining one wall. Tarik motions for us to sit. I watch Avi as he sits down on an orange pillow and I follow his lead, sitting down on a light blue one.

"I came with my father for the summer," I say.

I watch as a woman, wearing her head covered and in full traditional Muslim attire, brings a tray of fruit and sets it in front of Tarik. She doesn't say anything, just sets it down and leaves.

Tarik picks up an orange and hands it to me. "From our tree outside. I bet it's better than in America."

I look at Avi, who takes a cluster of grapes off of the tray and starts eating them. Only after I start peeling my orange does Tarik take his own. Is that his custom, to let his guests eat first?

I just can't believe I'm sitting in a Palestinian's house and he's feeding an Israeli Jew and an American stranger. With a smile on his face, no less.

"Are you two dating?" Tarik asks.

"Only for the summer," I chime in as my face gets hot with embarrassment. "That's all."

Tarik laughs. "And after the summer?"

He directs the question to me, but Avi says, "After the summer she goes back to her country. She's got a boyfriend back there."

"Ah, the story gets more interesting now. I think I like these American women."

Avi pops a large, green grape into his mouth. "Please, Tarik, don't let her fool you. Amy *lsanha taweel.*"

"Excuse me?" I say. "If you're going to talk about me, speak English so I can defend myself."

Tarik looks at me with a mischievous look on his face. "He says you have a sharp tongue, like a snake."

My mouth opens wide and I say, "I do not. Apologize," I tell Avi.

"Amy, you should know this guy doesn't apologize," Tarik says. "It's not in his nature."

Avi chuckles as he pops another green grape into his mouth, finishing the last one. "Tarik, you should be a lawyer instead of a doctor. You like to argue both sides of an argument, confusing everyone."

Shuffles from the door interrupt us as two girls come into the room with cups and a teapot. They set the cups down in front of us.

"These are my sisters, Madiha and Yara."

Gosh, my life is so different from these girls. They smile and bow slightly in greeting and I stand up and do the same although I feel a little underdressed. I wonder what they think of me. I don't cover my head or wear long robes like they do and I imagine how different our lives are.

After they leave, I sit back down and take a bite of my orange. It is as sweet as if I licked a spoonful of sugar. Yum!

When the sisters leave us alone Avi says to Tarik, "Amy thinks all Israelis hate Palestinians."

The last thing I want to do is start a political discussion with these two and here Avi is, bringing it up. I almost choke on my orange. When I'm finally able to swallow, I open my mouth to say something. Nothing comes out.

Tarik leans back and says, "The Palestinians hold claim to the same land as the Israelis. There's no way around that fact."

"But," Avi continues, "not every Palestinian hates every Israeli and not every Israeli hates every Palestinian."

"How can you guys be friends?" I ask. I turn to Tarik and say, "He's going into the Israeli army!"

Tarik shrugs. "This is his life, what he must do. Mine is not so different. But my people have chosen to fight in a different way; it's the only way my people think is effective."

"Nobody wins," I say. "Why can't you just come to some kind of agreement and stick with it?"

"Hopefully in the future things will change," Tarik admits. "To some, peace with the Israelis is not an option. Me? I want peace, but I also want my people to live their lives respectfully."

Avi looks at me and says, "Many Israelis want the same thing, Amy. Peace, but with the guarantee our women and children can walk in the streets or ride buses without having to worry about their safety."

"But what comes first?" Tarik asks.

"In the Middle East, nothing has ever been simple," Avi says.

"Right," Tarik agrees. "We are both strong people in our beliefs."

I shift uncomfortably on the pillow. "If you saw Avi on the battlefield, would you kill him?"

Tarik looks straight at Avi and says in a bold voice, "Yes. And I would expect no less from him."

Avi leans forward and takes my hand in his. "I brought you here to show you we're not all filled with hatred and here you are asking if two friends would kill each other. Way to make this meeting turn around, sweetheart. Listen, we both do what we have to do to survive. It's our way of life."

We stay at Tarik's house for a little while longer, the guys laughing about school and their families and asking me about my friends back home. They stopped the political discussion; it seems like they know their limits in talking about it. It feels good to discuss stuff without feeling like I have to act a certain way or answer a certain way to fit in.

I like Tarik. And I have newfound respect for Avi because I know he puts aside his political beliefs and befriends Tarik because he's a guy with a good heart and mind. The news makes it look so different from the reality; I think news programs should show the positive sides of people instead of focusing on the negative.

When we're ready to leave, Tarik gives me a hug goodbye and says, "Take care of my friend."

God, I feel like a weight is on my shoulders now. Life in Israel is hard compared to the teenage life in America. Our biggest worries back home are what movie to go see or what outfit we're going to buy. And after high school, we obsess about what college we'll get into. September Eleventh changed our lives, but we still have it easier than the people in the Middle East.

Israelis don't even go to college after high school. They have to put their lives on the line and enter the army. *Take care of my friend*, Tarik just said.

It's not as easy as one might think, especially when that statement comes from a guy who is on the other side.

My own life and the way I've pushed Ron away flashes before my eyes and I feel a little sick. I do have a family here in Israel, maybe I should act like I care about them. If Avi and Tarik can care about each other, maybe I can find a little piece of my heart to love Ron. And *Safta*. And, dare I even think it, Snotty.

I mean, Osnat.

But what if they disappoint me?

I watch as Avi and Tarik shake hands and slap each other on the back. A smile crosses my face. Because I know, even if they don't, they would protect each other with all of their power even if face to face on the battlefield. Both of these guys have pure, true spirits.

Peace between the Israelis and Palestinians? Who knows? Anything is possible. Maybe, just maybe, the friendship between these two strong-willed guys is a sign of hope for the future.

28

---

*There's a lot to learn by venturing
off the beaten path.*

"How did you meet Tarik?" I ask as we're driving back to
the hotel.

"Let's just say I helped him when he needed a friend,
and he did the same."

"I'm glad you took me to meet him," I say.

"And I'm glad you're here with me," he says, then
adds, "I knew you wouldn't believe me if I told you not all
Israelis hate Palestinians. You're the kind of girl who needs
proof. You shouldn't rely on television so much."

"I don't trust people in general."

"I bet if you did it would open your eyes to a more
colorful world out there."

"Probably. But at least I don't get let down too often because I already expect people are going to disappoint me."

He slows the car and stops it on the side of the road. Then he turns to me. "I want to thank you."

Suddenly my mouth is dry. "For what?"

"For making me remember there's a world out here worth living."

"How did I do that?" I ask.

"You're the first person to make the pain of my brother's death bearable." He kisses me, right here in the car on the side of the barren desert road. "When I'm with you, I'm whole again."

I smile, inside and out. But I'm embarrassed so I look down and finger the heavy silver chain hanging from his wrist.

"You want it?" he asks.

"If you want to give it to me," I say back shyly.

He takes it off and fastens it to my wrist.

"It's like you're telling everyone you're mine," he says. "At least for now."

I lean toward Avi and recapture his lips with mine. Like before, his kisses are drugging me and I'm feeling dreamy and lightheaded.

Before I realize it, I'm lying on top of him. I can feel his hard body under me, the warmth and strength of his muscles beneath mine.

"We should stop," he says.

I nibble on his ear and say, "Uh huh."

He throws his head back and moans. "I mean it, Amy. We're in a rental car on the side of the road."

This time I lick a path from his earlobe to his mouth. "Uh huh."

"You want to wear me down, don't you?"

"Uh huh."

I like the way I make him feel when we're together. I also really like the wild sensations running through my body right now, too, as I move my body against his.

When I feel him start to give in to my hands and mouth, I stop and sit up. I mean, we're in public and anyone could just peek in the window. Would the windows steam up if we continued? I didn't think it could get hotter in the car than outside, but I'm feeling pretty toasty even though the air conditioning is on.

He licks his lips slowly and opens his eyes. "I can't move."

I laugh. "Did I make you forget to be angry all the time?"

"Definitely."

"Good. I can do this forever if it'll make you happy."

His fingers move to my shoulder and he slides the strap on my tank down. "I wish . . ." he says, leaning his head forward and lightly kissing my shoulder.

I know what he wants to say. I want him to say it, but then I remember our little agreement. No getting too involved.

Too bad, I'm already so into him it's scary.

But I know he would regret it if we did go too far. And we are, in fact, parked on the side of a road. "If you don't stop kissing me like that, I'm going to rip all your clothes off," I say.

A little moan escapes from his mouth and he leans back. "I'm crazy about you."

"Good. Remember that when some pretty Israeli girl hits on you after I'm gone. Now let's get back to the others, or I really am going to follow through with my threat."

A half hour later, when we turn onto the road leading to the hotel, Avi says, "So what's the story with your parents?"

He asks me this loaded question and I turn toward the window. "I don't want to talk about it."

"Why not? Lots of parents get divorced."

Yeah, only my parents were never married to begin with. Try telling that story to your peers at school. I always feel they think my mom just slept with a random guy in college and got pregnant. And the sucky part about it is, it's not far from the truth.

"Tell me about *your* parents," I counter. "I never hear much about them from Ron or my aunt and uncle."

"There's not much to tell. My mom works as a teacher on the moshav and my father is your uncle's partner. Okay, your turn."

I take a deep breath. "My parents were never married and I should never have been born. I was, shall we say, a mistake. A very big sixteen-year-old mistake."

There, I said it. My face is hot and my eyes are watery. I'm holding myself together as best I can under the circumstances. I've thought about my life and what a mistake it is about a million times. I've never actually voiced it aloud before.

We arrive at the hotel and Avi parks the car in the parking lot. "I'm not a very religious guy," he says, "but I know there's a very important reason you were born."

"You sound like a rabbi," I say.

"No, I'm just a sheep farmer."

"Avi, you are SO much more than that and you know it," I lean back in the passenger seat and sigh. "I don't want today to end."

He flashes me one of his dazzling smiles. "Me either."

I look into his eyes and he holds my gaze for a long minute. We don't say anything more, there's no words that can say what I want to say to him. Or are there? "Avi—"

"Shh," he whispers, covering my lips with his fingers. "I know."

I reluctantly get out of the car and head for the lobby of the hotel.

The rest of the gang is waiting for us.

When I spot Snotty . . . make that Osnat . . . sitting alone in the corner, I go up to her. "I'm sorry I said you wear short shirts, tight pants, and have a sorry excuse for breasts."

Osnat shakes her head in confusion.

I shift my feet and look at the ground. "I mean, you do wear tight pants . . . and your breasts are smaller than mine. But they're lovely breasts. And I'm sure it's the style in Israel to have tight pants."

Her eyebrows are raised as she says, "Are you trying to apologize to me? If you are, you're doing a lousy job."

I open my arms out wide and say, "Give me a break here, I'm not used to being all gushy and apologetic."

Osnat stands up and says, "I'm sorry I said your breasts sag. Your sagging breasts aren't bad, either." Then she holds her hand out for me to shake it. "Truce?"

Wait just one itty-bitty second.

"You never told me my breasts sag!" I say, ignoring her fake truce.

"Not to your face, I didn't," she admits.

I guess I deserved the insult. And I'll keep to myself I've called her Snotty almost since I met her.

We both start laughing hysterically and everybody else is looking at us like we're mashed potatoes. Two mashed potato cousins.

"Can we go for a walk?" she asks.

"Sure."

We exit the hotel and start walking aimlessly in the parking lot.

I kick a rock down the road as I walk. "I didn't want to come to Israel this summer," I say. "And I didn't want to like anyone here."

She kicks the same rock, continuing its journey down the road. "And I was shocked Ron had a secret daughter. I guess in some way I was jealous of you."

Me? A *secret* daughter? Being thought of as a secret sure beats being thought of as illegitimate. "Believe me, you have nothing to be jealous about. At least you have parents who love each other."

"But Ron has the best job ever. You must be so proud of him."

Okay, so you're probably wondering what Ron does for a living. All I know is he's in the security business.

"It's no big deal," I say. After all, everybody's in the security business these days.

Osnat pulls my shoulder back and stops me from walking. "Are you kidding?" she says. "My mom told me he's been hired as a consultant to the Director of Homeland Security in the U.S."

What? I didn't know that. I guess I never even asked him. I've been too busy being pissed off at him for not being Superdad.

"Yeah, well, he doesn't talk about it much."

"He probably can't because it's classified."

I'm having a hard time thinking of Ron as a super-security consultant hired by the U.S. government. After all, I'm used to thinking of him as the Sperm Donor.

Osnat turns to me and says, "You didn't know what he did until I told you, right?"

"I wouldn't be called a daddy's girl, if that's what you mean," I say. "In fact, I'm not close to anyone in my family. My mom's kind of in her own world and Ron isn't exactly the best father. I don't even have a cousin who likes me. Well, besides your brother, but he can't even speak English. If he did he probably wouldn't like me, either."

"You aren't exactly the funnest person around," Osnat says.

"Are you kidding? I have a lot to offer," I say. "For example, I can show you how to put on makeup so it won't look overdone and won't smear. I'm a whiz when it comes to hairstyles, I can even French braid hair. And I can beat most people I know in tennis. What have you got to offer?" I ask, putting my hands on my hips as I wait for an answer.

"I can ride a horse bareback and I'm really good at dancing. And I'm a great person once you get to know me," she says, absolutely certain she's won me over.

I can imagine riding a horse bareback isn't much different from riding in that Jeep on the rocks, but it does have merit.

"And?"

"And I can tell you Avi has changed since he met you. He smiles now . . . something rare since his brother died. I guess I don't mind you've gotten together since you make him happy."

We hug and I feel lucky to have a cousin who can ride bareback. And to be a friend, too.

29

*The threat of taking something
away makes us appreciate it more.*

Two days later, all seven of us are back in the Jeep heading
back to the moshav. I'm anxious to see Ron and tell him I
want a fresh start.

We all enter Osnat's house and it seems like the whole
neighborhood is crowded inside. And they all have their
eyes glued to the television screen. I see my little curlyhead
cousin Matan and *Doda* Yucky. I don't see Ron or Uncle
Chime.

The mood is definitely somber.

"What's going on?" I ask. I can't understand the news-
caster who is obviously covering a very important story.

The house erupts with Hebrew, everyone explaining to Osnat, Ofra, Avi, Doo-Doo, O'dead, and Moron what they're so upset about. Except I don't understand any of it.

"There's been a bombing," Avi explains to me after listening to the others. "In Tel Aviv."

"Where's my dad?" I ask in a panic. "Where's Ron?" I need him now more than ever.

Avi pulls me into an embrace. "Amy, it'll be fine."

Tears fill my eyes and I say again, this time directing the question to *Doda* Yucky, "Where is he?"

I don't get an answer and I feel bile rising to my throat. I pull back from Avi 'cause I want to throw up.

"Your *aba* drove to Tel Aviv with Chime to deliver some meat to some restaurants there," she explains.

"They're fine, right, *Doda* Yucky?" I say, crying fully now and not caring a bit.

Tears are running down her face, too. "I don't know. There's a lot of confusion. After one bombing, people ran to help . . . a second bomber . . ."

"Ohmygod," I say.

I may not know Ron well, but I definitely know if people were hurt, he would be one of the first to run and help. The second bomber . . . I can't think about it.

"We don't know where they are," she says. "The cell phone isn't working."

Going into Osnat's room, I frantically rummage through my backpack. In one of my jean pockets I fish out the Jewish star *Safta* gave me. The diamonds are shining back at me, almost as if telling me I'm a Jew just like the rest of my family. We've survived thousands of years even though we've suffered through most of them, I remind myself.

Walking back into the main room, I put my hands over my face. I don't want anyone looking at me right now. I feel so helpless. How many people were injured or died today? I feel sick just thinking about it. I try to push the image of Ron's body lying in the street out of my mind. But what if he's dead and I wasn't there to help him? I need strength because I think I've lost all of mine. I put my hands down and my gaze rests on Avi.

I need him.

I need him so much I don't know what to do with myself.

"Avi," I say as I run into his chest and hold him tight. "Please don't leave me; I don't think I can handle this without you."

"I'm here," he assures me in a soft voice as he strokes my hair. "And I'm not leaving."

That's right, he lost his brother in a bombing. He must be rehashing the pain of his own loss. We can help each other through this.

Holding out the necklace to him I say, "Will you put this on me?"

We wait the longest hour of my life as Avi and I sit by *Safta* in her room and avoid watching the news report. She tells me about her childhood in Israel and her experience when she first came to what she calls 'the holy land'. She's scared, I can tell. The loss of two sons would devastate her.

When the phone rings, I jump up and run to the kitchen.

Doda Yucky is on the phone, and she looks directly at me as she answers it.

My heart is racing.

"Amy," she says, and I lean against Avi for support as I'm preparing for bad news. "It's your *mudder*."

My *mudder!* I hurry to the phone and clutch it to my ear. "Mom!"

"Hi, sweetheart. I heard on the news there's been a bombing in Israel. I'm just calling to make sure you're okay. Jessica called and she's worried, too."

"I'm . . . I'm okay," I say, barely able to make the words out through my sobs. "But . . . I was traveling and Ron was in Tel Aviv . . . and we haven't heard from him and I'm freaking out. I don't know what to do. We're waiting for a phone call but . . ."

"Oh, no. This is terrible, I never thought—"

"Mom, I got to get off the phone in case he calls."

"Okay, okay," she says in a panic. "I'll hang up. Call me back when you hear something . . . anything. Okay? And you stay put. I need you to come back to me in one piece."

"I will, Mom," I say.

When I hang up, the phone rings again. I hand it to Osnat, who's as anxious and scared as I am.

"Ze aba!" she screams to the crowd after talking to the person on the other end of the line. *"Hakol beseder!"*

Avi picks me up and twirls me around. "They're okay!"

I can't believe it. I go into *Safta's* room and tell her the good news. I learn from *Doda* Yucky that Uncle Chime and Ron had stayed at the bombing site to help the forty-plus wounded.

There's a lot of hugging and rejoicing even though we're all full of sorrow for the poor souls whose lives were lost today in the bombings. It's a strange thing to be happy and sad at the same time. I don't know how Israelis deal with it all the time.

Avi waits at the front entrance to the moshav with me, along with Mutt. The little guy is lying next to me, almost as if he's my protector.

"I can't believe what happened. This has been such a nightmare," I say. "I almost lost my father. Before I really even knew him." It's too scary to think about.

Avi says thoughtfully, "But you get a second chance."

I lean against him. "Yeah, I do. And from now on I'm going to make every second count."

"Me too," he says, and gives me one of his amazing kisses to prove it.

When the gate opens and I see headlights from a car, I stand up. The car stops and my daddy, whose shirt has blood splattered on it, hops out and pulls me into his arms.

"Are you okay?" I'm staring at his stained shirt.

"Don't worry, I'm fine."

"*Aba,*" I say to him in Hebrew. "I love you so much."

"Oh, Amy, I love you, too."

I pull back and wipe my tears with the back of my hand. "I'm so sorry I didn't say it before. I know I've been treating you badly. I want you to be a big part of my life now. I want to be Jewish, too. And I want to learn Hebrew. Can you teach me?"

"Slow down, I can't catch up with you. I'm still basking in the '*I love you, Aba*' part." I see his eyes getting red and watery. "I never want you thinking I didn't fight to be with you, sweetheart. I screwed up real bad in so many ways."

He wipes a tear streaming down his face and I'm dumbfounded.

"I was hoping this trip to Israel would change everything. I don't want to lose you to Marc. You're *my* daughter, not his," he says as he embraces me.

He's crying like a baby. So am I.

"I thought I lost you," I say as we walk back to the house, letting Uncle Chime drive back all by himself.

Avi has left us alone, too, giving me and my dad privacy.

"I lost you a long time ago, daughter. I'm glad we've finally found each other."

"Do you think you could find room in your apartment for me?"

"You mean it? I'd love for you to move in with me. For a year. For weekends. Forever. I'll take whatever you want to give."

"If you're not too busy with the Director of Homeland Security, that is."

He chuckles and puts his arm around my shoulder. "I always have room in my house for my number one girl and don't you ever forget it."

"You sure you don't have a girlfriend?" I ask.

"Not anyone important enough to bring home to my daughter."

"I think you need someone . . . to take the edge off of you."

"And who should I thank for taking my daughter's edge away? Or maybe I don't want to know."

"He's been a perfect gentleman."

"Who? Doo-Doo?"

"Can you see me with a guy named after feces?"

"His real name is David."

"Huh?"

"Doo-Doo is a nickname for David."

Stupid nickname if you ask me. "It's Avi."

Ron's face is serious now. "He's eighteen years old, Amy. And he lost his *brudder* . . ."

"I know all that. We've helped each other during our trip and I . . . I love him."

My dad's jaw tightens and the muscle in the side of it starts to twitch.

"It's not like *that*. He respects me and I respect him. Maybe too much."

"I have to get used to having a teenage daughter," he says.

I look at him straight in the eye. "No. You have to get used to me."

30

> *You don't even know what you*
> *want until it's put in your lap.*

Well, it's the day before I have to leave for Chicago. Avi and I are going on an double date with Osnat and O'dead.

I glance at my cousin, who looks great now that I've shown her how to put on makeup so she doesn't look like a dartboard.

She's watching me pick out clothes to wear. I can tell by the way she's staring longingly at my Ralph Lauren sundress that she likes it.

"I don't like this dress," I say. "You want it?"

Her eyes light up. "Really?"

"Absolutely. It makes my butt look big," I say, and toss it to her.

I end up wearing a short, slinky, navy skirt and white top with frilly sleeves. It's the first time I've dressed this nice since I've been in Israel. I hope Avi likes it—all he's seen me in is jeans and shorts.

When I hear Avi's voice in the hallway, my whole body is filled with anticipation and I can't stand it.

Mitch is really going to be pissed when he realizes I've fallen for another guy, but it would be impossible to ignore the excitement I feel when I even think about Avi.

Just as I'm about to walk out the bedroom door, my *aba* walks in the room. He sits on my bed and does a double-take. "You're beautiful," he says. "Like your mother. It scares me."

"Would you rather I was butt-ugly?"

His mouth curves into a twisted smile. "Maybe."

"You want me to cancel my date to make you feel better?" I ask seriously.

He looks up. "No, of course not."

"Good. 'Cause I wasn't going to."

"Amy . . ." he says in a warning tone.

"Get a grip, Dad. I'm not going to do anything you wouldn't do at my age."

He stands up and says, "That's it. You're canceling this date."

Osnat walks out of the room and comes back with her mom. *Doda* Yucky says something to Dad in Hebrew. He sits back down, obviously defeated, and then *Doda* Yucky leads me out to the foyer.

Avi takes one look at me, smiles, and his hand goes to his heart. "Wow."

Great reaction.

Then he takes my hand, squeezes it, and leads me to his car. Osnat and O'dead are already waiting in the back seat.

"Where are we going?" I ask.

"The disco," he answers.

The disco place? I don't really have visions of spending my last night in Israel in a loud, crowded, smoky bar. But I keep my opinions to myself. He's trying, even if my heart is a little deflated at the moment.

When we reach the place, I notice the line is longer than the last time we were here. Great, now I'm going to spend the better part of this evening in a line. What a bummer.

Avi drives up to the front of the club. Osnat and O'dead get out, and I open my car door.

"Where are you going?" Avi asks.

"Uh, to wait in line like the rest of the people who want to go in," I say sarcastically.

"I'm taking you somewhere else."

I furrow my eyebrows. "You said we were going to 'the disco.' I specifically heard you say the word 'disco'."

He says, "We are. But only to drop Osnat and O'dead off."

When Avi winks at me, I settle back in the car and close the door. I really do have butterflies in my stomach, because now I'm alone with him. I've never felt like this about anyone else in my life.

He holds my hand as we drive away from the club and head up a winding dirt road that probably hasn't been traveled in centuries.

He stops the car, turns to me, and shows me a hand-kerchief.

"Is my nose running?" I ask. I mean, is that a hint or what?

"It's to blindfold you, Amy. Close your eyes."

I close them, lean into him and feel him tie the blindfold around my head while he brushes a gentle kiss across my lips. After he helps me out of the car, he leads me somewhere.

This is exciting, he's exciting. I can't wait for all the surprises he's planned for me.

He takes the blindfold off. "Open your eyes."

I blink a few times before I can focus in the dark.

Candles. Lots of them. Two pillows. And between the pillows is an empty plate.

"Sit."

I follow his instructions.

"Okay, wait here." He sounds nervous, which is so cute. Usually he's so calm and cool.

I take in my surroundings. We're in the middle of nowhere, on some barren, deserted land with crickets ser-enading us. I sit down on one of the pillows and wait. Avi comes back with a Styrofoam carton.

He hesitates before opening it. "Are you hungry?"

"For what?"

One of his eyebrows raises. "You tell me. I have food here but if you're hungry for something else—"

"Food's great," I say, interrupting him.

He gives me one of his awesome smiles, sits down next to me, and opens the carton. When I see what's in there, I get so choked up I have to swallow a lump in my throat.

"You bought me sushi! My very favorite food in the whole world. How did you know?"

The sushi rolls are like little, round happy faces smiling at me.

He hands me a set of chopsticks. "Ron told me."

"I've been going through sushi withdrawal these past few months," I explain. "Do you know what quitting cold turkey like that will do to a person?"

He's looking at me like I'm nuts. But I don't care.

"Want some?" I ask, my mouth already full with a spicy tuna roll. I'm moaning in pleasure as I eat the sweet, tangy roll, the sound coming from my throat automatically.

Avi admits he's never eaten sushi, so I coach him. We share the meal, Avi tentatively trying small bites while I'm shoving the stuff very unlady-like into my mouth. I'll have to remember to tell Jessica Israelis make great sushi.

When we finish the meal, Avi stands up. "I have another surprise for you."

"What is it?" I ask, totally excited. So far this evening is absolutely perfect.

"Shoot, I forgot something." He goes off and comes back with a small bouquet of flowers.

Okay, I'm not trying to be bitchy here. But *Safta* got a whole flower shop from my grandfather. And what does Avi expect me to do with flowers when I'm going on a twelve-hour flight tomorrow? I try not to show my disappointment as he places them in front of me, so I smile as sweetly as I can.

"You don't like the flowers?"

"I do," I say.

He takes a red rose out of the bouquet and breaks off part of the stem. Then he kneels next to me and places the rose in my hair. "I wanted to get you something to remember me by, but I didn't know what you'd like."

"So you got me flowers. That's nice."

He chuckles. "The flowers were from my mom. She's old-fashioned. To be honest, she bought them for me to give to you."

This is not the romantic guy I thought he was. "The sushi was great," I say. "But you're losing brownie points fast, buddy."

"Wait here," he says. "I have one last surprise." When he comes back and I see what he's holding, I can't believe it.

Avi is holding Mutt. The puppy has a blue ribbon around his neck. And he's beautiful. "You washed him," I say, tears streaming down my cheeks.

"He's officially yours now," he says, and places Mutt in my lap. "I've arranged for you to take him back to the States."

I can't believe how fluffy and soft he is now that he's clean. "Arg!"

"Can I really take him home?"

"Yep. He'll probably have to go through a quarantine period, but—"

I smother his words with my lips, because this is the most perfect night of my life.

We spend the rest of the evening talking, making out, fooling around, and playing with Mutt. Right before we pack up the pillows and candles, I know we have to have The Talk.

"So . . . I guess our summer fling is over," I blurt out, fingering his bracelet still on my wrist. I undo the clasp and hold it out to him.

Avi leans forward, resting his elbows on his bent knees. "Keep it. So you won't forget me."

As if. "I'll never forget you. And I realize I am a spoiled American bitch."

"Amy, I'm sorry I ever said that . . ."

"No," I say. "I'm spoiled because I want us to keep in touch and maybe one day, after you finish the army, we could, you know, get together again."

"It's a long way off," he says. "What if you're dating someone?"

"What if *you* are?" I counter.

He laughs.

"You've taught me so much about myself."

He smoothes the stray hair in my face and tucks it behind my ear, his fingertips lingering on my earlobe. When his fingers trail down to the Jewish star still around my neck he says, "You really are a gift from God, Amy."

"No, you are."

When he leans down to kiss me for the last time, I know for a fact somewhere, sometime, someplace, I'll be kissing Avi again.

And next time, it might just be on the top of Mount Masada.

*The end of one thing is just the
beginning of another.*

I'm back home in Chicago. Yep, Dad and I actually made the long plane ride back.

I was kind of nervous to tell Mitch about Avi, but when Jessica spilled the beans and told me she and Mitch kind of got together after their Ravinia night, I felt a lot better. Of course I made them both sweat it out for a couple of hours. Then I spilled my own beans and told them about Avi.

My Israeli non-boyfriend is in the army now, training to be a kickass commando. He writes when he can, which is about once a week. I realize from his letters O'dead's name is spelled Oded and Moron is actually spelled Moran (thank goodness for them). Doo-Doo still goes by his nickname, but I hope to change that next summer.

Avi never told me he loved me, but he doesn't have to say it. I know he's worried about me worrying about him and he loves me. He has a hard time saying it out loud. I'm okay with that, for now.

My dad and I are going to spend my summer break in Israel next year. This time, I'm planning a two-week-long camping trip throughout the country. I can teach Dad a few things this time, like when to duck when an alpaca starts to make gurgling noises. Avi will be able to take two weeks off then; I can't wait to see him. *Safta* is doing okay—she starts her next set of chemo treatments next month. I'm sending her a care package today.

The wedding between my mom and Marc with a "c" was okay. Marc and I had a talk before the wedding. I told him he could be a friend to me, but I already have a father. He took the news better than I expected. Ron was at the wedding; he was a great dance partner for me.

I've been living at my dad's apartment until Marc and Mom's new house in the 'burbs (which they decided to build from scratch) is ready, which will be months from now. While I'm here, I have a lot of work to do . . . like teaching Ron how to dress to impress a woman. He's not there yet, but he's on his way to becoming a retired bachelor. All I have to do is find the right woman for him. In the meantime, he's teaching me Hebrew and swears to his friends I'm a natural when it comes to herding sheep.

Me and my religion? Well, I'm taking conversion classes with Rabbi Glassman over at Bait Chaverim (which for you non-Hebrew speakers means House of Friends). Mom was shocked when I told her I'm becoming Jewish. I've made her promise to make sure there are no pork or shellfish products in the food she makes for me. Keeping kosher is part of who I am now.

"Arg!"

Yes, that's Mutt. And yes, my dog has a speech impediment. I can't help but love the little bugger. He eats most of Mom's shoes, but knows to leave mine alone. He also thinks he's a lap dog although he's going to be about ninety pounds when he's full grown. We've been through a lot together and he's teaching me to love animals.

My name is Amy Nelson Barak and I went to Israel for my summer vacation. I learned about my family, my heritage, a beautiful land full of rich history, and love. Wouldn't you know, my ruined summer vacation turned out to be the best three months of my life.

*How to Ruin
My Teenage Life*

1

In conversion class, Rabbi Glassman told me that every word in the Torah is meant to be there for a reason. No wasted words. It makes me think about all the wasted words I've used in my life.

My name is Amy Nelson-Barak. My mom is a Nelson and my dad is a Barak. And no, they were never married. Being an illegitimate kid used to freak me out, but I guess this past summer when my Israeli dad took me to his homeland I got over it.

Mom got married a few months ago to Marc *"with a c."* He's okay, I guess, if you like the über-conservative type. They moved to the 'burbs after the wedding, as if marriage somehow warrants moving to a place where you have to drive a car to get to the nearest Starbucks.

I'm living with my father in Chicago. I call him *Aba*, which means Dad in Hebrew. He owns this cool condo in a building in Chicago on the fortieth floor. He was pretty non-existent in my life up until a few months ago. To make a long story short, this past summer my dad and I got to know each other and worked out our issues. He's learning how to be a dad to a teenage girl (me) and I'm learning how to deal with an overprotective father. I've decided to live with him until I graduate high school so I don't have to change schools. The best part about his place is it's situated directly next to a coffee shop called Perk Me Up! It's like a Starbucks, only it has better coffee.

Okay, so I don't *exactly* drink coffee. I just turned seventeen in December and haven't gotten that acquired taste thing goin' on. But that's not the point. I'm a city girl. And a coffee shop steps away from your front door equals city.

I'm sitting at Perk Me Up! right now, doing algebra homework on this frosty January day. Winter break ended a week ago, but I'm still struggling to get into the swing of things at school. I could go upstairs and study in a quiet place, but since my dad is coming home late tonight I'm vegging out here. Besides, the owner of Perk Me Up!, Marla, is super cool. She always piles the whipped cream on my hot chocolate extra high.

Did you know whipped cream has little or no carbs? It's true. You could spray a whole can of whipped cream into your mouth all in one sitting and still have less carbs in your system than one nutritious apple. Nothing compares with extra whipped cream, unless it's a spicy tuna roll from my fave sushi restaurant, Hanabi. Okay, so I admit sushi rolls surrounded by rice aren't exactly lacking in the carb intake department. Sushi rolls are my obsession and addiction, so I give them a wide berth when it comes to counting sushi as high in carb content.

"Your dad working late again?" Marla asks as she wipes off the table next to mine.

I close my algebra book. "Yep. I swear, it's as if the world will collapse if he misses one day."

"He's a dedicated man," Marla says, a newspaper in her hand from someone who left it on a table. "It's admirable."

"I guess."

New customers walk in the door. Marla heads to the register, leaving the newspaper on my table. I notice it's open to the personals. Men seeking women. Women seeking men.

Man, how desperate are people? I mean, who would actually need to go out and advertise for a date?

"What are you doing?" a familiar voice says.

I look up at my best friend, Jessica. She's got dark hair and dark eyes, just like her parents. And her brother and sister. And her cousins. They all look like dark-haired, dark-eyed clones of each other. I swear there's not one recessive gene in her entire Jewish family tree.

"Me? I'm not doing anything." I say, then shove the paper in my backpack.

"Amy," Jess says. "I saw you reading the personals."

"Okay, you caught me." I show her the paper. "Get a load of these ads, Jess. They're so…personal." I feel like I'm *peeping tomming* into these people's lives.

Jess leans in and we both read:

Big-Hearted Taurus
SWF, 38, 5'10", lazy but likes music, dancing,
casinos, dining out. Seeking SWM, 30-42, who
likes lazy women for LTR.

"She can't be serious," I say.

Jess snickers. "Who'd want a lazy gambler?"

We lean our heads together and read more:

Professional Model
Sexy SWF, 28, 5'4", 110 lbs., blonde hair, blue
eyes, enjoys trying new things and having fun.
Seeking SWM, 25-65, for LTR.

Seriously, I'm confused. "Can you please tell me what an LTR is?"

"Long-term telationship."

Oh. I guess I don't have the personals lingo down pat. "Why would a skinny blonde model want a sixty-five-year-old?" I could understand the lazy chick, but the model?

I call Marla over to our table.

"Need more whipped cream, honey?"

"No, thanks," I say. "Why would a model advertise for an LTR in the paper?"

"Huh?"

Jess shakes her head. "Long-term relationship." She holds out the paper to Marla.

"Don't knock it," Marla says. "I know plenty of people who've met their soul mate online or in the personals section."

Jess takes a sip of my hot chocolate. "Amy can't understand. Avi is the perfect guy, right?"

I smile at the mention of my non-boyfriend, who is serving in the Israeli army. We can't really be boyfriend and girlfriend with him a billion miles away. And he's not perfect. A perfect boyfriend wouldn't be living in another country. "What about Mitch?" I ask Jess. "Last week you told me God made him just for you."

She makes a yuck face. "Don't even mention his name around me."

This doesn't sound promising. "All right, what's up?"

Jess sighs. "Well, he hasn't called in two days and the Valentine's Dance is right around the corner. You'd think if he was going to ask me he'd have done it already. My mom wants to go dress shopping but I don't even have a date." She's about to cry. "And I checked my smile in the mirror this morning and realized my face is crooked."

"It is not."

"Is too. See," she says, smiling like she's in pain. "The right side of my mouth droops down."

"Let's go to the dog park," I say, heading off a huge rampage about how bad Mitch is and how crooked her face is. Does she really think God can make everyone totally symmetrical...I mean, give the Big Guy upstairs a break. Besides, Jess has been a hypochondriac and hypercritical of herself ever since third grade when she thought she had lice but it was just bad hair spray flaking. She just needs to chill and redirect her energy into positive thoughts. "I need to walk Mutt."

Mutt's my dog. And yes, he's a mutt. Avi gave Mutt to me before I left Israel. No purebred anything in his blood. He used to be a little fur ball, but in the past two months he's tripled in size.

Back at our condo I fetch my dog and the poop bags. Jess and her one-one-hundredth-of-an-inch crooked face is waiting for me when I walk back outside.

"Oh my God, he's even bigger than when I last saw him," she says, each breath causing puffs of steam in the winter cold.

"I know. If he grows any more I'll have to buy a king-size bed just to fit the both of us," I say, bundling my North Face jacket around me. Visitors here wonder why we Chicagoans brave the cold weather when we could be wearing shorts right now if we lived in Arizona. I'll admit Chicago winters suck if you hate cold weather. I love the cold, I love Chicago, and I love the change in seasons. I need to live in a place where in autumn the leaves actually fall off the trees.

Jessica bites her bottom lip. "You don't think Mitch'll be at the dog park with Zeus, do you?"

Yes. "No. Jess, why don't you just ask him to the dance?"

"So I can be the loser chick of the entire school?"

A bit of an exaggeration, dont'cha think? But I don't disagree with her. Sometimes you challenge Jess, and other times you don't. This would be one of those other times.

Besides, Mitch probably hasn't even thought about the Valentine's Day dance. It's January and the dance isn't until the middle of next month. Guys are a different breed, I tell you. I glance at Jessica, who has this pathetic, sad look on her face.

We're walking down the street with my white, furry monstrosity practically pulling my arm out of my socket. Mutt gets über-excited just going out for a walk. But when he realizes we're going to the dog park, watch out. He's a total spaz about the dog park.

"Can't you send him to doggy boot camp or something?" Jess says as she tries to catch up with us.

"He just came to this country five months ago," I argue. "And he had to be quarantined. I refuse to put him in another stressful situation, the poor guy will need therapy."

Jess shakes her head. "He's a *dog*, Amy. You spoil him way too much."

I do not.

Okay, I do.

But Mutt is my companion. He protects me. He makes me laugh. He's everything to me.

We arrive at the dog park and Mutt can't contain himself. As soon as I close the gate and unlatch the leash from his collar, he romps toward his dog buddies to play.

Mr. Obermeyer, the grumpy old man from the fourteenth floor of our building, sneers at me. "Keep that dog of yours away from Princess."

Princess is Mr. Obermeyer's champion poodle. He hates Mutt. That's just fine because I hate poodles named Princess.

"Don't worry, Mr. Obermeyer," I say. Why the old

man even hangs out at the park is beyond me. He doesn't talk to anyone, except to balk and tell people to keep their dogs away from his pampered pooch.

"Look, there's Mitch!" Jess whispers, then hides behind me.

I look over at the other end of the park and see Mitch. "Let's go talk to him."

"No! Amy, you knew he was gonna be here. Admit it."

It gets to be a problem when people call you out on your passive-aggressive behavior.

"Jess, he's your boyfriend." Okay, Mitch used to be my boyfriend, but that's another story. I'm not into him at all. Besides, I'm content with my non-boyfriend. Well, sort of. I hate the "non" part of it. I wish Avi didn't have me promise not to make any formal commitment to him and vice versa.

Jess peeks over my shoulder. "Don't you see who he's with?"

I crane my neck. A flurry of red hair attached to a long-legged girl comes into view.

Roxanne Jeffries.

I hate Roxanne Jeffries almost as much as I hate dogs named Princess.

She's smiling at Mitch. The *ho*. "Jess, get your ass over there," I order, then move out of the way.

"He's smiling at her! Roxanne doesn't have crooked features, just a crooked personality. Do you think he asked her to the Valentine's Dance?"

"No," I say. "He's *your* boyfriend. What's making you

all insecure? You've got gorgeous straight hair I'd die for, perfect features, and perky boobs. Now go over there and claim your man."

There's no way we can stay undetected. Mutt is the biggest, fluffiest, friendliest dog in the place. In fact, everyone in the neighborhood knows Mutt. And everyone in the neighborhood knows Mutt is my dog. Mitch, who thinks he's too cool to wear a jacket in twenty-five-degree weather, has already spotted my beast and waves to me.

"He sees me," I tell Jess.

"Shit," Jess mutters into my back.

Okay, I've had enough. "He can't ask you if you don't talk to him." I start walking over to Mitch, assuming Jess will follow. "Hi," I say to Mitch and Roxanne. Only now I look back and realize Jess hasn't followed.

Mitch gives me a half wave. "Hey, Amy."

Roxanne, bundled up with a scarf, leather gloves, and a new winter coat I heard she got at Barney's and cost over five hundred dollars, doesn't greet me with a hey, hello, or even a hi. Instead she says, "Your dog is humping Zeus."

I look over at Mutt. She wasn't kidding; he's humping Mitch's black lab like there's no tomorrow. "He's showing Zeus who's the alpha male," I say matter-of-factly.

Roxanne gives Mitch a disgusted look. Mitch laughs.

Mutt hops off Zeus, then takes a huge, steaming dump. Seriously, before I had a dog I would never have thought I'd be okay picking up raunchy, hot steaming dog poop with a plastic bag being the only thing separating me and the excrement.

"Where's Jess going?" Mitch asks.

I quickly scan the dog park and catch sight of Jessica's retreating back. She's leaving. "Come on, Mutt!" I order, then run toward the gate. Mutt is preoccupied with sniffing a pug's butt. Damn. I open the gate, say, "Mutt, treat!" and he comes faster than a horse at the Kentucky Derby.

I have the warm poop bag in one hand and Mutt's leash in the other. The problem is that, instead of stopping so I can put on his leash and dump the poop, Mutt flies right past me, through the open gate, and onto the crowded Chicago street.

"Mutt, get back here!" I yell at the top of my lungs. I swear, when I catch the beast, he's toast.

You'd think my dear dog would listen to me. But no. He's bolting so fast I imagine him singing "Born Free" like I heard on one of those animal shows.

I run about two city blocks which, I might add, are way bigger than any suburban blocks. And my boobs are flapping together, which is not a pretty sight no matter what your gender is. I'm panting and it feels like my lungs are running out of air and shriveling up. I still see a blur of white puffy fur and a wagging tail, but it's getting farther and farther away.

I give a little curse to the snow that melted and is now frozen ice on the sidewalks. I'm slipping and sliding in my boots, which I picked out for fashion and not traction, while trying to avoid the barricades in front of most buildings. If you live or work in Chicago, you know it's a hazard just walking down the streets in winter when ice melts off the tops of the skyscrapers. Ice falls to the street and the people below are targets. Once I got tagged by a chunk of ice from a building. Luckily, I put my head down so I only had a huge lump and serious bruise on top of my head. If I was looking up…well, let's just say I would have either died or my nose would have been broken. I'm careful to look straight ahead and ignore the sounds or warnings of falling ice.

"Mutt!" I scream, but in my state of decreased lung capacity it comes out as a squeak.

I'm about to give up when I see Mutt halt. Thank the Lord. I slide up to the person who stopped him.

A teenager, wearing a geeky button-down plaid shirt and corduroys, is kneeling down and holding Mutt's collar. "Is he yours?" he asks while pushing his glasses high up on his nose as I come to a halt.

I'm huffing and puffing, but I manage a yeah.

Before I can catch my breath and formally thank the guy, he stands up and says, "He should be on a leash, you know. It's the law."

"Thanks for the tip," I say between puffs, then reach out and clip Mutt's leash on.

"Seriously," he says. "He could have been hit by a car."

"Seriously," I say. "I know."

The guy steps toward me. "Do you realize how many dogs are hit by cars or end up in shelters because of careless owners?"

Is this dude kidding me? The last thing I need is a lecture on dog safety. I wave the poop bag, which is still in my hand, at the guy. "Listen, I am not a careless owner. Careless owners do not carry poop bags. And, as you can see, my dog is safe and sound."

He holds his hands up in mock surrender. "Don't get all angry with me. I'm just a concerned citizen."

"Whatever. Thanks for catching my dog," I say, then walk toward home with the poop bag still in my hand.

"Arg!" Mutt barks as we walk.

I look down at my dog and give him my famous sneer, the one where my lip curls up just the right amount. "You are in *so* much trouble."

My dog farts in response. It's a steaming one, too. Yuck.

Talk about passive-aggressive.

2

God talked to Moses (Exodus 3:4).
Does God still talk to people?
And how come when I talk to God,
he never seems to answer back?

On Sunday I drive to Mom's new house in Deerfield with Mutt. Since I moved in with my dad, I visit her on the weekends. Mutt springs inside the house before I even open the door all the way.

"Arg! Arg!"

I don't need to guess where Mom is. Her little shriek alerts me she's in her kitchen. "Amy!"

Here she goes. "What?" I say extremely unenthusiastically.

"Did you have to bring the mutt?"

"Mutt, Mom. His name is Mutt." Okay, so he's also technically a mutt.

"Arg!" Mutt responds.

"Why does he bark like that?"

"I already told you, he's got a speech impediment." It runs in the family. My dad can't say the "th" sound because Israelis don't have the "th" sound in their language. I'm used to it, though, and I don't even hear his accent. It's the same way with Mutt.

"Maybe he's got something wrong with him," she says, backing up. "Did he get all his shots?"

I roll my eyes. "And you call me the drama queen. He's perfectly healthy."

"Just…let him outside, okay? Marc is allergic."

I feel bad leaving Mutt in the cold, especially because I got him in Israel and he's used to the heat. But, hey, he's got a fur coat on so I shouldn't worry. Right?

"Mutt. Out," I order while I open the back door. He doesn't seem to mind going outside, actually, and bounds out the door.

To be honest, I think Marc is allergic to the *idea* of having a dog around. He's a clean freak. And Mutt is a slobbering, shedding animal.

I turn around and find my mom staring at my chest.

"They're looking a little saggy lately. I think it's time to go buy you new bras."

"Mom," I say, horrified. "My bras are fine."

"When was the last time you were fitted properly?"

Oh, no, here we go again. As if I'm going to stand inside a dressing room and have a lady come in, size me up, and watch/help me shove my boobs into bras. Once my mom made me go to one of those specialty bra boutiques.

It was the most embarrassing moment of my life. (Okay, so I've had a ton of embarrassing moments in my life, but that one is high on the list.)

"Can we not talk about my boobs, please?"

Great. Now O Holy Allergic One is walking into the kitchen. I hope he didn't hear the convo about my saggy boobs. "Hi, Amy," he says.

I mumble a "hi."

He leans over my mom and kisses her. Eww! Seriously, if he starts making out with her I'm outta here.

"Ah-choo!"

"Oh, sweetie," Mom says (not referring to me). "Amy's dog was in the house."

"It's okay," he says.

Kiss-ass.

I can't stand all this lovey-dovey stuff. "I'm taking Mutt for a walk."

"Wait. We want to ask you something."

I turn to Mom. "What?"

"Just…come sit down."

I plop down in a chair in the kitchen. Mom sits down beside me. Marc sits next to Mom. She reaches out to hold my hand.

Okay, this is bigger than boob talk. I can tell just by the way Mom is squeezing my hand.

"How would you like to be a big sister?"

I shrug. "I wouldn't."

I like my life just how it is. I have my mom, I have my dad, I have Jessica, I have my non-boyfriend Avi, and

I have Mutt. My life is fine, why would I want a little brat screwing it up?

Mom's excitement deflates.

"Why, were you thinking about adopting a baby? Listen, Mom, I doubt people would even allow you adopt at your age."

"I beg your pardon. I'm only thirty-seven."

Duh! "You're almost forty!"

"Besides," she says, ignoring me. "We're not thinking of adopting. I'm pregnant."

Pause.

Silence.

Back up. Did I hear right?

"You're *pregnant*? As in you're going to have a baby *pregnant*?"

Marc smiles wide. "Yep."

I stand up. "And you didn't consult me on this?" I mean, you'd think they would have at least talked to me about it. Are they replacing me because I moved in with my dad? It's not like I don't come around the 'burbs. I do. But Mom just up and sold our condo in the city. I couldn't move schools my junior year. Then I would have to make all new friends. Oh, man. And they're so excited about it, too. Like the new, shiny kid is going to be way better than the old, used model.

A baby.

There's no getting around the fact that I'm being replaced.

"I'm not changing diapers," I blurt out. Yes, I know

it was immature and childish to say that, but it just came out. Sue me for being a teenager.

Mom gives me a tearful look. "You don't have to change diapers."

I'm sorry, I just can't stand here calmly. My mind is whirling with questions. "Was this planned?"

Marc and Mom look at each other. "Well, yeah," he says.

"And you didn't think it was important to ask my opinion?"

"Amy, Marc and I want to have children together. I thought you'd be as excited as we are."

I swallow, which is no easy feat because I have a lump in my throat the size of a basketball.

"I gotta go," I say, and get Mutt. "Come on, boy," I say, leading him to the front of the yard. I need to get away from the house and figure out where I fit in my so-called family.

My mom runs after me. "Amy, stay. I don't want you to be angry."

I sigh. "I'm not angry, Mom. I just need to sort this all out in my head." In my car, I flip open my phone to text Jessica.

Me: Guess who's pregnant?
Jess: u?
Me: Get real.
Jess: ur mom?
Me: yep

Jess: Mazel tov!?
Me: Don't congratulate me, plz
Jess: Could b worse
Me: How?
Jess: Could b u?
Me: I'm a virgin.
Jess: Nobody's perfect.
Me: Don't make me laugh.
Jess: Better than crying, right?

Leave it to my best friend to put it into perspective. But Jessica doesn't know that there's history with my mom and dad. History that I think still stings for one of my parents. And that is no laughing matter.

When I get back to the city, I swear the temperature in the city has decreased by at least twenty degrees. It mimics the chill in my body.

Crying isn't my thing, but my eyes water on their own. Damn.

I feel sorry for my dad, even more now that I know Mom and Marc are really going to have a new family. My poor dad is alone. He'll never get my mom back now. When he finds out about the baby, he's really going to get depressed. I'll have to do something about that, sooner rather than later. My perfect family life just blew up in my face.

Are families supposed to drive you crazy? I need to talk to someone about this. I'd like to talk to my non-boyfriend, but he's somewhere in the middle of Israel in training. No phone calls during boot camp.

I glance at the picture of Avi on my nightstand. He's in his army fatigues, a machine gun strapped to his shoulder. And he's smiling. Smiling. As if being stuck in the middle of the hot Negev Desert during military boot camp is no biggie. I miss him more than anything right now. He's so strong, inside and out. I wish I was like that.

In his last letter he wrote about stars. He said in the Negev Desert at night he looked up and the sky was so clear he could swear he saw a billion stars.

He said he thought of me right there, wondering what I was doing under the same stars. My heart just about melted into garlic butter sauce (which I love to dip my pizza in) when I read his letter. Sometimes I feel like he has the right perspective on life. Me? I'd probably look up at billions of stars and think, *I'm so insignificant.*

I sit on my bed and open my backpack. There, staring back at me, is the personals section. I must have shoved it in there accidentally. I wipe my eyes and focus on the paper.

A small idea, as tiny as a faraway star, starts forming in the back of my mind.

If Mom and Marc can create their own little suburban family, I'm going to create one of my own for my bachelor dad…right here in the city.

After all, what's wrong with placing a personal ad for my dad? Maybe, as Marla said, he could meet his own soul mate.

3

Kosher question # 1: In Leviticus (11:1), God lists what's kosher and what's not. Nowhere in the entire Bible does it mention anything about spicy tuna sushi rolls with little pieces of tempura crunch inside.

Hunky, brooding single Jewish dad with an adorable teenage daughter seeks woman for dinners, dancing, and walks in the park. Needs to like dogs and be free of any neurosis or hang-ups.

"Amy, I'm home. And I brought sushi for you."

I shove the draft into my backpack and rush for the door. Okay, okay, I know the ad needs a little tweaking. But I'll deal with that later. Sushi can't wait. "Did you get spicy tuna rolls?"

"Yes."

I kiss him on the cheek and say, "You're the best. Did you remember to ask for tempura flakes inside?"

"Sorry, I forgot. I hope they're still edible."

He's joking with me because he's well aware I'll devour the spicy tuna rolls with or without the tempura crunch.

My dad is sifting through the mail by the front door. He lives for mail. Sundays he positively goes nuts not having any. When Monday rolls around, he's like a hawk.

I snatch the white takeout bag off the table by the front door. My mouth is already watering in anticipation of eating freshly made sushi. "How was work?"

"Hectic as usual. How was school?"

"Hectic as usual."

He looks sideways at me.

"Well, it was," I say. "I had three tests, one I probably failed, two hours of homework, and I have no date for the Valentine's Dance. Top that."

We walk into the kitchen together. "Avi is in Israel," he says as if I'm pining for a relationship that's bound to fail. Talk about the "like father, like daughter" syndrome.

"I know," I say.

My dad gives me a weak smile and shrugs. "I just don't want you to miss out."

Mutt bounds into the kitchen and starts jumping on me. "Arg!"

"We have to get him fixed," he says.

I sit on the kitchen floor with Mutt and pat his springy hair. "We aren't going to do that," I tell my dog. "Only mean people do that to their dogs."

Mutt responds by licking my face. There's no way I'm having my dog's balls cut off.

My dad takes extra food for himself out of the refrigerator because he mistakingly treats sushi as an appetizer. He says sushi doesn't fill him up. "Amy…"

I give him my I-am-not-backing-down stare. "What?"

"The vet said—"

"Yeah, and the vet thought Mutt was a goldendoodle, too. Can you believe that? A *designer* mutt, no less. I don't trust that guy." Give me a break. My dog is a pure, un-poodleized mutt.

My dad takes a piece of pita and swipes it into a container of hummus. It's his staple food. Israelis are to hummus as frat boys are to beer. (We've been studying analogies in English. Can you tell?)

"Don't double dip," I warn him.

"I wouldn't dream of it," he says, stuffing the pita into his mouth.

"Maybe you haven't had a date in a while because you shove food into your mouth when you eat," I say.

"Maybe I haven't had a date in a while because I've been busy," he says back.

Yeah, right. "So what kind of woman do you like?"

"Why?"

"Maybe I can help you."

"Amy, we are not having this discussion."

"But—"

"But nothing. Stop thinking about finding me a date and start concentrating on your schoolwork."

I assure you schoolwork is a lot more boring. "You know what your problem is?" I ask him.

"Yes. I have a daughter who insists she knows everything."

"That's not your problem, *Aba*. That's your blessing."

My dad chuckles, then sets our dinner on the table.

Taking the chopsticks from the takeout bag, I pick up a spicy tuna roll from the platter and dip it into a little container of soy sauce. I'm so glad he got sushi from my favorite place. They always have the tuna without any stringy white veins attached. I do not eat sushi with stringy white veins attached. After I pop the roll into my mouth, my insides smile.

"I forgot to ask," my dad says. "How was it at your mom's yesterday?"

I gauge his reaction as I say, "She's pregnant."

The poor man puts down his fork and stares at me. "Really?"

I nod. I can't talk now even if I wanted to. I refuse to get emotional.

"Wow."

He goes back to eating after his "wow" comment. I want to apologize even though it's not my fault. He's probably devastated my mom chose a dork over him. Now she's not only married to the new guy, but she's had sex with him to procreate. Eww. The thought of my mom having sex at her age is just plain gross. The fact that she's having it with my stepdad is even grosser.

The only way to fix this situation is to find my dad a wife. Not for procreation, but so he doesn't feel like the odd one without a partner. He's for sure hiding his true feelings, covering up his devastation of losing my mom to make me feel better.

After we finish dinner, he goes to the workout room in the building while I make a beeline for the computer.

I'm web surfing. Don't worry, I know not to give out any personal information when I'm in chat rooms. My dad is a consultant for the Department of Homeland Security and has bored me to death with the dangers of the Internet until I thought my ears would bleed.

I'm not interested in chat rooms, no siree bob. I'm focused purely on finding my dad a wife. Now…where can I find the perfect woman?

I surf the Net until I finally find it. Yeah!

Professional Jewish Singles Network.

They guarantee *you will find the Jewish mate a matchmaker would be jealous of.*

I saw *Fiddler on the Roof.* This is the best possible news.

My heart races as I read the home page and the requirements to join the PJSN. Need to be single. Duh! Need to be between the ages of twenty-one and seventy-five. Check. My dad is a whopping thirty-seven. Need to have a college degree. Check. My dad has a degree from the University of Illinois. Need to have a credit card to pay the $59.99 monthly fee.

Okay, the credit card thing is going to take a little manipulation.

My eyes dart over to the front door. His wallet is on

the table where we put the mail. I know his credit card is inside.

I saunter over to his wallet. I've used my mom's credit card before. Of course I had permission then.

It wouldn't hurt just to take the card out. Just to look at it. I slowly open his wallet. Yep, in one slot the top of a shiny gold credit card is staring back at me. I slip it out and glance nervously at the front door.

I have at least thirty minutes before he comes back. After I put the wallet back on the table I trot back to the computer with his credit card in my hand. I'm not thinking about how it's probably illegal that I'm using someone else's card—this is about helping my father.

The words in my head are chanting *soul mate, soul mate, soul mate*. My dad can't just live the rest of his life in solitary misery.

I click the word *Register*. The computer prompts me to answer a list of questions. My fingers automatically type in the info.

Name: Ron Barak
Age: 37
Hair color: dark brown
Eye color: dark brown
Children: one *delightful* seventeen-year-old
Occupation: security consultant
State: Illinois
Hobbies: reading, hiking, tennis, baseball

Okay, I'm having a tough time with the hobbies question. And, to be completely honest, I've fudged a few of the hobbies I listed. My dad doesn't know the first thing about baseball. It's not exactly a popular Israeli sport. But if you live in Chicago, you gotta be into either baseball, basketball, hockey, or football. This is a sport-centered town. I'm not even going to get into the Cubs/Sox, North Side/South Side rivalry.

On to the next question: *Describe yourself in two words.*

Hmm…what two words will attract women? I type in *Israeli* and *hunk* something quick and click *enter*. It prompts me to scan a picture for his profile and I find one from our trip to Israel.

Finally, it asks for my credit card number. I mean *his* credit card number. I punch in the numbers and before you can say "stolen credit card," my dad has his own profile, PJSN e-mail, and is ready to meet his soul mate. Oh man, oh man, I am excited. My dad is in the Professional Jewish Singles Network and is ready to join the dating scene.

Oh, shit. I hear the door opening and I still have my dad's credit card in my hot little hand. *Do something quick,* my mind tells me.

I slide the credit card under the keyboard and close all of the open windows on the computer. I'll place the Visa back in his wallet later. By the time he figures out I used it, he'll be so thrilled to have met his future wife he won't get pissed off. In fact, he'll be thanking me all the way to the rabbi who'll marry them.

"Amy?"

He's onto me. He knows I took his credit card without permission. Oh, no. I swallow, hard. "Yeah?"

"Don't you think Mutt needs to go out?"

I let out a breath. "Uh, I guess."

"Well…"

I stand up, put the leash on Mutt, and dash to the elevator. As soon as the elevator door opens, I'm pushed back by a huge cardboard box and almost fall backwards. My boobs are squished, I tell you. I probably just went from a saggy C+ cup to an A– cup.

"Hey!" I yell.

"Sorry," a masculine voice murmurs, then the guy puts down the box.

But he's not a man, at least not a real one. It's the boy from yesterday who caught Mutt and gave me the *concerned citizen* lecture.

Today he's wearing a green plaid shirt and jeans with a waist way too high. And I swear cranky Mr. Obermeyer has those same gym shoes.

"Arg!" Mutt barks, then tries to sniff his crotch as if he's hiding a treat in there.

Concerned Citizen covers his privates with his hands like a soccer player during a penalty kick. Then he pushes his glasses high up on his nose, the rims circling his green eyes. "Oh, it's you."

I pull Mutt away from his pants. "Just watch where you're going next time. As a *concerned citizen*," I add, "you should know not to crash into people with large boxes."

With my rant I miss the elevator. Damn. I push the down arrow again.

He steps forward and trips over the box. "Are you always this friendly?"

I don't even answer him. Where does he come off challenging me? Thankfully the elevator dings and the door opens. I hurry inside with Mutt. There's no way I'm missing my second chance at freedom.

"Arg!"

As the elevator door closes, he bends over to pick up the box again. I wonder what this boy is doing in my building, on my floor, in my life.

Avi says everything happens for a reason. I hate to disagree, but he's wrong.

4

I've seen Fiddler on the Roof. *There was this one lady, Yente, who was the matchmaker—that was her job in the village. Right now I'm the matchmaker. Maybe I've found my calling...*

"Hey, girl," Marla says as I walk into Perk Me Up! after school the next day. "Jessica is at the computer corner."

Marla said she put in the computers because people wanted to be connected to the Internet and their e-mail no matter where they are. And if they want free, convenient Internet while they're drinking her coffee, all the better.

I stand behind Jessica. "What are you doing?"

Her hands are busy clicking away. "Checking Mitch's e-mail."

"Sneaky, Jess. How'd you get his password?"

"I have my ways. See, that bitch Roxanne is e-mailing him," Jess says, pointing to the screen.

Oooh, gossip. I know it's bad, but gossip is seriously addictive and underrated. "What does she say?"

"Just that she needs help in biology, yadda yadda."

"You better watch out for her," I say. "Now get off the computer so I can check something."

"I'm still mad at you, you know."

Me? Innocent, little me? "You'll get over it. Besides, whatever I did was probably for your own good."

"You took me to the dog park knowing Mitch would be there. Stop meddling in my life."

I huff. "I'm Jewish, what do you expect? I was born to meddle."

Jessica shakes her head. Okay, so she has more Jewish blood because both her parents are Jewish and my dad is the one who gave me my Jewish genes. My mom gave me good fashion sense genes.

While Jessica goes to the bathroom, I quickly check the PJSN website and log into my father's profile.

Oh. My. God.

I've got thirty-seven responses from women who want to date me...I mean, my dad. And, checking the home page, my dad has gotten the most hits on the PJSN website in the past twenty-four hours.

It brings popularity to a whole new level.

I'm almost giddy (does anyone use that word anymore??) as I scan the responses of women.

Three make sexual innuendos. They're out.

Ten live in the suburbs. Definitely out.

Five don't put their pictures on the site. Questionable. What if the supposed woman is a man?

Seven are over fifty. Ten have more than two kids. Out. Out. My dad can hardly handle me. How would he be able to handle a whole tribe?

That leaves two.

One is in human resources, the other a lawyer. I e-mail both of them and ask them if they want to have coffee sometime. Okay, it's a little creepy asking women out on dates. But even more daunting is having to manipulate my dad somehow to get him to go on the date. I know meeting for coffee isn't the most original date, but at least it's not a dinner or lunch where you have to sit and talk the entire time, waiting for that uncomfortable silence when you both want to escape.

"Does your dad know about this?"

I shriek and scold Jessica. "Didn't your mother tell you it's not nice to sneak up on people?"

"No."

My best friend shakes her head and puts her hand over her eyes. "Please tell me you didn't sign your dad up for an online dating service."

"I didn't sign my dad up for an online dating service."

"You're lying, Amy."

"Of course I'm lying."

"Amy, one of these days your little plans are gonna backfire and come crashing in your face."

"Oh, ye of little faith," I say. "My dad will have a girlfriend by Passover."

"Oh, ye of too many scatterbrained ideas," Jess says. "Your head is getting bigger than your boobs."

"Shut up. Haven't you ever needed something you didn't want?"

"Yeah, a flu shot. And it hurt me way more than it hurt my mom who made me get one."

Jessica doesn't understand. "You don't expect me to sit around as my mom makes babies with Marc while my dad stays alone for the rest of his life, do you?" It makes me sad thinking he's pining for my mom.

"Your dad doesn't seem to mind," Jess says.

I turn in my chair and face her. I admit my dad doesn't outwardly show his unhappiness, but it's in there. Deep down. And he's starting to age. "He's got a few gray hairs already."

"Your parents are way younger than mine, Amy. My dad is totally bald and my mom's almost fifty and is totally white . . . well, underneath all of the hair dye she's as white as a snowball."

"Great. In a few years my mom'll turn gray and people will think my little sister or brother is my own kid. They'll think my mom is the grandma."

"People in their late thirties have babies all the time. Don't stress about it."

I put my hands over my heart. "Me, stress? I never stress about anything."

Jess raises her eyebrows at me and chuckles. Because we both know it's not true.

My cell phone is ringing. I click the little green button. It's my dad. "Hey, *Aba*."

"Amy, I just took my clients out for dinner. I'm about to pay the bill."

"So?"

"So," he says in a distressed voice. "Do you by any chance know where my credit card is?"

Oh, no. I forgot to put it back in his wallet after my run-in with Geek Boy. "Umm...*Aba*...you're not gonna believe this—"

5

To make a sin offering to God:
a) sacrifice an animal to the Lord (Leviticus 6:18) or
b) wait until Yom Kippur and fast a whole day.
(Leviticus 16:29)
So good to know I can erase my sins.
(Erasing guilt is outlined in Leviticus 5.
If God can forgive, surely humans should, too.)

I'm grounded for the rest of my life.

My dad laid down that law a few minutes ago, and he sounded dead serious. Now I hear his little outbursts of anger coming from the kitchen.

The phone rings. It's probably Jessica.

"Don't you *dare* pick dat phone up!" he yells from the other end of the condo, his thick Hebrew accent getting thicker by the minute. I swear, the neighbors are going to start calling the police soon if he doesn't calm down.

I hear him stomping closer to my room. He opens the door and scowls at me while running a hand through his hair, his signature and patented I-am-frustrated-and-don't-know-what-to-do-with-my-teenage-daughter move. "Do you not understand what you did was wrong on so many levels, Amy? You stole my credit card—"

"Borrowed it," I correct him.

"You made me look like a fool in front of clients. You sign me up for a dating service...what's next?"

Before I can open my mouth to defend myself, he says, "How much did it cost me?"

"The dating service?"

He nods.

"Um...less than sixty dollars a month," I answer.

"How much less?"

"One penny."

"Go on the computer now and cancel it before I have to pay for two months."

"Um, *Aba*?"

"What?"

"I got you a six-month subscription. It was cheaper to pay it all up front. I got a deal. Think of me as your Yente from *Fiddler on the Roof*. Your personal matchmaker."

This time he laughs, and I think he's broken way past the anger barrier and is quickly gliding toward delirium. A delirious Israeli ex-commando is not a good thing.

"What's the problem with a dating service? It's for *Jews*," I interject, hoping to lessen the blow. "You gotta love Jewish women. You're Israeli."

"That's not the point. You used my credit card without asking."

"Yeah, well, I don't exactly have one of my own."

I swear I hear him praising that fact under his breath.

The doorbell rings. Mutt is going nuts, barking non-stop. "Arg! Arg! Arg! Arg!" It gets my dad's attention. He's afraid he'll have to pay a fine if we get too many complaints from the neighbors about Mutt's excessive barking. I'm saved from my dad's rant for now. *Thank you, Mutt!*

"Stay here," my dad orders, leaving my room.

So now I'm sitting on my bed, alone once again. And I'm grounded. I wonder how long I'll be stuck here before he gives in.

"Amy, come here!" he calls out.

"Yeah?" I say innocently as I head to the foyer of our condo. Dad is holding Mutt's collar, holding him back from jumping on and sniffing the crotch of whoever is at the door. I've had the talk with Mutt, but he doesn't listen. I don't know what the big deal about crotches is. I assume once you've smelled one, you've smelled them all. Not that I'd know. I have no desire to go near anyone else's to test my theory.

"You know Mrs. Keener, don't you?"

I scan the suit and tailored attire of the woman, sure she hasn't smiled in at least a year. Can she pull that 1970s bun tighter on her skull? I turn my gaze to the person beside her. Oh, no. It's Concerned Citizen Boy, in the flesh.

Mrs. Keener pushes him closer to us and directs her conversation to my dad. "This is my nephew, Nathan. He's come to live with us for a while." She shakes her head as she says, "It's a long story. I know your daughter is about the same age and was wondering if she'd be able to show him around the city."

Nathan looks about as happy as I do to be in this situation. But I suppose being grounded and stuck in my room is worse than being stuck with Nathan Keener.

Nathan Keener.

Just the name alone could get a kid beat up.

"Amy's grounded," my dad says.

Thanks a lot for sharing that humiliating piece of information, Dad.

"Oh," Mrs. Keener says, obviously put in an awkward situation.

"But I guess if she takes Mutt for a walk, she could go out for a bit—"

Needing no further push, I grab Mutt's leash off our hall tree and snap it on his collar. "Come on, Nathan," I call over my shoulder as I hurry to the elevator with a very excited and very large puppy.

Nathan, it seems, needs no further push either. He follows right behind me and enters the elevator as soon as Mutt and I step inside.

We have no elevator music in our building, so it's just silence except for heavy panting courtesy of my dog.

"You don't have to babysit me, you know," he says while crossing his arms over his chest, trying to look tough. He doesn't.

"Your aunt seems to think I do," I reply.

The elevator door opens. Nathan Keener is right behind me, not missing a step when I exit our building. But once I turn toward the dog park, I don't hear his footsteps behind me anymore. Turning around, I find Nathan walking in the opposite direction. With his long, corduroy-wrapped legs, he's already half a block away.

Mutt is pulling me toward the park. "Hey, Nathan!" I yell, but the guy doesn't turn around. Now what am I supposed to do?

6

---

*Chicken soup can help heal you
when you're sick. Is there a recipe for healing
relationships?*

If you can believe it, I found out this morning Nathan Keener is going to my school, a private prep school called Chicago Academy. Yep, it's true. I also have the pleasure of sitting behind him in English class and he's even in gym class with me. It wouldn't be so bad, but he's already the talk of the entire school.

What is it about transfer students that fascinates people so much? If I hear one more time, *Amy, did you see the new guy?* I swear I'm gonna scream. It's fifth period. I have study hall. I sit next to Kyle Sanderson, the varsity center for Chicago Academy's basketball team and all-around popular guy. The only flaw is that Kyle wears no less than a half a bottle of cologne every day. You can tell when Kyle leaves a classroom that he's been there. He's like a bear, leaving his scent behind for girls.

"What's up, Nelson?" he says, calling me by my last name as he slides skillfully into the seat next to me. Do you think he practices that move?

I'm not about to tell him I've been hyphenating my last name since the beginning of the school year, using both my parents' last names. I'm now Amy Nelson-Barak. I'm not telling Kyle because 1) he wouldn't care and 2) he wouldn't remember even if I did tell him.

"Not much," I respond.

"That's not what I heard."

Huh?

"What'd you hear?" I ask him. Is there a rumor about me?

"That you signed up for a dating service."

"Who told you that?" It's not true…exactly.

Kyle leans his chair back on two legs. "The new guy. You know, the one with glasses and dorky clothes."

"Nathan?"

Kyle shrugs his big shoulders and says, "Yep. The dude's my bio partner this week."

I'm going to kill that tall, lanky jerk who wouldn't know the difference between Dana Buchman and Armani. How dare he spread rumors about me!

"So…are you that hard up?" Kyle asks. "'Cause you're kinda cute, Nelson, and you got great boobage."

I whip my head around and glare at him. "Boobage? Jeez, Kyle, do you make these words up?"

He puts his hands up in question. "You'd rather I said tits?"

"Shut up," I say before opening my trig book and sticking my head in it. I swear, if he keeps staring at my chest I'm going to make sure he can't pass the ball at the next basketball game.

"Miss Barak, would you care to share your conversation with the rest of us?" Mr. Hennesey barks out from the front of the room. Mr. Hennesey is the gym teacher as well as study hall monitor. Study hall policeman is more like it.

If Kyle mentions my *boobage* to the rest of the room, I'm going to kill him…along with Nathan Keener.

"Nope," I say.

"Then I suggest you both quit talking or I'll have to separate you." I wish.

Ten minutes later, Mr. Hennesey walks out of the room. As everyone knows, when a teacher walks out of the room it's an invitation to start talking. Right now I don't want to talk.

"You need a date for the Valentine's Dance?" Kyle says, loudly I might add.

I cock my head to the side and answer sweetly, "Why? Are you asking me?" Ha! Right back at ya. Nothing like a lowly junior putting a popular senior boy on the spot.

I'm sure everyone in the entire room hears our conversation. The snickers and looks in our direction are a clue. I think the words "Valentine's Dance" alone would turn heads. It's on everyone's mind since the posters went up last week.

"I will, if you want to do a threesome. I already asked Caroleen Connors, but I'm man enough to take you both on at once."

Kyle has the nerve to wink at me. Eww! The guy needs a serious ego adjustment.

Mr. Hennesey walks back into the room, so I can't respond. So now I'm sitting here, seething at Kyle for being a male chauvinist pig and at Nathan for spreading rumors about me.

After study hall, I walk to social studies while plotting ways to confront the geek who moved into my building. Is he *that* socially inept he has to stoop to spreading rumors about me just to get attention?

"Did you see the new guy?"

I look up at my friend Raine, who has no clue my heart rate just jumped and my veins tensed at the mention of him. I look up at her with my patented sneer.

"What did I do?" Raine asks, wide-eyed.

"Nothing," I say. "Just please don't talk about Nathan Keener."

A guy's voice behind me says, "FYI, it's Nathan Greyson."

I'm left with my mouth wide open, staring at my neighbor and his oversized tortoise-rimmed glasses slipping down the bridge of his nose.

Raine says, "Nice pants," and walks away giggling.

"You and your friends really know how to throw out the welcome mat," Nathan says with a fake smile. "Private schools are a breeding ground for fake, plastic people. This school is no exception."

I don't understand this guy. He's geeky, but he's got

an attitude that doesn't mix with his outward appearance. "Who *are* you?" I ask.

"Hell if I know," he responds, and without another word walks away.

Leaving me to wonder if he's a vampire or alien in human form.

I walk into social studies and the last thing on my mind is current affairs. But Mrs. Moore is obsessed with vibrant class discussions on the president, his policies, and making sure we all know what's going on in this great country of ours. I think the mere act of looking at the American flag brings her to tears.

When the bell rings at the end of the day, I stuff my homework in my book bag and trudge through the slush to the bus stop with Jessica, Cami, and Raine. Mitch is standing at the bus stop already, and when Jessica walks close he casually puts his arm across her shoulders. I can tell Jess is still upset he hasn't asked her to the dance. She's as stiff as the icicles hanging from the bus stop sign.

"Seriously, Amy. Did you join a dating service to get a date for the Valentine's Dance?" Roxanne says, and laughs like a hyena giving painful birth to twins.

I *really* hate her. She knows it, too, because last year we almost came to blows in tennis when I bumped her down from the varsity team to JV. The cheat always pretends to hyperventilate in the middle of a match she's losing so she can take a break and regroup. Nice try, Roxy. I still beat your butt.

"She's got a boyfriend," Jessica chimes in while rolling her eyes. "Leave her alone, Roxanne."

I want to cheer *Go Jessica Go!*, but don't. Jessica doesn't reveal the fact that I signed my dad up on PJSN because she knows it would embarrass me. One of these days Roxanne is going to find herself banned from the bus stop if her mouth keeps running like diarrhea.

Unfortunately, we have to wait ten more minutes for the bus to come. We all live on the Gold Coast and have to take public transportation to school. It doesn't make sense to have a car when you live and go to school in the city. So we're at the mercy of the Chicago Transit Authority. It's cool during the summer and spring, but when snow dumps itself on Chicago it can get pretty rough. We ususally wait inside the school until the last possible minute, then trudge outside and freeze our butts off until the bus stops and opens its doors.

As if standing next to Roxanne wasn't bad enough, Nathan comes sidling up the sidewalk and stands with us. He's got his iPod headphones in his ears, highlighting that he doesn't care to start conversations with fake, plastic people. Kyle kind of nods his head in acknowledgment of him. Nathan nods back, then pushes his glasses up again. Someone should clue him in that they sell non-slip glasses now.

The bus turns down the street. Relief time! I'm the first one on, ready to get out of Roxanne and Nathan's sight even if it's for ten seconds. I head to the back of the bus where we hang until our stop. Jess and Mitch—"the couple"—sit across from me. Cami and Raine sit together, so do Kyle and Roxanne. That leaves Nathan and me, the singles.

Nathan doesn't even contemplate sitting next to me as he and his headphones plop themselves down onto a bench in the front of the bus. He makes it very clear he doesn't consider himself one of us.

I have no clue why this irks me so much.

Maybe it's because he insulted my school and my friends. And me.

Whatever. I don't care what Nathan ~~Keener~~ Greyson thinks about me. I have my own friends and boyfriend, even if he does live halfway around the globe.

Ugh. I miss Avi, especially at times like these when I need someone just to ramble to. Jess has been depressed lately—I have no clue if it's really about Mitch or if something else is bugging her. She won't open up to me.

Cami is studiously doing her homework so she has less to do when she gets home. And Raine is just the opposite, concentrating on putting her lip-gloss on to keep it fresh. She doesn't give a crap about homework. In fact, I bet she probably has her mom do it for her.

Roxanne is flirting with Kyle. Maybe she's moving on to someone who doesn't have a girlfriend. I wonder if she knows he's going to the Valentine's Dance with Caroleen Connors. Probably not by the way she's leaning into him and touching him as if he's her property. I swear, Kyle just eats up the attention. But thank God he's focused on her *boobage* now instead of mine.

The bus stops on the corner of Dearborn and Superior, where I get off. Of course Nathan gets off the bus, too, and we walk into our building together. Elevators are a strange place to begin with. The creaky sounds and rattling of the doors can put anyone on edge. But when you're in the elevator with someone you don't particularly like, the place can make even a non-claustrophobe feel like they're stuck in a coffin.

I'm on one side of the elevator; Nathan is on the other. He still has his iPod earbuds in his ears, but I have no clue if there's music playing in them. I almost want to say something to test him. I know people who pretend they're listening to music but are really eavesdropping on conversations when others think they can't hear.

"I'm not plastic," I say to him. "Or fake."

No reaction, except for a little twitch of his jaw. And his breathing halted, just for a millimeter of a second.

It's true. I'm as real as they get, no holds barred. My dad says sometimes it's a good trait, and sometimes it's a horrible one.

We finally reach the fortieth floor.

"Check ya later, Barbie," Nathan mumbles.

Did I just hear right?

Barbie? Um…that's not gonna fly with me. No way, no how.

I stop dead in my tracks and turn around. "What did you call me?" I ask.

I should have known the guy would ignore me. Ignoring is apparently Nathan's specialty.

Inside my condo, Mutt greets me with a pounce and a germ-infested lick. Most people say that a dog's mouth is cleaner than a person's mouth. But most people haven't tested my dog's mouth. He licks too many private parts to be considered clean by anyone's standards.

I look up when Mutt runs over to his leash. To my surprise, my dad is sitting at the dining room table.

"You get fired?" I ask.

My dad looks up. "No. Just wanted to be here when you got home."

That's a first. "Why?"

My dad's attention is taken by Mutt, holding the leash in his mouth and wagging his tail around like a lance. "Let's talk about it after you take Mutt out."

This doesn't sound too good. "Tell me now."

"He's going to have an accident on the floor if you don't take him."

"I'm going to freak out if you don't tell me. What's worse?"

My dad takes a deep breath and says, "I'm new at being a fadder, but I have to try my best. You used my credit card without my permission. You signed me up for a dating service without my permission. That six-month membership is costing me over three hundred dollars."

That about sums it up. "I said I was sorry."

"This time, Amy, sorry isn't good enough."

Now I'm starting to panic. Does he want me to leave and go live with my mom and her hyper-allergic husband? There's no way they'll let me keep Mutt in their pristine suburban house with the new baby coming. And will I have to start a new school with kids I don't know? High school is tough enough without being the new kid, and I'm not going to think about Nathan right now because he doesn't deserve my sympathy.

"I'll do anything, *Aba*. Please don't send me away."

My dad stands. I can tell he's going to break the bad news right now and I wince. "I'm not going to send you away, sweetheart."

"You're not?"

"No. I got you a job."

7

Moses had incredible negotiation skills. He made God, The
#1 Top Guy, *change his mind about destroying all of the
Jewish people (Exodus 32:13). If that doesn't prove anyone
can change the course of their life, nothing will. I wish I
had Moses's negotiation skills when dealing with my dad.*

"Amy, what are you doing here so early? Conversion class
doesn't start for another ten minutes."

I'm standing in the doorway of Rabbi Glassman's office
at Temple Beit Chaverim. The rabbi is reading over papers
while he rubs his gray and black beard.

"I need to talk to someone," I tell him.

Putting his papers aside, Rabbi Glassman motions for
me to sit at the chair opposite his desk. "I'm always here to
listen if someone needs an ear. That's my job."

"Listening to people complain?"

"Among other things," he says with a smile, then leans
back in his large cushioned chair. "What's on your mind?"

Lots of stuff, but I'm going to pick out the top one bugging me. "I got in trouble."

"With the law?" he prompts.

"With my dad. I took his credit card without his permission and now he wants me to pay him back the money I charged." I look to the rabbi, to make sure he's not keeling over in shock or shame.

"What did you charge, if I may ask?"

I put my hands up. "I know this is gonna sound weird, but it was for a good reason. I signed up for PJSN…you know, the Professional Jewish Singles Network. It's a dating service. And I did it for my dad."

The rabbi's eyebrows raise up. "You signed your father up for a dating service without his permission?"

I nod. "He needs a wife."

Rabbi Glassman sighs, then says in a quiet voice, "Amy, sometimes you have to let people choose their own paths in life."

"Yeah, but what if they're taking the wrong one?"

"Everyone makes mistakes. Even rabbis. We're all human."

I seem to be making more than my share of human mistakes lately. "So you're saying I should let my dad live his life alone and lonely?"

"Nonsense. He has you, doesn't he? Some things aren't measured by their size, but by their importance."

"That's very philosophical, Rabbi," I say, smiling.

"You caught me on a good day."

I bite the inside of my cheek. "I haven't had a lot of those lately."

"Ah, but you can't appreciate a great day unless you've experienced bad ones."

"Like Jonah had when God made the whale eat him?"

"I see you've been studying for class."

I lean forward and whisper, "Yeah, although I don't really buy it all, Rabbi. It's a little far-fetched for me, if you know what I mean. Can I still be a Jew if my brain can't grasp around certain Bible stories?"

The reason I can talk to Rabbi Glassman honestly is because he's never judged me or laughed at my opinions or arguments in class. He makes me feel like everything I have to say is really important and smart. Even when I'm disagreeing with him.

Rabbi Glassman leans forward and whispers back, "Amy, I think it's far-fetched, too."

My mouth goes wide. "You do? Don't worry, Rabbi. Your secret is safe with me."

Rabbi Glassman smiles and says, "I think it all comes down to faith and trust."

"In people?" I ask.

He shrugs, as if he doesn't have all the answers to all of his questions. "In people…in God…in yourself. Do you think you have faith and trust?"

I look up at him. "Should I answer that now?"

My rabbi shakes his head. "I don't know if you're ready to answer that yet. Why don't you think about it for a while and get back to me when you're…let's say…twenty years old."

I stand up, taking in all the information Rabbi Glassman

gave me as I leave his office. "See you at class, Rabbi," I call over my shoulder. "And thanks for the talk."

"Any time," he calls back.

Five minutes later, I'm in conversion class with five other people. Even though my father is Jewish, my mother isn't. I've lived with my mom most of my life, and she raised me without any religion. I went to Israel this past summer and realized I was missing something in my life: being Jewish. So I'm learning as much about my faith as I can.

Hence the conversion class.

We meet once a week. Rabbi Glassman has us read stories from the Bible and we discuss our opinions and reflect on the meaning or lessons behind the stories. He also teaches us about the different Jewish holidays and laws. The rabbi says a lot of Judaism comes from traditions. Since I don't really have any Jewish traditions, I'm going to have to make up some myself.

Back at home, I take Mutt out then walk over to Perk Me Up! Yes, I'm officially a Perk Me Up! employee, thanks to my father and Marla. My punishment is a job at my favorite café, and I'm not thrilled about it.

Marla greets me with a huge smile. "Nice to see we're all perky this evening."

"It's been a long day."

"Oh, then maybe I'll just have you sweep floors and wipe off tables so you don't have to interact with the customers."

I put a fake smile on my face.

"Thatta girl," Marla says. "That's what my customers like to see."

Marla directs me behind the counter, has me sign forms, then holds out a yellow apron. "Here, put this on. You can shadow me until your shift ends."

Yellow isn't really my color, but I hang the sunshiny thing around my neck and tie the wrap at my waist without complaint. Even though it's seven o'clock, there are still customers hanging out and ordering pastries. They're even drinking coffee this late, especially the ones who pull all-nighters.

The most all-nighters I see are lawyers. The ones who have to head to court in the morning or prepare for what they call depositions. Do you think the money they make is worth it for the amount of sleep they're missing? There's no way I could ever be a lawyer. I like my sleep too much.

After fifteen minutes, Marla hands me a white rag with antibacterial stuff on it and tells me to wipe off the tables.

I was really hoping to hide behind the counter all night until my shift was up, but Marla's having none of that. I'm just thankful she hasn't asked me to clean out the bathrooms so I shuffle over to the tables and start wiping them off.

I start cleaning the private nook where a couch and two cushy chairs are located, then I freeze. Sitting in the chair, reading, is none other than Nathan *Keener's-not—my-last-name* Greyson. He looks up and I can tell he's about as thrilled to see me as I am to see him. The cup stops short of his lips.

Ignoring the urge to confront him about spreading rumors about me, I hurriedly wipe his table before he sets whatever he's drinking back down.

"You missed a spot," Nathan mumbles. I huff. I did not miss a spot.

"All the tables are clean," I tell Marla back at the register.

She seems pleased as she does an eye scan of the café. For the next thirty minutes, Marla gives me the rundown on how to make the espressos, cold drinks, blended drinks, and tells me the particulars of some of her customers. She also explains how to use the cash register. I'm dizzy from the information overload, but I think I got it. Or at the very least I'll make it look like I got it.

"You think you can hold down the fort for five minutes while I call in an order for more cups?" Marla asks. "And don't forget to smile. Remember, the café is called Perk Me Up!"

Just call me the Smiling Barista Extraordinare. Well, not really—I don't know how to "garnish," as Marla puts it, with cinnamon, nutmeg, and other fancy stuff. I've been hanging out at Perk Me Up! ever since I moved in with my dad, so I pretty much know the basic routine. It's the non-basic that throws me off.

While I'm counting how many cups we have left, the door to the café opens.

My first real customer. I smile and look up then relax as I realize who my customer is.

My dad.

"Welcome to Perk Me Up!" I tell him in an overly formal tone. "Can I help you?"

He walks up to the counter and surveys the scene. "You look good as a working woman," he says, looking proud.

"Cut the crap. What do you want?"

I hear a gasp beside me. Oops, it's Marla. And she can't see I'm talking to my dad instead of a real customer. "Amy!" she chastises.

But when she reaches me, she breathes a sigh of relief.

"Boy, you've got tough employees," my dad says, then gives Marla a wink. "Okay, Amy, give me a large cup of your house coffee, black, with a shot of espresso."

"You're never gonna fall asleep," I tell him.

"Good. I've got a lot of work to do tonight."

It's a wonder my father isn't a lawyer. He never tells me the specifics of his work. I guess it's cool that he's got a top-secret job, so I don't bug him about working late.

I pour the mixture into a cup while Marla watches me closely. She smiles as I finish; then I hand it to my dad. He takes a sip right away, not even waiting for it to cool off. "*Best*-tasting coffee I've ever had in my life," he tells Marla, his overzealous reaction totally obvious.

I roll my eyes. "*Aba*, go sit down already."

"Why don't you join him," Marla says. "Your shift is over."

"I've only been here an hour. How can it be over?"

"That's our deal," my dad chimes in. "An hour a day on the weekdays, three hours on Sundays. I didn't want it to interfere with your schoolwork."

Eight hours a week isn't so bad, especially because I'll still have my Saturday nights free.

I hand Marla my yellow apron, but she says to bring it back tomorrow when I work. Then I grab my purse from the locked cabinet and sit down with my dad at one of the tables.

My dad takes out mail from his briefcase and starts rummaging through it. I'm craning my neck to see if there's a letter from Avi. It's been over two weeks since I've gotten one. It's unlike him.

"Well?" I ask.

My dad has this mischievous smile that gives it away.

I hold my hand out. "Give."

He holds out a letter and I snatch it out of his hand. My heart skips a beat and my stomach feels like little butterflies are flying around inside me as I run my fingers over the return address.

Since Avi and I have this long-distance relationship, I get insecure. When I'm in bed at night, thinking about how much I miss him, I wonder: Did he forget about me? Has he met someone else who's cuter or nicer or just...doesn't have as many hang-ups as me?

I'm feeling a bit better as I rip open the letter, but then notice my dad staring at me...gauging my reaction.

"Why don't you read it out loud," he suggests.

"Yeah, right," I say sarcastically. I stick the letter in my pocket, I'll read it later when I'm in bed...alone.

"Wait!" Marla calls out as we're about to leave. She's

holding a backpack. "Do you know that boy who was sitting on one of the chairs over there? He left this."

"It's Nathan's," I say. "I'm sure he'll realize it and come back to get it."

"Don't be silly, Amy," my dad says. "You can return it to him on the way home."

8

Deborah was a great prophetess of Israel, even led Israel
for a time (Judges 4:4). She ordered a man named Barak
(relation to me, perhaps?) to take ten thousand men into
battle. Barak told Deborah that he'd only do it if Debo-
rah came with him. Kind of parallels my life, doesn't it?
Also reinforces that men need women to back them up.

I want to protest, but the backpack is being shoved into my hands. "Dad, I'm sure he'll come back to get it once he realizes—"

"Amy, don't be a snob."

My mouth opens wide in shock. My own flesh and blood just called me a snob. I head out the door and into our condo building entrance. I wave to the doorman, who buzzes me into the elevator banks.

"Amy, come back here," my dad says.

I put my hands on my hips. "I can't believe you, of all people, called me a snob."

My dad never backs down. I guess being an ex-commando makes you act like a tough guy in your personal as well as army life. Occupational hazard. "Just because he doesn't look like the kids you hang out with doesn't mean you can't be friends with him."

"Dad, he told Kyle Sanderson I joined a dating service because I couldn't get a date for the Valentine's Dance."

Who's the snob now?

My dad looks concerned; his eyebrows are furrowed as he contemplates this new piece of information. Taking a deep breath, he tells me, "Then confront him about it."

Spoken like a true Israeli.

We're in the elevator, which has just reached our floor. Stepping off, I turn around to face my father and hold out Nathan's backpack (which weighs a ton, I might add). "You give it to him. Then you can ream him out for spreading rumors about your daughter."

"We'll go together."

Ooh, partners in crime. "Fine."

"Fine."

I follow him to Nathan's aunt and uncle's condo right down the hall from us. My dad knocks obnoxiously loud, like he doesn't know the power of his own strength. *That's my dad.*

Mr. Keener opens the door, but doesn't invite us in.

"Nathan left his backpack in the café," my dad says. "Amy wanted to bring it back to him."

Mr. Keener smiles and opens the door. "You can go give it to him. He's in the guest room. It's the second door on the right."

My dad puts his hand on the small of my back and

pushes me forward. I've never been into their condo. Mr. and Mrs. Keener keep pretty much to themselves. I step inside the foyer. I'm feeling awkward so I'm glad my dad is backing me up.

A cell phone rings; it's my dad's ring tone. The national anthem of Israel. Dorky, but totally *him*. He's still in the hallway as he answers the call. "Sorry, *motek*, I have to take this," he says as he waves and leaves me in the Keeners' condo.

Oh, just great.

So now I'm faced with going into Nathan's room. All alone. With absolutely no backup.

Mr. Keener waves me toward Nathan's room. Okay, I'll do it. I'm not afraid of that guy. In fact, after I shove his backpack at him, I'm going to give him a piece of my mind.

Because nobody makes a fool out of Amy Nelson-Barak.

I walk with purpose to the second door on the right. The door is closed, so I have to knock. Looking back, I see Mr. Keener hasn't followed. I knock lightly at first with the hand not holding the backpack. No response. I knock a little harder.

After I get no response again, I think he might not be home after all. Which is a good thing, I think. I mean, I want to confront him and everything but I'm not sure I want to do it on his turf. I know the advantage to warfare. On your own turf you have the upper hand.

I check the doorknob to see if it's locked. Nope. I turn the knob and crack the door open so I can peek inside.

Nathan's in the room, but he's listening to his iPod while banging a pencil against a binder, so he can't hear me.

Sure enough, as soon as I look at his face I catch two green eyes narrowing at me.

"I can see you," he says.

Damn. I open the door wide and walk in, watching as he takes the earphones out of his ears. "You left your backpack at Perk Me Up! I brought it as a goodwill gesture."

The guy just shrugs. *Thanks* would have been nice. Nathan is in dire need of etiquette lessons.

As I drop his backpack, I scan the room. It's obviously the guest room. Old bookshelves line the side wall and a pullout bed is open and takes up most of the room. Nathan is leaning on the bed, against the back, just staring at me.

"Who's the girl?" I ask, picking up a picture of a cute blonde girl in a bikini with short hair and abs I can't even imagine having. "Your sister?"

Nathan pushes his glasses up his nose and says, "It's my girlfriend."

Yeah, right. There is absolutely no way this is Nathan's girlfriend. I'd bet my dog on it.

"What's her name?" I ask, curiosity getting the best of me.

"Bicky."

Wait. What did he say? "Becky?" I ask. The other alternative is downright ludicrous.

"Bicky," he says again.

"*Bicky?*"

"Now you're acting Barbie all over again."

"Was she born with that name or is it a nickname?" I ask, ignoring the insult.

Nathan slides off the bed and snatches the picture out of my hand. "Her name is Bicky. No nickname. Just Bicky."

While he shoves the picture into his half-zippered suitcase, I say, "You accuse me of being so Barbie when you're the one who's deliberately spreading untrue rumors about me just so you could seem cool."

"I did no such thing," he says. "And I definitely don't want to hang around with your friends, if that's what you mean."

"You told Kyle I joined a dating service. For your information...and not that it's any of your business, but I signed my dad up."

Nathan shrugs, as if falsely tarnishing my reputation is no biggie.

"Why do you hate me so much?"

He rubs his hand on top of his shaggy, light brown hair that resembles the color of maple syrup, and sighs. "I don't hate you, Amy. I just hate people like you."

"Same difference," I say, then storm out of the condo. When I stomp into my own place, my dad is sitting at the dining room table, still on the phone as he shuffles through some papers.

Men. I feel the taste for revenge. I head to the back office, where the computer is, and type in *www.pjsn.com*. It prompts me to type in my login name and password.

I have fifty-five new people who left messages on my

dad's profile and the two women I asked out for my dad responded. Wow. The human resources worker, Kelly, would love to do coffee, how about next week? and the lawyer, Wendy, says she's looking for an American guy so she's not interested.

Good. I didn't want a lawyer to be my stepmom anyway. Lawyers probably follow all the rules and regs in life. That's not my style. I live inside the gray areas and love it.

I e-mail the human resources lady back and ask her to meet me (aka my dad) at Perk Me Up! tomorrow night at seven.

As I settle into the chair, I hear a crinkling sound from my back pocket. Oh my God. I can't believe I forgot with all the Nathan-and-my-dad commotion to open Avi's letter. Is my forgetfulness a betrayal of our relationship?

Uncrinkling it, I sink back in my bed and open the envelope.

"Sorry, Avi." He can't hear me, but maybe my conscience can.

As I unfold the letter, my heartbeat starts racing.

Amy,

You know I'm not good with letters, but I promised to write so I'm writing. I'm assigned to a new army base, but I can't tell you where it is. Top secret stuff. I can tell you that I shot a new gun today. I know you hate guns, but this one was cool. It shoots around corners. We run every day until I think my legs are going to fall off. Tomorrow my unit will be dropped off in the Negev in the middle of the night to see if we can navigate with nothing but the stars to guide us through the desert. I guess that's it. If I survive desert training I'll write you again. You know I miss you, don't you?

Avi

I hold the letter to my chest, concentrating on the last sentence. *You know I miss you, don't you?* Avi isn't one of those sappy guys; he's guarded because he lost his brother in a bombing and hasn't let himself open up, be vulnerable, and grieve. And I know he doesn't want me to wait around for him while he spends his required three years in the Israeli military, so he doesn't write romantic and mushy letters.

I don't want a romantic and mushy guy, anyway. I want Avi. Oh, I know I'm not going to even see him until the summer when I go back to Israel. I'm not holding my breath that he'll be waiting for me. Okay, I am. But I'm not admitting it publicly.

Leaning over my nightstand, I open the drawer and pull out Avi's silver chain link bracelet. He gave it to me after we started dating this past summer. I also pull out a picture of him. It was after our last official date, when he gave me Mutt and a sushi dinner. I snatched a photo with my dad's camera right before our last goodbye.

I stare at the picture, him with his mocha eyes and thick head of dark hair to match. Not to mention his signature half-smile, which can make my heart stop. There is no way the girls in Israel are going to leave him alone; that's a given. It scares me and brings out my worst insecurities. I'm not pretty enough, my boobs are too big, I'm not skinny enough.

Ugh, I hate when I pick myself apart and focus on the negatives. Avi likes me for who I am. I know he does.

Kissing his picture would be the dorkiest thing. I'd never do that. But I do clutch his picture to my chest and hug it. It's still dorky, but less so than actually kissing it.

"Amy, I'm sorry but it was an important call."

Great, now my dad is invading my personal space and witnessed me hugging a picture. The only thing keeping me from telling him how important knocking on a teenager's door is the revenge date I'm setting him up on. "You know what your problem is?" I tell him.

"What."

"You think work is more important than your personal life."

He takes life way too seriously, but I'm trying to help him loosen up and not be such a stiff. It's the work part that worries me. I swear he's gonna have a heart attack one of these days if he doesn't let up on the work hours.

He walks closer to my bed and I slip the picture of Avi and his letter under my pillow.

"I have responsibilities, Amy. Ones I've committed to long ago."

"Yeah, yeah," I say, sitting up. "I've heard the spiel before. What now, the president of the United States needs you to act as his bodyguard?"

"The Secret Service does that."

"Then what's so important?" I ask him.

"I have to go out of town. That's what the call was about. It can't be postponed, not this time."

Cool. So I'll get the condo all to myself? The possibilities are endless.

"When?" I say a little too eagerly.

"On Friday morning. I'll be back on Sunday."

Two whole nights without parental figures! Brighter times are definitely ahead. "Can I use your car?"

"Only to go to your mother's house. That's where you'll be staying. I just got off the phone with her. You can have my car to drive to her place."

Nope, not okay. "I am *not* staying with Mom and Marc. What would I do with Mutt? Besides, I think Marc is allergic to both of us."

"We'll put him in a kennel."

I wish he were talking about Marc, but I'm not that lucky. This time I stand up, ready for battle. "First of all, Mutt and I are a package deal. He is not going to a kennel. Period, end of story."

It takes me exactly fifty-six minutes to convince my dad I'm old enough to stay at the condo without parents.

Brighter times are definitely ahead.

9

Kosher question #2: You can't mix milk and meat because
God commanded "You shall not boil a kid (baby lamb)
in its mother's milk" (Exodus 23:19). So why can't I mix
milk with chicken? You can't milk a chicken.

"Why do you keep glancing at the door every two seconds?" Marla asks me the next day at work.

Umm...maybe it's because my dad's date is gonna be here any second, followed by my dad who still doesn't know he's going on a date. He thinks Marla needs to talk to him about my work schedule. I made up some ridiculous story to get him into the café at seven o'clock.

"I'm watching for my dad," I tell my boss guiltily.

The door to the café opens. It's a woman I've never seen before. Is it Kelly, my dad's date? Or is it someone else? Kelly wrote in her e-mail that she has strawberry blonde hair. This woman kind of has strawberry blonde hair, although it's really frizzy and she needs some expensive hair products to help tame that mane of hers. That picture she posted online was with her hair straight, but maybe she forgot to flatiron it today.

She walks up to the counter and suddenly I'm feeling self-conscious, like I have to impress the woman. "Are you Kelly?" I ask.

The woman shakes her Brillo pad head. "No."

"Oh, good."

When she frowns at me, I try and recover quick. "Can I take your order?"

She looks up at our board of specialty coffees, taking her time. I have the urge to give her a snoring sound (I'm good at those) but don't think Marla will appreciate my humor. So I wait with a smile on my face. And wait.

And wait.

And wait.

I swear, any more of this waiting and I'm going to frown. My mouth can't take all this fake smiling. I start humming, but I don't even realize it until the woman looks down at me with a stern expression. Seriously, thank goodness this woman isn't my dad's strawberry blonde date.

The door dings. Another customer. "Are you ready?" I ask the woman who can't make up her mind. I could just see her as my stepmom, me waiting for her to pick me up from school, taking forever to pick out groceries, and waiting for her to order a simple spicy tuna roll from Hanabi.

Looking around her, another woman who could pass for strawberry blonde walks up to the counter. I suck in my breath. This woman is really large. And I'm being nice.

Maybe the picture she posted was pre-weight gain. My dad is a workout and health nut, and this woman looks like she's snacked on a few too many Kit Kats if you know what I mean. She has a friendly face, though. Hey, maybe Dad can put her on a boot camp diet plan and she'd lose those extra pounds in no time at all.

Ignoring the wishy-washy lady, I ask the overweight one, "Are you Kelly?"

"No. But I'd like a large caramel latte with whipped cream."

I keep up the Perk Me Up! smile, although I'm tempted to suggest the skim latte instead of the caramel one. While I'm ringing her up, the wishy-washy lady signals to me she's ready. Can't she see I'm ringing up someone else?

Marla is in the office and I don't want her to think I can't take care of the customers. I turn to the wishy-washer. "Did you decide?"

"What's the calorie count of the medium vanilla coffee? Is it the same as the regular?"

Is she kidding me? I look under the counter to see if there's a calorie listing for the drinks, but there isn't. Now I don't know what to do. Should I make the other lady's drink or call Marla to help?

I look at my watch. It's seven on the dot. Kelly will be here any second. My dad will be here any second.

And Miss Wishy-Washy is worried about a calorie count.

I knock on the door to the office and call Marla out to the register. I hurry to make the large caramel latte while

Marla takes care of the frizzy-haired, high-maintenance customer. The chime rings on the door and a woman walks into the café who definitely looks like Kelly's PJSN profile pic.

She scans the café, then sits down at a vacant table to wait for my unsuspecting dad.

Sure enough, my dad walks in the door next. My heart is palpitating a hundred beats a second right now. My dad waves to me and walks up to the register. Kelly must recognize him from the picture I posted on his profile. She moves up behind him and is about to tap him on the shoulder.

"I have to tell you something," I say at the same time Kelly taps him and says, "Ron?"

He turns to her. "Can I help you?"

"Dad, it's important."

He puts his fingertips together on one hand and moves it up and down, the unique Israeli sign for *wait a second*. The problem is, I can't wait a second. I need to tell him that, even though he's unaware of it, he's on his first PJSN date.

"I'm Kelly. Are you Ron?" Kelly asks.

"Yes."

"From the Professional Jewish Singles Network?"

Pause.

"Um…could you hold that thought for one second," my dad says to Kelly. Then he turns to me. "Tell me what this is all about, Amy. Right. Now. I'm assuming Marla doesn't want to talk to me about adjusting your work schedule."

"*Aba*, you're going to laugh when I tell you this."

"I doubt it."

Kelly looks upset and embarrassed. "Am I missing something here?"

Okay, it's time to fess up. I thought it'd be easier than it is. I have the urge to hide in a dark corner. "I set up the date. I'm his daughter," I tell her.

Getting it, Kelly steps back. "Oh." She adjusts the Coach bag hanging on her shoulder. "Well, that makes me look stupid."

"Actually, it makes me look stupid," I tell her.

"And me," my dad chimes in. "I'll tell you what, Kelly. Why don't we sit down and have my daughter serve us the most expensive drinks in the place. It'll be her treat."

Kelly shrugs and nods her head in agreement. "Sounds good to me."

It doesn't sound good to me at all!

"I'm hungry, actually. How about one of the scones?" my dad asks. I'm adding the bill in my head, knowing I'll have to work at least two more hours in order to pay for the food bill.

"Scones sound wonderful," Kelly says, smiling. "Don't they have Eli's cheesecake, too? Grab me a slice of that, would you, dear?"

I'm not liking Kelly with the strawberry blonde hair as much as my dad seems to like her. Teaching me a lesson is not how I imagined this date going. My dad sits down with Kelly while I bring them over Double Dutch Coffee Delight drinks. (I add a couple extra shots of espresso as a bonus…I hope they both are up all night and can't sleep.) Those specialty drinks are four dollars and twenty-five cents each, along with the two-dollar-and-fifty-five-cent cheesecake and two-dollar-and-thirty-five-cent scones.

As if my day isn't disastrous enough, when Marla tells me to sweep the floor of the café I find Nathan at his usual spot in the corner. "You got caught in one of your lies, Barbie?" Nathan says. "I have a piece of advice. Next time you set your dad up on a date, you should probably tell him about it beforehand."

I shoot him a nasty glare. "At least I have parents," I say, then want to take back my words right after they've left my mouth. Nathan's face goes ashen and he starts packing up his stuff.

Maybe his parents are dead or in the hospital somewhere. I'm a jerk. "I'm sorry," I quickly say.

As he shoves the last book into his backpack, he looks up at me. "No you're not." Then he leaves me standing here while he storms out of the café, leaving me to pick up his used cup which is still three-quarters of the way full with tea. Now I'm feeling even worse than before.

I glance over at my dad, who's shaking hands with Kelly. She exits the café, leaving my dad alone at the table until I saunter up to him and say, "So?"

He looks up at me from his chair. "So what?"

"How was the date?"

"Fine."

Fine is probably the most non-committal and non-descriptive word in the English language. I hate the word *fine*. It doesn't even mean anything. I try a different approach, one that can't be answered with a "fine." "Are you gonna see her again?"

"Maybe."

Great, another non-descriptive word. "Did you get her number?"

My dad stands now, which is not a good thing because he's way taller than me. "Listen to me, Amy, and listen good. Don't set me up on another date without my knowledge or you'll find yourself without a cell phone. Got it?"

"Fine."

10

Rosh Hashanah: Two nights of huge festive meals.
Hanukkah: Eat foods cooked in oil.
Passover: The Haggadah (Passover prayer book) specifically
says, Eat The Festive Meal.
Sukkot: Build a sukkah and invite friends to eat in it.
Yom Kippur: Eat three meals at once
to make up for the day just fasted.
I see a pattern here.
Why are so many Jewish holidays centered around food?

Since my dad went out of town this morning, Jessica invited me over for Shabbat dinner. So after school I go home, walk Mutt, then take a cab to Jessica's. I might also add that Nathan ignored me the entire day. Even when I tried to apologize again, he turned around and blatantly dissed me.

"Come in, Amy," Jessica's mom says when she opens the door to their six-flat. "Jessica is in her room."

I climb the familiar whitewashed staircase and catch Jessica sitting at her desk, punching the keyboard of her computer. "You're not checking Mitch's e-mail again, are you?"

Without looking at me she responds, "You bet I am.

He has no clue. I check them all and mark them as 'unread' e-mail."

"Jess, break up with him if you don't trust him."

Jess swivels her chair around to face me. "He told me he loved me on New Year's Eve, Amy. I haven't had a guy tell me he loved me since That Guy."

That Guy is Michael Greenberg, who Jessica lost her virginity to last year. He blew her off right after their big night together and she's been insecure about guys ever since. She won't even give me, her bestest friend in the entire world, details about what happened with Michael. I can't even say his name without her walking out of the room.

"Did he tell you he loved you in the heat of passion?"

"His hands were under my shirt."

Okay, so I'm not going to state the obvious. He gave her the ol' "I love you, let's get it on" crap. I look back at her and know she doesn't want to talk about it anymore.

I look inside Jessica's closet to see what new clothes she's gotten that I can borrow. I pick out a vintage gray shirt with pink writing. "Where did you get this?"

"I have no clue. My mom got it for me."

"It's cool." As always, I make myself at home. Best friends share clothes, secrets, and beauty tips. I guess we also share guys because I dated Mitch for about a millisecond before he started dating Jessica. Taking my own shirt off, I try on her gray one. It fits, except when I look in her long mirror on the back of her door my nipples stick out because the fabric of the shirt is too thin.

Depressed, I pull the shirt off and study my bra-covered boobs in the mirror.

"What are you doing?" Jess asks.

I hold my arms at my sides and look down at my pink lacy bra. "Do my boobs sag in this bra?" Testing what it would look like if they were perkier, I cup the bottom of my boobs and lift them up.

"Now they're too close to your chin." Jess lets out a frustrated sigh. "I wish I had your boobs. Guys *love* your boobs."

"They droop," I say, my hands letting go of them.

"How can they not, they weigh what…five pounds each?"

I'll have you know I've never weighed my boobs. And I'm sure they don't weigh more than two pounds each. I turn to my best friend. "Jess, you have perfect, perky boobs."

"Otherwise known as virtually non-existent," Jess says. "They only look perfect because I bought this Fantasy Bra last week." She pulls up her shirt to show me a padded pushup bra that's more padded than my mom's down winter coat. "I need this in order to look like I have *something.*"

The door to Jessica's room flies open. It's her twelve-year-old annoying and testosterone-charged brother Ben. His eyes go wide at the sight of us in our bras. I screech and hold my hands out to cover my chest.

"Get out, you little creep!" Jess yells, pulling her shirt back down.

"Are you guys comparing boobies?" Ben says while laughing. "Amy, are those real?"

Jessica and I both grab pillows off her bed and fling them at the door while Ben slams it shut. "By the way, dinner's ready," he says, still laughing.

When we enter the dining room a few minutes later, Jess flicks her brother hard on the back of the head before sitting down.

"Ow!"

"If you don't knock next time, I'm going to take a picture of you while you're in the shower and e-mail it to your entire school."

"That's enough," Mr. Katz says, putting on his *kippah* and motioning for Ben to put his on, too.

In the kitchen, Jess and I help place soup bowls filled with matzoh ball soup on the table.

Mrs. Katz sets up two Shabbat candlesticks with candles in them and takes matches out of a decanter on the credenza. "Amy, would you like to do the honors?"

Me? I usually watch while Jessica or her mom lights the candles and does the Hebrew prayer. "Are you sure?"

"Absolutely."

The entire room is silent as I clear my throat. Striking the match, I light both candles. When they're lit, I cover my eyes with my palms and say, "*Baruch ata Adonai Eloheinu, melech ha'olam, asher kid'shanu b'mitzvotav v'tzivanu l'hadlik ner shel Shabbat.* Blessed are You, Lord our God, King of the universe, who has made us holy through His commandments and commanded us to kindle the Sabbath light."

I take my seat at the table, abandoning the candles in the corner, when Mrs. Katz says, "Amy, did you make a wish?"

"A wish?"

"Yes, over the candles. It's our custom to do the prayer, then make a silent wish to God. Or a thank-you to God...whatever your heart feels like saying."

Standing up and walking back to the bright yellow burning candles, I cover my eyes again and think about what I want to say.

"Ask God for Ben to accidentally have his orthodontist wire his mouth shut," Jess says.

"Ask for Jess to grow boobs," Ben's voice chimes in.

Ignoring both of them, I say to God, *Please take care of my Safta in Israel. She has cancer and needs your help. And also, thanks for giving me this family to have dinner with tonight so I'm not alone.*

I look up, expecting everyone to be staring at me and to ask me what I wished for. But they're not; they respect my private Shabbat wish and thanks to God. I love Jessica and her family. Even Ben.

"I saw Amy's boobies upstairs," Ben says, then wags his eyebrows up and down at me.

Okay, maybe not Ben.

Mrs. Katz slams her hand on the table. "Can I please have a respectful Shabbat?"

"Listen to your mother," Mr. Katz says. He stands while picking up the silver Shabbat wine cup and pours the red wine until it's almost overflowing. "*Baruch ata Adonai Eloheinu, melech ha'olam, boray pri ha-gafen.* Amen."

After he takes a sip from the cup, he passes it around for everyone else to take a sip. Ben puts on a big show of gulping down the wine, but then he coughs so it splatters across the white tablecloth.

Jess rolls her eyes, takes a sip, and passes the cup to me. I'm not a wine drinker, but this wine is so sweet it's like drinking sugary children's cough syrup.

Ben lifts the embroidered cloth cover off of the challah, the Shabbat bread which is expertly braided at the kosher bakery down the street. "*Baruch ata Adonai Eloheinu, melech ha'olam, ha-motze lechem min ha'aretz,*" he says, then makes a big show of singing, "Aaa, aaah, maaaaaaiiiiinnn."

Jess and I mumble, "Amen."

Ben tears a chunk of the challah off and tosses everyone a small piece from the chunk. I think he tried tossing it into my cleavage, but I'm not sure. And when it comes to tossing a piece to Jess, he whips it at her. I think the kid needs to go to therapy, or at least be locked up until he turns eighteen.

"How is the conversion class going, Amy?" Mr. Katz asks me as he takes a spoonful of matzoh ball soup.

"Good. Rabbi Glassman is really nice."

Mrs. Katz puts her hand over her husband's. "He married us, you know. Twenty-two years ago."

I wonder if Rabbi Glassman will officiate my wedding one day. Even though he's not Orthodox, he won't officiate a marriage between a Jewish person and a non-Jew.

He's kind of strict about that, even refused to marry his own sister because she married a Christian guy. I want to marry someone Jewish because I think it will head off lots of arguments. It's important that my kids are Jewish; it's important that my family doesn't eat pork or shellfish...or mix meat and milk products.

"Are you going to the youth group meeting tomorrow?" Mrs. Katz asks.

Jessica nods her head and says, "Are you coming, Amy?"

"I wasn't planning on it."

"You should go. It's fun."

After dinner, Jess and I convince her parents to let us go back to my place to crash. We spend the rest of the evening Ben-less, talking about boys and bras and books until we're tired. Then we take out ice cream from the freezer and watch movies on TV until I convince Jessica to call Mitch.

He isn't answering his cell, so she tries his house. Unfortunately, she gets reamed out by Mitch's dad for calling past eleven o'clock. He doesn't even tell her if Mitch is home or not.

What do two parentless teenagers do at eleven at night? I have a brilliant idea. "Let's call my cousin in Israel. It's eight hours ahead there."

Before Jess can tell me it's a horrible idea, I start dialing the gazillion digits to get access to the Israeli phone system. "Allo?" my Doda Yucky answers.

"Doda Yucky, it's Amy," I yell into the receiver.

"Ah, Amy'leh. *Mah nishmah?*" The woman thinks I'm

fluent in Hebrew, but really my dad told me *mah nishmah* means "how is everything?" It's a staple phrase for Israelis.

"Great. Is Osnat there?"

"She's right here. Give your *aba* my love, *tov*?"

"*Tov*."

"Amy?" Osnat asks.

"Yeah, it's your American cousin. Remember me?"

"How could I forget. Our sheep still has a Mohawk from when you shaved it."

Ha, ha. Very funny. Okay, so my sheep-shearing skills are definitely lacking, but I did make a valiant effort. "*Mah nishmah*?" I ask her.

"*Ah, evreet shelach mitzuyan.*"

"Okay, cut the Hebrew. You know I have no clue what you're saying. How's Avi?"

"Looking hot."

"You've seen him?"

"Yeah. Why, hasn't he called you since his basic training was over?"

No. "I'm sure he was busy." He wrote that he'd be in basic training for another week. I wonder what he's doing back home. Even more, I wonder why he hasn't called. You know what they say: if they're not into you, they don't call. If they're into you, they'll find the time.

My stomach muscles clench up, but I continue talking to Osnat and then talk to *Safta*, my grandmother, who tells me the doctors think her tumor shrunk since her last set of chemo treatments. She insists she's doing fine, but her voice is weaker than I remember. I promise to call next week and she promises she'll stay healthy and strong until I come to Israel for summer break.

Jess is thumbing through my CD collection, looking more depressed than I am. I come up with an idea. "Try texting Mitch."

"I tried before. He ignored it."

I grab her phone and start texting.

Jess sits on the bed next to me. "What are you doing?"

"Getting your boyfriend's attention," I tell her. Mitch is obsessed with his cell phone. He'll for sure have it with him. If he's ignoring Jess on purpose, I'll kill him.

> Me: *Mitch, it's Amy. Jess is XOXOing another dude*
> Mitch: *What?*
> Me: *Just kidding. Where R U?*
> Mitch: *At a movie w/friends. Can't talk.*
> Me: *Call your gf tomorrow. Or else.*
> Mitch: *U don't scare me, Amy.*
> Me: *Y not?*
> Mitch: *Bark worse than bite.*
> Me: *I don't bite.*
> Mitch: *I dated U. U bite.*

I turn off the phone and look up at Jess. "He said he'll call you tomorrow."

"Really?" she asks, looking hopeful. "Where is he?"

"At a movie with friends."

"I talked to him earlier. He didn't say anything about a movie. Since when can't I go with him and his friends to a movie?"

I shrug. I can't figure out my own boyfriend. How am I supposed to figure out hers?

I lie in bed later thinking about all the promises I forgot to get from Avi. Maybe I'm delirious thinking he's waiting for me to come back to Israel. If he's not thinking of me, why am I so obsessed with him?

11

"When a woman at childbirth bears a male,
she shall be unclean seven days...
If she bears a female, she shall be unclean two weeks."
(Leviticus 12:2-5)
Umm... does this mean boys are viewed
as cleaner than females? Has God seen the boys' restroom
at Chicago Academy lately?

"Do you know if it's a boy or girl?"

It's Sunday and I'm in the 'burbs with my mom. We're sitting in her car, heading to a maternity-clothes shop. She looked so excited about this little excursion; I couldn't say no.

My mom rubs the bump in her stomach, like a prego person in the movies would. "We want it to be a surprise."

"What if it's twins?" I ask her.

When she smiles at me, the corners of her light blue eyes crinkle. Isn't she too old to have a baby? "There was only one heartbeat. No twins."

The baby is due in six months and already my mom's stomach looks like a small bowling ball. I can't believe I haven't noticed it before. Maybe she's been trying to hide it with those ponchos she's overly fond of lately.

When we drive up to a place called Modern Maternity I feel stupid. I'm seventeen years old. I could seriously be a mother myself.

"Marc and I both want you to be involved in this pregnancy," she says. "It's important to us."

My mom's not Jewish, but she definitely has the Jewish guilt thing down pat.

I put on a huge, toothy smile. I'm probably overdoing it, but the reality is I want my mom to be happy. "I'm so happy for you," I gush. "And I want to be a part of this new family, too!"

"Amy, I'm your mom. I can see right through you."

We're still sitting in the car. I watch her face turn from elation to unhappiness in a matter of seconds. Oh, no. I gotta talk to her before she starts crying. "Mom, I *am* happy for you and Marc. It's just weird for me. First the wedding, now the baby. I just need time to get used to it, okay?"

I remember back to when my mom took me to my first ballet lesson. I'd begged for her to sign me up and practically dragged her to Miss Gertie's Dance Studio where Jessica was already taking lessons. My mom paid the hefty tuition, bought me ballet slippers and a cute leotard, and off we went to the first class. Only there was one problem: I refused to go inside the studio. For some unknown reason (even to me) I cried in the car until my mom dragged me kicking and screaming into that studio.

She forced me to go.

In retaliation, I sat in the corner of the studio and refused to move even one pink ballet-slippered foot the entire time. This routine continued lesson after lesson until the costumes came in for the recital. My class danced to a song called "The Buzy Bees." We were little bees with black and yellow sparkly sequined leotards and black springy sparkly antennas. What can I say, all those sparkles would turn any reluctant kid into an instant ballerina just waiting to go on stage. The day those costumes came in, I stood up from my usual spot and danced and buzzed around as if I was making up for lost time.

Those ballet lessons made me learn one thing:

My mom is a patient parent beyond belief. And she'll wait anything out until I cave.

"Amy, I know it's not easy for you. Too many changes in such a short time." She looks up at the sign to Modern Maternity. "Should we just go back home? Or go bra shopping for you? I can do this another day."

"No, we're already here. You might as well get some clothes that won't strangle the baby." Besides, I don't want to go bra shopping with my mom. She'll probably pick out those big hefty white ones that resemble tablecloths with straps.

Mom needs no further encouragement. She's out of the car as if someone was pushing her enlarged butt forward. I swear, my mom used to have a body an aerobics instructor would be jealous of. Now…well, let's just say she's changed a *lot*.

I follow her into the store, silently hoping the salesperson doesn't mistake me for the customer.

"Can I help you ladies?" the short and perky salesperson asks, looking from my mom to me and back.

My mom touches her stomach again. "Well, I'm about three months along now and am outgrowing my clothes already."

The lady claps her hands together. "Are we looking for casual or business attire...or do you need something for a specific occasion?"

I'd like to cut the word "we" from the woman's vocabulary.

"Casual. And business."

While the lady shows my mom around the store, I follow in silence. To be honest, though, some of the clothes aren't too bad. And before long my mom is trying the stuff on, making me go with her into the dressing room.

On the bench I catch sight of something weird. It's like a cream-colored pouch with strings coming out of it. "I think someone left something in here," I tell the saleslady, pointing to the strange object.

"No, there's one in every dressing room. It's to strap to your stomach to make you look five to six months pregnant."

I can't help the giggle that escapes my mouth. My mom shushes me, then closes the dressing room door.

"Can I try it on?" I ask.

Before my mom can stop me, I pick up my shirt, tie the pouch around my waist, and pull my shirt back down.

"That's not really the image I want of my seventeen-year-old daughter," Mom says, eyeing me rub my tummy like she does.

I wonder what it would be like to be pregnant. A baby growing inside your body until it can survive on its own. Turning sideways, I check myself out in the mirror. Do I want kids? I mean, I feel sorry for my parents that they have to deal with me. Sometimes I think I'm not normal, that I'm long overdue for a psychotherapist to straighten me out. Then at other times I feel like everyone else is a mashed-potato nutcase and I'm the only sane one.

Maybe Mom's banking on this new kid to be the normal one, the one who's freak-out resistant.

I stare at my mom's stomach as she tries on a black and white suit with a stretchy panel in the front of the pants. It makes me realize what a big deal this must be for her. She's not just getting big; she's creating another human being, one she'll be responsible for forever.

"You can touch my stomach if you want," she says.

I do, but I don't. I remember I used to lay my head on her stomach and laugh as I heard gurgling noises coming from it. Now there's a baby growing inside there...

I guess she senses my hesitation, because she takes my hand and places it on her bulging tummy. "Can you feel it moving?" I ask.

"Not yet."

I gaze at my hand on her belly, close to my half brother or sister. As much as I know it's weird for my mom to have a kid, I'm feeling unusually protective of it right now. I pull my hand away; this is getting a little too weird for me.

She tries on a big white shirt with an arrow pointing down saying *Future Physician*. "What do you think?" she asks, holding her arms out wide to give me the full view.

"I think it's weak sauce."

"Weak sauce?" she says, scrunching up her face in confusion. "New slang I don't know about?"

"You know…same as lame. It's all about the sauce. If it's bad sauce, nobody likes it."

"Is this one lame sauce?"

I don't correct her and tell her it's *weak* sauce, not *lame* sauce.

Now she's holding out one that says *Almost done*.

"You can get it, but I'm not going out with you in public if you're wearing it. Don't they have one saying *I'm a Dorky Mom?*"

"I didn't see that one on the racks," she says, teasing me.

In the end, she picks out a pants suit for work, one dress, two pairs of jeans, and three T-shirts that don't have writing on them. I swear, before my mom was married and actually had a job, she dressed like she was a Vogue model. She knew everything about fashion and taught me so much. Now, my mom got married, quit her job, and seriously does not know what's in. I hope after the baby is born she'll change back into the same mom I had before.

"Are you staying over for dinner?" she asks when we're on the way back to her house.

"Sorry, can't. I'm going to some Jewish teen group thing with Jessica."

"You sure about this Jewish route, Amy? Marc and I

were discussing it the other day, and we just don't understand this sudden interest in conversion."

Mom doesn't understand that during my trip to Israel last summer I changed. It's like I found a missing piece of myself. It's a small piece, but sometimes I feel like when I find the missing pieces of myself I get closer to being whole. "It's not sudden, Mom."

"What does your father say? From what I know, he's not all that religious himself."

I look out the window, fighting the urge to argue with her. Converting to Judaism is something I feel strongly about. It has nothing to do with my dad or my mom. It has everything to do with me. To argue and try to make her see my side is pointless. My mom has her own opinions about organized religion and I don't share her view.

When *Safta* gave me a Jewish star pendant, I felt something I'd never felt before. A connection to people I had previously not acknowledged. And when I climbed Masada, it really hit me. My dad is Jewish, so half of me is Jewish. To ignore it suddenly felt like it would be dissing a part of who I am. I admit, learning about Judaism and reading the Tanakh (that would be the Torah and learning about the numerous Prophets) isn't easy. And, to be honest, I don't totally agree with or understand the Torah.

Rabbi Glassman encourages discussion, even disagreements. Which is great, because I'm disagreeable by nature. I question everything, like why Abraham really was going to kill his son. And it's obvious men wrote the Bible (it's a bit male-centered if I do say so myself.) But did the stories actually happen or were they made up?

"Dad supports me."

"But can't they consider you Jewish because your father is? It's seems silly to have you go through months of classes—"

"They're not *making* me do it, Mom." She just doesn't get it. Or maybe she doesn't want to get it. "I don't *have* to convert. I *want* to convert. Just…leave it alone, okay?"

Mom shrugs. "Okay, okay. I just want you to be happy."

"Then stop nagging me about religion. Nag me about something else instead."

Looking at me sideways, my mom smiles. Oops, I should never have said that. Because…you guessed it, she takes me to Sally's Intimate Boutique on the other side of town to get me fitted for bras.

Mom drives me back to the condo in the city after the bra run. I kiss her goodbye, get out of the car, and attempt to hide the girly pink bag under my arm. It's gotten so cold I pull my coat tight around me, but catch sight of Nathan standing on the curb with a bouquet of yellow tulips in his hand.

I'm still watching Nathan as my mom drives off. When the public bus heading to Evanston stops at the corner, Nathan gets on without a backward glance.

Hmm.

I wonder if he's going to see Binky…I mean Bicky. Not that I believe he's actually dating that girl in the picture in his room.

I still haven't figured him out. Why is he staying at his aunt and uncle's house? If it's *not* temporary, why is he still living out of his suitcase? If it's *not* temporary, why is he going to my school? The whole thing doesn't add up.

Shaking thoughts of Nathan from my head, I run up to my condo before my dad gets home. Hurriedly, I check my dad's still-open PJSN account. The only problem is he'll kill me if I set him up on another date. I have to come up with another scheme, something creative.

I've heard about speed dating, where a person goes on a bunch of three-minute dates in one night. Hmm...maybe I can convince Marla to host one of them at Perk Me Up! one night. I must admit I have the best ideas.

My dad walks in the door just as I'm closing out the PJSN account. He asks me about my weekend without him. I ask him about his trip. We eat dinner together while playing *shesh besh*, which is Hebrew for backgammon. It's something we both like to play. We even have a little rivalry going on.

I answer the phone when it rings after dinner, knowing before I even check the caller ID that it's Jessica. "I need best friend advice," Jess says.

"Me, too. I need to know what I should wear tonight." I mean, I haven't been to a youth group meeting in...well, never.

"I thought you were going to wear your Fuego jeans and that heather-gray top you got last week at Saks."

I lay down on my bed in frustration, petting Mutt who just jumped on my stomach and almost knocked the wind out of me. "I was, but decided against it. I was thinking about wearing my long print skirt and a plain white shirt."

There's a big huff on the other end of the line. "Amy, you don't have to dress religious for the group."

"Come over and help me pick something to wear tonight. Please? I'll do your makeup for you and listen to your Mitch problems at the same time."

Jessica loves when I do her makeup. She will absolutely come over. I know her weakness is the two Ms—Mitch and makeup. For the double Ms, she'll go through the torture of finding a parking spot on the overcrowded Chicago streets.

"Um…I'm picking up Miranda Cohen first," Jess says.

"Miranda Cohen?" I ask. "The girl who hyperventilated when we ran the mile in gym last year?" Poor Miranda. The Diet Coke she drinks just doesn't erase the other crap from her system.

"Miranda's in the youth group."

So? I'm not best friends with Miranda, but I'd rather hang with her than Roxanne. "Jess, I need your help. Bring Miranda."

"I don't want to talk about Mitch in front of her, Amy."

"Okay, so here's my advice on the boyfriend front. Give Mitch some space and let him come after you. Ignore him for a bit. He thrives on challenges, Jess, and maybe you're too accessible."

"But—"

"But nothing. Listen to me. I know what I'm talking about. I dated him, too. Remember?"

"Yeah, I remember."

"So, are you coming over now or what?"

"I'll come. Just remember to be nice to Miranda. She's sensitive."

"I'm always nice," I say, then hang up.

I wrap myself in a robe and wait for Jess and Miranda. Ten minutes later the doorman rings me to get my approval to let my friends up. When I open the door, Miranda is standing behind Jess, looking down at the ground. Miranda is wearing black stretch pants and a huge red sweater that hangs to her knees, as if she's trying to hide her body.

"Hi, Miranda," I say.

She manages a small "Hi," and follows Jess into the condo.

Leading them to my room, I open the door and Mutt, who was locked inside, goes right for poor Miranda's crotch.

"Leave her alone," I say to Mutt, who sniffs loudly then walks out of the room.

I open my closet doors. "Okay, what should I wear?"

I admit I've been blessed with a mom who came up with the *Everyone's a star at Starbucks* campaign. Don't knock it. My entire wardrobe was probably paid with jingles and slogans my mom created. The *Don't Baby Me* slogan for Precious Baby Finger Foods was a big hit along with the jingle *If you know someone who needs someone, call 1-800-Therapy.*

"Are those real Jimmy Choo shoes?" Miranda asks, wide-eyed.

My mom brought them back for me from a fashion show in New York last year. "Yeah. Want to try them on?"

Miranda takes a step back. "Oh, no. I'm so heavy I'd probably break the heel."

"Don't be ridiculous," I say, then grab the shoes and hand them to her. They're slingback and will practically fit anyone. "Just don't let my dog lick them."

Miranda hesitates, then slowly reaches out and takes them from my outstretched hand.

I look over at Jess when Miranda sits on the edge of my bed to take her gym shoes off and put the Jimmy Choos on. She's rummaging through my closet, taking stuff out and laying it over her arm. "I'll give you choices."

"Thanks, Mommy," I say sarcastically.

Jessica rolls her eyes as she lays out the outfit I wore on my last date with Avi. I know it sounds lame, but it's sacred. The memories of that night are attached to that skirt and top. I'm absolutely not wearing it. "Nope. Next."

She holds out a ripped jeans/tight sweater combination. "Nope. Too alternative."

A knock at the door interrupts us. "Amy, it's me." My dad.

When I tell him to come in, he surveys the clothes strewn around the room and Miranda trying to balance in the Choos. "You girls putting on a fashion show? I'll give you money if you'll make Amy clean her room."

"Dad, don't be a dork," I tell him, pushing him out of the room before he embarrasses me more. "I'm going to the youth group meeting tonight. Remember?"

"I remember. But I thought you said it started at four."

"It does."

He checks his watch. "It's five to. You better hurry."

When he's gone, I see the third outfit Jess has picked for me. Dark blue jeans and a simple pink long-sleeve tee with a gold O at the top. While I'm shimmying into the jeans, Miranda stumbles in the Choos over to my nightstand and picks up the picture of Avi. "Is he your boyfriend?"

Jess bites her bottom lip, probably to keep herself from blurting out, "He's her non-boyfriend."

I hesitate before saying, "Kind of."

Miranda looks from the picture of Avi to me. "He's a hottie."

A little part of my heart flips over. Turning around, I finish dressing and say, "I'm ready. Let's go," because I don't want to talk about him. I haven't even written him back and I don't call him at home because I don't want to act like stalker-girlfriend. I'm confused. I hate feeling like this.

When we arrive at the youth group meeting at the synagogue, I'm surprised at the amount of kids here. There must be at least forty kids hanging around the social hall. Some kids I recognize from school, but most I've never seen in my life.

A dark, curly-haired guy with a *kippah* on his head who's probably in his thirties tries to quiet everyone down.

"He's Rabbi Doug, the new assistant rabbi," Jess tells me.

Miranda stays close to Jess's side as we find a vacant place on the floor to sit. It takes a while for everyone else to shut up, but finally all eyes are on Rabbi Doug.

"Is everybody ready to build a *sukkah* for our play?"

Ask me a year ago and I couldn't tell you what a *sukkah* was. Now I know it's a small structure where you invite family and friends to eat the "harvest meal." Normally Jews build a *sukkah* sometime near October for the holiday of Sukkot, but the youth group is putting on a play for the Hebrew school students about the holidays and the *sukkah* is being built tonight.

Rabbi Doug proceeds to have us count off so we're in different groups. I'm in a group with a bunch of kids I don't know. This guy who assigns himself the leader of our group has us meet in the hallway.

A girl with curly black hair and bushy eyebrows is in my group, along with a couple of other girls and a bunch of guys. I sit next to Bushy Brow and give her a small smile.

"I'm Nikki. With an *i*," she says.

Oh, no. Flashbacks of my stepfather, Marc *with a c*, slam into my consciousness. "I'm Amy. With a *y*," I say back.

"Where do you go to school?"

"Chicago Academy. Where do you go?"

At the mention of Chicago Academy, Nikki blinks twice. What is it with people lately? I swear you'd think Chicago Academy was synonymous with School For Brats. "Mather," she replies.

"That's cool."

Nikki isn't über-friendly after I told her I go to Chicago Academy, like she's suddenly wary of me.

Luckily, a cool guy wearing a black hooded sweatshirt sits on the other side of me and starts talking. "What's up? I'm Wes."

"I'm Amy."

"I've never seen you here before," Wes says while checking me out. He's so obvious about it, a guy like that deserves to be played with.

"I'm a youth group virgin," I say.

Instead of being shocked, the guy laughs. "Cool. You might not want to hang with me. I'm so *not* a virgin I might scare you off."

"I go to Chicago Academy," I tell him. "I might scare you off."

Instead of being intimidated, Wes leans forward. "Ooh, one of those rich kids. Is it true your parents host teenage parties with booze and pot?"

"Absolutely," I lie. "What else would we do with all that excess money?"

He laughs and gives me a big, cocky smile. "I like you, Amy."

Rabbi Doug gives us our assignment. "You guys are in charge of hanging the fruit in the *sukkah*. The baskets, hooks, and string are in the back room. Be creative, people."

I follow the rest of the kids to the back room. Wes and I are instant friends, I find out he goes to Mather High, too, and sings in a band called Lickity Split. Nikki is starting to warm up to me, or maybe she likes Wes so she's acting all nicey-nice.

"Do you have a boyfriend?" Wes asks me while we're attempting to string bananas together.

I look over to Jessica's group, working with nails and wood to put up the *sukkah* structure. "Sort of."

"What do you mean by 'sort of'?" Nikki chimes in.

Is it really any of these people's business? "I have a boyfriend, but he's in Israel."

Wes plunges a needle and thread into the skin of the banana. "As in he lives there?"

"Yeah."

"How can he be your boyfriend when he's, like, a million miles away?"

I stop the banana threading. It's like everyone else is putting into words what's been on my mind lately. It's pissing me off. Ever since I talked to my Israeli cousin yesterday, I've been rethinking my relationship with Avi. Obviously I'm not his first priority. Why should he be mine?

Without answering Wes, I wander away from the youth group and stare out at the view of Lake Michigan. The backyard of the synagogue faces the lake, on prime real estate property. I'm sure my stepfather would love to get his hands on this piece of land. I envision myself on the sandy beach below.

An image of Nathan pops into my head, interrupting my thoughts of Avi. Why, I have no clue. It's just…well, Nathan kind of reminds me of Avi. Not his looks, by any means. Avi is drop-dead-oh-my-God gorgeous, the Abercrombie model come to life. Nathan is the opposite. He looks as awkward as he acts and doesn't even care that he's a loner. Avi has a bunch of loyal friends.

Avi and I fell for each other after hating each other for the better part of the summer. In the beginning, we fought every time we came within two feet of each other. When he kissed me, it was as explosive as the fighting and more incredible than any kiss I'd ever had.

I'm sure kissing Nathan would be nothing like kissing Avi.

I put my hands on either side of my head and squeeze my eyes shut. How can I think about kissing Nathan? Eww.

Okay, I'll admit he has unique green eyes. They have little specks of brown and gold in them, and when he looks at me I find myself searching for those specks. A guy like that shouldn't have such cool eyes.

"Hey, Amy, you okay?"

It's Jessica. I don't feel like talking right now, even to my best friend. I'm kind of fine being depressed all by myself. "I'm fine."

"You think the youth group is weak sauce, don't you? I'm sorry I made you—"

"It's not weak sauce."

"Then why are you all mopey?" My best friend rolls her eyes at me, if you can believe it. "Seriously, Amy, you're gonna have to get over Avi. You've been acting like a total recluse lately and it's getting on everyone's nerves, especially mine. Can't you move on? I guarantee Avi's not moping around, making his friends and everyone else around him miserable."

I stand here wide-eyed, not believing for a second Jessica just bitched me out. She's never done this before. We've always supported each other through guys and zits and parents and school. "I guess it's too much to ask for my best friend to support me when I need it the most," I say.

"You know what, Amy? I was thinking the same thing," she says, then stomps back to the *sukkah*-building activity.

What the hell was that all about? I'm too confused to think right now. All I want to do is go home. What's worse is that I'm at the mercy of Jessica because she drove me here.

Stomping back to my group, I plop myself down next to Wes from Lickity Split again.

"Amy, you just sat on a banana," Wes informs me, then bursts out laughing. Nikki and the rest of my group follow. All eyes are watching to see what I'm going to do next.

I could cry—that wouldn't take too much effort. In fact, I can feel a waterfall forming behind my eyelids.

Closing my eyes, my brain focuses on the wet, gushy mush soaking the jeans I spent over a half hour picking out. And on Jessica's tirade. And on my mom's pregnancy. And on Avi and Nathan and my dad's date disaster. And Mutt's insatiable addiction to sniffing everyone's crotch.

In case you haven't noticed, my teenage life is officially ruined.

12

*Rabbi Glassman said he realized he wanted to study to be
a rabbi when he was in high school.
To be honest, I think God chose him to be a rabbi
instead of the other way around.
He's too unbiased and wise to be a regular person.*

Yes, I had to last the rest of the night with wet, sticky banana-encrusted jeans. And no, Jessica and I still aren't talking. Miranda is, though.

"That was so much fun, wasn't it?" Miranda says as we get into Jessica's car at the end of the night. I put down a plastic bag before I sit in the back seat while the engine is warming up.

Jessica grunts and I say, "Yeah. Great fun." I love being laughed at by an entire group of high schoolers and smelling like baby food. Where can I sign up for the next meeting?

"Sorry about your pants," Miranda says from the front passenger seat. "I'm glad you came, though. There's not many kids from CA here."

"We don't necessarily have a huge Jewish population at the Academy," I say, leaning back and hearing the bag under my butt crinkle with every movement I make. Jewish kids probably make up fifteen or twenty percent of the student population at Chicago Academy, and CA isn't the biggest school in Chicago by far.

"They think we're rich snobs," I blurt out.

Miranda turns and faces me while Jessica concentrates on driving us home. "People don't think I'm a snob. They think of me as the fat girl. They think you're a snob because you're pretty and don't smile a lot."

"Smiling is overrated."

Jessica snorts.

Miranda looks animated now. She's going into excited mode. "Smiling takes years off your life. Did you know it takes more muscles to frown than it does to smile?"

"Did you know it takes more energy to talk than to be silent?"

Did I just say that? Oh, man. Miranda bites her lip and turns around, slinking down in the seat. I didn't mean it. I just wanted to stop feeling like I was bombarded with everyone pointing out what's wrong with me.

Jessica stops the car. I think she's so pissed she's going to dump me off the side of the road and order me to get out. But now I realize we're at my building.

Keeping up with the I'm-not-a-good-friend-and-I-don't-smile theme, I open the door to the car and step onto the sidewalk. I'm about to swallow my pride and thank Jess for the ride, but she blurts out, "Close the door."

As soon as I shut the door, Jessica's off like a NASCAR driver.

I feel like the biggest bitch. Maybe I am. Should I feel better that I'm a bitch with a conscience? Because I feel totally wretched.

I stay on the sidewalk for a minute before I turn and walk into the building. I want to smile. I want to be a good friend to Jessica and even Miranda. Miranda doesn't look or dress or act like me, but she's nice and smiles. Does she smile because she's genuinely nice or is she perceived to be nice because she smiles?

Does it even matter?

Exhausted physically and emotionally, I pass our night doorman Jorge who opens the door for me as I head for the elevator bank.

"Did you have a good evening with your friends, Miss Barak?" Jorge asks.

"Not particularly," I answer back.

"Some days are like that, I'm afraid."

"Yeah, some days are crap."

In the elevator, I lean my head against the wall. The doors start to close, until I hear someone stopping the doors from shutting with their hands. Those hands are attached to none other than Nathan.

Nathan enters the elevator in sweats and workout pants. A lady who I've only seen a few times who lives on the fifth floor follows in right behind him.

I close my eyes to block out everything. When we stop on the fifth floor to let the lady out, I open my eyes.

Nathan is staring right at me through his glasses. His eyes are as bright as Kermit the Frog and the gold specks in them are shining in the lights of the elevator. Stupid lights. Stupid elevator. They make my mind think stupid thoughts, like wondering what I could do to make Nathan like me.

He takes a drink from a water bottle he's carrying in his hand. I start breathing heavily, as if my mind is one big mashed potato. I stare at his lips. I've never noticed them before, but now they're shiny from that water.

Nathan hates me, but maybe…

No, I can't.

But he's looking right at me; our eyes are locked. I can't change anything else in my crappy life, but maybe I can change his attitude and animosity toward me.

If I don't try it, I'll never know. I drop my purse on the floor of the elevator and rush toward him, pressing my lips to his. I'm kissing Nathan in the elevator as we ride up from the fifth to fortieth floor, my eyes still locked on his while I'm waiting for some reaction from him.

I get none.

My hands. What should I do with my hands? I place them on his chest, which feels unusually hard for a guy like him, and tilt my head to attempt a more intimate kiss.

Nathan isn't responding. His lips are soft and inviting but he's standing stiffly with his arms at his side. He's not shoving me away from him, but he surely isn't acting like a guy who's being kissed by a girl. His lips are parted slightly against mine, his breath is warm and smells sweet. But he's not all here. He's not into it and I'm the one doing all the work.

When the elevator dings and the doors open, I lift my hands off his chest and lean back.

"Well, that was pleasant," I say as I lift my purse and step out of the elevator.

"For who?" Nathan responds, walking right past me.

We're in the hall on the fortieth floor of the building with nobody else around. Nathan is in front of his door and I'm in front of mine. I look down the hall at him while he fishes for his keys. "For nobody, Nathan. That was a joke. You obviously don't like girls."

He gives a short, cynical laugh. "Whatever you say, Barbie. Did anyone ever tell you you smell like fruit?"

"Stop calling me Barbie!" I yell, ignoring the fruit comment for the moment. Nathan doesn't respond as he opens the door to his condo and slams the door shut behind him.

The door quickly opens to my condo and my dad rushes at me. "What's wrong? Who are you yelling at?"

"Nobody, Dad."

"I heard you yelling. Are you okay?"

"Don't spaz on me. I'm fine," I say, then brush past him

My dad follows me to my bedroom, my private sanctuary where I go to be alone. "I'm your father. I have a right to spaz. Why are you acting like this? And why do you smell like bananas?"

I give him my famous sneer. "Acting like what?"

"Like you're angry with the world."

"I'm not angry with the world; the world is angry with me. And for your information, I sat on a banana. Now if you'll excuse me, I'd like some privacy so I can change." That gets him to leave pretty quick.

After I shimmy out of my now crusty jeans, I dress in pj's and head down the hall to brush my teeth and scrub my face. With all the stress I'm under, I'm bound to get a zit or two…or twenty. I'm in the bathroom, scrubbing my lips and that kiss away with a washcloth. Back in my room, I look up and see my dad standing in the doorway.

He leans against the door frame. "I admit I'm not used to teenage girl problems. But I'm here to listen."

I can tell he's mentally preparing for some heavy discussion. He's not used to heavy *teenage girl problem* discussions. My dad is such a guy. He needs some feminine influence in his life. "Why don't you want a girlfriend?"

"Because relationships are a time commitment."

I roll my eyes and say, "It's no secret you have commitment problems. Let's just get that out in the open. Are you refusing to date because you're in love with my mom?"

"I'm not talking about this with you."

"Why not? You're obviously not talking about it with anyone else. And if you think by working yourself to death you can hide from the truth, you can't."

"I'm committed to you, Amy. I hardly have time to spend with my own daughter these days, which is killing me inside. How can I add something else to take me away from my family?"

"You call two people a family?"

"Yes."

My poor dad doesn't get it. "What about when I go to college? You'll be all alone while Marc and Mom have more babies together. And what about after you retire? You'll be sitting at home by yourself with nothing to keep you company but a set of dentures and an old, wrinkly body."

The side of his mouth quirks up in amusement. "Thanks for painting the full picture. Consider me officially forewarned of my future fate."

"Great. Now will you go on a date?"

"No. But I'm coming home early tomorrow to spend time with you. After working at Perk Me Up!, I'll take you anywhere you want to go. *Tov?*"

Leave it to my dad to slide in a Hebrew word now and then. "*Tov,*" I say back.

When he leaves my room, I let out a long, frustrated sigh and look over at my cell phone. I was really rude to Miranda tonight in the car. I practically told her to shut up. And I hate fighting with Jessica. Every time we argue I feel sick.

I decide to text Jessica.

Me: You there?
Jess: No.
Me: Want to talk?
Jess: No.
Me: Fine.
Jess: Fine.

Crossing my room to my desk, I take out the CA student directory and dial Miranda's number.

"Hello?"

"Miranda?"

"Yeah."

"It's Amy. Um…I just wanted to say I'm sorry I was kinda rude tonight. I mean, if I hurt your feelings I didn't mean to. It was the banana incident and—"

"And your fight with Jessica," she says, stating the obvious.

"Yeah, that too. Well, I just wanted to apologize."

"Apology accepted."

Phew. One person to check off my list of people pissed with me. "Maybe we could hang out sometime."

I think Miranda just dropped the phone, 'cause I hear this big bang on the other end of the line. She recovers pretty quickly, though. "You really want to hang out with me?"

"Sure. I know you're in pretty much all AP classes and I'm not, but you were really cool tonight."

"Wow. Thanks," Miranda says excitedly. "You're way more popular than me, Amy, but you must know that. I just thought you would think I was lame like the other girls at school…well, except Jessica. Although Jessica and I don't hang out unless it's for the youth group."

Here's the thing about popularity: it's the ones who declare themselves popular who usually get pegged as popular. You've got to know how to talk big and act like you're someone important and people will treat you like you're big and important. My wonderful mother taught me to be who I want to be without making excuses. I admit sometimes I go a bit overboard with my comments and actions, but I have a conscience. I apologize.

Of course it's only to the people who deserve an apology.

I guess you can call me *apologetically selective*. (I think I just made that up, but I like it.)

"Don't you live next door to that new guy from school?" Miranda asks. "He's totally cute."

Ugh! "You mean Nathan?"

I can feel the vibration of excitement over the line. "Yeah. Nathan. He sits in front of me in calculus and has the coolest eyes. Like emeralds."

"Don't waste your breath, Miranda. He's not into girls."

13

From the beginning when the Israelites were slaves to Pharaoh in Egypt to the Nazis' attempt to annihilate the Jewish race, Jews have suffered—but in the end have prevailed and become stronger.
They've even overcome God's anger (Exodus 32:10).
Overcoming obstacles is in my Jewish blood.

"The whole school thinks I'm gay."

I'm standing at my locker, fishing for my U.S. history book. It's in here somewhere. "Did you say something?" I say sweetly to Nathan, still keeping my attention on the books stacked in my locker.

"Amy."

Oh, there it is. I reach out and grab my book, wondering when Mr. Krazinski will spring a pop quiz on us. Maybe I should take the book home tonight and read it.

Nathan grabs my arm, pulling me away from my locker. "Ouch," I say. He's stronger than I'd ever give him credit for, but it doesn't hurt. I rub my arm for effect.

"I didn't hurt you. Yet."

"What do you want from me, Nathan? I've got to get to class and I'm already late."

He's wearing a stark white button-down shirt and pleated navy pants. I'm not even concentrating on his lack of fashion sense because I'm trying not to look at his eyes. I keep thinking about that ludicrous comment Miranda said about emeralds.

"I want you to admit you told the entire school I'm gay."

Leaning back against the lockers while avoiding his eyes, I say, "Listen, Nathan. I didn't tell anyone you're gay. I *may* have said you're not into girls."

"Why, 'cause I'm not into you?"

"That's low, Nathan."

"Oh, I can get lower, Amy. Just try me." He steps forward and straddles both hands on the lockers behind me, locking me in. "Look at me."

I'd like to still keep my gaze on the wall opposite him, but that would be cowardly. I'm anything but a coward. He's tall and close. I can smell spicy cologne radiating off his body. And when I look up, I'm staring straight into his eyes because his glasses have slipped down. I swallow then say, "What's wrong with people thinking you're gay? Jason Hill is gay and he's probably the most popular guy in school—with girls as well as guys."

"If I was, I wouldn't give a shit. But I'm not."

"So tell everyone you're hetero. Just like I have to tell everyone I didn't join a dating service." I shove his arm out of the way and head to class, thinking all the while that his personality does not in any way match his looks. It's like dressing a buffalo up as a hyena. It's just not right.

Jessica is in my U.S. history class. I sit in my usual spot next to her after being grilled by Mr. Krazinski about why I was late. I lied and said it was *a feminine problem* and that quieted him real quick.

Jess looks horrible. I'd be surprised if she took a shower this morning, she looks so disheveled. Her brown hair is frizzed out; she's wearing sweats and no makeup. I don't care if she was insensitive to me last night. I need to find out what's going on. I've been best friends with Jess for twelve years. Our friendship can weather any fight.

I hope.

Now I'm worried. She won't even look in my direction, so I wait until the bell rings to corner her. I swear this school should be called Drama Academy instead of Chicago Academy today.

When the bell rings, Jess grabs her stuff and hurries out of the classroom faster than a jackrabbit being chased by a dog. I push the other students out of my way to catch up with her. I'm hearing curses from guys as I shove past them but all I can think about is my friend in trouble.

I find her in the girls' bathroom. "Jess, I know you're in here. I *saw* you." When I get no answer, I continue. "I admit I've been wrapped up in my own crap and have ignored you, but *please* let's talk about it."

The door to one of the stalls opens. It's Roxanne Jeffries.

With a toss of her red hair and a smirk on her face, she says, "I hear Mitch dumped Jessica for a freshman."

"Shut up, Roxy, or I'll tell people you got implants last summer when you told everyone you went to overnight camp," I hiss.

"You're a bitch," Roxanne says with a huff.

"So I've been told. Now scram. Your perfume is making me ill. Or maybe it's your B.O. that reeks."

Roxanne washes her hands, then storms out of the bathroom.

"You're not a bitch," Jessica's voice bellows from one of the stalls. I can tell from her tone she's been crying. "You're just preoccupied."

"No, I think everyone's right. I'm a bitch because no matter what's going on in my own life, I should never let down my best friend."

Jess pushes open the stall door with bundled-up tissue in her hand. "I'm sorry what I said about you and Avi."

"I'm sorry for not realizing earlier that you're having a crisis. What's up? Is what Roxanne just said true?"

Her eyes get watery and I hand her a paper towel. "Mitch called me before I left for the youth group thing last night. He said he had something important to talk to me about. I tried getting it out of him, but he said we'd just talk later. I asked him if it was good news and he said no."

I bite my bottom lip in fear. "He didn't?"

"Yep. After I got home from the youth group thing I called him. He broke up with me and said he was asking Kailey Pulson to the Valentine's Dance."

My eyebrows furrow in confusion. "Kailey Pulson? Freshman Kailey Pulson?" Kailey Pulson is a total jock girl. I think she rock climbs for fun.

Tears run down Jess's cheeks as she nods. "Now what am I gonna do?"

The bell rings again. I'm late for another class. "I'll figure something out, Jess. They don't call me your best friend for nothing. What we have to do is find us both hot dates for the dance. Leave it to me."

Jess sniffles. "To be honest, right now I don't want to go. The last thing I want to do is see Kailey and Mitch together."

She has a point. As I open the door to the bathroom, I turn back and face my best friend. "Then we'll just hang out, the two of us dateless girls. We'll watch DVDs, order pizza, and gossip all night. Sound good?"

"Thanks, Amy," Jess says.

I got to English class late because of my chitchat with Jess in the bathroom, but Miss Haskell has a sub so it wasn't a big deal. Can it be a sign of good karma coming my way?

At lunch I pay for the salad bar, then search for Mitch. I'm going to find my old boyfriend and give him a piece of my mind. Jessica told me not to. She wants me to leave him alone but I can't.

"Barbie," a male voice says from behind me. I whip around. Of course it's Nathan. Nobody else would have the nerve to call me Barbie. Without saying another word, he pulls me close and starts kissing me.

I mean *really* kissing me. To the point where I drop my food tray and don't even care I've just made a mess on the floor and on my shoes with a mixture of lettuce and vegetables and Thousand Island dressing. Nathan's soft, inviting lips are open to mine and just when I'm about to pull back and yell at him, he snakes his hand around my waist and pulls me closer.

My brain is telling me to pull away even though my lips are as involved as Nathan's are right now. I grab onto Nathan's biceps and attempt to push him away, but he's too strong and I'm not as determined as I want to be.

Nathan is the one to pull back first, after his glasses hit my face and I wince. He turns to the crowd with a huge grin after he pushes his glasses up and says, *"Fine*, I'll go to the Valentine's Dance with you."

Fine? Nothing is *fine* around here.

The cafeteria is in an uproar with cheers from the guys. I'm still in a daze when the lunchroom lady, Gladys, sees the salad mess on the floor and moves us aside with a look of disgust and comments about PDA rules at Chicago Academy.

When my eyes finally focus, I'm still in shock. Nathan tries to help pick up the mess with Gladys, but she shoos him away with a wave of her hand.

Without a word, I walk through the cafeteria and plop myself down at a lunch table next to an open-mouthed Miranda. I know. I never sit at Miranda's table. I just know Miranda and her friends don't gossip like my friends do.

I give her a small smile. Unfortunately Mr. Emerald Eyes follows my lead and sits down next to me.

"Here," he says, shoving a brown bag at me. "It's my lunch. You can have it since you dropped yours."

As if he's a gentleman. Puh*leaze*.

I look over at Jessica, sitting at the popular girls' table. Less than two hours ago I told her I'd stay home for the Valentine's Dance instead of going. She probably thinks I was lying and I'm hooking up with Nathan.

"I'm not hungry." I bark the words at Nathan. In fact, I don't think I could eat all day after that kiss.

14

I love listening to Hebrew prayers put to song.
I have no clue what the words mean,
but hearing the cantor and congregation sing together
makes me want to chant
right along with them.

Okay, I admit it. Nathan surprised me. I would have never guessed the guy would go ahead and do a crazy thing like kiss me in the cafeteria and declare us a Valentine's Dance couple. Now all the kids at school are whispering about us behind my back, in front of my back, and all around me. They're waiting with bated breath for another Amy/Nathan spotting.

I'm not gonna let that happen.

So after school I take a cab home instead of waiting for the bus. If Nathan has no problems kissing me in front of half of the student body, what other stunt is he going to pull on the bus ride home?

After I let Mutt do his duty, I walk over to Perk Me

Up! The rich smells coming from the café immediately make me feel energized and lift my spirits. I don't even need to consume the coffee in order to get the caffeine fix.

Marla hands me an apron and I'm immediately into Perk Me Up! employee mode. I clean off tables, start taking orders, and try to keep a big bright smile on my face. *Show teeth when you smile*, Marla told me last week. Yeah, I'm trying.

My toothy smile fades when Nathan walks in to the café. He has his backpack slung over his shoulder and I didn't notice it before, but he's got splotches of Thousand Island dressing on his white shirt. I don't think those stains are going to come out.

"I'm sorry," he says when he reaches the register. Unfortunately nobody else is in line behind him.

Marla stands beside me, watching and listening.

I ignore Nathan's apology and instead say to him, "Welcome to Perk Me Up! Can I take your order, sir?"

"Come on, Barbie. You kissed me yesterday. Why am I the villain for kissing you today?"

"You kissed him?" Marla asks.

I turn to her. "Only because I wanted him to stop hating me."

Marla's eyebrows furrow in fascination. "You kiss people who hate you?"

"I don't hate her," Nathan chimes in.

"Oh, really?" I say sarcastically, putting my hands on my hips. "Then why do you keep calling me Barbie? And why didn't you kiss me back yesterday when we were in the elevator, but today you have no problem making out with me with the entire school watching?"

"It was to prove a point."

"To prove you're not gay? Listen, you're not cute enough to be gay."

Nathan laughs. "Are you kidding me? You are the most stereotypical, insensitive, and obnoxious girl I've ever met."

"I take offense to that," I say, then cross my arms in front of my chest.

"Me, too," Marla interjects. "Amy's rough around the edges, but she's as good as gold."

"Oh, you're so sweet, Marla," I say, then hug her.

Nathan points to me. "She thinks I'm a dork because I wear old clothes and have glasses."

"Well, he thinks I'm a bitch because I say out loud what everyone else is thinking."

"You know what *I* think?" Marla says, stepping closer to the counter.

Nathan and I say, "What?" in unison.

"I think you two like each other."

I roll my eyes while Nathan does a shiver as if the thought of liking me grosses him out.

"Nope," he says.

"Not *at all*," I say. "Besides, I have Avi. And he's got Bucky."

"Bicky."

"Whatever."

"Yep," Marla says, then saunters to the supply room

like she knows what's going on. "You guys definitely like each other."

Nathan starts to laugh.

"It's not funny," I say. More customers come into the café, so it's my chance to say to Nathan, "Please order or step aside so I can wait on someone else."

"I'll have a medium green tea with ice, no sweetener," he says, diverting my attention back to him.

Figures he'd order something so plain.

After I take his money and turn around to make his boring drink, Nathan says so only I can hear, "Don't spit in it."

As if I would. Puh*leaze*.

I hand his drink to him and focus my attention on the other customers.

The hour goes by fast. Making drinks, cleaning off the tables, and ignoring Nathan typing away in the computer corner is exhausting, though. I sigh in relief when my dad walks through the door to pick me up.

My dad has already changed clothes from work. He's wearing dark jeans and a black long-sleeve tee. I've convinced him to grow his hair out a bit, so he resembles a cuter and cooler dad but he's still got about two months to go before he can get a good style going.

"Hey, *Aba*," I greet him.

Out of the corner of my eye I swear I see Nathan watching us.

"How was school today?" my dad asks.

I look over at Nathan. Now he's pretending to read the computer screen, but I know he's not reading a damn thing. He's wondering if I'll tell my dad what happened in the cafeteria. "Nothing much. What about you?"

My dad kisses the top of my head. "Just preparing for a presentation in D.C. You ready to go?"

"Yep."

"Great. Where to?"

I grab my dad's elbow and journey into the cold outside air. "Follow me," I say, leading him down State Street.

I lean into my dad to try and soak up some of the warmth of his strong commando arm. "I'm sorry I yelled at you yesterday," I say. "I just want you to be happy."

"I'm sorry, too. You didn't make any more dates for me, did you?"

"Here we are," I tell him as we turn down artsy Oak Street with the designer shops and upscale salons. I pull him into the first building we come to, a place called Sheer-Ahz. I purposely leave out the speed-dating thing I signed him up for at the last minute.

"You're getting a haircut?" he asks when he realizes Sheer-Ahz is a salon.

"Nope."

He halts his steps abruptly. "Then why the salon?"

I look up at him and smile widely as if he was a customer at Perk Me Up! "We're getting manicures."

"You mean *you're* getting a manicure."

"Nope. You heard me right the first time, *Aba.*"

"Men don't get manicures."

"Come, on. Haven't you heard of metrosexual men?"

My dad shakes his head. "No. And I'm sure I don't want to be one."

"Didn't you say I could pick what we do tonight?"

"Yes, but—"

I turn to my dad, one of the few people who takes my crap and loves me despite it. Maybe even more because of it. My dad pretends he's not afraid of anything, but I've just uncovered his weakness…getting his nails trimmed and shaped. Give me a break. "This is what *I* want to do. My nails are all dry and cracked. Think of it as daddy/daughter bonding time."

"Can't we bond by playing indoor soccer or something like that?" he says.

"I don't do soccer. I do manicures." I pull all six feet of him up to the front desk. "We have appointments for two manicures," I inform the lady. "For Amy and Ron Barak."

She doesn't flinch as she punches our names in the computer, writes something on two tickets, and hands them to us. "Feel free to have refreshments in the meditation room while you're waiting."

My dad turns to me and says, "Did she just say meditation room?" in his deep, manly voice. I swear he's making it sound deeper than usual.

Once inside the white silk-draped room with scented candles and soft music, he looks nervous. I don't think a retired Israeli commando has ever been in a place like this. He'd probably look more at home in the desert. Or in a war zone.

There are no other guys in the room, just a lady in

a terry cloth robe. I bet she's got nothing on underneath. She's reading one of the complimentary magazines and doesn't pay any attention to us.

"Sit down," I tell my dad while I sink into the plushy, soft, cream-colored chair and breathe to the rhythm of the slow music.

"I'd rather stand," he says tersely.

My eyes close as my mind drifts. "Suit yourself."

After a few minutes, two women dressed in long, white coats call out, "Ron and Amy Barak."

"That's us," he says, then clasps his hands together and rubs them back and forth. The sound is making me cringe and everyone is staring at him. Real smooth, Dad.

When we're sitting down next to each other, the nail technician takes my dad's hand and places it in a small container of soapy water.

"I don't want a color," he tells the woman right away.

I want to groan. Does he honestly think they're going to make his nails a brilliant red or fuchsia pink? "*Aba*, guys get clear. Or just a buff." Duh.

"Oh. Okay…I think."

Seriously, take a guy out of his element and he gets all confused and insecure. My own nail technician, Sue, is expertly massaging my wrists, palms, and hands as they turn to Jell-O under her skilled touch.

"My daughter made me come here," my dad tells the women, but he says it loud enough so everyone in the small salon can hear him. *Go, manly man! Yes, tell all women you a strong warrior man.* Spare me.

"*Aba*, you've got calluses and your skin is all dry and cracked. I swear you look like a dinosaur. Right, Sue? Just look at his paws."

Sue is extremely non-committal as she glances at my dad's hands. She smiles sweetly at him, then continues to work magic with my fingers.

I can tell when my dad's nail tech starts his own hand massage. His shoulders, for the first time since we got here, slump into relaxation mode.

His hair has curled from the dampness in the air, making him look younger and vulnerable. I wonder if he was ever insecure. As a teen did he go through an awkward stage or was he hard and manly and confident since the day he was born?

My dad looks Middle Eastern with his dark olive complexion, dark features, and strong chiseled nose. If he was a stranger, I wouldn't immediately think he was Jewish, though. I wonder if he ever wanted to be something other than what he is.

Because I never thought I'd want to be any religion, but now I feel different. Being Jewish isn't a choice; it's a part of me. A part I just discovered, but it's significant in any case.

"After I convert I want a bat mitzvah," I tell my dad, bringing him to attention.

"With a big party?" he asks.

Thinking about it more, I decide I don't want a big shindig. "I'd just like Jessica and a few other friends to come over afterward. And Mom and Marc. You know, if it's okay with you."

"It's fine. In fact, it's great."

He's watching intently as his cuticles are cut and fortified and his nails are shaped. I think he's enjoying it as much as I am, but I'm not sure if my "manly man" dad will admit it.

I pick a French manicure while he picks out a sheer, almost invisible bottle of polish.

When we're done, the nail techs lead us into the drying area and instruct us to place our wet nails under ultraviolet lights to get them to dry fast.

I put my hands under the lights while my dad picks up his ultra-violet light machine and examines it.

"Put that down before you get us in trouble," I whisper.

"Before I stick my hands under something, I'd like to know exactly what it is. Don't be so trusting, Amy," he advises, going into Homeland Security mode.

I chuckle. "Yeah, the nail technicians are the enemy. Be afraid. Be *very* afraid."

He puts the machine down but still doesn't stick his hands underneath the fluorescent blue light. "Let's talk about Avi," he says, still refusing to put his hands under the light.

"Why?"

He shrugs. "I just want to know if you're still an item."

"Dad, the word 'item' went out in the seventies but yes, I still like him. I mean, we haven't been able to see each other but I'm hoping in the summer when we go back to Israel he'll get time off." I take a sideways look at my dad. "You know he's my *non-boyfriend*, right?"

"What exactly does that mean?" he asks. "I've heard you and Jessica using the phrase, but I don't get it."

I check my nails to see if they're still tacky and need more ultra-violet rays but they're as dry as my stepdad's liquor cabinet. I hop off the stool I've been sitting on, trying to explain the relationship label Avi wanted. "It means we can see other people because we obviously can't physically be together. There's no commitment. We're casual, great friends. Get it?"

He nods. "Got it."

"Speaking of casual friends, I have a surprise for you."

"It's not another online date, is it?"

"Oh, no," I say, shaking my head vigorously. "It's a bunch of dates. Tonight. Speed dating at the Blues Bar on Chicago Avenue and you have to be there in fifteen minutes. Don't worry about impressing anyone. You only have three minutes for each date. It's all about making a connection."

15

Israel is tiny, yet everyone fights over it.
I guess it's true that the biggest and best things come in
small packages.

My manipulation skills obviously need help, because my
dad refused to even step one foot inside the bar for the speed
dating night.

Standing in front of the bar, I wait until the bouncer is
preoccupied and slink inside without him noticing.

"He's not coming?" Marla is there, wearing a black
scooped-neck dress. She got so excited when I told her
about the speed dating she decided to sign up, too. She
and my dad aren't compatible. She's into mushy romantic
guys and my dad is...well, he's not. He's Israeli.

I walk up to the guy running the program, a balding
guy with a ring of red hair around his scalp. He's got a
nametag on his chest with the word LARRY in big black

letters. "My dad couldn't make it," I tell Larry, looking over his notes. The bar is crowded. I refuse to cancel my dad's reservation to date twenty women in an hour and a half.

Larry looks up at me. "Your dad?"

"Yeah, I kind of signed him up."

"You can't do that. Did you read the rules?" The guy doesn't even question what a seventeen-year-old is doing in a bar in the first place.

Umm…"I'm not a rule kind of person."

"What's his name?"

"Ron…Ron Barak."

My mouth opens wide as he takes a big red pen and crosses off my dad's name from the list.

"You can't do that!" I say, totally upset now. I paid thirty-five dollars to sign my dad up for the speed dating night. Okay, to be completely honest Marla paid and I'm working it off. It's a little side business arrangement I made with her.

Marla takes a seat next to Larry and makes her lips all pouty. "Is there any way you could help her out?"

The guy shrugs. "What do you want me to do?"

Marla looks to me for an answer.

"Let me go on the dates in my dad's place." I admit it isn't the most brilliant idea, but it does have potential. If I could find the perfect woman for him, screen her person-ally…

Before the guy comes to his senses, I pull a nametag and scorecard off the table.

"Women, please sit at your assigned places. Men, you'll

go around to each woman, marking off either a 'yes' or a 'no' on the card. Women, you'll do the same for the men. Just write their number on your card and mark it with a 'yes' or 'no.' If you get two matching 'yes' marks, we'll e-mail you each other's contact information. Everyone got it?"

Nope. But I can't say anything because I'll be kicked out of this ridiculous shenanigan. Right now I'm not blaming my dad. I'm so nervous, as if I'm going to be judged for my looks and brains and…

"Start!"

I head to the only open seat in the place. I'm sitting across from a woman with the name Dru on her nametag. She looks really confused. It takes me a minute to explain myself. "Hi, I'm Amy. My dad was supposed to be here, but couldn't make it. Well, actually he didn't want to come. It's kind of a long story, but ultimately I'm looking for a wife for my dad. What kinds of qualifications do you—"

"Switch!"

Before I finish my question, I'm being rushed out of the chair. I take another empty seat and find myself across from another single, confused woman. She's looking a little old to be set up with my dad, and her gray roots need to be touched up. "How old are you?" I ask.

"Forty."

"Have you tried nighttime moisturizing face cream?"

"I beg your pardon? This is a speed dating function, not a cosmetic consultation."

"I know. I'm trying to find a woman for my dad, but—"

Oops, the lady is raising her hand, getting the attention of the organizers. I crane my neck to find Marla deep in conversation with a guy at the other end of the bar. At least one of us is having luck tonight.

"Switch!"

Larry stands over my chair. "Miss, you can't be here. This is a private function for adults only."

I stand up, defeated. "I'm going, I'm going," I say, then give a little wave to Marla and head outside.

In our condo, my dad is sitting at his desk, working.

"I'll have you know I went on two three-minute dates for you."

"How were they?"

"Terrible. You know how they say there's a pot for every lid? I think you've got a pot in the shape of a trapezoid."

"Is that bad?" he asks.

To be honest, the jury's out on that one. Being unique and different is good. But I suspect there's a fine line between being unique and needing major therapy.

16

> *Some people will think differently of me*
> *because I'm Jewish.*
> *Some people will call me names because I'm Jewish.*
> *Some people will hate me because I'm Jewish.*
> *Should I ignore them or confront them?*

Before school the next day, I spot Mitch by his locker.

"You don't break up with someone right before the Valentine's Dance," I tell him. "It's rude."

He furrows his bushy eyebrows, which at one time I thought made him look rugged and adorable. "What do you want me to say?" he says, then closes his locker and walks away from me.

Why can girls be strong enough to confront boys with issues, but boys can't do the same? They make asinine statements and run away. I'm going to make a generalized statement about boys, so brace yourself: *Boys have an aversion to confrontation.* (And commitment, but that's a whole different story.)

But I am persistent. Catching up with Mitch, I tap him on the back and say as we're walking, "You hurt Jessica. That wasn't cool."

Mitch stops, but his curly hair is still bouncing up and down on his head. "Lay off, Amy. I liked you, then I stopped liking you and fell for Jessica. Now I like someone else."

"Can't you commit to someone?"

"Yeah, while I like 'em. When it's over, it's done. I'm a teenage guy. I can afford to be picky."

I want to slap him.

While I'm still contemplating his egotistic statement, he leaves me in the hallway standing amongst the student body. How many of these teens are picky? Nathan told Marla I don't like him because he wears old clothes and has glasses.

That's not why.

I have the sudden urge to share with Nathan why I hate him. It's not that I'm picky, or rude, or think of myself as too good to be friends with him.

"Earth to Amy."

I blink out of my daydreaming. Cami and Raine are standing in front of me, waving their arms in front of my face. "Welcome back to reality," Cami says, laughing.

"What's on the menu for lunch?" I ask, trying to forget about Mitch and what he just told me. Besides, on Mondays sometimes they surprise us with Uno's pizza. (Another high carb food, I know…but just as worth it as sushi.)

"Forget lunch. Tell us about that Nathan guy and you going to the Valentine's Dance. Everyone's talking about it, if you haven't noticed. They're saying you've gone geek on us. First you kiss the guy in the lunchroom and then you sit at Miranda's table. What's gotten into you?"

I think about how cool Miranda was after I was rude and how quickly she took my apology without making me feel bad. She could have bitched me out, but she didn't. "Miranda's not so bad."

Raine puts her manicured hands up. "She smells like Swiss cheese, Amy. You'd think that big Jewish honker of hers would notice it."

And there it is. My first time since going through conversion someone saying a derogatory remark to me about Jews. More than derogatory. Racist, really. My heart is pounding faster and I feel my throat start to constrict. I'm getting a sick feeling in the pit of my stomach.

"*I'm* Jewish," I say, ready to defend my people even if it costs me popularity-wise. And let me tell you, being unpopular at Chicago Academy is like being a lone rabbit surrounded by a roomful of hunting dogs. Or wolves.

"Yeah, but not really. You're only half Jewish," Raine says, not getting it.

Eww. Half. Like I can never be whole because my mom isn't Jewish? Wrong. "Um, I gotta disagree with you there, Raine. I'm all Jew. If you want to start throwing around Jewish jokes or insults, it's not gonna fly with me."

Raine looks like she's smelling some bad cheese right about now. "Lighten up, Amy."

"Don't tell me to lighten up when you insult my people," I say.

"I insulted Miranda Cohen, Amy. Not you. Not the

entire Jewish population or *your people*. Geez," she says, then rolls her eyes.

I desperately want to walk away, to back down and remove myself from the situation like Mitch did to me. But I don't. Because I want Raine to know, or anyone else who wants to fling around Jewish insults, that it's not okay. It hurts. I can't even describe how much her words cut right through me, even though I know she doesn't realize it.

My heartbeat somewhat gets back to normal when Raine turns and walks away in a huff.

I turn to Cami, who's pretending to check in her book bag for something. I can tell she's just shuffling around stuff. "I'm not mad at you," I tell Cami.

Cami looks up. "That was intense."

"It wasn't meant to be."

So now we're just standing here and I have to say something to break the silence. "You headed for the cafeteria?"

Cami hesitates before saying, "Nope. I have to go to the Resource Lab first. I'll meet up with you later."

Yeah, sure. "Whatever," I say, as if I don't care.

Walking into the cafeteria, I survey my surroundings. Raine is already here; she's talking with a couple of other girls with their heads together in obvious gossip-mode. Did I say gossip was underrated? Well, now that I'm on the other end of the Gossip Trail I'm not so happy about it. Payback sucks.

I'm standing in line, picking out food. Yesterday was a disaster with Nathan's kiss. Now Raine is gossiping about me being Jewish. I'm sure she's twisting the story around to make me look bad. I'm determined to avoid drawing attention to myself.

Oh, no. Nathan just walked in the room. He's about six people behind me in the cafeteria line. He's talking to Kyle. Better to know where he is so I'm not given another surprise kiss without being prepared for it.

Today I don't take a salad, especially because the lunchroom lady Gladys is watching me like a hawk. I order a turkey sandwich on sourdough bread, freshly made at the deli counter, and scan the lunchroom tables.

Here's where life gets tricky.

The lunchroom. Where the students classify and separate themselves like little granola clusters. Usually I'm attached to Jessica. Wherever she sits, I sit. Right now she's at the condiment counter, squirting ketchup into a little white cup for her fries. She has no clue Raine is talking about how she made fun of Miranda's Jewish nose.

Miranda is sitting with her usual cluster. They are not all Jewish. The thing they have in common is they all need fashion advice. They're also straight A students. Miranda waves over to me, and I wave back. She probably thinks I'm going to sit at her table like yesterday.

Jess sits in Raine's cluster before I can get her attention.

Looking back, Nathan is at the cashier about to pay for his two slices of pizza and bottle of Arizona Iced Tea.

Okay, time to make a decision. Cluster with Jessica and Raine, where I usually sit. Or sit with Miranda and her friends again. No time to dawdle, Amy. Popular girls don't dawdle.

As if I'm a programmed robot, I sit with my usual friends. I feel like a traitor, although when I glance over at Miranda, she's in a heated conversation with someone else and doesn't even notice I've chosen the popular girls who know what DKNY means, instead of her table, where they're probably discussing $E=MC^2$.

When I take a seat next to Jessica, the table gets super quiet. Jess is confused.

"So, what's with you and the new guy Nathan?" Roxanne asks with a snicker. "You two put on a pretty good show yesterday. Any chance for a repeat performance?"

I take a bite of my turkey sandwich so I don't have to answer right away. I need time to think of a response, although I'm usually quick-witted.

Just as I'm swallowing my first bite, I hear Nathan's voice behind me. "Can I squeeze in?"

I look up at Nathan and want to say "No" because everyone is expecting us to start making out. Why doesn't he go sit with Kyle and his buddies? Or with the geeks at the geek table?

Jessica makes everyone move down so he can sit next to me. Ugh, all eyes are on us. I do want to talk to Nathan, but in private without being surrounded and stared at by the cluster.

"So, I hear you guys are going to the Valentine's Dance," Roxanne says, her beady eyes focusing on my reaction. "Are you two, like, dating?"

I feel like the entire lunchroom is listening to my response.

"Oh, yeah," I say. "Didn't you know? It was love at first sight. Right, Nathan?"

It's either going to be me and Nathan against Roxanne and the rest of the bunch, or me against everyone.

I turn my head and look at Nathan, sitting beside me. The fluorescent lights of the cafeteria are reflected in his glasses, so I can't see his eyes. But those circular frames are definitely directed at me. "Yeah, right," he says. "I guess it's true. Opposites attract."

I chow on another bite of my sandwich, staring down at my food so I don't have to talk.

But I do see Nathan's fingers, reaching for his pizza. Within three minutes he's picking up the second piece. It's probably a world record in pizza eating. By the time he's done with his second slice, students are still entering the cafeteria.

One gulp of iced tea and he's done. I'm still trying to choke down my sandwich.

Nathan murmurs something to me in my ear that I can't understand, and leaves.

"What did he say?" Jess asks, obviously confused. She knows Nathan and I aren't even friends. Okay, we did kiss. But it was for show. I wasn't even a willing participant the second time.

"No idea," I mumble, then take another bite.

After school, Jess catches up to me on the way to the bus stop.

"Amy," she says. "I don't get it. You think Nathan is a dork—don't even argue with me because I know you better than your own mom does. Then you kiss him in front of the entire school while you're still hung up on Avi. Raine is telling everyone you've gone wacko on her. It doesn't make sense."

"Life doesn't make sense, Jess. Do you hate me?"

"Why would I hate you? I may not understand you. I may get mad at you. But I could never hate you."

Nathan is walking toward us, his uptight gait is so dorky I want to wince. I swear the guy needs a lesson in loosening up and being crazy. He probably dances like a sixty-year-old.

Avi is an amazing dancer. I remember in Israel last summer he was dancing with a girl and I got jealous so I picked a guy at random and pulled him out on the dance floor. Biggest mistake. Let's just say the end result almost had me arrested by the Israeli police.

When Nathan reaches us, Jessica walks to the bus stop to give us privacy. She's such a good friend. Totally mistaken about the situation between me and Nathan, but her heart is in the right place.

I tap Nathan on his elbow. "We need to talk."

"Why? You want to kiss again?"

"And have your glasses whack me in the face again? I don't think so. I want to talk. The kind of talking where lips don't touch."

"Sorry. No can do."

The bus is turning the corner. "Well, we can't keep pretending to be dating."

"Sure we can," he says, putting his arm around me and leading me to the back so we sit with everyone else.

I shrug his arm off.

When we get to our stop, we climb off the bus and he puts his arm around my shoulders again as if we're a real couple. Before I can shrug him off again, I look up. My heart slams into my chest and I almost fall backward.

Standing at the front of my building, like an Abercrombie model posing without even meaning to, is Avi.

And he's watching me walk toward him with Nathan's arm around me. I'm too shocked to ask Avi how he got here, why he's here, how long he's going to stay, or if he still cares about me.

"Avi," I say softly when we get closer to him. I swear I'm still in a trance when I add, "What are you doing here?"

"Who's this guy?" he answers back.

17

If God made the world in six days (Genesis 2:2),
surely I can make sense of my life in seven.

I shrug Nathan's arm off me. He drops it from my shoulders, but still stands next to me. What, is Nathan waiting for a formal introduction? I'm not prepared to give it, even when I find myself saying, "Avi, this is Nathan. Nathan, this is my...this is Avi."

It was a big deal to Avi that we didn't label ourselves boyfriend and girlfriend, with him in the Israeli army for the next three years. As much as my mind agreed with it, my heart didn't. My ego didn't, either. So I end up telling everyone he's my non-boyfriend. Let them decide what it means.

I look at Avi; his stance is stiff and his jaw is tight. He's always been guarded and tough, and I can feel he's already putting up an invisible thick wall between us, ready to shut me out. And he's been with me less than two minutes.

Which actually pisses me off because he was the one who didn't want to be official boyfriend and girlfriend. I did.

I watch as Avi reaches out to shake Nathan's hand. They're so opposite. Avi is the model type and Nathan is this all-American boy-next-door (who needs a major makeover). They give one hard "shake and release" with their hands.

"I got time off," Avi says. "For a week. Surprise, surprise."

A week. I have a week with him. A part of me is giddy beyond belief that I'll have seven days to spend with him and the other half is mad because it's just a tease. Just when I'm ready to move on in my life, he shows up and messes it all back up.

Nathan is still standing beside me, watching me with those stupid emerald eyes. "Catch you later, Amy," he says, then opens the door to our building.

He doesn't call me Barbie. Why that fact should stick in my brain is beyond me.

"Don't you have a suitcase?" I ask Avi.

"I left my duffle with the security guy inside." He puts his hands in his jeans pockets and looks away from me. "This was a bad idea, Amy. I thought...well, screw what I thought. I have a friend at Northwestern I can stay with."

A gust of Chicago wind rushes through the street and chills me to the bone. "You shouldn't have surprised me. I hate surprises. Although I probably should have told you that a long time ago. But now that you know, don't do it again."

Avi's eyebrow quirks up. "I told your dad," he says. His voice is smooth and reminds me of dark chocolate milk.

"Great. My dad knows more about my boyf—about you than I do."

Ah, it all makes sense now, why my dad asked me how I felt about Avi when we had our manicures.

"I thought you'd want me to come."

"I do, Avi," I say, but I can tell by the way he's standing stiff he doesn't believe me.

Right now is the awkward stage. I mean, really, we haven't even touched or hugged or really, *really* looked at each other yet. I can tell him how much I've missed him until I'm blue in the face, though I'm already blue in the face because I'm freezing my ass off out here.

"Let's talk up in my condo, okay?"

He nods and follows my lead. The doorman gives Avi his huge, army green duffle as we pass.

In the elevator, Avi looks straight ahead while I stand behind him. I can't believe he's actually here, in America, in Chicago, in my elevator!

I have so many questions running through my head, number one being why is he here? I thought he'd be in training until February.

Glancing at him, I analyze the differences a few months can make. Wow, he looks taller and more muscular than he did last summer—he's obviously been working out. And I swear he's standing straighter and has a determined look to him that I don't remember. Raw confidence.

A commando in the making.

Although there's a caged animal energy radiating from him, as though being in an elevator is making him claustrophobic.

The door to the elevator opens and I lead him to my condo. Mutt greets us with energetic "Args!" and a tail wagging so hard I think it'll fall off if he gets any more excited.

Avi's eyes go wide. "He's *gadol*...big," he says in Hebrew and English as he leans over to pet Mutt. When Mutt goes for his crotch, Avi says in a calm, deep voice, "*Die.*"

"That's not nice to say to my dog," I say. Maybe Avi's not the guy I once thought he *was*. Telling my dog to die is not my idea of being cool.

Avi stands up tall. "*Die* means 'stop' in Hebrew, Amy. As in 'that's enough; I don't want your nose in my balls.' That okay with you?"

Oh, no. Things are not going well at all. "Yeah," I say sheepishly. "That's fine."

Mutt scratches the door and noses the leash. I wish Mutt would wait, but if you gotta go, you gotta go no matter if you're human or animal.

"I need to take him out or he'll pee on the floor," I say.

Avi drops his duffle and says, "I'll go with you."

The problem is we need to talk honestly and openly (at the dog park that's not going to happen). I don't want to alienate Avi more than I already have. "That's okay. It'll just take me a minute. I mean, it'll just take Mutt a minute. Wait here, okay?"

He nods. "Fine."

I hurry and clip Mutt's leash to his collar. In the elevator, Mutt looks up at me with his puppy dog eyes that are so expressive sometimes I think there's a human soul inside all of that fur. "Avi's here," I tell him. "And it's awkward. What can I do to make it all better?"

Mutt looks up at me, sticks his tongue out, and pants like a...like a dog who wants to pee.

No answers from this genius dog.

At the dog park, I unclip the leash when we're fenced inside the park. My mind isn't on Mutt. It's on Avi. I contemplate what I'm going to say to him when I get back upstairs.

Do I tell him I kissed Nathan...twice?

It didn't mean anything, and yet I did participate. But how much participating do you have to do before it can really be labeled cheating?

Although how can I cheat on someone who I'm not even officially dating? Does the label of "dating" matter, or is it the feelings in your heart that takes precedence? Oh, man, I am so screwed up. Can my life get any worse?

As if on cue, I hear screaming and a ruckus coming from the other end of the dog park. I turn around and my eyes go wide when I see Mutt humping another dog.

He's usually humping another male dog, showing him who's the boss.

But not this time.

My mutt Mutt is humping Princess. Mr. Obermeyer's prized purebread Princess.

And he is going at it but good. Oh, shit.

When I run over, Mr. Obermeyer is screaming at me, "Get your dog off her!"

I swallow, hard. "What…what do you want me to do?"

In a state of panic, I catch Mitch watching the whole obscene scene and laughing. Most of the other people have their mouths wide open in horror because everyone knows to keep their dog away from Princess and Mr. Obermeyer.

I start yelling words to make Mutt leave Princess alone. "Mutt, come! Treat! No! Get off! Leave her alone! *DIE!*" Yeah, even that last word Avi just taught me didn't work.

Now all I want to do is DIE.

"Do *something*, besides give commands your dog doesn't follow," Mr. Obermeyer yells. "Hurry!"

I take a step toward the two dogs in a romantic dance. "Get off Princess," I growl through clenched teeth. "She's not your type."

Mutt obviously has selective hearing.

When I move closer, I'm getting queasy. I'm not an all-natural-comfortable-in-nature kind of person. Interrupting two dogs in the middle of a very private moment in a very public setting is not my thing and never will be.

Taking a deep breath and bracing myself for humiliation, I step behind Mutt and wrap my arms across his middle. And pull. And pull. But Mutt refuses to let go. Damn.

As soon as I release my grip and give up, Mutt bounds away from Princess as if the entire thing was no big deal.

Mr. Obermeyer runs over to his bitch. "He's tainted her womb."

"Mr. Obermeyer, she's just a dog."

The old man blinks in shock and I think he just turned a paler shade of white, if it was possible. "Princess is a state champion in obedience."

"Obviously," I mutter.

Mr. Obermeyer regards the crowd, still gathered around. "Someone call the police."

I can just see me being dragged to jail because my dog humped a prized poodle named Princess. "Mr. Obermeyer...please."

"Who's going to pay for the veterinary costs for this fiasco? She's in heat and was supposed to be bred with a stud. Now she'll have a litter of mutts instead of purebreds. It's all because you can't control your *animal*."

The old man looks like he's about to have a coronary and his wrinkles threaten to crease further into his waxy skin. "I'm sorry," I say, trying to break the tension while thinking the only stud around here is my mutt.

Mr. Obermeyer holds his hands up. "Sorry?" he says. "How is your 'sorry' going to change the situation?"

It can't. "I don't know."

"If he's not a purebred, your responsibility is to have him fixed." Pursing his lips together, Mr. Obermeyer stalks off with Princess strutting beside him.

I don't care if Mutt isn't a purebred. He's mine. And

Avi gave him to me, which makes him more valuable than any purebred.

Oh, no! Avi.

I run over to Mutt and clasp the leash on him. I walk back home, but stay a safe distance behind Mr. Obermeyer and his bitch, waiting long enough for them to reach the condo before I venture into the elevator with my stud.

I find Avi sitting on our couch, his elbows resting on his knees and his hands clasped together.

"Sorry it took so long," I say, releasing Mutt and hanging the leash back on the hook. "There was kind of a commotion at the dog park." I look over at Mutt, who is now stretched out on his back on the floor looking more relaxed and content than I've ever seen him.

What am I going to tell my dad about Princess and Mutt?

"I thought you ditched me," Avi says, the side of his mouth quirked up. "Amy, the more I'm here, the more I realize this was a bad idea."

I step around the couch and sit next to him. "Don't say that. There's just a lot going on right now."

His midnight eyes are so different from Nathan's. They're brooding, just like my dad's. I can tell he's been through a lot just by staring into them. He's worried about something but he's trying not to show it.

"How's the Israeli army?" I ask.

"*Sababa*," he says.

"What's *sababa*?"

"It means 'cool, awesome, no problem.'" He talks in

that deep, dark voice of his that can melt my own invisible walls I've built around myself.

"You look bigger and more muscular than this summer." Most American guys I know don't look as serious or manly at eighteen years old.

"Survival training will do that to a guy."

I nod. Survival training. My survival training consists of running to the racks at Neiman Marcus on the opening day of their winter blowout sale. It doesn't tone my muscles, but it definitely does hone my skills in sniffing out the best deals before anyone else can get to them. Kinda different than being stuck in a desert with a gun as your only companion. Although Neiman Marcus can be considered a battleground on those winter blowout days.

"I missed you," I say. I omit the fact that I've thought about him every single day since I came back from my trip to Israel. I also fail to mention that I've been having doubts about our relationship...or non-relationship, as it might be. And even though I'm totally blown away with seeing him again, I don't want to be a "friend with benefits." I want more.

Does he? And where does Nathan fit into all of this?

Ugh, I'm an emotional mess.

Avi's hand reaches out to mine. As he takes hold of it, the warmth and comfort I've been missing since the summer comes rushing back to me. His other hand touches my shoulder and slowly moves up, caressing my neck and cheek. I lean my cheek into his palm, the warmth of it drawing me in.

"I missed you, too," he says.

I tentatively lick my lips, scared for this first kiss that will tell both of us where we stand in this relationship. We've got a lot to live up to. Our summer makeout sessions were sensual and emotional and made me feel drugged without any chemicals or alcohol.

He leans forward, watching me. His eyes are fixed on mine. "I shouldn't want you so bad," he says, then his full lips capture mine.

It starts off like before. He brushes his lips over mine as if he's painting them...memorizing the shape and softness. I'm totally getting into it, but then my mind wanders. I have no clue why. Thoughts of Nathan, and Mutt's fiasco, and my mom's pregnancy, and the dates I keep bungling and...

When Avi's tongue reaches for mine, the events of the day are swirling in my head. And I have this nagging feeling I'm forgetting something really important, but I can't remember what. Especially while Avi's trying to take our kisses to the next level, concentrating is impossible.

I lean back and break the kiss.

Those beautiful brooding eyes are staring back at me. "What's going on? Is it that guy? Just *tell* me," he says.

Now I remember! With his lips on mine I couldn't think, but now my brain starts to function again. "I have to go to work," I say and hop off the couch.

18

Jonah tried to dis God by refusing to go to Nineveh as God commanded. The poor guy was thrown into the sea and sat in a fish's belly for three days as punishment (Jonah 2:1). Didn't Jonah know you can't hide from God—He knows everything. My boyfriend, however, doesn't. (Except when my friends open their big mouths.)

Avi insists on accompanying me to work.

When we enter the elevator again, I want to tell him everything that's been on my mind and why I'm confused. But there's no time. My life is spinning out of control and there's no button or switch to stop it. Time sucks that way.

"Avi," I say. I don't really have anything to tell him, I just want him to stop looking away from me.

"Yeah?" he says, turning to me. I wish I could tell what he's thinking.

"I'll see if I can get some time off work this week so we can do some Chicago sightseeing."

"I don't need sightseeing, Amy."

He doesn't have to say he came here for me. The fact

that he came all this way to spend a week in Chicago is flattering and overwhelming at the same time.

At the Perk Me Up! counter, I introduce Marla to Avi. Marla smiles wide and drops the cup she's holding so she can shake his hand. Then she giggles, which I've never seen her do before.

When I first met Avi it was a really confusing and awkward time in my life. To be honest, I was rebelling. Avi is the only guy who has ever challenged me. He stayed in the fight long enough to duke it out...mentally, of course. He's as strong on the inside as he is on the outside.

I'm taking care of customers. Avi sits on one of the big cushy chairs and waits. He's leaning back with his arms crossed in front of his chest and I can't believe he's actually here while I'm making skim vanilla lattes instead of spending time with him.

I glance over at him every time I have a free second. And when there's nobody else in the café, I ask Marla if I can make Avi one of my fave hot chocolate drinks.

"You didn't tell me he was visiting," Marla whispers while I'm mixing the drink.

"Yeah, well I didn't know. My dad did, though," I inform her as I top off the cocoa with a triple dose of vanilla-flavored whipped cream.

"And he forgot to tell you?"

"I guess they wanted it to be a surprise." I have yet to tell my dad I hate surprises. Surprises are like having your period in the middle of class. Initially you're shocked and confused, then you're embarrassed and have to deal with everyone staring at you. I'm self-conscious enough as it is; I don't need surprises in my life to make me feel more aware of people gawking at me.

Marla holds out a cup holder for me so I can slip it onto the perfectly made hot cocoa. "I miss my teenage years," she says with a wistful smile on her face. "Boys, school, friends. Enjoy it before you grow up and have more responsibilities than you ever signed up for."

I already feel like I have more responsibilities than I signed up for. And I'm only seventeen.

My specialty drink in hand, I walk over to Avi just as the door to Perk Me Up! opens. It's Jessica.

"I heard about what happened at the dog park today. Amy, are you okay?" Her hair is brown and stick-straight and her eyes look darker than usual because she's wearing a black top. It takes her a second to focus on the guy in the chair, but when she does, a little shriek escapes from her mouth. "Avi?" she asks, totally pointing like a little kid.

Avi stands and I clear my throat. "Jessica, this is Avi. Avi, this is my best friend Jessica."

"Call me Jess," she says, smiling so wide I think her cheeks are going to crack and her lips stretch out so much she reminds me of that elastic woman from the cartoon movie.

"Why didn't you tell me he was coming?" she says through gritted teeth although Avi can hear every word that's coming out of her mouth. Duh! He's standing right here.

"I didn't know," I say back. "It was a surprise."

"Oh."

Jess knows I hate surprises, thus the understanding "Oh" comment.

"What happened at the dog park today?" Avi asks.

I didn't really want to share the disaster so I just say, "Um…"

"Mutt humped another dog and impregnated her right in front of everyone," Jess blurts out. "The owner of the other dog almost called the cops."

"It was no big deal," I say, trying to blow it off. Well, at least I'm trying to make it look like I'm blowing it off. It actually is a major deal and my dad is going to kill me when he finds out Princess's womb is ruined because of my dog. And the fact that he might be a grandpa to a basketful of puppies in a few months.

"Amy, are you *kidding*? *Everyone* knows," Jess says.

Avi leans forward with a confused look on his face. "Why didn't you tell me?"

"I…I don't know." It's the truth.

I'd like to give Avi the hot chocolate concoction I made him, but the whipped cream is melting and running down the side of the cup onto my hand and it doesn't look as decadent and appetizing as it did before Jess came in the café. And now my hand is all grody and sticky from the melting, now lopsided whipped cream.

"I'm going for a walk," Avi says, obviously upset I've shut him out. I can't even blame him for being pissed as I watch him open the door and step out into the cold. I wish I could tell him what's going on, but how can I express it to him when I don't even have it all figured out.

So now it's just Jessica and me standing together. "Ooh, can I have that?" she says, eyeing the drink in my hand.

I shove my "Avi peace offering" at her and go back to working behind the counter.

Why can't things go my way? Is this God's way of entertaining me so I don't have a boring life? I swear, for once I'd like to have a calm, uneventful day.

Marla is in the middle of blending the new Tango Mango Crème Blend for a customer. The entire café now smells like mangoes.

"Can I have the rest of the week off?" I ask her. "I'll work double the hours next week."

"It's okay with me."

Jessica has parked herself at a computer terminal when I start wiping down the tables. "Can you please *not* tell Avi about my life?" I ask her.

"Why not?"

"Because if I want him to know something, I'll tell him. He doesn't need to hear it secondhand from my friends."

Jess cocks her head to the side and says, "What are you trying to hide from him, Amy?"

"Nothing."

Okay, that's not the honest truth. I'd like to hide the bad parts of me, and only share the awesome parts. You can't blame me. He's only here for a week. If he knows I screw up all the time there's no way he'll want to be my...non-boyfriend.

I'm seriously sick of referring to him as the "non."

Something in my life seriously needs to change.

19

Even though the Israeli army is strong, I worry about Israel. I pray for the safety of my family living in Israel and my boyfriend who is in the military there. Is there anything I can do to make this a more peaceful world?

I'm almost done with my shift at Perk Me Up! when, you guessed it, Nathan comes sauntering in. He walks up to the counter and says, "Medium green tea with ice, no sweetener."

He doesn't even look at me. He's focused on the sugar packets next to the register. And he's obviously not interested in sugar packets because he doesn't like his drinks sweetened.

Marla is standing next to me, humming a little tune as she's purposely trying not to pay attention to the interaction between me and Nathan.

When I hand Nathan his drink, he says, "Where's Abi?"

"His name is Avi, and you know it."

Nathan takes a sip of his cold tea while looking at me above the rim of the cup. When he stops drinking he says, "Whatever…" mimicking our previous conversation. "Did he ditch you already?"

It wouldn't hurt so bad if it wasn't so close to the truth. "No. Can't you see I'm working?"

"I'm a customer. I think you're supposed to be nice to customers."

I turn to Marla, who is not pretending to ignore our conversation anymore. "Go on," she says. "Don't mind me. This is extremely entertaining. I think I might even start charging admission…or start a Perk Me Up! open mic night."

Taking a deep breath, I shake my head and turn back to Nathan. He's still standing at the counter. The guy won't leave.

He leans forward and whispers, "You don't like me because I'm a geek…dork…lame…weak sauce…whatever you want to label me."

"That's not true," I say.

"Oh, yeah? Then why are you so hung up on this Avi dude? Tell me his brain is as big as his biceps."

"Not that it's any of your business, but as a matter of fact he's really smart. You don't always have to judge people by their grades. Being fun and outgoing and street-smart is important, too."

"If you're so hung up on the guy, why did you kiss me in the elevator? Oh, that's right. You did it as a joke."

"Did not."

"Yeah, right. Plastic girls like you like to play with people's lives. You never think about the consequences of your actions or who you'll hurt."

My mouth goes wide. Is Nathan kidding? I wouldn't kiss him as a joke, or even a dare. I kissed him because I wanted the upper hand. If he started liking me because of our kiss, I could control our relationship. I could make him hate me or like me. I admit it was manipulative.

Nathan's glasses slip on his nose and he pushes them back up. "I bet if I acted cool and dressed cool you'd dump that Avi guy and want to date me."

"Wanna bet?"

The door to the café opens. It's Avi. And he doesn't look happy that I'm talking to Nathan. Nathan must sense my hesitation because he takes his iced tea without sweetener and stomps off to his usual chair to study.

Marla taps me on the shoulder. "You can go, Amy. Your shift is up."

Thank the Lord.

I peel off the yellow apron. I lift myself on my tiptoes and give Avi a huge smooch while wrapping my arms around him. That'll show him how much I missed him, Nathan how much Avi means to me, and everyone else (including Jessica) how important Avi is in my life.

Taking my cue, Avi wraps his arms around me. "Let's get out of here," he whispers against my mouth, then takes my hand and we leave the café together as a couple.

I think the ice has broken between us as we step out into the cold night air. My cell phone rings. It's my dad. "Hey, *Aba*," I say into my phone.

"Did you get a big surprise today?"

"Yep. He's standing right beside me." I'll talk to my dad later about the new "no surprise rule" I'm about to set up.

"Let's all meet for dinner. How about Rosebud?"

Rosebud is an unbelievable Italian place on Rush Street right near our building. On a Saturday night it's one of the most crowded restaurants in the city. "Sure."

"I'll be there in a half hour."

"Cool. See you there."

I hang up and hadn't even realized I was leading Avi away from our building and Rosebud. I notice we're not holding hands anymore. We're headed toward the beach even though Lake Michigan is freezing and the wind is blowing hard enough to make my face freeze up, making it hard to talk.

"I thought if I told you I was coming you'd tell me not to," Avi says. We're still walking, both of us looking straight ahead at the lake peeking through the city streets.

I want to grab his hand and hold it as we walk, but he's got both of his fists stuffed inside the front pockets of his jeans. "I thought you forgot about me," I say.

He gives a short laugh. "I didn't have time, Amy. I was in basic training, remember?"

I'm totally aware that other girls walking past us on the Chicago city streets are checking him out. Will it always be like that? Does he exude that charisma and confidence on purpose? "What if you did have time, Avi?" I ask him. "Would you find someone else, some pretty Israeli girl to replace me?"

"Why? So you wouldn't feel guilty starting a relationship with that guy Nathan?"

"I kissed you in front of him, Avi. Like I'd do that if I liked him."

"You did it to make him jealous," he says matter-of-factly.

"Did not. Besides, you don't even want a real relationship. You made that clear last summer. No commitments, no boyfriend/girlfriend stuff. You know what I tell my friends…that you're my *non*-boyfriend. Do you know how that makes me feel? Well, I'll tell you, Mr. Israeli Tough Guy. It makes me feel terrible, like I'm not worth the time or effort or emotion to put into a real relationship."

I swallow, but it's not easy because my throat is starting to close up from emotion. Most of the time I try to keep my emotions deep inside, far from the surface. So this sucks, doubly so because it's Avi, the one person I don't want to get too emotional with because I know it'll just push him away.

He tries to pull me toward him, but I swat his hand away. I don't want his sympathy. I want his love.

What feels the worst is that I don't even think he's capable of giving it. God knows he'd never say it.

"I don't know what you want," he says, totally frustrated now. "Amy, I'm sorry. I thought we had this all worked out."

"Yeah, well, we don't. Why did you come here? Just to screw around with my life?"

"No," he says, pulling me into his chest and this time

doesn't let me resist. Holding me tight, he whispers into my hair, "I finished combat basic training and am assigned to a specialized fighting unit. The IDF is taking a different approach to terrorism; they're going to teach us how to think, act, and be the enemy." He takes a deep breath and says, "I don't know if I'll get authorization to contact you in the summer when you visit."

20

Jacob had twelve sons. Each became one of the twelve
tribes of Israel (Numbers 1:4).
I wonder what tribe my decendants are from. I'm sure the
Internet doesn't track birth records from that far back.

It takes a few minutes for me to comprehend what Avi just told me. Specialized fighting unit. Being the enemy. I pull back and look into his eyes. "We're supposed to see each other next summer when I come to visit. You promised me."

"I got time off now instead."

"Where are you going to be living in the summer?"

Avi gives me a small smile. "I'll be traveling a lot."

"In the Middle East?" I ask.

"Yes. And Europe."

"I don't like that," I tell him. "Not one bit." Taking a look at my watch, I realize we better head to Rosebud or my dad will be worried. "My dad's meeting us for dinner," I tell Avi, then start walking but I feel like I'm in a trance.

Avi takes his place right next to me. "Did I freak you out?" he asks.

"Yep." Totally freaked me out. All these thoughts are running through my head, especially the ones where men are captured and tortured and mutilated. I mean, it's inhumane what's going on in the world. I seriously like my life right here, as safe as I could be in a big city like Chicago.

I'm silent the rest of the walk to Rosebud. My dad is already there, sitting and waiting at a table. He waves us over and stands up to shake Avi's hand and to pat him on the back. Does my dad know? Does he have any idea Avi is about to risk his life for Israel just like he did at Avi's age?

I roll my eyes as they immediately start speaking in Hebrew, strange words and sounds pouring out of their mouths super fast. My phone vibrates with a text message. I read it under the table.

Jess: Where did you run off to?
Me: Dinner
Jess: Avi ok?
Me: Yep.
Jess: Does he know you XOXOed Nathan?
Me: NO!!!!!!!!!!!!!!!

The waitress is standing over to our table, but the guys are oblivious.

"I'll have a Coke," I tell her. "No ice. No lemon." There's nothing worse than watered-down Coke.

"Got it. And for the gentlemen?"

The *gentlemen* are gurgling and gargling their way

through a very intense conversation. They're probably talking about Avi's army training because my dad is totally concentrated and impressed with whatever Avi's talking about. Boys and their gun talk…

I just want to forget about guns and army and elite forces these next seven days. I'm going to treat his military service as if it doesn't exist. Ignorance keeps me sane sometimes. "When you're ready to speak Engish, just wake me up," I say, then lay my head down on the table.

"Sorry, sweetheart," my dad says. "I was just telling Avi your mom is pregnant."

"Thanks, *Aba*," I tell him sarcastically. "I'm sure I couldn't have told him that myself." I don't understand why everyone in my life just can't keep their mouths shut.

As my temperature is rising and my heart is pounding, I feel Avi's hand reach under the table for mine. As soon as our fingers touch, I take a calming breath. It's as if Avi knew I was starting to panic about everything. He gets big brownie points for this.

Even though I'm usually carb-conscious, I can't resist the warm bread at Rosebud. The loaf is crunchy on the outside and soft and warm on the inside. Taking the jug of olive oil, I pour some of the golden liquid onto my little appetizer plate and spoon parmesan cheese on top.

Avi is staring at me strangely. "What are you doing?"

"Tell me you've never dipped bread in oil and parmesan."

"I've dipped pita into hummus," he says.

"Not the same." I rip off a piece of bread and hand it to Avi. "Here, try it."

He tries it and nods. "That's awesome. Totally unhealthy, but awesome."

When our dishes come, Avi digs in to his food with gusto.

His mouth is going to get spoiled eating Chicago food. We have the best restaurants in the entire country, the largest portions, and probably one of the highest obesity rates.

"Are you watching me eat?" Avi asks, slowing his chewing rate.

"I just want to make sure you like it."

"Amy, in the army you get eggs, jam, bread, and slow-cooked meat. As long as I'm not eating any of those, I'm in heaven."

My dad laughs, then goes into a long, detailed story on the horrible food they served when he was in the army. I stop listening when he talks about bees being stuck in the jam. The rest of the dinner is okay, except that it's mostly my dad and Avi talking and me just wondering when I can get some alone time with my non-boyfriend.

I guess now is better than ever to break it to my dad before he finds out from someone else. "Mutt kind of had an incident this afternoon at the dog park."

Both of them look at me.

"What kind of incident?" my dad asks.

I start peeling away the nail polish from the manicure I just had. "He sort of impregnated Princess. Well, I'm not one hundred percent sure, but Mr. Obermeyer seems to think he did and he's more of an expert on these things than I am."

My dad's hand slaps over his face and he squeezes his eyes shut. "Please tell me you're joking."

"Mr. Obermeyer almost called the police." Then I blurt out, "But he didn't, so it's okay."

"Okay? *Okay*? Amy, I told you Mutt needs to be fixed."

I throw my hands up in the air and say, "I get it, Dad."

"A little late, don't you think?"

I stand up, glad the meal is over, and start walking out of the restaurant. The last thing I need is for Avi to see me and my dad fight. He probably already thinks I'm the drama queen everyone accuses me of being.

Avi catches up to me at the front door. "Amy," he calls out.

I stop and turn around. "I'm not the girl you thought I was, Avi. I screw up my life, like ninety-nine percent of the time. I'm like a mistake that won't stop." I was born a mistake and will always be one.

Avi grabs my shoulders and makes me face him. "Say one good thing."

"Huh?"

"One thing that's not a mistake. One thing you don't screw up."

I search through the recesses of my brain to come up with something, with no luck. "That's the problem, Avi. I screw up *everything*."

My dad comes out of the restaurant before we can finish our conversation. He looks tired and worn out.

"*Aba*, I'm sorry about the Mutt fiasco," I say. "I didn't mean for it to happen."

"I know," my dad says. "I know," he repeats. "Listen, I'll take care of Mr. Obermeyer, Amy. You just keep a better eye on Mutt. Deal?"

"Deal."

We start walking back to the condo and Avi takes my hand in his, then blows on my fingers with his warm breath. It feels so good. I want to moan and give him my other hand, too, but then I'd have to shuffle sideways and that would be dorky.

At the condo, Mutt runs into the foyer so fast he can't stop on the tile floor and flies into the wall. I look over at Avi, who's smiling with those sexy lips of his that were on mine a few hours ago. Avi, his lips, and that kiss stressed me out.

Right now, those lips formed in a tender smile make me less stressed.

"Mutt needs a walk," I say, then grab his leash and clip it to his collar.

I have to say, that's one negative thing about living in the city. In the 'burbs, people just open their doors and dogs run outside in their own yards and do their thing. In the city, it's a whole ordeal. Poop bags, leashes, elevators…

"I'll take him," my dad says, stepping forward and taking the leash from me.

"Cool." I give him a kiss on the cheek. "Thanks, *Aba*."

My dad says something in Hebrew to Avi which I obviously can't understand. Avi steps away from me. Oh, God, I hope my dad didn't warn Avi away from me like he did over the summer. Sometimes fathers can be too overprotective. If anything, this summer Avi was the one who stopped us from going too far physically, not me. It was like one minute I was a sane sixteen-year-old who had always vowed to be a virgin when I got married to one who was questioning everything because I was caught up in the moment with a guy who I had a major connection with.

"Be good," my dad says right before he leaves us alone in the foyer.

Parents shouldn't say "be good." If they know teenagers rebel against authority, saying "be good" to a teen is asking for trouble. I'm tempted not to "be good" just to show him how independent I am.

"What are you thinking?" Avi asks.

I swallow, hard. "Nothing. Nothing at all."

"You seem nervous. You don't have to be nervous."

Yeah, I do, when I'm thinking about being a rebel. "I'm not," I say, then start walking backward. "Do you want a tour of the condo?"

"*Ken.*" I know enough Hebrew to know that *ken* means "yes."

I start rambling while showing him the kitchen, the bathroom, the office, my dad's room, and finally my own bedroom.

In my room, Avi eyes the perfumes on my dresser and the messy, unmade bed. I lean down nonchalantly and pick up yesterday's panties off the floor and throw them into the closet with the rest of the clothes I have to wash. "I'm not usually this messy, and if I knew you were coming and you didn't *surprise* me, I would have actually cleaned up for you."

Avi picks up a picture of me, Jessica, and Cami on Halloween last year. We dressed as the three blind mice. We all wore black leotards with tails, ears, and black sunglasses. "Cute," he says.

I sit on my bed and hug an old Care Bear my mom bought me when I was six and had gotten my tooth knocked out when I was learning how to ride a bike. She let go and instead of me pedaling faster, I turned my head to make sure she was still holding on. When I realized she wasn't, I totally panicked and stopped so fast the bike fell over and I hit the pavement teeth first. I was okay, until I saw my mom's face. She was panicked, and when I wiped my mouth with the sleeve of my shirt and saw it full of blood, I cried so hard it took me over an hour to stop doing that heavy, jerky I'm-trying-to-stop-crying-but-can't breathing.

I bet if Avi saw me back then, in hysterics and snot running down my bloody face, he wouldn't think I was so cute.

I've grown up since then. Well, sort of. I still hate riding bikes. I prefer walking. And deep water scares me, but Avi already knows that.

Avi studies my tennis trophies I won, lined up on my shelf. "You still play?" he asks.

"Not on the team." I didn't make the team this year, partly due to the fact that I didn't go to tennis camp last summer. It's also partly because I've been really busy with conversion class and hanging with friends. Being on a team at CA is totally time-consuming and I missed a whole day of tryouts to go on Jess's parents' boat the day before they were going to sail it to Wisconsin and dock it there for the winter. Before this year I would have never thought anything was more important than getting on the tennis team.

Avi focuses on the picture of him on my nightstand. "I remember that picture. It was your last day in Israel."

"It was before you were in the army."

He nods slowly.

"Do you hate it?"

"What, the army? I'm proud to serve my country, if that's what you mean. All guys get a high on the range, shooting a weapon so strong it could take out an entire three-story building. Makes you feel invincible."

"But you're not."

"You learn that, too. Especially during combat training. With an instructor trained in kicking ass, watch out."

"Eww." I'd be flunking combat training for sure. I'm not into physical pain, inflicting it on myself OR others. It's no surprise Mutt isn't neutered.

"It's not the torture that'll mess with people. It's the mind games." Leaning back on my dresser, he catches his bottom lip with his teeth and looks straight at me.

He looks so adorable I just want to run over to him and hug him tight until I feel all safe and secure in his arms. "What?" I say, totally self-conscious that he's staring at me as if he's memorizing my face.

"I think of you. During the toughest training, when my mind gets weak and I have dark thoughts, I've thought of you."

"Me? I'm Disaster Girl, remember?"

"No. You're the only girl I know who expects life to be perfect and gets pissed off when it's not. You're the girl who's not only beautiful and has a kick-ass body, but you're funny when you don't mean to be and would rather eat dirt than back down from a fight."

"I hate most things."

"Give me one thing you hate."

"Olives."

"But you love sushi."

"I'm not fond of my stepdad, Marc."

"But you're close with your dad now."

"My room is messy."

His eyes rest on my closet and the clothes bursting out of it. "Yeah, it is."

Taking my Care Bear, I throw it at him. He catches the stuffed animal with one hand. "Be careful who you throw things at, Amy."

"Why? What're you going to do?" I take one of my pillows and fling it at him. With his free hand, he catches it without flinching.

He cocks an eyebrow. "You're just asking for trouble."

"I'm already trouble." Picking up my last pillow, I pull it back. "You have no more hands," I tell him. "What are you going to do now?"

Before I have a chance to fling it, Avi pounces on the

bed and pins me down while holding my hands at my sides and my legs with his feet.

"Is this what you learned in combat training?" I ask him, laughing and trying to escape so I can best him, but no such luck. The guy is pure, lean muscle. I'll bet he has, like, zero percent body fat. I'll bet my boobs alone have more body fat than his entire body.

He's sitting on top of me, but with just enough weight for it not to hurt. "Judge your enemy's strengths…and weaknesses," he says.

"Am I the enemy, Avi?"

"Are you? Because right now I can sense you're scheming. That overactive mind of yours is planning an escape."

"How did you know?"

"I can see it in your eyes," he says. "And I feel the adrenaline radiating off your body."

My heart is beating fast and I'm anxious, but not because I want to escape. I haven't been this close to a boy since this summer, when Avi and I went touring through Israel. I want him to kiss me now, like before. But he doesn't. Why?

"Amy, I'm back!" I hear my dad's voice yell from the foyer. Avi jumps off my bed faster than he got on it and reclaims his position leaning on my dresser.

When my dad peeks his head in the doorway of my room, he looks from me to Avi. I've managed to sit upright, but my comforter is all messed up and I'm sure my hair isn't much better.

"Avi, why don't you wait in the living room while I talk to Amy a minute."

Avi rubs his hand over his crew cut, stalling, and I can tell he wants to stay and be my protector.

"Dad, you're embarrassing me," I say after I tell Avi to wait in the living room so he doesn't have to hear my dad's lecture.

"This won't take long, Amy. Just cool it."

"If it's about sex, Mom already told me about it."

"Yeah, well now you're going to get the Dad version, okay?" He rubs his hands together as if he's about to do some heavy weightlifting. The noise of his dry hands making sandpaper sounds makes me wish I'd forced him to buy the hand cream the manicure lady suggested he get. He clears his throat and says, "No sex."

"Got it. Thanks for the talk, Dad. Totally helped. Glad we're on the same page."

"Amy…" he says in a warning tone.

I moan, situate my pillows which are strewn across my bed, and lean back on them. "What?"

"Avi is eighteen, a man. You *just* turned seventeen—"

"Over a month ago," I interrupt.

"Yes, well, guys are different than girls. Guys, um, have urges and, um, so you have to be careful, and uh, your own body is changing and, uh, you know. You might be having, um, feelings, too…"

All those ums and uhs are making my brain twitch.

"*Aba*, maybe you should have gone to that seminar our school had last year about talking to your kids about sex.

Mom went. She said to be careful; there's a lot of diseases. And to protect myself at all times, no matter what. And that if a guy tells me I have to do something in order for him to like me, then I should give him the old heave-ho. And that the risks of having sex at my age *so* outweigh the benefits. And that I can still be a teenager and liked without exploiting myself or my values. Does that cover it?"

He looks stunned. "I guess so."

"Don't you trust Avi?"

"Honey, I don't trust any guy with my daughter. And something funky was going on here between you two before I came back."

"*Aba*, nothing was going on."

My dad bends down, picks up my Care Bear from the floor, and tosses it to me. "You can't pull the wool over these Israeli eyes."

"You're an Israeli with paranoid eyes," I tell him.

"That's a good thing. Call it an occupational hazard. We need to set up a few rules now that Avi's here."

I hate the word "rules." It diminishes your fun, freedom, and spontaneity. "Hit me with 'em," I say, knowing it's no use arguing.

"No boys in your bedroom. You and Avi can hang out in the family room, living room, and kitchen."

"*Aba*, I was just giving him a tour of the condo."

"Sure," he says, obviously not believing me. "Rule number two: no sneaking out to the living room to visit Avi in the middle of the night."

"Why don't you just lock me in the room so I don't escape," I say sarcastically.

"Don't tempt me, Amy."

I roll my eyes. "Dad, a lot of my friends are more experienced than I am."

"That's their parents' problem, not mine."

I stand and face him. "I mean, if I wanted to do something I'd have done it. I'm not ready. Don't worry."

Before he can continue his lecture, I open the door and find Avi. He's going through his duffle in the living room.

"Everything okay?" he asks.

"I got the sex lecture," I tell him.

"Avi, *boyenna b'vakasha*," my dad calls out.

Oh, no. "What did he say?"

Avi stands. "I think I'm about to get the sex lecture, too." He walks to the back of the condo, where my dad is. Oh, great.

Why doesn't my dad trust me? I mean, I'm not the kind of kid who usually rebels by hanging out with druggies and drinkers. I'm clean cut. Okay, so I've stolen my dad's credit card and this summer I had feelings for Avi that surprised me...and I tested those feelings. But isn't that what teenagers are supposed to do?

I eye Avi's open duffle. Not much in there besides jeans, socks, shirts, and underwear—those tight boxer-ones like the ones in the Calvin Klein ads.

Behind me someone's clearing their throat. I jerk myself up, startled, and turn to Avi.

He nods, then says, "I got the sex lecture."

"Was it harsh?"

"Let's just say your dad tried to convince me he has the knowledge to kill me with one finger."

My dad walks into the room, looking pretty smug I might add. Sure, he just threatened Avi's life if he probably so much as looked at me.

"Arg!"

Mutt is oblivious as he takes a squeaky hamburger in his mouth and drops it at my feet. I pick it up and throw it down the hallway. He bolts after it and brings it back for another round.

"I met with Mr. Obermeyer downstairs when I took Mutt for his walk," my dad informs me as he watches Mutt slide past him. "We had a long talk, which seems to be the theme of my day."

"And?"

"And he said he's taking Princess to the vet tomorrow to see if she's pregnant. If she is, we'll deal with the consequences then."

"Thanks, *Aba*."

"It'll all work out; don't worry. Listen, I've got some work to do and you've got school tomorrow, so I think you should both say your goodnights and go to bed."

Since Avi's bed is the couch, I pull out of the hall closet bed linens and a blanket. I feel Avi's eyes on me as we make the bed together. "I wish we were back in Israel," I say. "This summer we had no rules to deal with, nobody telling us what we can and can't do...it was awesome."

"This is your dad's territory, his house, and his rules."

"Goodie for me." Isn't this my territory and my house, too? When can I start making my own rules up? Or be trusted enough not to have any rules?

When the couch is transformed into a bed, I turn to Avi. "You can use the bathroom to get ready first."

"*Todah*," he says, grabbing a toothbrush, toothpaste, and blue flannel pants.

"You're welcome."

I hurry into my room and dress in a tank and shorts, my usual pajama attire. I sit on my bed and stare at the picture of Avi on my nightstand and can't believe he's really here . . . in my house, in my life again. It's not as perfect as it was in Israel, but there's something about Avi that calms my soul.

At the same time, I try to warn myself that he's only here for a week and not forever. He's leaving soon and I'll be left alone again...no date for the Valentine's Dance, no date for New Year's Eve, no date for Valentine's Day, and no date for the Fourth of July fireworks if the summer trip to Israel doesn't go through.

Nathan'll be around, though. Every day.

Why am I thinking about Nathan when Avi is here? I don't even like Nathan, or his emerald eyes.

Surely I gave Avi enough time to change and brush his teeth. But the door to the bathroom opens just as I reach it and Avi comes out...shirtless, with his hair wet from showering.

Bronzed skin, chocolate eyes, hair that looks almost black when wet. "Hi," I say.

He rakes his fingers through his wet hair. "Sorry I took so long. I needed a shower. I felt dirty from the flight and all."

"I think I'm gonna need that sex talk again," I whisper, then give him a self-conscious smile and move past him to lock myself in the bathroom.

Looking at myself in the bathroom mirror, I wonder what makes Avi think I'm on the same level looks-wise as him. My teeth aren't perfect, my top lip disappears when I smile, my hair is too frizzy, and my boobs are a cup size too big. I even kept my bra on with my pjs because I don't want Avi noticing how much my *boobage* sags when I unleash "the girls."

He said that he likes me because I expect life to be perfect. Who doesn't fight for things to go their way? I guess some people, even Jessica, settle for the status quo. It's in my nature to fight. I guess I can blame that trait on my dad.

I've also come to realize that with turning seventeen, I've become boy crazy. I think about them all the time. It started when I met Avi, and hasn't stopped. Sometimes I'll think about boys at the strangest times, like in conversion class or even when I'm shopping. Last week when Jessica was telling me about her dance competition, my mind wrapped around the word "dance" and my thoughts wandered to when I was in Israel this past summer at a disco and I watched Avi dance. He's an amazing dancer, so comfortable moving his body to music, unlike most guys I know.

Maybe the rules are a good thing, after all.

I peek into the living room before I go to bed. Avi is

laying on the couch, the blanket covering his bottom half but his toned chest is exposed. He's got one arm resting behind his head, which makes his bicep tense up.

"What?"

"Are you on steroids or something?"

He laughs. "You ever try holding a Kalashnikov assault rifle over your head while walking five kilometers in water up to your waist twice a day. Your arms would be just as big. The gun touches the water, you get another kilometer tacked on."

No thank you very much. "I thought you trained in the desert."

"We did that, too. It's either holding the *jerikon* full of water, which is over twenty kilos, or being one of four supporting the heaviest guy in the unit on a stretcher while running. And no matter where you are, if the unit leader tells you to drop on the ground, you go down…whether it's on sharp rocks or not."

"How did you get the scars on your arms?" I ask, now focused on the raw skin on his forearms.

"Ground-crawling exercises. Fun stuff. Now can we stop talking about the army?"

"What do you want to talk about?" I sit on the edge of the mahogany coffee table in front of the couch.

"Tell me about your city. What makes it so special?"

Chicago is unique, unlike any place in the world. I can say just one thing about it and start rambling. "We have world-famous museums, the largest indoor aquarium, every sport team you could imagine with dedicated-to-the-death fans. We have Lincoln Park Zoo, one of the only free zoos in the country and the Harold Washington library, which is the largest of its kind in the world. We have three of the tallest buildings in the world and the best food in the entire country, which includes pizza, sushi, hot dogs, and Italian beef. You want me to go on?"

Avi sits up. "Your eyes light up when you talk about your city."

"I love Chicago. I was born at Weiss Memorial not too far away from here and have lived here my whole life. My mom moved to the suburbs so now I live with my dad. I can't stand not being here. The energy of the city is contagious. My mom and her new husband are having a baby in their new house, anyway, and don't need me hanging around."

"Does it bother you that they're going to have a kid?"

I chip more polish off my nails. "Yeah. It's going to change our whole family. Just when I'm trying to get used to a permanent man in my mom's life, I now have to deal with a baby. It's totally strange. I'm, like, confused about where my family begins and where it ends. No small nuclear family for me. In fact, I don't even know who my immediate family is anymore."

I've never been a fan of change, and my life has changed way too much in the past six months.

"Amy, I thought you were in bed," my dad says from the hallway.

"I was just saying goodnight to Avi."

My dad watches us as if he's a guard in the Israeli military.

"*Lyla tov*, Amy," Avi says, then winks at me.

I guess my night is over, whether I want it to be or not. "Goodnight," I say, then go back to my room and text Jessica.

> *Me: You there?*
> *Jess: Yep, was waiting 4 u to text me. How's the hottie?*
> *Me: Kewl*
> *Jess: What, no details?*
> *Me: There are none*
> *Jess: Liar. U kiss him yet?*
> *Me: Yes*
> *Jess: And?*
> *Me:*
> *Jess: What's wrong?*
> *Me: Wasn't the same.*
> *Jess: Can I have him, then?*
> *Me: NO!!!!!!!!!!!!!!!!!!!!!!!!!!!!*
> *Jess: Just kidding. Gee, Amy, no need 2 yell. Didn't know u were so territorial.*
> *Me: I'm not. OK I am.*
> *Jess: U confuse me.*
> *Me: I confuse myself. And I'm tired.*
> *Jess: Me, 2*
> *Me: I'm going to bed. C u tomorrow.*
> *Jess: Bye, chica*
> *Me: Lyla tov*

21

Oil production of Saudi Arabia: 9.475 million barrels per day
Oil production of Iran: 3.979 million barrels per day
Oil production of Iraq: 2.093 million barrels per day
Oil production of Egypt: 700,000 barrels per day
Oil production of Syria: 403,800 barrels per day
Oil production of Israel: 2,740 barrels per day
Do you think Moses made a wrong turn somewhere?

The next day I leave Avi with a map of Chicago and a key to our condo before I catch the bus to school. No amount of begging my dad to stay home and ditch the algebra/trig test today so I can stay home with Avi worked. Nathan isn't at the bus stop, so I'm standing alone. On the bus, Jess is eager to grill me.

"So? How was it last night after we texted each other?" she asks before I even sit down.

"Uneventful. I went to bed." And neglected to do my homework, but I'm hoping to ignore that issue until I'm forced to deal with it. A person can only handle so much at one time.

"And this morning?"

"I took a shower, ate breakfast with Avi and my dad, and left for school."

Jess looks disappointed there isn't more to the story. I am, too. I wish I had more exciting news to tell her, but I'm not about to make anything up.

"I hear you're going to be a mom," Kyle says from the seat behind us.

"Don't know yet," I say, playing along so no one realizes how freaked out I am about Mutt's little escapade yesterday.

Mitch, who has been hiding in the back row of the public CTA bus in an obvious attempt to avoid being confronted by a jilted Jessica, says, "Dude, that dog is an *animal.*"

Yes, he is. And yes, he's mine.

"Where's Nathan, Amy?" Roxanne asks.

"How would I know?"

"He's your boyfriend, isn't he? Or are you just going to the Valentine's Dance with him out of pity?"

Pity? Nathan doesn't need pity from me. Okay, so he needs a new wardrobe...but not pity.

"For your information," Jess says, turning around, "Amy has a boyfriend, and he's in town visiting her. Nathan was just a...a brain fart."

Oh, I'm sure Nathan will definitely appreciate being described as a fart. Sometimes Jess gets me in more trouble than I'm already in and has no clue she's done it.

"You guys should come to my place tonight," Kyle says.

"My p's are out of town. A bunch of us are gonna hang out."

Jessica says, "I can't."

"What about you, Amy? You can even pick one of the guys in your harem to bring," Kyle says.

It is Friday, and I am committed to showing Avi a great time while he's here. It wouldn't hurt to stop by Kyle's and hang out. Avi might actually like it. In the dark recesses of my mind, I'm a little excited to show Avi off to Roxanne, who'll inevitably show her face. She's always hanging on Kyle and his friends like one of those disgusting neck skin tags.

I find myself promising I'll be at the party with Avi. I turn back around and lean in to Jessica. "Where are you going tonight?"

"Youth group meeting."

Oops. I forgot I was supposed to go with her and Miranda again. "Are you upset if I don't go with you guys? I mean, Avi is here and all…"

"That's cool," she says. "We're supposed to do a scavenger hunt together, but Miranda and I can do it without you."

I think Avi would think a scavenger hunt with the teen youth group would be lame. I'm convinced he'll have a better time at a party where everyone is dancing and hanging out. Besides, I think he's had enough organized activities in Israel lately; he doesn't need another one while he's on vacation.

During lunch, Jess is sitting at Miranda's table and not at our usual spot. Nathan is sitting next to Miranda. They're all in a deep conversation.

I take my tray of the Chef's Pizza Special and sit next to Jessica. "What's so interesting?"

Miranda glances up and then back down at the paper she was writing on. She mumbles, "We're figuring out strategy for tonight."

"For the youth group thing?"

Jess looks up. "Yeah. We're dividing the city up into monuments, parks, and sports arenas."

I look up at Nathan. "Are you going?"

He puts his arm around Miranda and smiles at her. "Miranda invited me."

The poor girl looks nervous. "You don't mind, do you, Amy?"

"Why would I mind?"

"Well, you guys seem pretty close and everyone thinks you two have something going on." She says it as a statement and a question.

"Nathan has a girlfriend," I inform her.

"And Amy has a boyfriend," Nathan blurts out.

"Wait, I don't get it. If you have a boyfriend and he has a girlfriend, why are you going to the Valentine's Dance together?"

I open my mouth to say something, but nothing comes out.

Nathan takes his arm from Miranda's shoulder. "Now *that* is a great question."

"So what's the answer?" Jess asks impatiently.

"Well, since Avi will be back in Israel, and Bicky…well, I'm not convinced she's real but if she's not a figment of

Nathan's imagination she's, nonetheless, not in Chicago. So we're going together...as friends. Right?"

Nathan puts his hands up. "That pretty much sums it up, except for the part about my girlfriend being a figment of my imagination. She's real."

"What school does she go to?" Miranda asks.

Instead of answering, Nathan gathers his lunch, shoves it into his bag, and stands up. "I just remembered I forgot to study for my chem exam. I'll catch you guys after school."

"Sure thing," Jessica says. "What's his issue?" she asks when he's out of earshot.

Looking at the door Nathan just bolted out of, I say, "No clue. But if you guys find out, you gotta tell me. He lives with his aunt and uncle, he doesn't talk about his past or his parents, and never talks about any brothers or sisters. Something's off."

"Maybe he's an undercover police officer investigating something illegal at school. Or maybe he's a reporter doing an exposé on private schools."

I roll my eyes. "Miranda, I think you've been watching too much television." Nathan is definitely a teenager, as messed up and confused as I am.

I catch up to that messed up kid at his locker after school. "Miranda thinks you're an undercover reporter doing an exposé on private schools...or a cop." With those glasses and skinny frame you'd think he was Clark Kent. Nah, he's too skinny and wouldn't be able to fill out any Superman outfit.

"Cool."

"So, what's your deal? Why are you living out of a suit-case? Why do you bring flowers to someone every week? Why do you say you have a girlfriend but she's never around?"

Nathan shoves his books into his backpack. "Why do you care?"

"I don't know."

He slings the backpack around his back and glares at me. "Well, when you do know maybe then I'll tell you."

22

I was preparing for conversion class today and read the Bible scenario if a man suspects his wife was not a virgin when they got married. The woman, if found guilty, gets stoned to death by the men in her village. If the man is found to be proven wrong, he gets fined and flogged (Deuteronomy 22:18). I seriously need to have a talk with Rabbi Glassman about this. Because there are just so many things wrong with this scenario.

I take Avi to Kyle's party in the evening, ready to show my boyfriend off to all my school friends (besides Jessica, Miranda, and Nathan, who are doing the temple youth group scavenger hunt). With a huge smile on my face, I take Avi's hand and lead him through Kyle's condo. It's bigger than my dad's—Kyle's dad owns one of the best steak houses in Chicago and likes to show off his wealth with big cars, big condos, and big boats.

In the kitchen, Kyle passes out cans of beer. "Dude, you must be Amy's boyfriend," Kyle says with a slurred voice. He's plastered.

Avi declines the beer and Kyle tosses the can to me.

"You're not drinking, are you?" Avi asks.

To be honest, I think beer is gross. "Nope," I say, and toss the can back to Kyle, who mumbles something under his breath about sober people being boring.

Leading Avi to the back of the house where most of the crowd has gathered, we find an unoccupied chair. Avi sits on it and I park myself on his lap.

The music is loud in the back room, almost to the point that my ears are pounding to the bass of the song. While everyone else is either drinking or making out or trying to talk above the music, I lean into Avi's chest while he holds me close.

When I catch sight of Roxanne arriving, I quickly turn my head toward Avi and start to kiss him. Our lips touch first, then I slide my tongue over his while I slip my arms up his chest and around his neck. As I pull back, I lick my lips and give him a sexy, knowing smile.

He nuzzles his mouth close to my ear and says, "Why the big show?"

I turn my head and try to say to him so only he can hear me above the blaring song, "Don't you want to kiss me?"

"Yeah. But not with a bunch of drunk kids watching us."

"Are you saying I'm a kid?"

Before he answers, I hear Roxanne's squeaky voice saying, "Hi, Amy. Hi, Nathan."

I look up. Roxanne is standing next to us, her fingers over her open mouth while she gasps. "Oh, I'm sorry. I thought you were Nathan."

I'm in trouble. Avi is expressionless, but his arm loosens from around my waist.

"Why would she think you were kissing Nathan?" he asks me.

I clear my throat. "I can explain." Roxanne is still standing over us, a wicked smirk painted on her face. "Do you mind?"

Ignoring me, Roxanne holds out her hand. "I'm Roxanne."

"I'm Avi," he tells her in his slow, sexy Israeli accent as he shakes her hand. I swear she turns her hand as if she expects him to kiss the back of it. "I'm Amy's boyfriend from Israel."

Roxanne bursts out laughing. "Oh, I heard about you. So glad you and Amy decided to see other people. You're such an understanding guy."

When he releases her hand, I wave my fingers at her and say, "Shoo, go away." She's like an annoying gnat that I wish I could squash.

Roxanne moves away when Kyle walks in the room with a bottle of champagne.

"Did you kiss Nathan?" Avi asks.

Umm…"No. Roxanne is the enemy, Avi. Don't listen to her. She just likes spreading lies about me."

He stands (I have to pretend not to have fallen off his lap) and walks over to Roxanne. She cocks her head to the side and says, "Wanna play Spin the Bottle? You can, you know, switch partners. Amy likes switching partners, right?"

I try pulling Avi's hand to make him leave the room, but he's planted where he is like a stubborn tree root.

"I don't like people spreading rumors about my girl-friend."

I pull his arm more. "Avi, let's just leave."

Roxanne laughs. "Rumors? Dude, you're the second guy she's been locking lips with this week. And speak of the devil. Hi, Nathan. We were just talking about you and Amy's hot show in the cafeteria."

Oh, man. I'm toast. I look at the door and see Miranda, Jess, and Nathan walking toward us.

The entire room is silent for the moment while the next CD is put into the slot.

"Hey," Jess says. "We finished with the scavenger hunt and wanted to see if you were still here."

Avi knows the truth. He saw the way Nathan and I looked at each other just now. Is the guilt transparent in my eyes?

"You lied to me," he says.

Right in front of everyone he lets go of my hand and leaves me standing here in the middle of Kyle's party.

23

It's not so easy to convert as one might think. I still have to go before three respected Jewish community members called a "Bet Din" and take a verbal test. Rabbi Glassman told me not to stress over it; it's not like the SATs. Life is full of little SAT tests, though, isn't it?

"You made an ass out of me," he says after I catch up with him at the entrance to my building.

"Avi, I'm sorry. I didn't expect you to go up to Roxanne and get details."

He turns to me while we're in the elevator. "You looked me right in the eye and lied to me."

I put my hands up in surrender. "Okay, I admit it. I lied to you. Are you happy now?"

"Don't turn this around to make me the bad guy. Do you always go around kissing guys?" he asks when we reach my floor and step off the elevator. "Where's your loyalty and honor?"

I roll my eyes and say, "We're not in the army now, Avi."

"Maybe we should be."

"What's that supposed to mean?" When I open the door and walk inside my condo I turn to him, "Besides, where's *your* commitment?"

"Please, Amy. What would you know about commitment?"

I open my mouth wide in shock. "Screw you!" I yell, then go to my room and slam the door shut.

I can't remember how long it's been since I had a good cry. You know, one of those cries where you can't catch your breath and just when you think there can't possibly be any more tears coming out of your eyes, a new wave of desperation washes over you and you bawl all over again.

That's the way I'm crying right now. I feel so horrible I messed up with Avi. I feel so horrible that I want to figure out Nathan and what makes him the way he is. Nathan told me I liked Avi because of his looks and warned me if he looked as good I'd be after him, too.

I'm a terrible person. It's not Avi's fault, either. It's mine.

Avi knocks on my door after about a while.

"What?"

"Open the door and let me in."

"You aren't allowed in my room, remember?"

He knocks again, louder. "Then just open the door."

When I do, I see that he's got his duffle slung over his shoulder. "What are you doing?"

"This isn't working. You and I both know it. I'm going to stay with Tarik over at the Northwestern dorms. You remember Tarik, don't you?"

"Yeah, but—"

"He'll be here soon. Listen, Amy…you want to kiss other guys, that's cool. This thing between us wasn't going to last anyway."

"You *told* me not to wait. You *wanted* to be the non-boyfriend, remember?"

"What's in here," he says, pointing to his head, "and what's in here," he says, fist pounding on his heart, "are two different things."

I step forward and hold out my hand, wanting to ease his insecurity and the tension between us. "Avi…come here."

Instead of stepping forward, he steps back and points to his head. "Gotta keep my mind clear," he says. "Remember what I told you about the mind games?"

"Yeah. They're worse than the torture."

"God, I can't tell you how many irrational things are running through my head right now. Kissing you until you can't think straight. Kicking that Nathan guy's ass. Smashing the wall with my fist because you've been looking at other guys."

"I told you I'm the Disaster Girl."

"No, Amy. You've got your life here. Mine is in Israel or wherever the army sends me. It's the way it is; it's the way it was always meant to be. Who were we kidding, thinking this thing between us could work?"

I did, but I don't tell him. He's obviously given up the fight. "You're really leaving?"

"Tarik is probably downstairs waiting for me."

New tears start to come, damn it. I will them to stop, but

they won't. "I don't want you to go." I want to beg, plead, grab his leg and hang on until he agrees to stay...but I can't.

When he pets Mutt and walks to the door, I let him. And then I stay with him and walk outside where I recognize his friend Tarik in a car outside my building. Tarik steps out of the car and gives me a small hug. "Hey, Amy," he says. "It's been a while, huh?"

I wipe my nose and watery eyes with my sleeve. "How's school?" I ask.

"Tough, but I'm getting used to it." Tarik looks from me (obviously overwrought and devastated) to stone-faced Avi. "Um...you want me to get involved in this?"

"No," Avi says emphatically, while I tilt my head to the side and contemplate asking for intervention. Maybe what Avi and I need is third-party arbitration. I learned about arbitration in my social studies class last week and the magic of an unbiased party deciding your fate.

"Well, then...I guess I'll leave you two to say your goodbyes." Tarik heads back to the driver's side, but calls over his shoulder, "If you need me, just give a holler."

I'm tempted to holler.

Avi tosses his duffle into the back seat of Tarik's car, then turns to me. "I'll call you before I leave Chicago."

"I wanted to take you to the top of the Sears Tower. Every tourist has to go there."

"I'll go on my own."

"And what about Oz Park? Did you know the guy who wrote *The Wizard of Oz* lived here?"

"I'll figure it out."

"But what if you don't, Avi? What if you go back to Israel without seeing what Chicago has to offer?"

Avi cups my cheek with his palm. "It doesn't all have to be perfect. Life isn't perfect."

"I want it to be."

His thumb slowly caresses my face. "I know. It's what makes you unique." He squeezes his eyes shut, then says, "I gotta go before I do something stupid."

I watch as he sits in the passenger seat, says something to Tarik, and the car drives off.

After he leaves me alone, crying, and devastated, I want to kneel right here and start bawling all over again.

"You're not crying over that guy, are you?" I hear Nathan's voice behind me.

I face him and squint my eyes accusingly. "Have you been spying on me this whole time?"

"Nope. Why, was it a good breakup? 'Cause if it was, I'm sorry I missed it."

I walk up to Nathan, take my finger, and poke it into his chest. "You are the *rudest*, most *self-centered*, *dragon-eyed*, *inconsiderate*, *egotistical...*" I'm racking my brain to think of more words when Nathan takes my finger into his hand and stops me from poking him again.

Nathan's touch doesn't affect me like Avi's does. And for the first time it's clear Nathan isn't "The One" and never has been. I have a connection to him, but it's oh, so different than the connection I have with Avi.

I'm too weak to do anything else but slump my shoulders and cry. The pain is too great, like someone is ripping open my heart and squeezing it tight. My knees start to buckle and Nathan catches me.

"You really *are* upset, aren't you?" he says, staring at me with his eyebrows down and furrowed in sympathy. I've never seen Nathan have sympathy for anyone, especially me.

I squeeze my eyes shut. "I'm not as plastic as you accuse me of being."

"I guess not. Listen, Amy. I'm sorry. You're right about me. Well, except for the dragon-eyed part."

"What?"

"I played you. I played your boyfriend. It wasn't fair, I know. Sometimes I want everyone's life to be as screwed up as mine. Call it a self-defense mechanism."

He helps me stand. I wipe my nose and eyes with the sleeve of my shirt. "What's so wrong with your life, Nathan? Who are you? Make me feel better about my crappy life by sharing yours."

I understand why I'm insecure: my dad just came back into my life, my mom and her new husband are planning a family without me...and I don't know where my family life begins and where it ends.

"I'm a foster kid. Parents gave me up when I was ten because they couldn't afford all eight kids they had. I've been tossed from one foster home to another since then."

Wait, I don't get it. "I thought Mr. and Mrs. Keener were your aunt and uncle?"

"No other foster home would take me after they took a look at my file, so they were kind of forced into it by the courts. My aunt and uncle aren't on speaking terms with my parents. They cut all ties a long time ago. Something about marrying trailer trash makes you trailer trash."

I can't imagine my parents giving me away. Even when my dad and I weren't talking, he still tried. It was me who pushed him away. My mom raised me since she was in college, going to school and working while trying to juggle having a kid and getting a career going. I admire her so much. I don't think she ever considered giving me up.

"Why do you dress like—"

"Like I'm a dork?"

"Well, yeah."

"My aunt wants me to dress conservative. Thinks if I dress like a bad kid, I'll be a bad kid."

"Are you bad, Nathan?"

He focuses on the ground and shrugs. "I have been. You don't get kicked out of thirteen foster homes in seven years for being a model kid. "

"And now?"

"I guess I'm still fucked up." He looks at me. "I shouldn't have kissed you in front of everyone in the cafeteria. And…I have to admit…I knew your boyfriend was going to be at the party tonight and was secretly happy he found out we kissed. I know I hurt you, Amy."

The truth is I hurt myself. I let my insecurity and confused emotions overcome what I knew deep in my heart was right all along. I play a tough game, but inside I'm weak. Just like Nathan.

I hook my arm through Nathan's and say, "Do you have any ice cream at your place?"

"I think so. Vanilla, maybe."

"That'll do."

"You want to hang out with me?" he asks, totally shocked.

"Yeah. Isn't that what friends are supposed to do?"

"I've got to admit, I haven't had a friend in a long time. Don't know if I even know how to be one."

"What about Bicky?" I ask when we get in the elevator and head to the fortieth floor.

"She's a foster kid, too. I met her in a home in Freeport last summer."

"Where is she now?"

He takes a deep breath and says, "Rehab. She got into some bad stuff and is all messed up. I bring her flowers every Saturday, but they won't let me see her or talk to her. She receives my letters and notes, though."

Wow. And I thought my family life and love life were rough. I have the urge to go hug my mom and dad and thank them for hanging in there with me.

When we step into Nathan's condo, he turns to me. "Will you please change your shirt, it's got snot all over the sleeve. As your friend, I just want to be honest with you."

I look down at my snot-encrusted shirt. It is grotesque. "I'll be right back," I say, then trot over to my door.

I change my shirt and go back to the Keeners' place. When we're in Nathan's room, we hang out on his bed and dig into a tub of ice cream.

I look at Nathan. If you look past his geeky attire, you can see that he could possibly be cool. With a LOT of help.

"What are you looking at?" he asks, turning to me with his bright green eyes.

"I was just thinking that you don't have to dress different to appease your aunt and uncle. You should be yourself. If they kick you out for being you, well…I'm sure you could come live with me and my dad."

"We could be like brother and sister?"

"Yeah," I say, totally serious and meaning every single word. "Like brother and sister. And friends…great friends," I say, taking a spoonful of vanilla ice cream.

Those green eyes are starting to water.

"Nathan, are you crying?"

One lone tear falls down his cheek. "Yeah." He looks down and swipes the tear from his face. "I haven't had a sibling in a long time, Amy."

I hug him. To be honest, I think it's the first sisterly hug he's had in years.

"Do you really play the guitar?" I ask him, eyeing the black leather case on the floor while I try and lighten the mood.

"Used to be in a band, but it's kind of tough being a member of a group when you move as often as I have."

Picking up the guitar, I hand it to him. "Play something for me."

"Like what."

"A song. For me."

"Do you want me to make it up?"

"If you can."

"Okay…let's see. I'll call it 'My Sister Barbie.'"

Tzedakah is the commitment a Jew makes to give charity.
Tzedakah doesn't have to be all about money. It can be
doing mitzvahs (good deeds) for others less fortunate, too.
My friend Nathan needs a little Tzedakah thrown his way.

I bring Nathan to my mom's house in Deerfield the next morning for moral support. Last night Nathan convinced me to be honest with her and Marc about questions I have concerning the new baby.

My mom rushes out of the house and hugs Nathan. I think her emotional hormones are in overdrive. "Avi, it's so nice to finally meet you," she says with a big smile. "Amy's told me so much about you."

"Mom—"

"How are you liking being in our big city?" she says, ignoring me. "Amy must be showing you a grand old time."

"Mom, this isn't Avi."

"It's not?"

"No. It's Nathan. Nathan, this is my mom," I say as I unleash Mutt and let him loose in my mom and Marc's house.

"Oh. I thought his name was Avi."

"No, his name is Nathan. Avi is another guy."

"Then where's this Avi?"

"I don't know."

"Oh. Well, Nathan, why don't you come in and have lunch with us."

While we're eating lunch in the kitchen, Nathan kicks me under the table. It's my cue to start bringing up issues I've been avoiding. "When the baby is born, where's it going to sleep?"

My mom looks to Marc. "In our room, at first."

"Well, we only have two bedrooms because the third is used as an office," Marc chimes in.

"What are you asking?"

"Well, I don't want to be sleeping on the couch when I stay here. I want to keep my room. I may not live here permanently, but I still want a room when I visit. It's important to me."

"Can't you share one with the baby?"

I raise my eyebrows and chuckle. "I'm a teenager. Like I really want to share a room with someone in diapers."

Marc puts his fork down while he thinks. "Maybe I can move the office into the basement."

"There's no windows down there and little ventilation, Marc," Mom coos. "What about your allergies?"

"Amy has a point about the room situation. I can take

my allergy medicine before I go down there. Is that fair? You keep your bedroom and the baby will get the office."

I guess Marc isn't such a bad guy, after all. He just needs to get used to having a daughter like me around...and a dog like Mutt. Maybe I should suggest he take his allergy medicine every day.

My mom sits up straight, or as straight as she can with a protruding belly. "As long as we're making concessions, how about if I request one of my own?" she says.

I brace myself. "Shoot."

"After the baby's born, you babysit one weekend night a month. Changing diapers and all."

"Fine. But if it pukes all over my clothes you're paying for the dry cleaning."

"It's a deal."

After lunch, the four of us sit and play Scrabble.

"So...are you two an item?" my mom asks before one of her turns.

"We're just friends," Nathan blurts out.

"Yeah," I confirm. "Just great friends."

Marc wins Scrabble by a landslide with a triple word score with the word zareba. We all challenged him and he won. Zareba is a word, if you can believe it. Then Nathan and I take Mutt for a walk around the block before we head back to the city. It feels good to have Nathan as a friend, to give me the guy perspective on stuff.

My phone buzzes with a text message when we're driving back to the city.

"Can you read it to me?" I ask Nathan.

"It's Jessica. She wants to know why you want Wes's number."

"Text her back and tell her it's a surprise."

I hear Nathan typing away on my cell phone.

"She says you have enough guys in your life and need to take a breather."

I steer the car to the side of the road and grab my cell out of Nathan's hands.

"What are you doing?"

"Bribing my best friend." I smile when she finally texts me Wes's number. I dial it and wait for an answer.

"Wes, this is Amy. You know, the virgin from the youth group meeting."

"I remember. The girl with the dark hair and clear blue eyes. Are you breathing heavy on purpose?"

"No, that's just my dog panting in my ear."

"Yeah, right," he says, totally not believing me.

"Listen, if you ever need a guitar player for Lickity Split, my friend Nath—I mean Nate—Nate Greyson is his name and he rocks."

"I sing, too," Nathan whispers beside me.

"He sings, too," I add.

"We're rehearsing today at Lounge Ax. If he wants to come by and jam with us, that's cool. Can't say he's in the band, but we're always lookin' for subs."

I hang up and toss the phone into Nathan's lap.

"Thanks," he says. "I think I once called you inconsiderate and rude. You're not."

"Yeah, well, you caught me when I'm heartsick and weak."

I tell Nathan to be at Lounge Ax later. I have to pick up Jess and take her to dinner. The bribe dinner.

At Hanabi, our favorite sushi place, I order the Jewish Chef's Special without crab or shellfish, a spicy tuna roll and spicy tuna rice bowls with tempura crunch. Jess orders the Hwe Dup Bob bowl of kosher sushi, lettuce, and brown rice.

Jess takes the first bite of her special concoction and moans with delight. "This is *so* good."

"It better be. It's costing me sixteen dollars."

She shoves another forkful into her mouth. "First Avi, then Nathan…now Wes. I think you've gone off the deep end here. I have to say giving you Wes's cell number was *so* worth this dinner."

Frustrated, I tell Jessica the truth. "The number was for Nathan. He plays guitar and needed guys to jam with."

"So you just spent sixteen dollars on my dinner for doing something nice for Nathan?"

I shove a spicy tuna roll into my mouth and nod.

Jess puts her fork down. "So you're not into Wes?"

I shake my head. "Nope."

"What about Nathan?"

Another shake. "Nope."

"And Avi?"

At the mention of his name, my heart stings. "He's staying at Northwestern with a friend. It's over."

"Why?"

"Because he wants it to be. I kissed another guy, I humiliated him in front of everybody, and because he's in the Israeli military for the next three years."

"Do you still like him?"

"Oh, man, Jess, you can't imagine. It's like he took a piece of me when he left. I really screwed up. I wish I knew where he was, but even if I did I wouldn't know what to say to him."

"Too bad you can't kidnap him."

Yeah. Too bad. If I could kidnap him then I could tell him that it doesn't matter that we're apart. It doesn't matter that I kissed another guy. My heart still belongs to my Israeli soldier and nobody can take that away...not time or a kiss. But why *can't* I kidnap him? Why can't I make him listen to what he might not want to hear? While my mind is churning, I'm getting more excited by the second.

"That's it. Jess, you're a genius!" I say.

She looks at me, confused and clueless. "I think I missed something."

"No, you're right. I need to kidnap Avi. Secret military operation style—it's right up his alley."

"Jess, you don't even know what dorm he's staying in."

"We'll find out. Doesn't Miranda's aunt work in admissions? That's why she thinks she's automatically getting in?"

"Okay, so suppose you know where he's staying. Then what? We're going to handcuff him and take him in a getaway car? I've only seen him a few times, but I know he could overpower the two of us no problem."

She's right. I need more muscle on my side—a guy. "Nathan will help."

"Nathan?"

I convince her he's the only one who'll help. Besides, our kiss was fifty percent his fault.

In the evening, I recruit Nathan and Miranda. Nathan's skeptical, but Miranda's on board. We plan the mission for Friday, after school.

Two days from today.

25

What is God's definition of a family?
I've been trying to figure out my own definition, but I
can't come up with one that makes complete sense.

I'm going to be a grandmother. For real. My dad talked to Mr. Obermeyer's vet on the phone, confirming the results. Mutt really is a stud.

Not wanting bad blood with Mutt's father-in-law, I bake homemade doggie cookies and knock on Mr. Obermeyer's door. The creak on his floor alerts me he's home, although I'm not sure when he peeps through his peephole and realizes it's me he'll open the door.

Lucky (or not) for me, he opens the door. He does not look happy to see me. "What do you want now?"

Holding out the bag of cookies that I tied with a pink ribbon, I say, "These are for Princess."

His lips unpurse for a millisecond. Opening the door

wider to let me in, I'm not sure I want to actually walk into Mr. Obermeyer's condo. He's probably going to make me take my shoes off to protect his pristine floor and has plastic covering his furniture so nobody gets any marks on it.

I walk inside his place. He's got jazz playing softly in the background. "You like jazz?" I ask, trying to make conversation, at the same time wondering when I can make a smooth exit without insulting the old man. The last thing I want to do is upset Mr. Obermeyer. His grumpy threshold is very thin.

Reaching into the bag, he pulls out a homemade treat and hands it to Princess, who's lying on a pink plushy dog bed with her name embroidered on it. Her water bowl is right next to it. The pampered pooch doesn't even have to get up to drink; she can hang her head over the side of the bed and lap up her refreshment.

What a life!

"Your mutt really messed things up, didn't he?"

I bite my bottom lip. "I know it's my fault, Mr. Obermeyer. And I'll pay for the vet bills and even take all the puppies and sell them after they're weaned if you want so you don't have to look at them more than you have to. Just...I'd appreciate it if you'd not terminate the pregnancy." Tears are coming to my eyes, which sucks because even though I'm emotional I hate to show it to other people.

"Wait here a second," Mr. Obermeyer says, leaving me alone while he disappears down the hall with his feet shuffling slowly across the floor. He shuffles back, holding a picture of an old woman beside a huge silver cup. A poodle is sitting next to her. The woman is grinning from ear to ear. You can tell she's deliriously proud. So is the dog.

"Is that Princess?"

"Yes, with my wife. Esther died last year, right after the dog show." Mr. Obermeyer gazes at the picture longingly. "I miss her."

"I'm sorry I ruined your dog's uterus," I say, taking advantage of the sentimental moment and praying he'll forgive me.

The old man shakes his head. "You didn't ruin her. It's just…well, I'm a little overprotective of Princess."

Ya think? "What about the puppies?"

"My wife wanted to breed Princess and create champion purebreds."

"What do *you* want, Mr. Obermeyer?"

"I just want my wife back."

His dedication to his wife makes me think of Avi. And for the first time since I moved into my dad's building, I can relate to the old man. He's not bitter. He's jealous that I have a dad and friends and he's got nobody. Well, nobody except an ugly dog.

Here I was thinking all along that two people can't possibly make up a family, but I think I was wrong. Yes, it does happen that I'm wrong. Not often, but on the rare occasion.

"Mr. Obermeyer, how about you join us for a family Shabbat dinner next Friday."

"I'm not Jewish."

"You don't have to be Jewish in order to be in my family, Mr. Obermeyer. Just ask my mom."

26

> *I love the Lord*
> *for He hears my voice, my pleas;*
> *for He turns His ear to me*
> *whenever I call (Psalms 116:1).*
> *Sometimes my brilliant ideas get me in trouble*
> *and I need a little help from above.*

"Knit caps?"

Miranda holds out our newly purchased hats for our kidnapping operation. "Check."

"Black clothes?"

Miranda does a scan of me, Nathan, Jess, and herself. "Check."

"Flashlights?"

We all click them on to make sure they're working. "Check."

"Walkie-talkies?"

Jess holds up four Motorola ones her parents use when they go to Disneyland every year so nobody gets separated for too long.

"Handcuffs?"

I hold up the plastic ones I bought at Walgreens.

"Lipstick and scrunchies?"

"Now here's where I draw the line," Nathan says, flicking the light from his flashlight in my face.

"Nathan, obviously I didn't mean you. Miranda, you've got the keys?"

Miranda jingles her keys in front of her. "Got your dad's keys, your dad's car, and the address. You ready for this, Amy?"

Considering my heart is beating a million times a second and I haven't eaten for two days because I've been nervously looking forward to today, I'm ready.

We pile into my dad's Lexus and drive north toward Evanston. Miranda is driving. I'm in the front passenger seat. Jess and Nathan are in back. When we're close, I order everyone to put on their knitted caps from their back pockets.

"Do I have to?" Jess asks. "My hair will get all flat."

I roll my eyes. "Do you think commandos worry about their hair being flat?"

"Amy, we're not real commandos. And Avi will know it's you. This isn't a real military operation. It's a girl who wants her guy back."

It's a real operation to me.

At Allison Hall, we park out front.

"Now what?" Miranda asks.

I scan the area, analyzing the best place to plant ourselves.

"How do you know he's even here?" Jess asks. "He could be out for the night, staying in for the rest of the night…"

"Jess, you're not helping," Nathan chimes in.

Jess shuts up.

"Okay, here's the deal," I say. "Jess, you go inside and ask around. Pretend you're a student and ask if people know where Tarik is."

She puts her hand on the handle to the car door, but pauses before she opens it. "What's his last name?"

"I don't know. But I'm sure there's not an abundance of Tariks in the dorm."

While I watch her saunter to the front doors of the dorm. Manicure be damned, I peel off the remaining nail polish from my fingernails, then start to chew on each nail.

"Stop that," Nathan orders. "Nail biting creeps me out. Listen, if he likes you he likes you and if he doesn't…well, that's his loss. Either way, whether you bite your nails or not isn't going to change the outcome."

"You're heartless," I tell him.

"I'm a realist," he argues.

I disagree. As a person who thinks when life gets shitty you can plow right through the shittiness and change the course of your life, I'm going to do what I can to change it. I do think I can change my destiny.

Every guy who enters the dorm I think is Avi. Every girl who enters the dorm I think is there to see him. Oh, man, I know what Avi means about how dangerous your mind can be.

"Is that him?" Miranda says excitedly for the millionth time.

"No."

Ten minutes go by and my great kidnapping idea maybe isn't so great, after all. When Jessica finally comes back to the car I'm ready to ditch the plan and trek back home.

"Tarik left about a half hour ago with a guy I'm assuming is Avi."

I grill her with questions. "How do you know? Did you ask a guy or a girl? Do they know where they were going? Do you know when they'll be back? Who else was with them?"

"Amy," Jess says. "Why don't you go in there and ask the guy yourself. I got the info you wanted. He's not at the dorm. Do you want to stay and kidnap him when he comes back, or do you want to abort the mission?"

I consider both options. Leaving here means I'm giving up on him...on us. Leaving here means that my insecurities and self-doubt have overpowered and won over my desire to change the course of my life for the better.

"We're staying on course," I tell them.

"Can we abort the stupid knit hats, at least?" Jess asks.

"No."

I hand everyone their walkie-talkies and we sync our channels. "You all know what he looks like, right?"

Miranda bites her bottom lip. "I've only seen him once in real life and once in a picture. It's dark out, but I'll do my best."

"Good enough," I say. "Nathan, you wait by that tree on that side of the dorm and Jess...you wait over there by that statue. When you see Avi, Tarik, or both of them, announce it on the walkie-talkies and we'll surround them. Got it?"

Nathan shoves the black knit cap on his head and heads for the tree with the walkie-talkie in hand.

Jess puts her cap on, but leans over the front seat and turns the rearview mirror toward her so she can see what she looks like. After loosening some curly wisps of tendrils from beneath the cap she says, "I'm doing this because we're best friends, you know."

"I know. And I love you for it."

"Uh huh. You owe me big for this, Amy," she says, and jumps out of the car, marching toward her lookout spot.

"Where are you going to stalk him... I mean, stake him out?" Miranda asks.

I stick the handcuffs in my back pocket and shove my hair under the cap. Then I stumble out of the car, toss my cell phone at Miranda, and say, "I'll be across the street. I've got to have all sides of the building covered."

With a walkie-talkie in hand, the cuffs hidden in my back pocket, and my hair hidden from sight, I seriously feel like I'm undercover.

I sit on a bench at a bus stop across the street from the dorm. And wait. And wait some more. I think we've been on the stakeout for over fifteen minutes.

"Ten-four, do you read?" Jessica's voice calls over the walkie-talkie.

I press the talk button. "Do you see him?"

"No. I just wanted to know what our operation's name is. Every operation has a code name."

"Yeah," Miranda chimes in. "How about Operation Wildcat. You know, for the Northwestern Wildcats."

"How about Operation Kidnap Avi," Jessica chimes in.

"How about Operation Stupidity, *ten-four*," our fourth accomplice chimes in.

"Nathan, shut up," Jessica says.

"I was just wondering…" Nathan says. I'm trying to keep the walkie-talkie on a low sound level so no one else can hear us. I didn't know my recruits were going to be so chatty. "What do you want me to do if I see him?"

Well-thought-out plans are not my strong point. I say, "Stall him."

"How?"

"I don't know…do whatever it takes to stop him," I whisper into my walkie-talkie. "Just make sure he stays still long enough for me to handcuff him and lead him in the getaway car."

"THIS IS NORTHWESTERN CAMPUS SECURITY," an unfamiliar and very authoritative voice comes through the walkie-talkie speaker in my hand. "IDENTIFY YOURSELF AND YOUR LOCATION IMMEDIATELY."

"Don't give out any information," Nathan says. "They'll never find us."

Spoken like a true bad boy.

"I'm scared, Amy," Miranda's voice comes through the walkie-talkie.

I bang my head against the lightpost I'm leaning on. "You just said my name."

"I'm sorry. I didn't mean to. I'm turning this thing off right now."

"THIS IS CHIEF OF SECURITY ON NORTH-WESTERN CAMPUS," the walkie-talkie bellows. "AMY, YOU'RE ON A CAMPUS RADIO FREQUENCY AND WE HAVE YOUR ENTIRE CONFESSION RECORDED. IF ANYONE IS ASSAULTED ON MY CAMPUS, WE'VE GOT EVIDENCE AGAINST YOU."

His threat gets met with silence until Nathan chimes in with, "I'm hungry."

"I'm cold," Jess says.

I think I need new recruits.

Just as I'm about to send everyone home, I see two guys out of the corner of my eye who look just like Avi and Tarik. In fact, I'm sure it's them. I quickly press the talk button. "I see them! Nathan, they're headed to Allison Hall, almost reaching you right now."

I hear a "Stop right now!" and the walkie-talkie goes dead. I run across the street, aware Jessica is behind me trying to catch up.

The area is dark and is surrounded by trees, but I can make out the scene without light. Nathan is moaning on the ground, Avi is in deep commando mode with his hands in fists, and Tarik is standing behind them.

I run and kneel on the ground beside Nathan. "Are you okay? Oh my God, you're bleeding," I screech when the side of his face catches the light.

"He punched me and did that Israeli self-defense stuff on me," Nathan says while staying in the fetal position.

Avi holds his hands up as if he did nothing wrong. "Are you kidding me? You tried to tackle me." He takes a look at me and Nathan, then at Jessica. "Wait, why are you all dressed like burglars?"

"We're kidnappers, not burglars," Jessica corrects him.

"Who're you going to kidnap?"

I stand up and whip out the handcuffs. "You."

Avi looks down at the cuffs dangling from my fingers. "They're plastic."

And cost me a dollar ninety-nine. "Yep. Now turn around and put your hands behind your back so I can complete this mission."

Avi turns to Tarik. "I guess we're not hanging out tonight."

Tarik is smiling wide. "This is better than reality television, man. I'd do what the girl wants."

Following my instructions, Avi places his hands behind his back and I secure the handcuffs to his wrists.

Just as I'm ready to escort him to the car, flashing lights and campus security cars screech beside the sidewalk. Security personnel come running at us from all directions. There's no escape.

"Which one of you is Amy?" a big guy who I swear could double as a WWE wrestler asks.

"Listen," Avi says to the guy, stepping between me and the security guard. "I'm responsible for this whole thing."

"Are you Amy?"

I think Avi is sizing up the guy, seeing if he could take him and his attitude on while handcuffed. My Israeli knight in shining armor.

"I'm Amy," I tell the guy while slowly raising my hand and peeking my head around Avi.

"Amy, I can handle this," Avi says.

"I can, too," I tell him. "Besides, you're handcuffed. I wouldn't be arguing while handcuffed."

Avi gives a short laugh. "Do you ever think there's consequences to your actions?"

"Not usually."

The security guy clears his throat, getting our attention. "Are you done with your private conversation?" Shaking his head, he points at Nathan on the ground, looking like a wounded puppy. "Are you hurt?"

"Yes. And my ego is, too," Nathan responds.

The big guy surveys the situation. "We have a hazing policy on campus," he says. "I warn you; for breaking the policy you not only get stripped of your Greek affiliation, you get kicked out of the university."

"Lucky we're not students here, then," Nathan says groggily.

"Is there a reason this guy is in handcuffs?" the big guy asks, eyeing Avi and getting more annoyed by the second.

Letting out a breath I say, "Okay, here's the truth." I point to Avi. "This is my boyfriend…well, sort of. And he came to visit me but when he found out I kissed him…" I point to Nathan, "he left and stayed with him…" I point to Tarik. "My best friend is here for stakeout purposes and moral support," I say as I point to Jessica (who has taken off her hat), "and I have another friend in the getaway car over there," I say, pointing to the car.

By this time a large crowd has gathered around us and I think a photographer from the campus newspaper just took a picture of us. When my parents find out about this, I'm probably going to be grounded for life.

"Let me get this straight. This guy in handcuffs is your sort-of boyfriend. And you kissed that guy bleeding on the ground over there."

"Yep."

"And none of you are students at Northwestern?"

I nod enthusiastically and say, "You got it." No need to needlessly involve the innocent bystander, Tarik.

The security guys look over at Nathan. "Sir, would you like to press charges against anyone here for assaulting you?"

Nathan looks at Avi and says, "I don't think so."

"Does *anyone* here want to press charges?"

We're all silent.

He walks over to Avi. "Sir, turn around so I can release you from those handcuffs."

"Um…I'd like to keep them on," Avi says.

The security guard puts his fingers to his temples and starts rubbing as if he's got a migraine. "Well, then, whoever is not a student at this school should leave University property as soon as you get this all straightened out." I hear the guy mumbling about crazy teenagers as he walks away and tries to disperse the gaping crowd.

Out of the corner of my eye I spot Miranda stumbling out of my car to join us. But I'm not really focused on her; I'm concentrating on Avi…his eyes piercing mine as we stand by the Northwestern dorm with people watch-

458

ing and Nathan bleeding and Tarik all confused and Jess primping and Miranda trying to look innocent.

Avi's hands are pinned behind his back, still bound by the toy handcuffs. "What now?" he asks me. I've missed his deep, sexy voice.

I lick my lips nervously. "Well, the plan was to kidnap you."

"It was Amy's scatterbrained plan," Nathan chimes in while working his jaw back and forth. "I had nothing to do with it."

"Me, either," Miranda says, standing behind Nathan for protection.

I roll my eyes. My accomplices are such weak sauce.

Jessica, who is now fluffing her hair up, says to Tarik, "I suppose you're Tarik."

He holds out a hand to her. "And you're?"

"Amy's best friend Jessica. But everyone calls me Jess. And that's Nathan and Miranda."

Tarik looks at me, his eyes smiling but his words serious. "What are you planning on doing with him?"

"Do you care?" I ask.

Tarik shrugs. "I might. Then again, I might not."

"Whatever you're going to do," Avi says, "do it. If you haven't realized it, I'm standing handcuffed in the middle of the school campus and people are staring."

Tarik jangles keys from his fingers. "Amy, why don't I take your friends back home while you two work out…whatever you need to work out."

"Really?" I say, giving him my best impression of a thankful puppy dog.

"But if he ends up floating in Lake Michigan tomorrow, I'm not covering for you."

Leaning forward, I kiss Tarik on the cheek and whisper in his ear, "You're a good friend."

After saying my thank-yous to my accomplices and assuring them they'll be well taken care of by Tarik, I grasp Avi's elbow like a police officer would and lead him to the car.

When we reach the car, I open the door for him and gesture toward the seat.

"Aren't you going to take the cuffs off before I get in?"

"Nope."

27

Freedom.

Does it mean freedom from persecution?

Freedom to do whatever you want?

Or is freedom a state of mind?

Maybe it's all of those mixed together.

"You don't trust me?"

I give a short laugh. "I didn't cause that whole scene just to let you go free. Get in."

He bends his head, his hands still bound behind his back, and sits in the passenger seat. He's forced to situate himself so he's not leaning against the uncomfortable cuffs, which makes me want to unshackle him, but what if he decides to leave me after I free him? No, I need him to hear me out, no matter what.

I have to lean over him to put his seatbelt on. He can't do it himself while his hands are bound behind his back. I can feel his breath on my neck as I reach over his body to fasten the seatbelt. It's the law, you know. I think I just heard him give a little grunt/moan combination, but I'm not sure.

"Are you wearing a new perfume?" he asks, his breath hot on my skin. "You smell different."

I don't answer, although it's either the French fries I had at lunch or the Pleasure perfume I sprayed on an hour ago.

"Where are we going?" he asks when I drive off campus, heading north on Sheridan Road.

"You're my prisoner. Prisoners aren't usually told where they're going to be held hostage. And they don't talk." To be honest, I don't know where I'm headed. Somewhere we can be alone, somewhere nobody can find us. If there was a button I could press to whisk us away to a stranded island, I'd do it. He needs to hear me out. After that, well...I'll hold my breath while I wait for his response.

When I reach a red light, I look over at him. He's wearing a gray long-sleeve T-shirt with some logo in Hebrew on it, along with faded jeans with a small rip on one of the knees. I wonder if that rip happened tonight when Nathan jumped him. I can't read Avi's face; he's a master at hiding emotion. Is that something he's been taught, or was he born with that talent?

"Amy, you don't have to do all this," he says.

"Oh, yes. I do," I tell him before I push on the accelerator and start driving again.

"Listen, Amy, when I came to Chicago I didn't know—"

"Avi, wait until you hear me out before you say anything. Okay? I mean, I have some things I have to get off my chest before you tell me how much of a mistake it was that you came here and you're going back home in two days never to see me again."

"Whatever you want," he says, looking out the window and taking a deep, frustrated breath.

Oh, great. Now I've pissed him off. I'm passing the Baha'i Temple, which looks like the Planetarium. It's so huge and brilliantly lit up.

"It's the Baha'i temple," I explain when Avi's eyes go wide from seeing such a unique building.

"Whoa," Avi says. "The one in Haifa by my aunt's house has a gold dome. Stuck in the middle of the mountain you can see it from miles away."

I drive past the temple, past Gillson Park, past the million dollar houses on Sheridan Road *only people who have old money can afford*, my mom says. By the time we pass Glencoe I know my destination.

Rosewood Beach.

It's a small beach in Highland Park my mom took me to one summer when I was little. I remember the wind was so strong my blanket flew up and threw sand in my face. I wasn't a sand person to begin with. It was too messy and got all over and it took days to get out of my hair and shoes. And as much as my mom wanted to get me in that Lake Michigan water, I resisted. I saw the kids who played with their buckets in the water and splashed around…eventually they had to come out of the water and walk on the sand. That dry sand stuck to their feet and legs and hands and…ugh, all over.

Turning into the little driveway leading down to the tiny parking lot, I think of how messy situations can sometimes be a good thing. I think I'm just learning that.

I park the car in the darkened parking lot right near the edge of the beach overlooking the lake. No other car is in sight. We're the only ones here in this secluded place.

Almost as if we're on an island alone.

"Are you going to take the cuffs off now?" he asks.

"Nope. Not until you hear what I have to say." I turn in my seat so I'm facing him. The only thing between us is the arm rest and cup holders. And our strained relationship, if you want to get technical.

I reach over and unbuckle his seatbelt, the click releasing him from the harness. He's as comfortable as he's gonna get with his hands secured behind his back.

His eyes are shining in the bright moonlight. I can feel them on me as though they were his hands.

"Don't look at me," I tell him.

"Why not?"

"It embarrasses me. What I'm about to say embarrasses me."

"So let me talk," he says in his smooth, confident voice. "I'm not embarrassed."

I tilt my head and raise my eyebrows. "Just turn around."

He shakes his head in confusion, but turns and stares out the opposite window.

I brace myself for the worst and start talking. "Last

summer was the best summer of my life. Meeting someone I really liked surprised me more than anything."

"Same here," he says to the window.

"Yeah, but you told me not to wait for you. You didn't want to get involved, you didn't want a relationship...all you wanted was a summer fling."

"It was awesome."

"Yeah. But then it was over. You went to the army and I came back home. When things go wrong with Jess, I can't call you. When things go wrong with friends at school or my family, you're not here to calm me down and tell me not to freak out or hold my hand in that familiar way."

This time he turns to me, his jaw clenched. "So you replaced me with Nathan?"

With my index finger, I twirl it in cirlces to remind him to turn around.

He looks at the window again and repeats, "So you replaced me with Nathan. I get it, Amy, you don't have to state the obvious."

"I admit it," I say quietly. "I kissed Nathan. Twice. And he was a good kisser. Well, the first time he wasn't, but the second time was considerably better."

"I don't want to hear it," Avi says, his voice tight.

"Yes, you do. I don't want secrets between us, Avi. And I don't want you running away from me when things get tough."

"I don't run."

"You left so fast I didn't have a chance to figure things out in my own head," I say, putting my hand on his thigh.

I need to touch him, to make him realize how much I care. Will he know by my touch how much I want him back in my life, how there's a void in my heart only he can fill?

He looks down at my hand. "Did you figure it out?"

"I didn't kidnap you for nothing, you know. Stay with me, Avi. Stick with me through my mistakes and through my crap and through my crabbiness and through my doubts because…oh, God, I love you."

I'm waiting for him to say it back to me, not that it even matters. My love won't waver. I can list one reason, or a hundred reasons, why I love him. There's a connection when we laugh, when we fight, and when we kiss…there's a restlessness that burns inside me for him when he's not with me. I'm calmer when we're together.

He's in the Israeli army, I know. And I won't likely be seeing him for a long time. Maybe he'll get leave in the summer; maybe he won't. It doesn't even matter to me, as long as we take the time now to say whatever, whenever.

"Come here," he says.

I look over at the small space in the front seat, the cup holders and arm rest between us. "Um, where do you want me to go, Avi? There's not much room here."

"You're smart. Figure it out."

Don't ask me how it is that my prisoner is giving me the orders now, but I'm totally okay with it. I squeeze my way over the hump of the armrest and wiggle my way over to the passenger side, finally able to sit comfortably while straddling his legs.

"I'm selfish," Avi says, his dark chocolate eyes boring

into mine. "Because I don't want to share you." He bends his head down, says something in Hebrew to himself that sounds like a curse, and says, "My ego took a beating when I found out you kissed Nathan. I left you because my damn ego was bruised."

I twist my head down so he can see my face. "If you can forgive me, I can forgive you...and your ego," I say. "I just want to spend every second together before you go back to Israel."

"And after I go back, what's between us? I've got three years in the army. Who knows what'll happen."

"I don't want to break up, Avi."

"Me, either. How about a don't ask, don't tell relationship until I'm out of the army?"

Don't ask, don't tell. That sounds fair. "Sababa. Does that mean I can call you my boyfriend instead of my *non*-boyfriend?"

The side of his mouth quirks up. "Definitely."

"Do we have a contract drawn up? Do we shake on it?"

"How about we seal the deal with a kiss. No distractions this time."

We both lean forward, meeting in the middle. Just as our lips are about to touch, my cell phone rings.

"Aren't you going to get it? It might be your dad."

Tilting my head to the side and brushing my lips against his, I say, "No distractions, remember?"

Ignoring the persistent phone, we start kissing softly, the way it was the first time he ever touched me. Sweet and slow, with passion and hunger lurking behind as if waiting to be unleashed with a vengeance.

Lips against lips, I caress his face before moving my hands down to the hard planes of his chest, exploring my way while he's still bound and we're still kissing.

"One day we're going to do this somewhere else than in a car," he says, his voice and breath coming harder than before. Through his shirt I can feel his heart racing faster, too. I smile, knowing that I can bring him to feel this way, that he wants me as much as I want him.

Wiggling closer to him and putting the seat into a reclining position, I realize I'm playing with fire but it feels too good to stop. Groaning sounds fill the car. I'm not even sure if they're coming from me or him. Avi nuzzles my neck with his lips, licking and kissing a path down to the V in my shirt while my fingers are wandering around his body giving caresses of their own.

With a shift of his body, suddenly Avi's hands are on my waist, moving up my spine and cradling my head. His breathing is heavy and erratic and his eyes are so intense when he looks into mine it makes my breath hitch.

"You're free from the handcuffs?" I whisper, feeling weak from his kisses and caresses and hands and words.

Between kissing me, he says, "Yeah. There was a release button on them."

I lean back, separating our lips and bodies for a second. "When did you find it?"

"About ten seconds after you put them on me." His fingers brush stray strands of hair away from my face. "The funny thing is, you don't need handcuffs to bind me to you. I'm yours without them."

I pull his head toward mine, and we kiss and continue exploring as we move in rhythm against each other.

"I want to forget how inexperienced you are," he groans the words into my ear.

"So teach me," I say. I bite my lower lip as I sit up and unbutton the top two buttons of my shirt.

"Look at me?" Avi asks.

"Why?"

"So I can see your eyes."

Avi's eyes are totally focused on my face and not my shirt as I move my hands lower and start unbuttoning the rest of the buttons. My hands are shaking. I'm not sure if it's from the cold car or my trembling nerves.

"Didn't you listen when your dad had the sex talk? Didn't he tell you boys only want one thing?"

"Do you, Avi? Do you only want one thing?" I say as I open my shirt and reveal my bra beneath it.

"To be honest, my body's only thinking about one thing right now."

"Me, too. Aren't you going to take your shirt off?"

As his hands reach for the hem of his shirt he says in a strained voice, "Your dad's gonna kill me," then he lifts his shirt over his head and tosses it onto the drivers seat with his eyes never leaving me.

Brushing the tips of his fingers across my abdomen, my body tingles in response and I shiver. "Are you okay with this?" he asks, his face serious.

I nod and give him a small smile. "I'll let you know when I'm not."

As I lean down to press our bodies against each other, his hands reach around under my open shirt and pull me toward him. "Your body...so warm."

His hands are like a fire, consuming my body with his touch. I lean my head on his chest, hearing his heart beating in the same erratic rhythm as my own while his hands move up and caress my hair, my bare back, and my breasts.

I reclaim his lips and my raw emotions and new wonderful feelings whirl in my consciousness. I'm fully aware I'm not ready to have sex, but I'm ready to experience more... "Avi," I say, letting my tone say more than my words. I want...

As if he understands, Avi shifts again, this time moving our bodies so he's on top of me. "Ow," he says.

"What?" Did I do something to hurt him?

"I just banged my head on the mirror."

"I think the seatbelt is digging into my back," I tell him. Or maybe it's the handcuffs digging into my back. Or both. All I know is that we're both uncomfortable right now.

He puts his forehead against mine and groans in frustration as he attempts to stretch his legs out so they're not pinning mine under his. I think one of his legs is under the steering wheel, but I can't be sure.

My hands are on his shoulders, my feet scrunched

under the dashboard, and I think Avi's elbow is stuck in the cup holder.

And now my cell phone is ringing again.

"This isn't working, is it?" he says.

I scan our position, the awkwardness of it all. "I guess you're right," I say, totally frustrated.

He leans into the back seat, retrieves the ringing phone, and hands it to me.

Flipping it open, I say, "Hey, *Aba*."

Avi twists himself and ends up sitting in the driver's seat.

"Are you okay?" my dad barks on the other end of the line.

"Yeah." More than okay.

"Then I'm going to kill you. Where are you? I've been calling and calling. Why get you a cell phone if you won't answer it?"

"I didn't hear the phone," I lie, interrupting his tirade. "I must have been in a bad cell area." That is such a lame answer, but I'm not too good at coming up with lies on the fly.

"Where are you? I asked Nathan, but he's keeping his lips tighter than a submarine door. Are you in some kind of trouble?"

"I'm with Avi," I finally say while tossing the handcuffs into the back seat so they're not pressing into my back anymore.

"I thought he went to stay with his friend at Northwestern. You told me it was over between you two."

"It was…but not anymore. He's coming back home to

stay with us." I say the words, then look over at Avi hoping he'll agree to sleep at our condo tonight and every night until his plane leaves.

"Are you with him now?"

"Yes."

"Alone?"

I look out over the empty parking lot, the deserted beach, and the frozen Lake Michigan water glittering in the moonlight. "Yes," I say.

"Put Avi on the phone. Right. Now."

"*Aba*, don't embarrass me."

"Let me tell you this much, Amy. If you don't put him on the phone, I'm taking away your cell phone, your computer privileges, car privileges, and that boy is not allowed in my home. Got it?"

My dad is a total buzz kill. I hold out the phone to Avi. "He wants to talk to you."

Avi takes the phone with all seriousness. "*Ken*," he says. Yes.

I only hear Avi's part of the conversation, but it doesn't even matter because he's in full-blown Hebrew mode.

"*Ani shomer aleha. Ken. He beseder. Ken, ani rotze lishmor al kol chelkay hagouf sheli.*"

"What's he saying?" I whisper.

Avi holds his hand over the mouthpiece. "He's going through a list of my body parts he'll rearrange if I 'compromise' you."

I slap my hand over my eyes. Seriously, my dad could

drive any guy away from me, even a commando in the Israel Defense Forces.

"Ron, *ta'ameen li…ani ohev et habat shelcha ve lo ya'aseh cloom lif'goah bah.*"

After Avi said that last part, there's silence on the other end of the line for a second. I can feel the tension ebb and flow between the two men in my life.

"*Beseder,*" Avi says.

"*Beseder,*" he repeats.

"*Beseder,*" he says again.

The suspense is killing me. "What does *beseder* mean?"

Instead of answering me, he collapses the phone, disconnecting the line. Then he tosses the phone into the back seat. "It means 'fine', or 'okay.'"

"Did he really threaten you?"

"Especially after I told him I loved you."

Heart palpitation here. "You told him you loved me?"

He nods.

I tilt my head to the side and say with a smile, "You know you're supposed to declare your love to the girl before you tell her father. Unless it's the olden days, in which you'd be giving my dad goats, gifts, and gold in exchange for permission to marry me."

"My family owns half of the goats on the *moshav,*" he says, lifting his eyebrows. "How about I offer our half to your dad?"

I was at the *moshav* over the summer. My uncle owns

the other half of the goat farm. "That's a lot of goats," I say. "How do you know I'm worth it?"

Avi looks into my eyes. "You're worth it, Amy," he says, once again cradling my head in his hands. "Trust me, life with you would be an adventure," he whispers.

As I'm about to pull him closer, I feel him tugging my shirt together. "What are you doing?"

"Buttoning your shirt," he says as his hands deftly move up and button my shirt back up.

"Why?"

"Because I'd rather have you not tell our kids their dad declared his love in the back seat of a car."

"We're in the front seat."

"Yeah, well…and as much as I think I could take your dad on and give him a pretty good run for his money, I'd rather not get into it with him."

Avi puts his own shirt on, covering that six-pack and bronzed chest I once thought didn't affect me. It does.

"Let's take a walk on the beach."

I look out the window and know it's a cold, breezy night in northern Illinois. "It's freezing out there."

"Stay close, then. I'll keep you warm."

We step out of the car. Avi puts his arm around me as we walk down the dark, sandy beach. He's right. His embrace does keep me warm on this chilly night. After a few minutes, Avi halts his steps and turns to me. He takes my hands in his, weaving my fingers through his own. "Amy," he says, his voice laced with seriousness.

My eyes are filled with emotion. He's going to say it…I know it's so hard for him. His brother died in a bombing and Avi's been struggling with his emotions ever since.

He squeezes his eyes shut as if trying desperately to pull out the words. "Wait here." Taking my car keys from his back pocket, he runs to the car and back. "Here," he says, holding out my cell phone. "Call your voicemail."

"Why?"

"Just do it."

I dial my voicemail number. The first call was from five o'clock…before I kidnapped him.

"Hi, Amy, it's Avi. I've, uh, been thinking a lot this week and the truth is…well, I miss you. Too much. It's killing me inside not being close to you. I mean, I understand if you want to never call or see me again because I left like a wounded ass, but…well…if you find it in your heart…or even your mind…to forgive me for having an ego as big as the Sears Tower I visited yesterday, call me back on this number – it's Tarik's cell."

I press nine on my cell and turn to him. "That was so sweet," I say. And it means so much to me that he called before I kidnapped him.

"Wait, listen to the next message."

The next message? I put my ear back on the phone to hear the next message.

"It's Avi again. Did I tell you your eyes remind me of blown glass? I can see your soul through those eyes, Amy. They get darker when you're trying to be sexy and they shine when

you smile. And when you think you're in trouble you blink double the amount that you usually do. And when you're sad, the corners of your eyes turn down. I miss your eyes. And I don't want the sad ones to be my last memory of you."

I save the second message, too, then look up at Avi. "There's another one, isn't there?"

He nods.

I press the button and forward to the next message.

"*It's Avi. And I want to say something to you. Not because I want you to say it back, either. (deep breath) I…I love you. It's not that kind of conditional love…it's the kind that'll be around forever. Even if you don't call. Even if you like Nathan or any other guy. We can be friends. We can be more. Just…call me back.*"

I press the forward button. Avi looks like he wants to bite his nails right now, he's so embarrassed.

"*Did I mention when I first met you I was so attracted to you it scared me? Me, scared. I still am when I'm around you, because now I want you in my life forever. How long is forever, Amy?*"

I shut the phone off.

"Don't you want to hear the rest of the messages?"

I slip the phone into my back pocket while tears well in my eyes. "No." Well, actually I'll listen to them when I'm alone in my room at night and want to hear his voice before I fall asleep. Right now all I want to do is be with my boyfriend and enjoy the small amount of time we have left with each other.

"Avi?"

"Yeah."

"Now I have to tell our kids you declared your love over a cell phone."

He smiles wide, then laughs. "How about this, then…" he says, then picks me up effortlessly in his strong arms and lays me gently down on the sand.

I have to say, I'm much less worried about the sand in my hair or stuck to my designer clothes than the words about to come out of Avi's mouth.

He leans over me. His hands once again take mine in his and he weaves his fingers through mine. "I love you, Amy Nelson-Barak. From the moment I laid eyes on you I couldn't stop looking at you. From the moment we talked I couldn't stop arguing with you. From the moment we kissed I couldn't stop kissing you. And from the moment we shared our hopes, fears, and insecurities I couldn't stop loving you."

Oh, that's good. Twice.

Is today Tuesday?

28

King Solomon didn't ask God to be rich or to live long. He asked for wisdom and knowledge (Kings 3:9). I have to be honest…I'm more selfish than King Solomon. Abercrombie & Fitch is having a sale next week and, well…

It's after midnight when we get back to my condo. We had to retrieve Avi's duffle from Tarik's dorm at Northwestern before coming back home where my dad has been waiting for us like an overprotective lion waiting for his precious cub to return from her first hunt.

My dad situated one of our dining room chairs right in front of the door so his face is the first thing we see. His hair is all messed up, no doubt from running his hands through it a million times.

"Hey, *Aba*," I say, giving him a peck on his cheek while trying to keep the atmosphere light. Mutt jumps over to me, totally excited and wagging his tail furiously. I pet him, then look back at my stoic dad.

His eyes are narrowed at Avi, who is standing in the doorway with his duffle in hand.

Showdown time.

I put my purse on the table, wondering how long these two can stare each other down. "Avi, why don't you come in while I get the sheets for your bed."

Avi looks to my dad for approval. Oh, no. I seriously think my dad might just kick him out right now.

Is anyone else going to talk? Or are the two guys going to stand here staring each other down until one of them gives in and looks away? They're like dogs.

"If you loved my daughter you'd have her home at a decent hour."

Avi opens his mouth as if he's going to say something back, but then closes it. My dad seems content with the silence coming from Avi, as if he's not even expecting a response. I go to the hall closet to get the sheets because I'm too embarrassed to witness my dad going off on my boyfriend and know I can't stop it from happening.

When I walk back into the living room, the scene has changed. Avi is sitting on the couch while my dad has moved the dining room chair into the living room. He's sitting in the chair, facing Avi and watching him.

While Avi and I arrange the sheets, my dad doesn't change expression or flinch. When I hand Avi a pillow and our hands lightly brush against each other, I wonder if my dad can tell how electric that instantaneous touch was.

As soon as the couch is transformed into a bed, my dad barks, "Time for bed."

I change into pj's in my room and pass Avi in the hallway when I go to the bathroom to brush my teeth and wash my face. Looking at myself in the mirror, I see a happy person who's content with her life. It's not perfect, that's for sure. But I'm getting there.

Stepping out of the bathroom, I notice my dad has moved the chair from the living room into the hallway, directly between my room and the living room where Avi is sleeping.

"*Aba,* how long are you going to be sitting there?" I ask him.

"All night."

I can't even get mad at him. I know he just worries about me and questions his own effectiveness as a father. After all, I've only lived with him a few months and he's still getting used to having a teenage daughter around. He's probably wondering what to tell my mom if she grills him on my life. Considering last year I didn't even want to talk to him, I understand why he's sitting on a chair in the middle of the hallway and isn't willing to budge anytime soon.

Moving past him, I say, "I just want to say goodnight to Avi. Does that meet with your approval?"

"That depends on how long your goodnight will last," he says, abandoning his post to follow me.

Okay, so three's a crowd in this scenario. It's not easy

saying goodnight to the guy of your dreams when your dad is standing over your shoulder.

"Well, goodnight Avi," I say sheepishly when I get to the living room and wish we were still on the beach…without an overprotective chaperone.

Avi is sitting on the sofa, wearing baggy shorts and…well, that's about it. As much as I hate people staring at my chest, I have the hardest time not staring at his. I think he sits there half-dressed to tempt me.

Two can play at this game.

I can't do it now, but tomorrow I'm going to taunt him by wearing something extra low-cut and tight. Let's see how he reacts in the morning.

He's got this huge grin on his face. He has no clue I have ideas spinning in my head. "*Lyla tov*, Amy," he says, telling me goodnight in his native language.

I want to say more, but not with my bodyguard behind me, so I stroll back to my room. Although, one backward glance at Avi and I know I don't even have to say the words. He knows how I feel and what I want to say.

"Seriously, *Aba*, do you know how embarrassed you're making me?"

"Seriously, Amy, do you know I don't care?"

I roll my eyes. In bed, I wonder how long he'll stay perched on that chair in the middle of the hallway. I hope he falls asleep in that chair and gets a crick in his neck.

I cuddle under the covers of my bed, wishing I was cuddling with Avi instead of my Care Bear.

Two more nights until Avi leaves. How is my heart not going to crush into a million pieces? And how am I going to sleep tonight when I'm too excited to go to bed? I'm replaying the evening in my head, focusing on the "I love you" parts and conveniently skipping over the embarrassing parts on the Northwestern campus.

Because that can easily be erased from my memory.

Although...I wonder if Jess, Nathan, and Miranda are okay. If you want to get technical about it, I did ditch them tonight.

29

---

*Sarah gave birth to Isaac when she was ninety years old
and her husband, Abraham, was one hundred years old
(Genesis 17:17). I hope my mom and Marc aren't going
to keep having kids until they're that old.*

I love weekends. Especially when I don't have any homework and my boyfriend is in town.

In the morning, I walk out of my bedroom wearing a
black, extra-small wrap shirt that shows off way too much
cleavage. Jess and I both bought one last winter when they
were the hottest fashion, but we were too embarrassed to
wear them in public.

During breakfast, I make a big production out of bending down to pour Avi cereal. He's not looking; every time I
check his eyes are focused on his food. I keep bringing him
stuff…bread, hummus, orange juice. He looks at my face,
but definitely not my cleavage. What's up with that?

When my dad walks into the kitchen, he takes one

look at me and slaps his hands over his eyes. "Amy, where's the rest of your shirt?"

"This is it."

"Um…no. No. No. No. It doesn't cover your…parts." He points to Avi. "Close your eyes." He shakes the same finger at me, but still has one hand over his eyes. "Go back in your room and put on something VERY conservative. That covers those girl things."

Avi's shoulders are shaking and I think he just spit out his cereal from trying to cover up his laughter.

I huff in frustration and look at my boyfriend. "Did you not notice my boobs practically hanging out?"

Avi looks from me to my dad. "Um…is this a talk we should be having in front of your *aba*?"

My dad holds up his hands, stopping the conversation. "This is a conversation that should not be happening *at all*. Amy, I'm calling your mom. *After* you change your shirt. This is out of my jurisdiction."

I change, then have to deal with my mom and dad talking on the phone about me for fifteen minutes.

"I noticed them, Amy," Avi says as I plunk myself back down at the kitchen table.

"Well, you weren't staring at 'em," I say accusingly.

"I didn't know you wanted me to."

He's got me there. Usually I hate people staring at my over-abundance of frontage that God "blessed me with" (my mom's phrase, not mine). Avi knows this. I know I'm being ridiculous and not making any sense.

"If it makes you feel any better, when you turned away I couldn't take my eyes off them."

Even though I know this entire conversation is ridiculous, I say, "Thank you, Avi."

He gives me one of his signature half-smiles. "It's all sababa."

"Yeah," I say. "It is."

After my mom has a "talk" with me over the phone about private parts remaining private, I drag Avi to the Museum of Science and Industry. It's my favorite museum, especially the dead baby exhibit. Okay, so technically it's called the neonatal exhibit, showcasing embryos and fetuses in formaldehyde. I've always been fascinated with the exhibit: seeing how human life starts as a speck and ends up a real person. Total miracle, I can't describe it any other way.

Makes you believe in God all over again.

I thought Avi would be bored looking at the dead babies, but when I glance over at him and catch him riveted to the exhibit I know he feels the same way about it that I do. As I study the stages of development, my heart goes out to the mothers of these children who weren't able to grow up. They lost their lives before life even started. But they're doing more for people than most do in a lifetime, surely more than I've done in my seventeen years. They've made people more educated, they've made people aware of what it's like inside of a woman's body as she's pregnant with a child, and they even bring people closer to God.

Avi takes my hand in his as we stop at each stage of development and study the fetuses. They're labeled as male or female (even identical twins are labeled) and how many weeks old they are.

Avi puts his hand up to the glass, right in front of the fetus that looks fully developed except it's so small. "I've never seen anything like this," he says.

I know it's not everyone's favorite exhibit, and if you really think about it it's kind of creepy. But it makes me feel good knowing I've shared it with Avi and he appreciates it as much as I do. Maybe one day…

I look over at Avi. He smiles. I can tell he's thinking the same thing.

In the afternoon, I take him along with Mutt to my mom's house. I can't have Avi go back to Israel without meeting the other half of my nuclear family, although I'm not sure how Marc and Mom will act around him. And now that we've just seen the neonatal exhibit at the Museum of Science and Industry, I hope my mom being pregnant doesn't freak Avi out.

As soon Mom sees Mutt, she says, "Do you have to bring the animal?" she says.

"Mom, you have a yard he can run in. He loves your yard."

Since I'm keeping Mutt on an extender leash at the park so he doesn't impregnate anyone else's dog, my mom's place is like Freedom City for him.

"Last time you didn't pick up all of his poop, Amy. Marc stepped in a little present last week."

Way to go, Mutt! "Sorry, Mom," I try and say sincerely, although in the back of my head I think God had something to do with it. *B'shert*, right? Meant to be.

"Amy, don't tell me you're sorry. Tell Marc."

After I let Mutt loose in the backyard, my mom says, "I'm going to assume you're Avi."

Avi gives her one of his killer smiles, putting on the Avi charm, and shakes her hand. My heart flips over because I know he's doing it for me, that it's important to him that my mom likes him. And maybe because he's lost some brownie points with my dad after last night and he wants to rack some up with my mom before he leaves. Smart guy.

"So, how old are you again?" Mom asks as she pats down her model blonde hair. If I didn't know better, I'd think my mom was trying to rack up brownie points with Avi.

Amy, don't go off on her. She's not embarrassing you on purpose. Wait to interfere when she pulls out the naked baby pictures.

"Eighteen," Avi replies.

"And you're in the Israeli army?"

"Yes."

My mom sits down at the kitchen table and says, "So…what do you do there?"

"Mom, he's training to be a commando," I say, interrupting. "He can't tell you what he does all day."

"Do you shoot guns?"

Avi looks from me to my mom and back. "When we have to," he says.

I need a Coke. This is harder than I thought. I open the refrigerator, but there's no Coke…no Diet Coke, no Cherry Coke, no Vanilla Coke. There's not even a Coke Zero. "Uh, Mom, where's the Coke?"

"We don't have any in the house. It's not good for the baby," she says, then touches her stomach.

As I stare at her hand caressing her abdomen, I think about the neonatal exhibit we saw today. For the first time, I can picture what my little brother or sister looks like right now. The size of my fist…or maybe even smaller.

Marc stumbles into the kitchen, introduces himself to Avi, and the two shake hands. "Do you play golf?" Marc asks, then sneezes into a handkerchief he just pulled from his pocket.

"No. Soccer's my sport," Avi says, then looks to me. I shrug, confused. Does Marc want to go hit a few at the range with Avi to test his skill with a club? Or is he desperately trying to have a manly sports conversation or, scarier yet, a sports competition?

"Why don't you boys see if there's a soccer game on TV while Amy helps me set the table?"

"I can help, too," Avi says.

"Go ahead," I say and push him gently out of the kitchen. I need private time to gossip about him with my mom.

While Marc and Avi settle into the living room, my mom and I set the table. Mom is smiling wide and staring at me as if I just got engaged or something. "He's adorable," she says. "I can see how you can be so hung up on him."

Hung up on him? I'm a little more than hung up on him, I'm full blown *in love* with the guy and even being one room away I realize is too far for me. I don't even want to think about tomorrow, when I have to drive him to the airport and watch a plane taking off with him inside.

Staring at the fresh flowers in the middle of the kitchen table, I say, "Mom, how many times have you been in love?"

"How many times did I *think* I was in love or how many times have I *really* been in love?"

"How do you know the difference?"

"You don't. Well, not at the time you're having the feelings. I was in love with Danny Peterson in high school; we dated my junior and senior year."

"What happened with Danny?"

"I caught him kissing Shayna Middleton under the bleachers during gym class. Guess he didn't love me as much as I loved him. Then there was your dad."

Deep in my mom's blue eyes I detect sadness. "Why didn't you marry him, Mom? I know he wanted to marry you, but you wouldn't."

She wrings her hands together on the table. "My parents…your grandparents…they didn't think your father was good for me. He was a foreigner, someone who might leave me and go back to Israel or who knows where. Or marry me just for citizenship and leave me."

"Do you wish things were different?" I ask. I mean, if she married my dad when she got pregnant then I wouldn't have to deal with a sneezing stepdad and my parents wouldn't live miles away from each other. We'd be a whole family, not a broken one.

She says softly, "To be honest…no. It would have never worked between your father and me. He's married to his work, and I need a man who'll pay attention to me. Marc maneuvers his work schedule around me, not the other way around."

A little piece of hope in my chest disappears with her words. Every birthday I prayed my parents would get together—every penny I threw into fountains, every time I blew an eyelash off of my finger. Now I realize all the hoping and praying wasn't going to change the course of things. There are some things I can't change, after all.

"Do you wish you'd never had me?" I say with a lump in my throat.

Her eyes go wide, "No! Amy, I wouldn't change having you for anything in the world."

"Mom, I was a mistake. Face it, you didn't mean to get pregnant in college on a one-night stand."

"Let's just say you weren't expected. But there was no way I was giving you up and when I held you in my arms the first time after giving birth to you, I cried so hard…from happiness, Amy. Because I'd never known how much I wanted you until I held you. From that moment on, you had my heart. I know I haven't been the best mom. I've grown up while raising you and made many mistakes."

We all make mistakes. "I have, too." But I'm trying to mend them.

Will my dad ever maneuver his work around a woman? Yeah, maybe when he's a hundred years old and is forced to slow down. I need to find out why he works so much, what drives him to put his personal life second to his work life.

"I'm sorry, Amy," Mom says, giving me a puppy dog look Mutt would be proud of. "I wish I could have given you the family you've always wanted."

I smile warmly and stop her hands from wringing by putting my hands over hers. "It's okay, Mom. For the first time in my life, I understand."

Dinner with my mom and Marc was nice. Since we couldn't have sushi because of my mom's pregnancy, we ordered Thai instead. Marc tried to engage Avi in conversation, but Marc isn't the most interesting person to chat with. Get him on a subject he knows, though, and he's a maniac. Like real estate. He could talk about prime Chicago real estate for hours. It's too bad nobody wants to listen.

After dinner Avi and I get in the car and cruise back to the city.

"Are we going back to the beach?" he asks. "Because I think another late night like yesterday and your dad really will pull out the Uzi."

"What's an Uzi?"

"An Israeli-made machine gun. Very popular during your dad's time in the military."

Yeah, I can see it. My dad waiting at the door sitting in the dining room chair with an Israeli machine gun strapped to his shoulder instead of just an angry stare.

"Nope. I'm taking you to a club. You took me to a club in Israel. It's time for me to show you what clubs are like here."

"I thought you had to be twenty-one to get into clubs in the States."

"Yeah, well, this one is lenient. Besides, I know the guy playing in the band."

30

We wait in line to get into Durty Nevin's until Jess pulls us out of line and leads us to the front door. She mumbles something about her uncle being part owner of the security company responsible for the bouncers. We walk straight up to the burly bouncer, he takes one look at Jess, and waves the three of us in.

I hold Avi's hand as we weave through the sea of people.

Miranda is sitting at a table up front. She's wearing her hair up in a ponytail and has actual makeup on. "Wow, Miranda, you look great!" I say to her.

The girl smiles as if I just told her she won a million-dollar lottery. "Jess did it for me."

I give Jess a thumbs-up sign, then join the others to snatch chairs for the three of us.

As soon as we sit, I reach for Avi's hand. His hand is already reaching for mine. Looking up, I swallow hard when he flashes me a private knowing wink.

"I'm glad you two worked it out, but if you start any major PDA I swear I'm banning you from this table," Jess says, eyeing our hands.

"What's PDA?" Avi says in my ear. Jess rolls her eyes, thinking he's whispering about how much he loves me and adores me and can't live without me.

I lean toward him, my hand braced on his chest as I whisper back, "Public display of affection. You know, making out in front of everyone."

Jess is pulling me off him. "I need to talk to you, Amy. It's important. If you could separate yourself from your man for one second, that is."

Tossing Avi an apologetic expression, I pry myself away and let Jessica pull me by my elbow into the hallway by the bathrooms. Music is blaring and pounding in my ears, but it sounds good. Anything would sound good to me right now. I'm happy.

Jess is flushed as she stops and faces me. This is serious. I can tell by the way her mouth and stance get all intense and stiff. "I'm in love, Amy. And I know it sounds weird and I don't want to get all dorky and googly-eyed like you and Avi, but I know he's 'The One.' And my parents are going to have a complete meltdown when they meet him because he's everything they've ever wanted for me. He's Jewish, he's Israeli, he's gorgeous, intelligent, he's sweeter than a cinnamon bun…he's every Jewish parent's wet dream—"

I put a hand up, wondering what this is all about. Cinnamon bun? Israeli? *Wet dream?* "Jess, the only Israeli you've been in contact with lately is Avi and my dad. Avi is taken and my dad…" I scrunch up my face in full grossout mode.

"I'm not in love with your dad, Amy," Jess says, her hands on her hips.

"Phew," I say, physically and mentally relieved. I just saved myself years of therapy.

"I'm in love with Tarik. You know, Avi's friend at Northwestern. After your kidnapping fiasco, he drove Miranda and Nathan home. Then we talked in the car for over an hour in front of my building." I can't stop the girl or get a word in. She's like a train that won't stop. More like a train wreck, because she's totally clueless. I listen to the rest of her rant before breaking the bad news. "He's the smartest guy, Amy. I can't believe you've known him since the summer, knew he was coming to Northwestern, but didn't introduce him to me. I would question your loyalty to me, but I'm so ridiculously in love. Did you ever think I would believe in love at first sight? I swear, I couldn't sleep last night thinking about him and this morning I had the biggest urge to go visit him and surprise him at the dorm. You know the way you feel about Avi? I feel the same way."

"Do you think I could talk now, Jess?" I ask her. She laughs, this crazy I-am-in-love-and-can't-be-normal laugh. Gee, I hope I'm not like that around Avi. Someone slap me please if I ever go over the deep end like that. "What did you guys talk about for an hour?"

"Everything. Life, family, friends."

"Jess, I hate to break it to you, but…" How do I tell her that 1: Love at first sight is a bunch of bull. And 2: He's—

"Wait. Before you tell me I'm crazy and go off on me that I'm supposed to be the friend who is realistic and sane, I need to know his last name. I don't even know my future husband's name."

"Muslim."

Jess cocks her head to the side in confusion. "Tarik Muslim? That's not a Jewish name, that's a religion. Amy, stop making fun of me and tell me his last name before I start getting pissed."

"He's Muslim, Jess," I say slowly with a serious expression on my face. It's really a pity expression, because I'm about to tell her that her cinnamon bun has raisins in it when she expected it to be plain.

"Amy, you said he was Israeli."

"No, I said he was Avi's friend from Israel. So as much as you like him, your parents would freak. Especially your dad. Isn't he the president of the men's club at the synagogue? I admit Tarik is awesome, Jess. But your parents want you to find a nice Jewish boy and I'm sure his parents want him to find a nice Muslim girl."

I shouldn't have put it like that. Just by looking at Jessica I can tell she's gone from elation to confusion to sorrow to defiance all in a matter of seconds. Defiance in my best friend is scary.

"He asked me out on Saturday night," she says matter-of-factly.

Oh, man. "And?"

"And of course I said yes. Crap," she says, as tears start filling her eyes. She turns and hurries into the restroom, leaving me to either go after her like a good friend or pay attention to my boyfriend who probably thinks I ditched him.

I peek around the corner to check out what my boyfriend is doing. He's abandoned the table and is talking to a couple of guys at the bar.

I decide to be a good friend and hope Avi can amuse himself for another five minutes.

In the restroom, Jess has some other girls from our school gathered around her, asking what's wrong. Mitch cruelly dumped her and now the guy of her dreams turns out to be a guy she's probably forbidden to date. Jessica goes to Hebrew school twice a week, Sunday school, and in the summers Jess rides a bus all the way to the middle of Wisconsin to spend four weeks at a Jewish overnight camp.

Needless to say it's been ingrained in Jessica's head

since she was born that she has to marry a Jewish boy. Her kids have to be Jewish, and it's her responsibility to carry on the Jewish traditions and religion.

But I never lose hope. There must be some loophole, some way Tarik and Jess can date without causing her Grandma Pearl to go into a nursing home prematurely.

Jessica waves the crowd away. "I'm fine. Really." She's trying to convince them. It's not working. First of all, her mascara is running down her face like streaks of ash with tears leading the way.

I push everyone else out of the way. Picking her chin up with my fingers, I say quietly, "Jess, don't cry. I'm sure once you explain the situation to your parents, it won't be such a big deal. You'll see."

Leading me to the side, away from everyone else, she says, "No, I won't. My mom's family was killed in the Holocaust, Amy. My great-grandfather has a number tattooed on his arm from when he was in a concentration camp. A reminder you can't wash away with soap and water. If I even mention a non-Jewish boy's name in his presence I feel guilty."

I still think God will take care of Jessica and look after her. I have complete faith. And there's always the guilt offering of a burnt animal…

Jess wipes her eyes, trying to compose herself. Grabbing paper towels and looking into the mirror, she witnesses the streaky mess her face is. "Take a look at me, Amy," she says. "I can't go out there looking like this."

"You have to. Nathan's counting on us being here."

New tears start streaming down her face and she turns to me. "Tarik said he'd be honored to go to the Valentine's Dance with me, Amy. *Honored*. When I spilled the beans about how I didn't have a date, he asked me. Right there in his car in front of my condo. And we had *a moment*. I know it sounds crazy and stupid, but we did."

A moment? Is she kidding me? A moment of lust, perhaps, but not love.

Oh, man. I know how much she wants to go to the Valentine's Dance. It's not about the dance. It's not about love. It's about being wanted and accepted.

I wish I could stop her from looking in the mirror again, but it's no use. One more wipe of the running mascara and I can see the defeat in her eyes. "I'm going home. Tell Nathan and Miranda I'll see them at school."

She moves past me and out the door. I don't even try and stop her because I've been best friends with Jessica long enough to know I can't convince her to stay. Besides, what more can I say? I can't tell her Tarik isn't awesome, because he is.

Speaking of awesome guys, I've left mine alone enough tonight. Heading back to the big crowd, I scan the area and find Avi sitting at the table with Miranda. They're surrounded by a bunch of people, talking and laughing. Two girls who I've never seen before are standing right near Avi. I can tell they're flirting by the way one is flipping her hair and the other girl is licking her lips. My protective radar goes off (okay, my jealousy radar goes off, too) and I weave through the mass of people with my chest held high, and steer toward my boyfriend like a paper clip to a magnet.

The hair-flipping girl is telling a story about her trip to Israel two summers ago and how she's *dying* to go back. It's hard to hear the details of her adventures because music is blaring in the background and I'm stuck standing behind Miranda. There's no room next to my boyfriend.

The lip-licker is laughing while lip-licking, which I think she's practiced in the mirror before. She does it frighteningly well. Avi is so intrigued with her conversation he doesn't know I'm standing here.

Miranda looks up at me. "Maya is telling us about her trip to Israel," Miranda tells me. "She went to *Gadna* for a week. It's a military training camp."

Oh, great. Flippy-haired Maya can talk guns with my commando boyfriend. I'm feeling sick and might just follow Jessica out the door so I can go home, too. "I went to Israel, too," I blurt out.

I have nothing else to say. I didn't go to an Israeli military training camp and I don't have hair I can flip over my shoulder and make it look like I just got it styled at a salon.

When I get Avi's attention, he gives me a small smile. The lip-licker sneers at me and the salon girl says, "Did you go on a Birthright trip or Shorashim?"

"Neither. I went with my dad…He's Israeli."

"Oh," she says, then her friend boasts about her trip to Ireland with her Irish family.

While everyone talks about their adventures abroad, Avi reaches out and snakes an arm around my waist and pulls me toward him. "There's no chair for me," I say to him.

Guiding me onto his lap, he says, "Yes, there is." He taps the hair-flipper on the shoulder and I'm wondering if he wants to keep up the military talk until I hear Avi tell her, "This is my girlfriend, Amy."

While my heart opens up and loves Avi for telling a girl who's obviously hitting on him that he belongs to me, Miss Hair-Flipper gives me a small nod and turns her back to us to talk to another guy.

"Why is it every time I turn around another girl is talking to you?"

"I was talking to everyone, Amy. Don't be so paranoid. That guy over there, Dale, is from the South Side and that dude, Kyle over there, goes to your school. He wondered if I met you on an online dating service."

"What did you tell him?"

"I said he should get a life. Where's Jessica?"

"She left. It's kind of a long story," I tell him.

I guess I shouldn't be jealous of any other girl. I know how Avi feels about me. I guess a little part of me...that insecure part that shows its ugly head once in a while, knows the reality of it all. He's going back to Israel and I'm here. In less than twenty-four hours Avi will be back on a plane flying far away from me. And who knows what'll happen. I know what I want to happen, but how realistic is it?

"Don't look all serious, Amy," Avi tells me as he guides my chin down so I'm face to face with him.

Avi and I are in our little imaginary cocoon looking into each other's eyes as if no one else in the world matters.

A loud "Ahem" interrupts us.

Looking up, I'm shocked at the person standing in front of me. Okay, I knew Nathan was going to be playing tonight at the bar. But I didn't know that Nathan was going to transform into a rock star look-alike. His hair is spiked up, he's got eyeliner on, ripped faded jeans with a faded gray vintage T-shirt, and a black leather necklace hanging from his neck. I might add that he's not wearing glasses, either.

"Nathan?" I ask, not really sure if the guy in front of us is a Nathan look-alike or the real deal.

Nathan leans in and says to me, "The guys in the band call me Nate. And…well, this is *me*. You said to be *me*, right?"

Wow. Talk about going from geek to…wow. "Yeah."

When he leans back, I'm aware that Avi's grip has gotten tighter around my waist. I look down at my boyfriend, whose eyes are a little darker and intense like he's ready to fight for me.

"Avi?" I say.

He's still glaring at Nathan when he says, "What?"

"Look at me."

He does.

"Nathan's my friend, like a brother. Stop glaring at him like he's the enemy."

"I can't help it. Besides, if he's going to be your friend I liked it better when he wore glasses and the pants that were too short."

"Dude, don't be so lame," Nathan says. "The girl is in love with you. Or are you really all muscles and lack in the brain department?"

I feel Avi's muscles tense up, but before he can respond, I wrap my arms around his neck and hold him back. Luckily, the announcer starts introducing the band and Nathan is all too happy to jump up on stage and avoid another confrontation with Avi. I notice Nathan still has a cut and bruise from yesterday when Avi decked him.

"Nathan looks *so* hot, doesn't he?" Miranda says as Nathan, now the lead singer for Lickity Split, takes the mic. Okay, so he's the substitute singer for Lickity Split. It's not permanent, but it's still super cool.

Avi pulls me closer. "I never want you to look at him the way you look at me, Amy."

Nathan aka Nate Greyson puts the mic to his mouth, points to me, and says, "Amy, this one's for you."

What?

Did he just dedicate a song to me?

My arms are still around my boyfriend, and his arm

is still holding me tight while Lickity Split starts the loud music. Nathan belts out lyrics I've never heard before:

She'll freak you out, she'll screw with your head
She'll kiss you once, then leave you for dead

I stop listening after the word *dead*. Nathan and I are going to have a long talk about this song. It's too angry. Is Nathan angry? I'm sure with his past there's a lot of anger built up inside, but I can help him with that. Isn't that what friends are for? And to set the record straight I kissed Nathan twice, not once. And I did not leave him for dead. I knew after Avi kicked his ass last night he was alive…and left in very good care.

I shake my head and listen to the rest of the song. I can tell the crowd is getting into the lyrics and the fast beat. Nathan is a hit. The song tells the story about a guy falling for a girl who he thinks is playing games with him but in the end is just being herself. He realizes that the friendship is the real deal; the attraction was just a façade.

The mass of people in the bar are jumping up and down, shaking their heads to the song, and waving their hands in the air like crazy people. Or more like people who are totally engrossed in the beat and lyrics. Nathan aka Nate is jumping on stage like the rest of the crowd, getting totally into the song.

"Let's dance," Avi says loudly so I can hear over the speakers right near our table.

Me? Jumping around and head-banging? Yeah, I might do that in my room with nobody watching, but there's a bunch of kids from school here and I'm not used to losing control in front of an audience. "You go," I say, standing so Avi can mingle with the crowd. "I'm not the getting-sweaty-in-front-of-other-people kind of person." I'd rather he stay with me, but I'm not going to be the loser girlfriend who tells him what he can and can't do. If he's not afraid of people staring at him . . .

Avi stands and pulls me into the middle of the dance floor, which has become a pit of sweaty people drowning themselves in the music. Nathan is on his second song. This one is about rough times and even tougher times ahead. Very depressing, if I say so myself…and I'm a pessimist.

Avi starts getting into the music. The music is so loud I think my brain is rattling and we're all going to suffer brain damage and wake up deaf tomorrow morning. I can't stop watching Avi and how masculine and cool he looks while he's waving his fist in the air and moving to the pounding bass.

"Come on," he says. "Lose control with me."

Me, lose control? Not my style. Besides, if I jump around then my boobs are going to bob up and down like a buoy in the middle of a tsunami. I shake my head, refusing to make a spectacle of myself.

Scanning the people around me, though, makes me realize that I'm making a spectacle of myself by being the only one in the crowd right now standing still. Even Miranda is jumping around, waving her hands in the air like she's about to take flight. And she's got bigger and sag-gier boobs than me.

I start by bending my knees up and down. Looking over at Avi, his hair wet from sweat, inspires me. I take a tentative jump to test my new bra to see how bounce-resis-tant my boobs really are when they're strapped in tight. I look down as I take another test jump. The bounce rate is acceptable. But when I look up and see Avi's eyebrows fur-rowed as he watches me, I bite my bottom lip.

"People will stare at me," I try to explain over the loud music.

Avi shakes his head in frustration. "Let go, Amy. I want to see you without your inhibitions. If people stare, they're just jealous they're not having as much fun as you are."

I look down at my boobs.

His eyebrows go up. "Just try it," he says. "I dare you."

I do not take dares lightly, and he probably knows it. With a deep breath and determination I never knew was in me, I start jumping to the music and shaking my head around like Mutt after he takes a swim in Lake Michigan. Surprisingly, it feels good to let go and lose control for once.

The pit of people has gotten more crowded, I'm being pushed and pulled around by the mass of dancing mani-acs. When I look up at the stage, Nathan is into his third song…or maybe his fourth. The words are seeping into my body:

Fight the fight worth fighting
Fight it to the death

Fight the fight worth fighting
And give up all the rest

As the words enter my consciousness, I wonder how many fights I've fought that weren't worth fighting. Nathan is totally into the performance. His face is fierce as he sings the words into the microphone. He's still trying to figure out where he fits in this world and why his parents gave him up.

When Nathan opens his eyes, he catches me watching him and winks at me before bending down and singing to some girl in the front row.

Soon the music stops and the band takes a break. While my ears adjust to the absence of blaring music, I head back to our table and plop myself down on an empty chair.

"You should let go more often," Avi says from behind me.

"I looked stupid," I say, which pretty much sums it up. Yes, I admit I had fun looking like a dork having my arms flailing and my boobs bopping around without caring what anyone thought. But in the end, I did look stupid. And in the end, I still do care what people think.

Avi bends down and kisses my neck. "You looked sexy, Amy."

"Will you two ever stop?" Nathan says as he joins our table.

I push Nathan away, but he's not paying attention to me. Something or someone at the other end of the bar is occupying him. I follow where his attention is focused.

"Bicky," Nathan whispers in shock.

The girl is even prettier in person and I hate her instantly. She has short, blonde hair pulled back with a headband and a half shirt showing off her amazing abs and bellybutton ring. And I swear her jeans must be painted on, they're hugging her body so tight. When I wear tight jeans I have to lie on my bed while I'm zipping them up. Bicky must have taken a dip in oil or grease in order to cram into her size zeros.

She sashays up to Nathan and puts her arms around his neck. "Aren't you going to introduce me to your friends?" she asks in a high, singsong voice.

Nathan is still in shock. His arms go slowly around her waist but he's looking at her like something isn't right. "What are you doing here? Did you break out of rehab?"

"You betcha." Bicky leans into him, almost tripping over her feet. "I heard you were performing. And besides, I wanted to meet the girl you kissed and wrote a song about." She looks me up and down. "You're her, aren't you?"

Oh, boy, am I busted. But before I can deny anything, Nathan says, "You're wasted, Bic."

"That I am, baby," she purrs, looking up at him. "You used to like getting wasted with me, until you turned all geek on me." She eyes his spiked hair and faded jeans. "Glad to see you're back to normal."

He grabs her wrists and pries her arms off him. "What we did wasn't normal, Bic. It was crazy and stupid."

Bicky is getting mad; her cheeks are red and splotchy and her eyes narrow into tiny slits making her look like an evil little pixie. "You used to like crazy and stupid, Nate. Or are you still going by Nathan? I can't keep up with all your personalities. Can she?" she says, pointing to me.

Everyone's eyes are on me now, analyzing my relationship with Nathan which is not good considering I just got back together with Avi.

"We're just friends," I blurt out, then hook my finger into Avi's belt loop making it obvious we're a couple. I hold my breath and peek at Avi's reaction to all of this.

Avi takes his hands off me, saying, "You don't have to defend yourself to me, Amy. I'll be at the bar while you work this out."

Is he serious? He doesn't have any doubts or insecurities about my friendship with Nathan? "You sure?"

"Yeah." He smiles and gives me a reassuring nod.

I watch his retreating back as he weaves his way through the crowd.

Wes, the guy from the Jewish youth group who helped me get Nathan in the band, weaves his way through the crowd. "Nate rocks, Amy. Thanks for bringing him by the other night. We're thinking of making him a permanent sub for Lickity Split."

"Cool," I say, but I'm not really paying attention to Wes or Bicky. Or Miranda, for that matter, even though she's in a deep conversation with a guy who I remember seeing at the youth group.

"Nathan..." I say, wanting to apologize for kissing him. I also want to tell him I'm sorry he has to deal with a screwed-up girlfriend on his first night singing with the band.

"It's cool, Amy."

"I can stay and help if you want."

"You've helped enough, bitch, don't you think?" Bicky slurs. I seriously think she wants to fight me, like in a physical fight. As I'm contemplating who would win in a fight between me and Bicky, I wonder if they teach tae kwon do in rehab. Because the only physical fight I've ever been in was with the sheep on the *moshav* last summer in Israel. And in the disco in Israel, but that was only because of the ear-licker—long story.

Bicky holds her hands out wide, "You want some of this?"

"Not really," I say. Is she joking?

Obviously not. My response really pisses her off, because now Nathan is trying to hold her back from charging me. I swear I'm living in the Twilight Zone. This girl seriously wants to deck me.

Not knowing what else to do, I close my fingers tightly into fists and hold them up by my face. The crowd around me starts moving backward. I think they're chanting "Chick Fight!" but I'm not sure. Whatever they're chanting, though, is fueling my bravery. Getting into the role, I start hopping around like boxers do. Maybe Bicky is too wasted and she'll fall to the ground on the first swing. It's wishful thinking, right?

If I break a nail I swear the chick is paying for a new manicure.

"You want some of this? Come and get me!" I say, playing the role while psyching myself up. I can seriously get into this, acting all tough and crazy. *Be afraid, everyone. Here comes the champion girl fighter of our time, Amy Nelson-Barak!*

From behind me, an arm snakes around my side and pulls me backward.

"What the…?"

I'm kicking whoever is holding me and punching at the arm, which is locked around me like a metal vice. Whoever it is drags me outside and sets me down on the sidewalk. I turn around and should have known nobody is as strong as my boyfriend who said he didn't want to deal with the drama, but ends up in the middle of it.

"What. Do. You. Think. You. Were. Doing?" Avi says each word slowly as if I'm an imbecile. His eyes are intense and his hands are shaking. I've never seen Avi shake before and it scares me.

"I'm sorry," I say.

He opens his hands out wide. "I leave you alone for two minutes and you're acting like a hellcat. How can I leave you for three years, Amy? I can't protect you while I'm in Israel."

I point to the club. "Bicky started it."

"So you took the bait?"

Uh, yeah. "What was I supposed to do, back down?"

"Yes," he says without hesitation.

"That's not me. Do you back down, Avi? Please tell me once in your life when you've backed down," I say, getting really riled up now because adrenaline is rushing through my body and I'm frightened because Avi's hands are still shaking.

No response.

Avi stares at his hands in horror, curses, then shoves them into the front pockets of his jeans. He swallows, looks away from me, and says, "Let's go."

I stay where I am, unmoving from this spot on the sidewalk in front of Durty Nevin's because I finally figured it out. What's making Avi shake.

His emotions are running rampant and he's not used to it.

Avi is a guy who is always in control of his body and mind. Even when I kidnapped him, he was in total control of the situation the entire time. Adrenaline he can handle, emotions he can't.

"You were afraid I was going to get hurt. That's why you're shaking," I blurt out.

He stops. His back is to me. "I don't shake."

"Then show me your hands."

"No."

"Avi, it's okay to be emotional."

"For you, maybe. But not for me."

I put my hand on his arm, knowing his pain about Micha's death is as raw in his chest now as it was when his brother first died. It has nothing to do with me and the fight. Avi can't let go of the pain of Micha's death, but still refuses to grieve. "You're only eighteen. And I hate to break the news to you, but you're human."

"I can't lose you, Amy," he says, his voice tense even though I sense he's trying to control his tone. "I came to America to prove to myself that I wasn't attached to you, that you weren't as important to me as my mind was telling me you were. I was wrong."

"You rode on a plane for twelve hours just to break up with me?" I say, totally confused and insulted now. I mean, seriously, to come all this way to prove I'm not worthy. "If that isn't the stupidest, most ridiculous, asinine thing I've ever heard," I say, then start walking across the street because I need space.

"A car is coming," he says.

Sure enough, I look behind me and a Honda Pilot is turning the corner and heads right to where I'm standing. "Aren't you going to save me?" I yell.

"Yeah, I am."

He walks fast to the curb and is about to step onto the street when I tell him, "If you take one step closer, it's over between us. I mean it."

"That car is gonna hit you," he says seriously, his eyes blazing with intensity. But he does stop cold in his tracks at the curb.

"They see me," I assure him.

Avi cocks his head to the side in confusion while his

hands come out of his pockets. He's trying to look relaxed, but I can tell he's ready to pounce and save me at any second.

"They'll stop," I say again, trying to prove a point that I'll be okay whether he's here to save me or not. He's not always going to be around to play Superman. Just like he wasn't around to save his brother when that bomber decided to kill innocent Israelis. My boyfriend is human and for once needs to let go and realize it.

Avi is looking at the car coming closer and then back at me. I can feel the struggle within him all the way over here. "Maybe they don't care," he says frantically to me. "Maybe they can't see you in the dark. Maybe the driver is drunk and—"

"Maybe I'll be okay, Avi."

"What if you're not? What if you die?"

I put my hand out. When the car reaches me, it comes to a halt. "Yo, chick, you gonna get out of the way?" a guy yells out the window.

"Everyone dies."

"Do you blame me for wanting to protect you, Amy? Now please get out of the street."

The guy in the car starts blowing his horn, really loud and it's hurting my already sensitive eardrums.

"I'm trying to teach my boyfriend a lesson," I scream at the driver. "Do you mind?"

"Yeah," he yells back. "Go teach him a lesson on Lower Wacker Drive where all the other wackos hang out."

"They give tickets for road rage in Chicago, you know," I say, then roll my eyes.

"Amy…I'm coming to get you in ten seconds."

"They give tickets for jaywalking in Chicago," the guy yells while intermittently beeping his horn. I get a little satisfaction he can't pass me because there's no room on the street.

"You have five more seconds to get your *ta'chat* over here."

"Do you love me, Avi?"

"Yes. Four seconds."

"Do you trust me?"

"Yes. Two seconds."

"Dude, if you don't get your crazy girlfriend out of my path I'm gonna move her myself."

"Amy," Avi says, closing his eyes tight and opening them again. Two seconds have come and gone. He has a pleading look in his eyes, eyes that are glassy with unshed tears. "*B'vakasha.* Please."

Okay, I give in. Because I've proven my point that I will be okay and Avi has proven that he can trust me. I walk over to him, my gaze never leaving his. The car screeches away. "You see. I survived."

His arms wrap around me, pulling me close.

"You're not shaking anymore," I say.

"I'm too angry with you to be scared."

"Angry? Listen, you've got to give up this superhuman theme going on in your life. Shit happens. *Life happens,*

515

okay? You're leaving tomorrow and who knows what'll happen. Am I gonna sit around my room so nothing terrible can possibly happen to me? No. Are you going to sit in your army barracks and tell your commander you can't protect Israel because your crabby girlfriend will die if you get so much as a scratch on that perfect bod or face of yours? No."

"Stop talking so I can kiss you."

"You can't shut me up with kisses, you know."

"Wanna bet?" he says, smiling with those perfect white teeth while putting his perfect hands on my body as he lowers his perfect full lips to mine and proves to me he's right.

"Let's go back to your place," he says when we come up for air.

I'm holding on to his biceps for support because his kisses still make me feel drunk. "My *aba* is there. If you even kiss me he'll probably kill you first and ask questions later."

Back at the apartment my dad is nowhere to be seen. I check the messages. There's one from him saying he has to stay late for an emergency meeting. Then he says to make sure Avi is listening to the message, too, and the rest of the message is all in Hebrew.

I roll my eyes. "Is he having another sex talk?"

"Oh, yeah. Big time."

I stop the machine before the message finishes and give Avi a mischievous look. "What are you thinking?"

"Which rooms your dad has strategically placed the hidden cameras."

I laugh. "That's ridiculous. My dad doesn't have any hidden cameras in this house."

"He sounded pretty convincing, but I have an idea."

We get ready for bed, like a married couple except for the fact that we're just two trusting teenagers in complete love with each other. Avi's bed is still the couch in the living room, but this time I snuggle under the covers with him because my overprotective father isn't home watching our every move.

"I like this," I say. "So what's your idea?"

Avi pulls the covers over our heads so we're cloaked in complete darkness.

I finger his stubble with my fingertips. "This is your big idea?"

"It was either under the blanket or inside the hall closet."

"It's all *sababa*," I say, and Avi laughs.

"Yeah, it is."

I will tell you that under the covers was an excellent choice and VERY *sababa*, although I'm one hundred percent sure my dad does not have any surveillance cameras inside the house tracking our every move. I know this because although my dad came home an hour later and I ran to my room and pretended to be fast asleep, those cameras would have caught Avi and I in some very compromising positions despite our attempt to keep the covers over us.

Oh, don't get all worried…I'm still a pure seventeen-year-old. I'm just…well…more knowledgeable about certain things. (Things I'm more curious about now than I ever was.)

In the morning, Tarik picked up Avi and drove us all to the airport. I was crying the entire time, although I tried to keep it together. Our goodbye kiss held more promise than last time, although we both know we have to go on and live our lives. Don't ask, don't tell. We're going to take it one day at a time and see what happens. Hopefully this summer when I go to Israel it'll be the same as last night…well, without the fighting.

I purposely didn't bring up Jessica to Tarik, although now Tarik and I are sitting at Perk Me Up! and Jess could walk in at any time.

Marla brings me hot chocolate with the whipped cream overflowing because she knows how upset I am. Do you think my bloodshot, teary eyes give my upsetness away? Marla hugs me, a warm hug my mom would give me if she were here.

An idea pops into my head. I can't believe I hadn't thought of it before. "Marla, what do you think of my dad? You know, if he smiled more and got a good haircut?"

Marla laughs and walks back to the register, ignoring my question. I think I saw her blush a little, though. My dad loves her coffee; he never drinks it anywhere else. In fact, I think he got me this job just so he could see her more and have an excuse to hang out at Perk Me Up! Hmm…

The door to Perk Me Up! opens and guess who walks

in…yep, Jess. Along with Miranda and a very sad Nathan. Poor Nathan. Poor Jess.

It's time I stop making a mess of my own life and focus on everyone else. I can do it. There's nothing that says I have to be a Disaster Girl all the time. I can live a squeaky-clean life while helping others un-screwup their lives. No more getting in trouble for Amy Nelson-Barak.

My cell phone is ringing. It's my dad. "Hey, *Aba*, what's up?"

"What's up? Please tell me what a pair of plastic hand-cuffs are doing in the back seat of my car."

Oops. Everything is *so* not *sababa*.

How to Ruin Your Boyfriend's Reputation

1

A vacation without parents is like a chocolate
brownie without the nuts—absolutely perfect!

Hi, my name is Amy Nelson-Barak. My mom is a Nelson
and my dad is a Barak and just in case you were wondering, I'm aware I have two last names. If you don't know
me, I'm a seventeen-year-old American teenager with red,
white, and blue blood running through my veins. You're
probably wondering why right now I'm on a bus in Israel
on my way to an Israeli military boot camp.

Yes, I did say I'm in Israel. No need to rub your eyes
and reread that.

And yes, I did say boot camp.

And before you think it's a boot camp for teens with
behavioral disorders, I volunteered for this summer program all on my own. (Although my parents often accuse

me of being a total drama queen, I don't think that counts as a true behavior disorder.) My friends signed up, too. Normally I wouldn't go anywhere near a program with the word "military" in it, especially during the summer between my junior and senior years of high school, but when I realized what military base the boot camp is held at, I jumped to sign up—as a volunteer trainee.

You see, my boyfriend Avi is Israeli. He's in the IDF—Israeli Defense Force—and since I live in the good ol' US of A (Chicago, to be exact), I haven't seen him since he visited me over five months ago. He's a commando, he's nineteen years old, and is just about the hottest, most gorgeous gift God has ever put on this planet. And he's all mine. Well, to be technical, the Israeli military owns his body until he turns twenty-one, but I own his heart. And he owns mine.

So I got this letter from Avi a few months back. He told me that after parachute training he's going to be at Base Nesher. He said if I was visiting Israel this summer, unfortunately he didn't think he could get any time off.

Then, when my best friend Jessica, along with this girl Miranda and my best guy friend Nathan (who I kissed once … okay, three times … but we're just friends), told me they were signing up for a program in Israel that included ten days in basic training boot camp, I laughed at them. I mean, what kind of idiot would go to a military boot camp on purpose?

But guess what? It's at Base Nesher—the same base Avi is at! When I figured that out, I begged my father to sign me up. I haven't told Avi that I'm coming—it's a surprise. I can't wait to see his reaction when he sees me. He's going to be as excited as I am!

I'm so thankful this bus is air conditioned and we have big, cushioned seats for the three-hour ride. We're on the bus with forty other American teens (half are girls, half are guys). The trip is called *Sababa*, which translates to "cool, awesome, a great way of life" or something like that. The tour starts out with the boot camp, then the rest of the summer is spent exploring and touring the country.

The director of the *Sababa* program gave me special permission to sign up for the boot camp portion of the trip only, because after boot camp I'll be staying at my aunt and uncle's house on their *moshav* (kinda like a community farm) in the Golan Heights. So I'll be with family while Miranda, Nathan, and Jessica spend the rest of the summer on the *Sababa* tour.

"Amy, I think Miranda is gonna puke," Nathan tells me. He's sitting next to Miranda, who has had anxiety about the boot camp part of the vacation. She's been stressing about it since we took the plane from Chicago to Tel Aviv (with a ridiculously long layover in New York). Miranda's a tad bit, uh, I don't know how to say this in a politically correct way...let's just say she's in the upper sixtieth percentile on the weight chart hanging in the nurse's office at our high school. (Probably closer to the seventy-fifth, but who's counting.) She's afraid they're going to ration her food at boot camp and make her run until her extra, overflowing muffin-top disappears.

I lean over my best friend Jessica, who's blocking my view of Miranda. "Miranda, it's not going to be like Camp Meltaway. I promise."

Miranda's parents sent her to a fat farm between seventh and eighth grade and she's never gotten over it. The girl cannot survive on granola for snack food. Believe it or not, during her second week at Camp Meltaway, meek and timid Miranda got caught trying to hitchhike into town in search of fast food.

Miranda smiles a little at the sight of a candy bar I pulled from my backpack. Seriously, one day I'll teach her that moderation is "the key" to weight loss. She can have a candy bar every day…just not three of them in one sitting.

Now for me, personally, if I could only get "the key" to smaller boobs (without surgery, since I'm not a fan of getting my little pinky parts cut off and reattached, thank you very much), I'd be the first in line. Yes siree, we all have our little personal issues, things we'd like to change or need to change about ourselves.

"I brought extra Kit Kats," I say, holding up the candy bar. Okay, so the label says *Kif-Kaf* in Hebrew, but it's the same thing.

Jessica slaps my hand down. "Don't show her that."

"Why not?"

"Because she wants to lose weight, Amy. Don't sabotage her."

I roll my eyes. Sometimes my best friend has to be enlightened. "Jess, you heard Nathan. Miranda is so scared she's about to *puke*. I'm just trying to comfort her."

"So comfort her with words and friendship, not candy bars," Jess whispers. "That stuff is poison."

Is she kidding me? Chocolate is my favorite comfort food. Well, it's actually #2 because everybody knows sushi is at the top of my list. Not all sushi, just spicy tuna rolls with little pieces of tempura crunch inside. Nothing, not even chocolate, beats that.

I rummage through my backpack. "Have you seen *these*?" I say, creating suspense as I slowly pull out a *Kif-Kaf* bar wrapped in a white package instead of the usual red one. "It's a Kit Kat bar in *white* chocolate, Jess. They were almost sold out at the store, but I found this one lonely package mixed in with the regular ones. I know you love white chocolate as much as I do." I wave it in front of her nose. "Smell the white chocolate…crave the white chocolate."

"I can't smell anything. It's still in the wrapper."

"I'm saving it for a special occasion."

Before I can stick my rare white chocolate find back in the special zippered compartment in my backpack, Nathan reaches across the bus aisle and snatches the *Kif-Kaf* out of my hand. "Cool, white chocolate Kit Kat. I've always wanted to try one of those. Thanks!"

"Give that back!" I yell.

Nathan, who is a total and complete dufus 90 percent of the time, rips the package open and takes a huge bite from the top. He doesn't even snap off one of the four sticks like any normal, decent person would do. No, he bites a quarter off the top, so now all the bars have a chunk out of them. "Damn, that's good."

My mouth is open wide in shock. "I can't believe you just did that."

"What?"

"First of all, I was just telling Jess I'm saving it for a special occasion. I only have one white chocolate, and you … you … you … " I can't even express how pissed I am at him.

Nathan shrugs, then holds out the rest of the uneaten bar. "Here, you want a bite?"

Yuck! "You bit off the whole top. You're supposed to snap off the sticks one at a time. Everyone knows that. Now the entire thing is tainted with your saliva germs."

"Come on, Amy. You've been exposed to my saliva germs before." He makes a smooching noise, then grins. "So what's the big deal?"

I pretend to gag. "Don't remind me."

You probably think I hate Nathan. I don't. Next to Jessica, he's my best friend and the most entertaining thing I have in my life, especially when Avi and I are apart. Nathan is like my very own live Elmo doll that walks, talks, and farts. Maybe that isn't the greatest analogy, but you get the idea.

"I'll have a bite," Miranda sheepishly chimes in, leaning toward the half-eaten chocolate.

Nathan sticks his tongue out at me and moves the chocolate closer to Miranda. She takes a bite, then Nathan finishes it off by popping the rest in his mouth. Miranda can be my guest and swap germs with Nathan all she wants.

"You owe me another *Kif-Kaf*," I tell him. "A *white chocolate* one."

"Whatever," he says, licking his fingers one by one, making those little sucking sounds on each one to annoy me.

"Keep doin' that, big guy. You forget that my strong, military commando boyfriend will kick your butt once I tell him you mutilated my white Kit Kat without my permission."

Nathan stops licking his fingers. "Seriously, tell that guy to stay away from me. I think I still have bruise marks on my face in the shape of his fist."

"Avi only hit you because you attacked him first," I remind him.

"You told me to, Amy," Nathan says defensively. "You know, during your stupid Operation Get-Avi-Back on the Northwestern campus."

Nathan's right—but it was only to stall Avi so I could let him know I was devastated we broke up during his trip to Chicago. I was desperate to get back together. It wasn't a stupid plan. It was brilliant, especially because it worked. "Well, that's old news. Avi doesn't even remember you."

Okay, so that's not exactly true. Sometimes Avi will ask about Nathan when we talk on the phone. He knows Nathan and I kissed ... he doesn't know it was *three* times, though. To be completely honest, the first time was awful, the third time was fake (it was actually last month—to make his ex-girlfriend Bicky believe he was dating me so she'd stop dropping into his life), but the second time ...

I don't want to think about that second time. So Nathan knows how to kiss when he puts a little effort into it. It's not a big deal.

It doesn't matter, anyway. Avi is the only guy I ever want to kiss. He knows nearly everything about me (of course, he's never heard me on the toilet because I run the water when I'm in the bathroom, and he has no clue I have a fear of spiders), and the guy still loves me. My dad warns me not to wait around for him, because he's in Israel and we have a long-distance relationship. He also says we're too young to say we'll be together forever.

As if my dad knows about love. My dad is single and has just started dating Marla, the woman who runs the coffee shop in the building next to our condo. I admit I set them up ... one night I invited her over, and when my dad came home I had Nathan come up with an excuse to get me out of there so they could have some alone-time. The rest is history; at least, it will be when my dad decides to ask Marla to marry him. Then I won't have to worry that he'll be without a partner the rest of his life.

The bus comes to a stop and I glance out the window. The security checkpoint, the gates, and the soldiers in green military uniforms clue me in that we've finally arrived at the base. Almost everywhere you go in Israel, you see someone in a military uniform and most have a rifle strapped to their backs.

I've only been to Israel once before (although this will be my first time on a military base) and I'm already desensitized to seeing military personnel everywhere I go, from the mall (they check your purse before you go inside to make sure you're not carrying an illegal bomb or weapon) to tourist and religious sites. They even have a security guy stationed outside the grocery store. It's totally different back home in Chicago. While the abundance of military presence in Israel isn't what I'm used to, it makes me feel tremendously safe.

I'll have to remember to pray for the day Israelis don't have to worry about war or terrorism. I also have to pray they can make some sort of peace with their neighbors, because I'm a huge "let's make love, not war" kind of person.

Speaking of love ... I look out the window and crane my neck to see if I can spot Avi. No such luck.

Pulling out my makeup case, I tell Jess to hold up the mirror so I can brush on more blush and fix any smudged eyeliner. Then I hold up the mirror for Jess so she can do the same.

"What are you girls doing?" Nathan asks, laughing.

"Fixing ourselves."

"This isn't a beauty pageant, you know. It's the IDF."

"We know," Jess says, dipping the lip gloss applicator in the tube and applying it to her lips. "But who says just because you're in the army you have to look like crap?"

"Seriously, Nathan. Don't you know anything about girls?"

"Apparently not." He turns to Miranda and puts his hands in a praying position. "Don't be like them, okay?"

"I like the way they look," Miranda tells him. "If I was as pretty as them, I'd do the same."

He slaps his palm against his forehead. "I cannot believe what I'm hearing. Miranda, you're fine as-is." *Great, Nathan, treat her as if she's a defective as-is item sold on the clearance rack.*

"Miranda, I need makeup to look good," I tell her.

"You're naturally pretty."

When the bus passes through the checkpoint, my heart starts racing. I wonder when we'll have free time to explore the base so I can search for Avi.

"Don't volunteer for anything," a guy in the seat behind us whispers through the space between the seats. "Pass it down."

I pass the message down.

"I heard if you volunteer, you'll be stuck doing some crappy assignment," Jess says.

Note taken. I will not volunteer. I have a major aversion to crappy assignments.

2

---

*Why couldn't God have given humans doggie sweat
glands, so we could gracefully pant our sweat away?*

Our military leaders, or *ha'mefa'ked* in Hebrew (if you say
it fast it sounds like *I'm a [insert cuss word]*), are named
Ronit and Susu. They're both Israeli, both in the military,
and *their* crappy assignment is being in charge of us during boot camp. Susu is in charge of the twenty guys and
Ronit is in charge of the twenty girls.

Ronit stands next to the bus driver with her clipboard
in hand. "Girls, please find your suitcases and follow me
to the *bittan*. Boys, follow Susu."

We gather our backpacks and file off the bus.

"If they're gonna separate the guys from the girls, can
we at least have co-ed showers?" Nathan mumbles.

"You're a pig," I tell him.

"Shh, don't say the word 'pig' so loud, Amy," Nathan whispers in my ear. "Pigs aren't kosher, you know."

"Whatever, Nathan. It's not like I'm gonna eat it. I just *said* it."

Some of the stronger American guys from our trip are unloading our luggage. I would be searching for my luggage, but I'm too consumed with Avi-scanning and fanning my face with my hand because it's so hot outside.

You'd think God's holy land wouldn't be as hot as hell, but it is.

"Find your luggage fast, ladies!" Ronit's voice booms from behind us. "And follow me!"

"Does she have to be so cheery all the time?" Jess asks. "It's irritating."

"Maybe she loves her job," Miranda chimes in.

I snort, on purpose. "Maybe she's got a personality disorder."

I watch as Nathan joins the other guys following Susu. I have to give major credit to Nathan for always fitting in as "one of the guys." He's never an outcast or out of place, because everyone likes him. It's a trait that totally annoys someone like me—I only feel comfortable with people who know me.

I spot my hot pink luggage that I bought for my trip. One big rolling suitcase and one smaller one. My father wanted me to buy a dorky duffel or some boring luggage that had been "rated highly" (my dad's words, not mine) by Consumer Reports, but I'd axed that suggestion because the only colors available were *black* and *black with dark gray trim.* I have one word to describe them: BOR-ING!

I want my luggage to reflect my personality. And I'm anything *but* boring. I pull out the handles to my girlie suitcases and start wheeling them away from the others.

Ronit holds her hand high in the air and says, "Follow me, girls!" as she heads down the road. "*Yala, zooz!* Hurry!"

Most of the girls in our group are lugging duffels (okay, I admit the brochure might have recommended them, but it'd be impossible to shove all my stuff in a duffel...and I'd never be able to carry it even if I could). How these girls can fit their necessities into one bag is beyond me.

Miranda, Jessica, and I are lagging behind. I mean, come on...who can hurry when it's so damn hot outside? Jessica has two pink suitcases, just like me, but hers have huge rhinestone/diamond studs spelling out JESSICA across the side. Miranda only has one painfully boring black suitcase. The poor girl is sweating so much there are wet spots in the shape of half-moons under her boobs.

"I think I'm going to die," Miranda says, yanking a portable fan out of her suitcase and hanging it around her neck. "Where are the barracks?"

I would feel sorry for her, except my boobs have the same half-moon wet spots and I don't have a portable fan.

3

*Everything from your sunglasses to your suitcase should
reflect your unique style and attitude.*

With my designer sunglasses protecting my eyes, my back-pack on my back, and a suitcase rolling in each hand, I'm walking slowly down the road. We're passing offices and off-white buildings made out of cement. I'm painfully aware of the many Israeli soldiers pointing to the three of us and snickering.

Yes, gawk at the American girls struggling with their luggage, I want to say, but don't. We must look totally out of place with our Abercrombie outfits and pimped-out suitcases. Listen, I don't blame them for laughing. I'm definitely out of my element.

I silently pray for Avi to come to my rescue and take my luggage to the barracks for me.

Sweat rolls down my forehead. Where is my boy-friend? And how big is this army base anyway?

"Come on, girls!" Ronit urges from far down the road.

Jess puts on a huge fake smile and waves to our leader. "We're coming!" she says, mimicking Ronit's cheery tone. Jess and I know she's making fun of Ronit, but I doubt anyone else does. "Don't they have a bellman?" She wipes her upper lip that's beading with sweat. "They better have air-conditioned rooms. I just got my lip waxed and don't have anything for the sweat to cling to."

"Ugh, TMI," I tell her.

"It's true, Amy. Do you have another portable fan with you, Miranda?"

She shakes her head.

I look left and right to see if I can catch a glimpse of my boyfriend. "Avi has got to be around here somewhere, right?"

Jess sighs. She misses Tarik, her boyfriend. He's Pales-tinian, and although he's not thrilled about her spending part of her summer on an Israeli military base, he under-stands her commitment to her religion because he feels the same about his.

Jessica is Jewish and Tarik is Muslim. You'd think they'd avoid each other like I avoid political debates, but ever since they met they've chosen to ignore the obvious obstacles in their relationship. So who am I to bring it up? I'm a huge fan of living in ignorant bliss.

I'm wondering when this lugging-luggage torture will

be over. My suitcases are kicking up dust from the gravel road. Now I'm not only sweaty, but dirty too. I pull harder. Visions of a hot shower with my papaya-scented bath gel and a nice relaxing nap on a featherbed dance in my brain.

Suddenly, I hear a snap and watch one of the wheels on my beautiful, designer, hot-pink suitcase roll away from me and bounce to the bottom of a ditch. I suck in a horrified breath.

4

It boggles my mind that there's a direct correlation
between lack of quality and bling.
At least in the suitcase department.

"Whoa, that sucks," Jess says slowly.

Miranda points to the offending wheel. "Amy, is that yours?"

"Yep." So now I have a broken piece of luggage and I'm still not at our barracks.

I swallow my ego and start walking toward the stupid broken wheel. I eye it in the ditch where it stopped. I'm wearing a pink tank and white jean shorts, and I know if I slip as I go down I'm going to have dirt all over me. Oh, don't go blaming me about wearing white shorts... climbing down into a ditch to retrieve a stupid wheel wasn't exactly one of the warnings in the *Sababa* brochure.

I take one step down. My foot slides a little, then stops.

I probably should tell you now that I'm wearing these really cute pink mules that aren't really made for traction—but they sure do match my tank perfectly. I'm not about to take out the gym shoes I bought for this trip, because they're at the bottom of one of my suitcases.

I take another step, and wobble because I'm walking on an angle.

"Be careful," Miranda warns.

Before I take another step, a boy in uniform walks up to us. "*Mah karah?*" he asks. He's got short hair and beautiful olive skin without a trace of acne.

"*Angleet, b'vakashah,*" I say. My dad taught me that phrase, which means "English, please."

"You need help?" He has a big Israeli accent along with a big Israeli smile (he's also got a big Israeli rifle slung on his back).

"Desperately," I admit, pointing to the wheel.

He scrambles down the bank as if he does it every day of his life, and picks up the wheel. On his way back up, he grabs my elbow and helps me back to the gravel road. Then attempts to reattach the wheel.

"This suitcase is a piece of *sheet*," he informs me. "It can't be fixed." He hands me the plastic wheel. I almost laugh at the word "sheet"—American profanity with an Israeli accent comes out really funny. But I'm sweaty and unhappy and cannot physically laugh right now.

I shove the wheel in the front pocket of my suitcase. "Well, thanks for trying."

"Yeah, thanks," Miranda chimes in.

The guy holds out his hand. "I'm Nimrod."

"No, really, what's your name?" I ask.

"Nimrod."

He did not just say *Nimrod*, did he? With the Israeli accent it sounds like *Nim-road*.

I put my sunglasses on top of my head, eyeing him suspiciously. "*Nimrod*?"

"Nimrod. I guess in America this is not a popular name, no?"

Jess is trying not to laugh. Miranda just looks confused. Some names in Israel do not translate to English well. Avi has friends named Doo-Doo, Moron, and O'dead. And my cousin's name is pronounced O'snot.

"I'm Amy. And this is Jessica and Miranda," I say, pointing to each of my friends.

Nimrod heaves the entire suitcase up into his arms. "Your group is at the *bittan* on the other side of the hill. I'll help you."

"Thanks," I say, noting that my hot pink suitcase looks very out of place in Nimrod's arms and I still have no clue what a *bittan* is. I roll my smaller suitcase behind him. As we pass other soldiers, they make comments in Hebrew to Nimrod, who laughs and shrugs as he leads us up the hill.

The guy isn't breaking a sweat in this heat, which is not normal. Looking around, I notice that none of the Israeli soldiers milling around are sweating. It makes me wonder if Israelis are born without sweat glands.

"Where are you girls from?" Nimrod asks.

"Chicago," I say.

"I've never been there, but there's a guy in my unit whose girlfriend lives there."

Could Nimrod know Avi? That would be so cool and easy if the first guy I meet on the base knows where Avi is. "Is his name Avi Gefen? Because I know he's stationed on this base for a few weeks this summer—"

Nimrod stops and his eyes bug out. "*You're* Gefen's girlfriend?"

I smile wide. I can't help it. "Yep."

I think I notice the corners of his mouth twitch, but I'm not sure. "Does Gefen know you're here?"

"No," I say sheepishly. "It's kind of a surprise."

"Oh, he will *definitely* be surprised." We all follow Nimrod to what I assume is the barracks (aka *bittan*). I spot them now. The barracks are off-white cement buildings (similar to every building on base), but they're one story and have only two small windows on each side.

"Amy! Jessica! Miranda!"

I wince at the sound of Ronit's voice. The four of us reach our very annoyed leader. She's standing next to a guy who resembles a Russian boxer I once saw in an old Rocky movie... or a WWE wrestler. He's over six feet tall with blond hair and blue eyes. And his arms are crossed on his chest, making his huge muscles bunch up. Avi's muscles are huge, but this guy must weightlift small cars to get his arms that bulky.

I point to the luggage in Nimrod's hand. "Sorry we lagged behind. One of my suitcases broke."

Nimrod sets my luggage down and salutes to the big, blond wrestler.

"Girls, this is Sergeant Ben-Shimon," Ronit says, introducing us to the big dude. "He'll be your unit commander."

"Oh, cool," I say. "Can we just call you Sergeant Ben?"

"No," he says in a stern voice. "The rest of your unit is already having lunch."

Great, they all left without us. "Well, I guess if you point us in the direction of the mess hall or whatever you call the place where we eat, that'll be great."

Ronit points to the open doorway. "Put your suitcases in the *bittan*, then follow me to the *cheder ochel*, where soldiers eat. There isn't much time left before your next activity."

The inside of the place we'll be sleeping for the next three weeks isn't pretty. Bunk beds are lined up in neat rows (just in case you were wondering, the bunks are made out of metal, not wood) and the mattresses don't resemble anything like featherbeds. The place is not air conditioned, and the windows are open. Unfortunately, the door to the room is open to the outside, too, so a few bees are flying around.

Do the *Sababa* tour people know that sleeping with bees is so *not sababa*?

Jessica and I eye each other. We don't even have to talk, because we've been best friends long enough to know what the other is thinking.

Miranda says, "This isn't so bad."

Jessica and I don't answer.

We all set our suitcases inside the barracks, then follow Ronit.

"Where are the bathrooms?" I ask. "I had an entire Diet Coke on the bus and I've got to pee."

"Me, too," Jessica says.

Miranda admits she's been holding it for the past two hours, so Ronit leads us to a small structure. It's bigger than a port-a-potty but smaller than the girls' bathroom at Chicago Academy, where I go to school.

"Here. But you better hurry, girls."

We file inside the bathroom. The stench of pee/poo/ bacterial disinfectant creeps up my nostrils immediately.

Jess takes her designer sunglasses off her nose slowly. "This place stinks so bad my eyes are starting to water."

I plug my nose. "Seriously, Mutt's farts aren't this bad." (Mutt is my crazy dog, and yes, he is a mutt.)

I hurry to pull back a curtain, which I assume is the equivalent to a bathroom stall back home. When I peek at what's behind the curtain, I can't believe my eyes.

It's a hole. In the ground.

Okay, so that's not entirely the right way to describe it.

It's a hole in the ground with two rubber non-skid mats in the shape of feet on either side of it … I guess for dumb people who have no clue where to place their feet.

"I can't pee in that," I say, but saying the word 'pee' makes my urge to do it that much stronger.

Jess whines. "Do you think I can hold it in for two weeks?"

I look back at Ronit. "Do you have any bathrooms with toilets?"

"This *is* a bathroom. And that's a toilet."

"No, that's a hole."

Ronit was previously cheery, but I think we've cracked her and now she's bordering on annoyed. She steps forward. "This isn't a hotel or spa, ladies. It's the IDF. Now either pee or not, I don't care. But you have three minutes to do your business and head to the *cheder ochel* to eat, or you'll be finding yourselves assigned to bathroom cleaning duties."

With that, Ronit leaves the three of us alone.

"I hate her," Jess says.

Miranda's mouth starts to quiver. I'm not sure if it's because she's late for lunch or because she doesn't know how to pee in a hole.

"My bladder is about to burst," I say, pushing past Jessica and closing the curtain shut.

"I'll go in the one next to you," Jess says.

I notice the graffiti on the side wall. In pen, someone etched words in English. It says: *Beware of the Loof!*

What or *who* is the Loof?

I don't have time to think about the Loof too hard. I put my feet on the rubber pads and pull down my shorts. But when I try and squat, they're in the way.

"I can't squat for this long," Jess says. "My thigh muscles are starting to quiver."

"I think I just peed on my leg," Miranda informs us. Eww!

When I'm finally in position, I can't relax because I'm listening to my two friends complain. "Shut up, guys. My pee is getting stage fright from listening to you both yapping."

"Thirty seconds!" Ronit yells from outside.

Yeah, as if pressure is going to help me relax.

I hear Miranda wash her hands and head outside. Then I hear Jess washing her hands by the sink. "Hurry up, Amy," she whispers loudly. "I don't want to do doo-doo duty."

I look down at the hole, to see if I am aiming in the right spot. "Oh, shit!" I yell. "My sunglasses fell in the hole!" I forgot they were on top of my head!

"If you stick your hand down there to get them, I cannot be best friends with you anymore. Just leave them!" Jess calls out. "And hurry up!"

"Those cost me $235."

"Now they're worth nothing. Come on!"

For a nanosecond I contemplate fishing them out of the crap (literally) below, but ... I just can't. I think if I did I'd require more therapy than I already need.

Wiping myself (with brown toilet paper resembling brown paper towels they have in the art room at school—which I now know is very scratchy and irritating on sensitive body parts) and putting my undies and shorts back on, I pray that I see Avi soon. Because this army experience is not me, and while I knew that the experience would be challenging, I also knew that seeing Avi for even a little bit would be worth it.

Now if I could just find my boyfriend ...

5

There are some things God never intended girls to do—
squatting when peeing is definitely high up on that list.

Lunch was in a hot and sweaty coed building. Well, to be specific, I was hot and sweaty ... the room was just hot. I caught a glimpse of Nathan, who seemed to be entertaining his table because everyone was focused on him. The meal consisted of overcooked chicken (considering I only eat white meat and came to lunch late, I was stuck eating legs and thighs), yellow rice, and a pea/mushroom concoction. Drinks were a choice of room-temperature tap water or room-temperature tap water (you guessed it, there wasn't a choice at all). And I'm not sure Israelis know what ice is, because every time I asked for it they got a confused look on their face.

Oh, yeah. They had hot coffee and hot tea as drink

alternatives, but I don't drink those and anyway who in their right mind would want a hot beverage when it feels like it's a hundred degrees outside? There wasn't even a Coke machine.

At the end of our hurried meal, we all place our garbage in cans and the plates/silverware in plastic bins, and are instructed to line up outside in neat rows.

Someone taps me on the shoulder. I turn around, hoping against all hope that it's Avi, but it's not. "Oh, it's you."

Nathan puts his arm around me. "Oh, come on. Admit that you missed me."

"We've only been apart for a little more than an hour, Nathan. Give me time to miss you." I shrug his arm off me. "I see you've made friends already."

"The guys in my unit are cool, but I'd rather bunk with you girls," he says as we line up with the others like good little soldiers. For over twenty minutes we're taught how to get in formation. Five rows of eight people each, an arm's length apart. "At ease" is hands behind your back with your legs spread shoulder width apart. "Attention" is saluting with your feet together.

Ronit is standing in front of the entire group, with Sergeant "Don't-Call-Me-Ben"-Shimon next to her.

"Let's just say I'm glad you're on the other side of the base," I whisper to Nathan as the sergeant starts talking.

"I can always sneak out with the guys and peek in on you girls while you're changing," he whispers back.

I wish I could talk louder but everyone is quiet, listening to the sergeant. I'll have to get briefed later on what he's saying, because I'm not listening. Instead, I whisper, "Nathan, you're a perv."

"We can call it Operation Boobie Watch," he whispers back, but emphasizes the word "boobie," which he knows I hate. *Boobage, boobie, jugs, hammocks,* etc … I hate all the nicknames for boobs.

Operation Boobie Watch? Eww! I know Nathan doesn't mean it. He's just trying to get a rise out of me because it entertains him. He knows how to push my buttons … especially when it comes to boobs.

God gave me this body, but I really wish he'd have given me less of it in the boob department.

In response to Nathan's comment, I shove him away from me. Which isn't the best idea in the world, because now Sergeant "Don't-Call-Me-Ben"-Shimon stops talking and focuses his ice-blue eyes on us.

"Tell me your names?"

Everyone is staring at us. We're in big trouble. Oh, crap. "Amy," I squeak out. Guess he didn't remember we already were introduced by the barracks.

"Nathan, sir!" I hear from my best guy friend/enemy/ annoyance beside me. He says it loud and clear, like he's been in the military his entire life instead of just one and a half hours.

"Amy, what was I just explaining?" the sergeant asks me.

Double oh-crap. I dare not tell the guy I was expecting

to get the shortened version by asking my friends. Deciding there's no other way around it, I tell him the truth.

"I don't know ... SIR!" I figure adding the 'sir' might earn *me* some brownie points—it seemed to work for Nathan. But from the sergeant's eyebrow-furrowing expression, I realize my 'sir' didn't work.

He stands in front of Nathan and asks the same question. Nathan's response is the same as mine.

"You and you," the sergeant says, pointing to each of us. "Follow me."

We follow the guy to the front of the entire American trainee unit. Looking ahead, I see Jessica with a worried expression. She knows I'm not into the whole military thing.

"Give me twenty," the sergeant commands, with his hands on his hips.

"You mean like dollars?" I ask. "Or shekels? I mean, I left my purse back in my suitcase."

Nathan nudges me. "He means pushups, Amy. Not money."

Oh. Right. "I knew that," I lie. I'm sorry if when someone says "give me twenty" my mind doesn't automatically think of physical activity.

Nathan flashes me a "loser" sign on his forehead.

The sergeant points to us, then the ground.

Nathan gets into position on the ground, supporting himself by his toes and hands.

"Can I do it the girlie way?" I ask. "Our gym teacher

Mr. Haraldson lets us." When the sergeant looks confused I add, "You know, with my knees on the ground."

"Fine."

I get in position next to Nathan, knowing my white shorts are now beyond repair. When Nathan starts, I start. My knees are on gravel, and rocks are digging into my skin.

After I do one pushup, sweat drips off my forehead and lands on the gravel beneath me. I do a few more, then stop to look over at Nathan. He's groaning after a few minutes and lies down on the dirt exhausted and sweaty like me.

"You both are weak. Get up."

The sergeant has Nathan and me stand side by side in front of everyone. "*Small* is left, *ya'mean* is right. When I say *small*, you march with your left foot. When I say *ya'mean*, you march with your right foot. Understand?"

Nathan says, "Yes, sir!" like a total kiss-ass army recruit.

I raise my hand. "Excuse me, I have a question."

The sergeant looks at me as if I'm the stupidest person on earth. Sure, when it comes to marching I might lack the basic natural instincts. But get me on my own turf and I know all there is to know about the city and how to maneuver in it. Some people call Chicago a jungle, but it's my jungle and my turf.

I'm not used to this military jungle, though.

"What *zee* problem?" he says impatiently. It's weird—when Israelis get upset their accent gets more pronounced. I know that from my dad, because he's Israeli.

Everyone is still watching, which makes me nervous. I even hear a few snickers from the American guys. Remind me to listen to every single syllable Sergeant "Don't-Call-Me-Ben"-Shimon (from now on referred to as Sergeant B-S) says from this second forward. I don't want to be put front and center again.

The sun is glaring in my eyes. I squint up at the sergeant and silently curse the poop hole I dropped my sunglasses in. "Yeah, I was um…I was wondering if you lift your foot on the *smalls* and *ya'means* or if you put your foot down on them. Could you clarify, please?"

"You put your foot down on them," my boyfriend's voice says from behind me.

6

Avoid public humiliation at all costs—
especially in front of your boyfriend.

I whirl around to see Avi. He's a few yards away, walking toward me. His face is tan and his profile is chiseled like a Roman statue. His hair is a little grown out from his buzz cut. He's so hot and sexy I can't help but stare in awe at my boyfriend who professed his love to me in letters (yes, he actually sits down and writes actual letters to me when he can't call), and in voicemail messages he left when he visited me in Chicago. I've saved them all and listen to them every time I need to hear his voice. Not being able to hold myself still any longer, I catapult forward and wrap my arms around his neck.

"Avi!" I cry into his chest. "Are you surprised?"

"Very." He gently takes my wrists and unwinds them

from around his neck. He salutes the sergeant, who says something in Hebrew. Avi answers.

So this is a time when I wish I knew Hebrew. I take Spanish. A few months ago I told my dad to stop speaking to me in English and only speak to me in Hebrew. That lasted about an hour, because I wanted to rip my hair out from not understanding him and got annoyed by his hand gestures when he pointed to objects, trying to give me hints. I wanted to learn Hebrew, not play charades.

Avi looks down at me. "We can't talk now."

Beside me, Nathan is tense. The last time I was reunited with Avi, back in January when he came to Chicago, he'd caught Nathan with his arm around my shoulders. It was not a happy time in our relationship, especially when Avi found out a few days later that Nathan and I had kissed in the cafeteria at school in front of half of the Chicago Academy student body.

But that was a long time ago. I'm here in Israel now, standing in front of my boyfriend who's in the Israeli military until he's at least twenty-one. Avi is wearing a sand-colored uniform, unlike most of the soldiers on the base who are wearing olive green. All of us Americans are still in our regular clothes, so we look out of place among the real soldiers.

"I know we can't talk right this second," I tell Avi. "But after I learn how to do the marching thing, do you have any free time so we can be alone? Just you and me."

"Amy, we can't go anywhere alone. It's against base rules."

"But I'm your *girlfriend*, not some *random*."

I hear snickers behind Avi. Leaning so I can see who's behind him, I notice Nimrod standing with four guys and a girl all in sand-colored uniforms like Avi's. The girl is covering her mouth to suppress her giggle. She's not wearing a stitch of makeup on her perfectly flawless skin, has long sandy blond hair with natural streaks in it tied up in a ponytail, and is really tall. To add insult to injury, she's got normal-sized, perfect boobs. I bet they stand at attention without a bra, while (as my mother always reminds me) God blessed me with boobs that need a little help being lifted.

I feel like an ogre next to this Israeli girl.

I would give her my famous sneer, but she's got a rifle so I figure it's in my best interest not to piss her off. I then notice they all have big rifles strapped to their backs. Avi does too.

Guns scare me. Especially big ones with bullets in them.

"Attention!" Sergeant B-S barks at me. I stand next to Nathan with my hands stiffly at my sides. We're still in front of everyone, so I guess our punishment for talking isn't over. This sucks.

The sergeant says something to Avi and his posse, then they all stand back and watch. "Ready," the sergeant says to Nathan and me. It's not a question.

Ready or not, I'm about to march. In front of the rest of my unit, and in front of Avi and his friends.

"*Small. Small. Small-ya'mean-small. Small. Small. Small-ya'mean-small.*" Nathan and I follow the sergeant as we demonstrate how to march. I'm all too aware of Avi's gaze on me, and I want to die from embarrassment because I'm royally screwing up. I'm *smalling* on the *ya'means* and *ya'meaning* on the *smalls*. It's not that I'm uncoordinated. I'm just nervous.

Glancing sideways, I catch sight of Avi. I can't tell what he's thinking because he's got a composed, soldier-like expression.

As my eyes meet Avi's, I stumble into the sergeant, who must have stopped and barked stopping orders while I was still *smalling* and *ya'meaning*. "Oops," I say as my nose bumps his back. Actually, my boobs bumped him first because they're a gazillion times bigger than my nose, but I hope nobody noticed.

"*B'amakom atz'or* means you stop." Ronit clues me in.

"Got it. Thanks." I salute her because I want to be all military-like, but the saluting just brings more snickers from Avi's friends until he glares at them.

Oh, God, I hope he's not ashamed of me. What if his feelings for me changed since he came to visit back in January? What if he likes the gorgeous streaked-blond girl with the big rifle?

That very girl whispers to my boyfriend, then looks in my direction. Avi nods. Our eyes meet again, and I wish I could speak telepathically. But he just keeps up that stern military expression. It's driving me nuts.

I've seen Avi smile and laugh. I've *made* Avi smile and laugh.

Ronit calls out, "Girls, follow me! Guys, follow Susu!"

While we're scrambling to obey, Avi is at my side. The warmth of his fingers on my elbow sends shivers down my spine.

"What are you doing here?" he asks me. "I thought you were staying on the *moshav* with your dad."

"I was. Until I realized Jess and Miranda and Nathan were going to be on the same base as you. I thought you'd be happy to see me. Obviously I was wrong."

"Gefen, *zooz*," the sergeant barks out.

Avi turns his head to the sergeant, who doesn't look happy that Avi's talking to me. "I gotta go."

"So go," I say sarcastically. Okay, I know I'm acting like a complete brat but seriously ... I came all the way to Israel and signed up to play soldier for ten days just to be with him, and he doesn't seem the least bit excited to see me.

"Amy ... " he says, but I shrug his hand off me.

"Go," I repeat.

He sighs and walks away.

7

Israel is .004% of the earth's surface.
They say the most valuable things come
in small packages.

So now I'm depressed and want to go home. Seeing Avi in all his military splendor grilling me on why I came here wasn't exactly how I imagined it. I'm sluggish as I follow the girls inside a building and we all sit in chairs in a classroom. To my surprise, the snickering girl from Avi's unit came with us and is obviously about to teach us something.

"This is Liron," Ronit explains. "She's one of the few female operations specialists assigned to a new IDF commando unit called Sayeret Tzefa. They've just come back from parachute training and are spending a few weeks on our base before they head off to Counter Terror School. We're very lucky to have them here to train you."

The other girls are immediately impressed by Liron. Even though she's not an official member of Sayeret Tzefa, by working alongside it she's as close as a female can get. We spend the next two hours listening to her talk about the state of Israel and the countries that surround it.

"Who can tell me why Israel is so significant?" she asks.

I definitely know why it's significant to me, especially since for the past year I've been taking conversion classes at my synagogue. My mom raised me with no religion, and my dad is Jewish. Last summer when I came to Israel, I connected with my Jewish heritage and wanted to learn all I could about it.

I raise my hand along with a couple of the other girls, totally ignoring the fact that my sweaty armpits smell like rotten eggs.

"You, in the pink tank top," Liron says, pointing to me. "Your name is Amy, right? Avi's *chaverah.*"

"His girlfriend," I clarify.

"*Chaverah* means girlfriend."

"I knew that."

Liron smiles at me, and I notice not only is her skin flawless, but her teeth are perfectly straight. "So Amy, why do you think Israel is significant?"

I sit up straight in my hot metal chair, which my thighs have stuck to from the heat. My skin rubs on the metal with each movement, making a squeaking sound. It hurts. I'll probably have thigh-burn later on. "Because it's the Jewish homeland," I answer.

Liron nods. "You're right. As Americans, you share the same democratic freedoms we do here in Israel."

"The Palestinians don't have it so easy here," Jess chimes in. "I mean, I'm proud to be Jewish and would never want to be anything else, but when will the fighting stop?"

Oh, no! While Tarik would be proud of Jess for sticking up for his people, I'm not sure this is the best place to debate the Palestinian/Israeli conflict. And while I am usually all for a knock-down-drag-out verbal sparring session, I'm not sure anything but trouble can come out of a political discussion on an Israeli military base.

I decide to intervene. "I think my friend Jess here is trying to say that, uh, while Israel is the Jewish homeland, not everyone feels the same way. No need to go into the specific differences, though. It's all cool. Discussion over."

Liron walks down the aisle and stands in front of my chair. "It's against regulation for a soldier to talk about the political situation in Israel while in an IDF uniform. But I guarantee that you can get into a long political discussion with any Israeli out of uniform. And I also guarantee that you'll get a hundred and fifty different opinions if you talk to a hundred Israelis."

Whoa, that's a lot of opinions.

"Girls, my job in the IDF is to protect Israel. As a private, or new trainee, *your* job is to take orders. You will be treated like a real Israeli soldier, and you will act like a real Israeli soldier. When we say 'get in formation,' you get in formation or you'll be doing twenty pushups. When we say 'run,' you run. When we wake you at the crack of dawn, you'll be ready and in formation within seven minutes. We're going to test your will and your spirit. We're going to test you physically and mentally. You're going to hate and curse your instructors while you're going through it, and love us and feel like a stronger person in the end. Any questions?"

I raise my hand. When Liron points to me, I say, "Do we get free time?"

"Maybe," she answers curtly. "Why are you here, Amy?"

To spend time with my boyfriend, so Israeli girls like you don't steal him away from me, I want to say. But instead I say, "To feel what it's like to be an Israeli soldier."

An instructor named Gili comes in and talks to us about the state of Israel. "Israel has a population of about six million Jews," she explains. "We are a minority in the Middle East. It's no secret we cannot afford to lose even one war. To do so might mean the end of the state of Israel. That's why every single Jewish Israeli citizen must serve in the military. Israeli Druze and Bedouins serve in our military as well."

For the next two hours, Liron and other instructors take turns teaching us. I haven't paid much attention to the other girls in my unit, but being in a small classroom gives me the opportunity to check them out.

During the bus ride to the base, I learned that five of the girls are friends from New York. They all have straight brown hair and the same basic "look." They're taking this whole boot camp thing seriously and are determined to be obedient soldiers. I swear these New York girls can't wait to get down and dirty in the Israeli dirt. I think they're under the impression that at the end of our military basic training program they'll be ready for the front lines of battle. I don't have the heart to tell them they've got a demented view of reality.

We have four girls from California. They're all really pretty and two of them are fakey-blond.

Then there's Tori, our resident bitch. She's a total loner, by choice. She rolls her eyes at everything, and makes snide comments to just about everyone on the trip. I think her goal in life is to insult every person she comes in contact with. Her hair is long and blond, but when she turns around and her hair parts you can see that underneath she has a sheath of black hair. It's totally two-tone, but I have no clue if she wants it that way or if it's a bad dye job. Either way, it's definitely unique.

The rest of the seven girls in our barracks are from different states scattered around the country, although two are actually from Canada and I want to laugh every time they say the word "about" because it comes out as "ah-boot."

Right now we're being dismissed from the classroom. How can I break it to Ronit that I'm "ah-boot" to go search for my boyfriend?

8

Breaking the rules feels great while you're breaking them,
but horrible while you're paying for them.

Getting free time here is proving to be nearly impossible. After our classroom discussion, we're led back to our *bittan* and are instructed to pick a bunk and unpack. This is also a bathroom break time, but I'm not going in that place again until I absolutely have to. There really isn't unpacking to do because each of us only has a little cubby to put our stuff in—just big enough to fit my shampoo, conditioner, and makeup bag. I'll just have to live out of my suitcases while I'm here.

Because Jess, Miranda, and I got to the *bittan* late, Jess and I can't share a bunk. I sit on an unoccupied one.

"That's mine," Tori says, standing over me. "I called it first. You can have the top bunk."

I look around for an empty bottom bunk, but there aren't any left.

"That's fine," I say to Tori, who seems pretty pleased to boss me around. I would argue that I didn't hear her "call it first" or that I'm afraid of heights and I'll probably fall off the top bunk while I sleep, but all I want to do is find Avi. I couldn't care less about Tori and her bottom bunk.

Just when I think free time has begun, it's time for the next activity. Ronit hands out pillows, sheets, and a very thin wool blanket. For the next hour, she teaches us how to make our beds. We have to keep unsheeting and re-sheeting until we get the A-okay from Ronit that we've finally done it to IDF standards (picture tight hospital corners). I can tell you right now that making tight hospital corners on a top bunk is tons harder than on a bottom bunk.

My bunk is two away from Miranda's and across from Jessica's. I can tell it'll be close to impossible to have private late-night chats.

"Everyone line up outside!" Ronit yells. "*Yala, zooz!*"

I don't exactly know what "*Yala, zooz*" means, but from her tone I guess it means "Come on, hurry up." I have a feeling I'll be hearing those words a lot while I'm here.

Jess pulls me aside before we go. "Switch bunks with me," she says. "You want a bottom bunk, right?"

"Yeah, but—"

"Well, it's right by the door so you can get fresh air." Jess is already bringing her stuff over to my cubby and switching my stuff out. "Just do it. We've got to hurry and get out outside before they make us do pushups. I hate pushups."

Liron and Ronit time how long it takes until we're all in formation outside. Ronit walks in front of us like a lion pacing in her cage. "It took you fourteen minutes. I think that's the worst I've ever seen! Next time," she says, "you'll do it in half the time—seven minutes. And then we'll cut it to three. March in formation to the *cheder ochel* for dinner! Ready?" she barks out.

She must not expect us to respond, because immediately she starts chanting the *small-ya'mean-smalls*. We're all out of line and out of sequence, bumping into each other. Ronit stops us. She makes us go back to the barracks each time we screw up until we get it right. The guys, who have obviously mastered marching in formation, have been gawking at us the entire time from the entrance to the *cheder ochel*.

We've attempted to get there six times. We're all getting crabby and tired. The seventh time, we're almost there when I spot Avi. He's standing by the American guys, watching me. I get so excited and nervous to see him that I totally screw up and step right on the back of Tori's foot, so hard that her shoe comes off.

"Stop!" Ronit says, then sighs in frustration. "Okay, girls. Back to the *bittan* for another try!"

Tori grabs her shoe. "What a *spaz*," she mutters.

Is she kidding me? "Oh, like you're so perfect with *your* marching?"

Tori flips her fake blond hair over her shoulder. "I've been dancing since I was five. I know how to count off."

I don't tell her that I've been dancing since I was four. I want to talk to Avi before he's whisked off so I ignore her. We line up again, and this time I look at the back of Tori's head so I don't mess up. In the end, it takes us thirty-five minutes to walk the three minutes to the *cheder ochel*.

On our way into the building, I look for Avi again. I spot him talking to other soldiers. While everyone rushes to stuff their faces with mediocre food, I walk up to my boyfriend. "Can we go somewhere private?"

"Amy, I can't."

"What? You can't talk to your girlfriend alone? You can't kiss your girlfriend you haven't seen for five months?"

"If someone catches us—"

"Let's go somewhere alone. For just a minute, Avi. *Please.*"

Before I even finish the word "please," Avi takes my hand and quickly whisks me away to a private alcove on the side of another building without windows. My mom says rules are made to be broken … or at least stretched.

My stomach is in knots, and I tell myself not to be emotional. I'm also very aware that we could be in big trouble if we're caught.

But looking at Avi's face brings me back to the first day I met him. He was working at the sheep pens on the *moshav*, lugging bales of hay. I was afraid of the huge herding dogs running toward me so I leaped into the pens for safety. Instead of landing on the soft hay, I landed on Avi. He broke my fall. When I opened my eyes, I was staring into the most mesmerizing eyes I'd ever seen.

Being here with him, alone, makes me forget about rules and regulations. It's times like these I'm happy that I live in the gray areas of life. Being with Avi makes everything that's crappy in my life bearable.

I wrap my arms around his neck. This time he doesn't pull away. "I missed you so much," I say.

He raises his hand to my cheek and brushes his fingers softly down my face. For such a tough guy, Avi's touch has always been super gentle. "I can't resist you," he says softly.

I'm relieved and excited when his lips touch mine. I wrap my arms around his waist and try to ignore the feel of his rifle against my fingers. When I urge him closer, our kiss gets more heated. As soon as his tongue touches mine, my insides feel like hot, molten lava.

My emotions are running high and I know a tear has escaped from the corner of my eye.

He pulls away a little. "Don't cry."

With the back of my hand, I quickly wipe whatever tears have escaped. "I'm not," I tell him.

He hesitates. "We need to talk. Seriously."

"About what?"

"About you being here. You said you'd be staying at the *moshav*."

I'm not going to lie to him. What would be the point?

"I'm here to be with you. To see you. To spend time with you."

"This is the military, Amy. I can't spend time with you here like we did last summer. I'm a soldier now."

"Well, now I'm a soldier too. At least for a little while. And we're spending time together right now, aren't we?"

"*Ze'heruit* Gefen," Nimrod calls out, startling me. "*Ata holech al chevel dok.*"

"*Sababa,*" Avi answers back, then says to me, "I can't do this."

"What did Nimrod just say?" I ask.

"He said I should watch out because I'm walking a thin line."

Nimrod frowns at us. Avi and I both stay silent, ignoring the warning, until Nimrod shrugs and walks away.

"What can't you do?" I finally answer. "Be specific."

Avi rakes his hand through his hair, even though in actuality he's just raking his hand over his growing-out buzz cut. He looks me straight in the eye and says, "I don't want you here."

I think my heart just dropped into the pit of my stomach. "Why not?"

A sound to our right makes Avi tense as he surveys the source of the noise. It's only an American guy from my unit on his way to the bathroom.

"I don't want to upset you, Amy, but ... I can't do my job when I have to check up on you, worry about you, or make sure you're okay," he explains when the guy is out of sight. "You're a distraction."

"And what about that Liron girl in your unit? She's a girl. Why aren't you worried or distracted by her?"

"She's not my girlfriend. You are. And she's Israeli—you're American."

"So if I was Israeli, you'd be fine with me being here?"

"If you were Israeli, you wouldn't have a choice. You'd be required to serve in the military. But you're American."

Yeah, technically. But... "My dad is Israeli, so that makes me half Israeli. And I'm Jewish. I've heard that every Jewish person can automatically get Israeli citizenship just because they're Jewish."

"But you're *not* Israeli, Amy. Tell me you're okay with trading in your designer sunglasses and designer clothes." He takes my hand in his and looks at my painted nails. "And your pink nails, for dirt buried under your fingernails."

I pull my hand away. "For your information, Avi, I don't even own designer sunglasses." Okay, so technically I owned them a few hours ago, before they fell into the pee/poop hole in the bathroom. But I'd rather die than admit that fact. "And even though I do have painted nails, and I'd rather be at the beach than learning how to march in formation," I continue, examining my nails and noticing a new chip in my polish on my index finger that I'll have to fix later, "I'm doing this for you...for us."

"Gefen!" a guy yells out. That guy just happens to be none other than Sergeant B-S.

Oh, no! We're totally busted!

Avi straightens and whirls around. "*Ken, Ha'mefa'ked!*" he says, then salutes to the sergeant.

Sergeant B-S barks out some command in Hebrew. Then he says, "Amy, go eat. Don't stop on your way there."

"It's my fault that Avi and I are alone," I tell Sergeant B-S. "I—"

Avi takes my elbow and gives it a gentle squeeze, cutting my explanation short. "Just do as he says. I would make that an order, because I'm a higher rank than you. But I know you better than to do that. So I'll say *please.*"

"I'm sorry I got you in trouble," I tell Avi quickly, then run to the *cheder ochel.*

Once there, everyone is busy eating dinner. Miranda waves me over. "Amy, over here!" I sit next to her and she pushes a plate full of food at me. "Here. I got you food."

I don't feel like eating, but know I need my strength. I nibble on bread and choke down the Israeli salad (which doesn't have any lettuce—what's up with that? It's just tomatoes, cucumbers, and onions). Every second or two I glance at the door to see if Avi walks in. I wonder how much trouble he's in and wish we could have avoided getting caught altogether.

Five minutes later (which means I checked the front entrance about three hundred times), Avi walks in with the sergeant. Neither look happy.

Avi's gaze briefly meets mine before he sits with the rest of the Sayeret Tzefa squad.

"Where were you?" Tori says to me from the opposite side of the table.

"In the bathroom," I lie.

"Oh, really? Because I saw you go off with that Israeli guy you hugged this morning and I was worried. I mean, I know the rules state we can get kicked out of the program if we're caught fooling around."

"So *you* told the sergeant?"

"Oh, no. Actually I told Ronit I was worried something happened to you. Of course she *was* talking to Sergeant Ben-Shimon at the time." Tori puts her fingers to her lips and sucks in a breath. "I didn't get you in trouble, did I?"

I don't buy her fake concern for a second. I let out a big, hearty chuckle. "No."

Tori is officially a person I will never trust. The girl is as manipulative as this girl Roxanne at my school.

Tori now gestures in the direction of Avi's table. "How do you know him?"

"He's her boyfriend," Miranda informs her cheerily. "They've been dating for a year."

"Wow. A long-distance relationship?"

"Yep," I say.

"So are you guys exclusive or what?"

That's a tricky question. Avi and I agreed to have a don't ask/don't tell policy since we're apart for such long periods of time. If I go on a casual date, I'm not going to tell Avi. He's not going to tell me if he's been on one, either. Avi and I are boyfriend and girlfriend, but we're trying to be realistic about our relationship.

"He's not available, if that's what you're thinking," I say, more defensively than I mean to.

If they weren't aware of it previously, our entire table now knows I'm dating Avi. I try not to glance at him while we're eating, but I can't help it. A few times I catch him looking back at me, but as soon as we make eye contact he breaks it.

This is definitely not turning out the way I expected. Has coming here been a huge mistake?

After we're done eating and scrape our plates into the big garbage bins (that don't have liners so I'm not sure how they clean them), we're excused to our barracks. I try to linger, hoping to exchange a few words with Avi, but Ronit comes up to me with a big frown on her face.

"Amy?" she says.

"Yeah."

"Follow me."

9

Is it any wonder the person who invented pushups hasn't come forward to claim their invention?

It's just me and Ronit walking away from everyone else. I follow my instructor to an open area, beyond the barracks. To my surprise, Avi and Sergeant B-S are waiting for us. Avi is standing at attention.

"Stand next to Avi," Ronit orders.

I have to get Avi out of trouble. I'm the one who lives in the gray areas of life, not Avi, so he shouldn't be reprimanded.

"We're very disappointed in both of you," Ronit says.

"It was my fault," I admit to our superiors. "I begged him to talk to me in priv—"

The sergeant, with a very pissed-off look on his face (which has just gone a dark shade of red resembling a very red grape), cuts me off in a stern loud voice. "Do not speak until spoken to!"

"But he—"

"Die!" (I learned back in January that *die* means "stop, enough!" in Hebrew . . . because when Avi told my dog to "die" when it was sniffing his crotch, I thought he was being rude, but he was just giving a command.)

I cover my mouth with my hands to stop myself from accidentally opening my lips and getting myself or Avi into more trouble.

Sergeant B-S steps between Avi and me. He gives Avi an order in Hebrew, then says, "Gefen, *Kadima*!" Then the sergeant turns to me. "Your job is to watch him. Come," he says, placing me a few feet in front of my boyfriend so I'm facing him.

"Watch him?" I question.

"Yes. Just stand and watch."

I know if I protest it's going to give him another reason to yell at me.

Avi, the ever-obedient soldier, gets on the gravel ground and does a pushup, then stands and our eyes meet. He repeats the pushup/standing exercise a few more times, and each time he stands our eyes meet. We can't talk, so our eye contact is the only way to communicate with each other.

Avi's straight, direct eye contact with me is telling me that he's okay . . . he's strong and he's fine.

I'm feeling worse than guilty. I wonder when he'll get to stop.

Avi is still going strong after five minutes, even though his back must be bruised from the rifle strapped to him. His palms are probably raw and bleeding from the gravel, too, but he doesn't give any sign he's in pain.

I hate watching this. The day has started to cool off, but I'm sweating again. Every time he goes down for another pushup, I wince. When he comes up, I want to tell him I'm sorry and won't lure him away again. After ten minutes, I swallow back tears and give Sergeant B-S a pleading look. He's got his arms folded in front of him, and doesn't show any sign of planning to let Avi stop any time soon.

I know when Avi is in pain, even though by looking at him you couldn't tell. I know it because he stops looking directly at me when he stands between those push-ups. He's looking forward, but not at me...he's looking through me. He's in "the zone" and is a robot now. It's a miracle he hasn't thrown up his dinner. I sure feel like throwing up mine.

My stomach twists. I can't deal with the fact that I'm just standing here doing nothing. I can't follow the order just to watch Avi. I know Avi won't stop until the sergeant says to, even if he's in pain.

I get it. Break down the soldier until they understand rules are not to be broken. Ever. Or else. Avi and I cannot go away in private even if we're dating. He knew this, but I lured him to break the rules and he did.

In the army there are no gray areas. I was wrong to ask him to break the rules, and Avi is paying the price for listening to me.

The next time he stands, I mimic him like a mirror and get on the ground to do a pushup with him. I try and do a manly pushup without putting my knees on the ground, even though my arms have the strength of a spaghetti noodle.

Silently I pray to God to give me strength.

When Avi and I both stand, this time he looks right at me and is not in "the zone" anymore. He shakes his head just the slightest bit, telling me to stop mimicking him. But I won't. I did the crime; it's not fair that he's the only one doing the time. The sergeant wanted to make me feel guilty. It worked.

I am back on the ground again, doing another pushup. Little pebbles get stuck to my sweaty palms, and it makes me cringe imagining what Avi's palms must feel like. But I don't stop.

"Die!" Sergeant B-S says.

For a second, I think he's giving an order for both of us to die on the spot...maybe he'll just take his gun and shoot us both. A harsh punishment for disobeying orders, but this is the army so maybe anything goes.

But then I remember it means "stop." Avi and I immediately stand at ease.

"I told you watch him. You're not good with following directions," the sergeant tells me.

I don't know if I'm supposed to answer or not, so I stay silent.

"Gefen tells me you and him are, uh, together. Is this the truth?"

My eyes stay on Avi when I say, "Yes, sir."

"This is a problem. On this base, between parachute training and Counter Terror School, Sayeret Tzefa trainees are assigned as instructors for the American volunteers. Special Ops soldiers must obey rules or they get reassigned. Eighty percent of Sayeret Tzefa trainees flunk training. Gefen might get reassigned as a driver if he doesn't obey the rules. And Gefen would rather die than be a driver. *Nachon*, Gefen?"

Avi stands tall and says, "*Ken, Ha'mefa'ked!*"

"I understand," I say. "It won't happen again."

"I don't care what you do off base or when Gefen is out of uniform. On my base, he's my soldier. Amy, you are a civilian trainee, don't forget that. Israeli soldiers are not to go off in private with civilian trainees of the opposite sex. Understand?"

"*Ken*, sir," I say, using the Hebrew word for "yes." It's one of the few Hebrew words that I actually know how to use correctly.

"You're both dismissed," he says. "*Zooz.*"

Avi does an immediate about-face and jogs away as if he hasn't just pushed his body to the limit. I want to run after him and apologize. I itch to examine his palms and take away whatever pain and cuts and bruises he's endured because of me.

I'm mentally drained and want this day to end. Sergeant B-S disappears while Ronit and I walk to the barracks. When we get inside, I notice that everyone has two sets of military olive green uniforms lying on their bunk, matching floppy hats, and a canteen with a strap. Liron is passing out towels.

"Shower time," Ronit informs me. "Each of you has seven minutes to shower."

I stand next to my bunk and receive my towel. Quickly collecting my papaya-scented bath gel, my poofy sponge, my shampoo, conditioner, and other essentials, I follow everyone to the showers.

Thank goodness the showers are next to, not *in*, the same room as the stinky bathrooms. There are six curtained stalls on either side. When it's our turn, I take the one next to Jessica.

The cement floor of the shower stall doesn't look blatantly dirty, but it's old and cracked. I can just imagine the amount of bacteria lurking on it, ready to attack bare skin and cause a foot fungus. Thank goodness for my shower shoes.

Foot fungus is not an option.

I hang my toiletries and PJs on the only hook in the stall. Getting undressed is not easy to do while you're wearing shower shoes. I balance on one foot as I slip out of my dirty shorts, but unfortunately my ballet skills aren't translating to shower balance.

Like a movie in slow motion, my naked body slips on the cement.

I make a huge noise that comes out as "Whoooaaa!" but it really sounds like that big ape-looking guy from *Star Wars* that Mitch made me watch when we dated. He made me come over to his house one Saturday and watch all six episodes. That's over twelve hours of movies in one day, if you include the deleted scenes. Once, in the middle of making out during Episode 5, Mitch asked if I wanted to see his Wookie. I sat up and slapped him. I mean, we'd only been going out for a few weeks and the thought of his "thingie" being a short, hairy thing grossed me out.

Mitch said later, after putting ice on his cheek to reduce the swelling from the hand-shaped red mark of my slap, that he only wanted to show me his set of Wookie figurines. As *if.*

"You okay?" I hear Jessica's voice echo in the other stall.

Okay, so now that I slipped/fell, I'm on all fours on the floor. I guarantee that no matter how fast I get up, the five-second rule doesn't count. I've for sure got things that grow in petri dishes on my hands, knees, and butt.

I turn the water on, refusing to be bacteria-ridden for even one more second. I'm ready to wash off the dirt and dust and bacteria and stress from my first day as an IDF trainee.

I stick my hand in the water to test the temperature. It's cold.

I turn the crank in the opposite direction, then test again.

It's still cold.

Maybe it needs time to warm up. So I wait a minute, then test again.

Still cold.

Now I'm starting to shiver, because I'm naked and the temperature has definitely dropped at least twenty degrees from this afternoon.

"Three more minutes!" Ronit yells from the door.

I pull the curtain aside and stick my head out. "Ronit, I think there's something wrong with my shower. There's no hot water."

"There's no hot water in mine either," Jessica cries out from her stall. "Brrr!"

"None of us have hot water," one of the girls from New York says as she gathers up her stuff and exits the shower. Seriously, she took an entire shower in less than four minutes…how clean can she be?

Ronit chuckles and says with a big smile, "Welcome to the IDF! You have two minutes left!"

With that warning, I quickly dip into the cold water. Wet and freezing, I quickly lather my hair with shampoo and squirt liquid soap on my poofy sponge. My teeth chatter as I soap myself and quickly plunge under the sprinkling showerhead.

As I'm rinsing, Ronit yells out, "One minute!"

I have to admit, my bottles of shampoo and liquid soap are scattered at my feet. I'm not thinking about bacteria anymore. I'm thinking about my hair conditioner, and how crappy my hair is going to look if I don't put it on. On top of that, I think I just bit my tongue because of my chattering teeth.

Halfway through squirting conditioner on my hair, I hear Ronit give us a "thirty seconds!" warning.

Oh, crap.

I don't even have my conditioner spread, and already I have to rinse it off. Does Ronit know how much Aveda minty-smelling conditioner costs? Not that she would care, but still.

"Amy, come on," Jessica whispers to me. "You have, like, ten seconds. Are you done?"

I pull my dirty clothes off the hook to get to my PJs from behind them. Unfortunately, my PJs fall onto the wet ground because the hook is too small. Taking a deep breath and pulling on my yellow polka-dot pajama bottoms (now wet in spots) and matching yellow top, I grab everything and run out.

"Tomorrow you'll have to do ten pushups for each minute you're late," Ronit informs me.

While we walk back to our barracks, Jessica blows hot air on her hands. "I'm freezing."

My teeth are still chattering as I look down at my thin nightshirt. "I think I'm going to be permanently nippy." I can't help but notice, again, that I have the biggest boobs out of our entire unit by far. I got my blue eyes from my Israeli grandmother, my black curly hair from my father, and my huge saggy boobs from my mom. Okay, so they're not as saggy as my mom's are … she's pregnant.

Did I mention that soon I'm not going to be an only child anymore? Yep, my mom and stepdad Marc *"with a c"* decided to have a baby. So now I'm going to have a brother or sister young enough to be my kid.

Back in the barracks, I open my suitcase and slip a University of Illinois sweatshirt over my wet, shivering head. Then I open my makeup case and do my nightly routine: take residue makeup off, put toner and moisturizer on, then spritz refresher spray for that extra misty-sparkle to make my skin look radiant (I know I sound like a commercial, but I did model once and my mom is in the advertising business).

After flat-ironing my hair, I pull out my favorite pillow from home. It's completely encased in a hot pink silk pillowcase. I set it on my bed. One of the New York girls, Victoria (aka Vic), is on my top bunk. Vic climbs up and the springs squeak as her weight presses down on the thin mattress.

I look up at the exposed springs. I hadn't noticed them before, but now I see why Jessica (who shall now be deemed the "manipulative traitor") wanted to switch bunks with me. The small springs keeping the mattress (and Vic) from falling on my face are attached with an S-type looking metal thingy. The problem is that almost every other spring is broken, missing, or super worn-out.

I'm not the claustrophobic type normally, but watching the mattress sink lower every time Vic moves makes me nervous.

I mean, seriously, what if Vic overstresses the *one* spring that's keeping all the rest from snapping off. It's like the game Jenga or that ice-breaking game. One wrong move and it's all over—SPLAT!

Out of the corner of my eye, I see Jess waving to get my attention. I narrow my eyes at my best friend. She puts her hand to her heart and mouths the word *sorry*, although she looks more amused than sorry. I think sometimes her brother Ben, aka *the demon from hell* (even though I'm Jewish and don't believe there's a hell), has rubbed off on her. One of his regular stunts is tossing chunks of *challah* bread across the Shabbat table with the purpose of getting one stuck in my cleavage. When he's successful, he grins and offers to take it out.

"Lights out in four minutes!" Ronit calls.

I wave to Miranda, who's on the bottom bunk two away from mine, across the aisle. I pull up my painfully thin blanket and try to get comfortable. It's not easy to relax with stretched-out springs squeaking overhead every time my bunkmate moves. I should watch all the food that goes into Vic's mouth during the next ten days. I can't risk her gaining weight while we're here, that's for sure … my life may depend on it.

Seriously, if the springs do give out in the middle of the night and she falls on me, will I suffocate and die? And if I do, will anyone care? Maybe I should sleep on my side, so if the springs collapse and the mattress and Vic fall on me, I might still have a little air pocket and live.

I'm definitely feeling sorry for myself tonight, but then I think of the Israeli soldiers who have to sleep on a bottom bunk staring up at missing and broken springs every night for years. I'm only here for a little over a week.

When Ronit flips off the lights, I turn on my side (partially because I like sleeping on my side) and think about Avi lying in his bunk.

Is he in pain from the pushups?

Is he lying on the top bunk, or bottom?

Is he thinking about me as much as I'm thinking about him?

When Avi stayed at my house back in January, he never wore a shirt to bed. I loved staring at his abs and biceps. I would kiss him good night and he'd flash me one of his rare smiles as he pulled me close (of course this was when my dad wasn't hawking us and ordering me back to my room).

I don't have my cell phone with me to listen to his old voicemail messages. He left them when we broke up during his visit and he was as desperate as I was to get back together. I know those messages by heart, and repeat them in my head…

> *Did I tell you your eyes remind me of blown glass? I can see your soul through those eyes, Amy. They get darker when you're trying to be sexy and they shine when you smile. And when you think you're in trouble you blink double the amount that you usually do. And when you're sad, the corners of your eyes turn down. I miss your eyes.*

> *I want to say something to you. Not because I want you to say it back, either.* (insert deep breath

here) *I... I love you. It's not that kind of conditional love ... it's the kind that'll be around forever. Even if you don't call. Even if you like Nathan or any other guy. We can be friends. We can be more. Just... call me back.*

Did I mention when I first met you I was so attracted to you it scared me? Me, scared. I still am when I'm around you, because now I want you in my life forever. How long is forever, Amy?"

I wish his arms were around me right now, assuring me that this is just another bump in the road of our rocky but passionate relationship.

I fall asleep, thinking of the day when Avi will hold me all night long without parental (or military) interference.

10

Lack of sleep has many, many negative consequences.

I'm dreaming that someone is turning on the lights and yelling in my ear.

"You have seven minutes to be dressed and outside! Bring your canteens!"

No, this isn't a dream. It's a nightmare. And I'm living it.

"I'm tired, Ronit. I just got to sleep," I hear Tori moan.

Her complaint is met by a "*Yala, zooz!*"

I hear some of the other girls talking, but instead of waking me up, the sound lulls me back to sleep.

"Amy, wake up!" Miranda says, shaking me like I'm the lulav branch during Sukkot.

"I'm up," I murmur.

"No, you're not. Come on! The guys from our unit are already outside."

I pull my pink silky pillow over my head. "I'm taking a mental health day."

"There are no mental health days in the military. Avi's there, too," she whispers in my ear.

I jump out of bed and give myself a nasty head rush. I strip off my PJs, strap on a bra, and get in my military uniform (which consists of an olive green button-down shirt and matching pants). I toss the matching floppy hat into my cubby because there's no way I'm wearing it, and slip on my new red high-tops. Opening my makeup case, I know I only have time for minimal application.

"What are you doing?" Tori asks with a stupid sneer on her face.

"What does it look like I'm doing? I'm putting on makeup."

Tori rolls her eyes. "Do you think you're going to a party?"

I sneer back, one of my famous sneers that beats hers hands-down. The only sneer that can rival mine is my cousin O'snot's.

I quickly apply eyeliner, mascara, and colored lip gloss while everyone scrambles around.

Once outside, with my canteen strapped on my shoulder like a very ugly purse, I get in formation while I watch Avi. It's still dark, but I can see him clearly in the lighted courtyard. He doesn't look tired; he doesn't look as if he's just woken up before God did. And today he's wearing a huge military vest with pockets, filled with ammunition or whatever military stuff he's supposed to carry. To top it off, he's got on a military backpack and his rifle. He looks as if he's about to go on some dangerous mission and is able, willing, and ready for war.

Nathan, on the other hand, looks horrible. He's got really bad bed-head, and is obviously super tired because his eyes are at half-mast.

Liron, with her ever-present big-ass rifle, asks Avi a question as she points to the papers on the clipboard she's carrying. He quickly glances at me, then nods to her.

I'm trying to concentrate on Ronit's lecture about time … something about time being important and how it could mean the difference between life and death in war. She says we have to move faster. But I'm not listening, because I'm too busy wondering what Liron and Avi were just talking about. Besides, someone needs to clue Ronit in that we're just civilian trainees on a "fun" summer program. The brochure didn't say anything about actually going into combat.

Sergeant B-S is mysteriously absent. I think he must be getting his beauty sleep. Avi, Nimrod, and three other Sayeret Tzefa trainees are in charge of our unit for this exercise. Ronit and Liron are coming along, too.

They make us stop by a big spigot coming out of the ground.

"Make a line and fill your canteens," Avi orders in a

loud Israeli accent. He stands in front of the spigot, supervising, as we wait our turn to fill our canteens.

When it's my turn, Avi puts his hand on the small of my back. I swear that electrons or protons, or whatever they taught us in biology class is in your body, zing up my spine. This boy, this man, this *soldier*... one minor touch from him reminds me of the time we were in my car on the beach back in Chicago. There were no parents, no friends, no military commanders around, no rules... it was just the two of us. My mind wanders back to that night...

"I want to forget how inexperienced you are," Avi groans as he leans back on the headrest of the car.

"So teach me," I say. I bite my lower lip as I reach up and unbutton the top two buttons of my shirt, well aware Avi's eyes are now totally focused on my task as I move my hands lower and start unbuttoning the rest. My hands are shaking—I'm not sure if it's from the cold car or my trembling nerves.

"Didn't you listen when your dad had the sex talk? Didn't he tell you boys only want one thing?"

"Do you, Avi? Do you only want one thing?" I say as I open my shirt and reveal my bra beneath it.

"I have to be honest and say my body's only thinking about one thing right now."

"Take your shirt off," I order.

As his hands reach for the hem of his shirt he says in a strained voice, "Your dad's gonna kill me." He lifts his shirt over his head and tosses it onto the driver's seat with his eyes never leaving me.

As he brushes the tips of his fingers across my abdomen, the tingles send wild sensations through my body. "Are you okay with this?" he asks, his face serious.

I nod and give him a small smile. "I'll let you know when I'm not."

As I lean down to press our bodies against each other, his hands reach around under my open shirt and pull me toward him. "Your body... so warm."

His hands are like a fire, consuming my body with his touch. I lean my head on his chest, hearing his heart beating the same erratic rhythm as my own while his hands move up and caress my hair, my bare back, and my breasts.

As I reclaim his lips, raw emotions and new wonderful feelings whirl in my consciousness. I'm fully aware I'm not ready to have sex, but I'm ready to experience more...

"You okay?" Avi asks me, bringing me back to the reality of my life called boot camp. I wish we were in my car right now instead of here.

"Uh, yeah. Are you?"

Avi wants to be a hardass in the IDF and not show

emotion. He once told me I'm the one person who makes him emotional, and that scares him.

I think of how I lured him to spend time alone with me yesterday. I guess deep down I knew if I begged him to go somewhere private with me he wouldn't refuse—even if it was against the rules. I have the power to make him forget the rules, and I abused that power.

Oh, no! I'm like Eve in the Garden of Eden, and he's poor Adam. Amy = The Dark Side.

My canteen is full, so I have to step aside. "Do you hate me?" I murmur.

He shakes his head and smiles. "No."

"I'm sorry you had to do pushups yesterday."

He examines his roughed-up palms. "I deserved it."

I feel a tension between us. I'm desperate for that tension to go away.

"Amy, I have to tell you something."

Good. I hope he says he loves me. I hope he says he's glad I'm here. I hope he says he wishes we were alone together. I gaze into his eyes and say in a hopeful voice, "What? What do you want to tell me?"

"Wear your hat."

"My hat?" Is he kidding me?

"Wear it. It's for your protection."

"I look dorky in hats, Avi. I'm not wearing it."

"You'll look worse with sunburn."

"Thanks for the tip," I say, kind of sarcastically, then head back into formation. I'm not wearing the hat, and

I'm sulking. I know I shouldn't expect Avi to say romantic stuff to me while we're here, but I want to hear those things coming out of his mouth nonetheless.

When everyone's canteen is full, we get fifteen minutes to scarf down breakfast, then we head out the gates of the army base in perfect formation. We march to Avi's *small-ya'mean-smalls* for a while. Every so often he orders all of us to drink from our canteens. It's no sparkling Perrier, and it's not cold, but it's wet and feels good going down my throat.

Avi and two other guys are standing in front of us, rifles cradled in their hands. The other Sayeret Tzefa trainees are flanking us on all sides.

You'd think I'd be freaked out with all the rifles and military precautions. But I'm not. I know the risks of being in Israel, and so do the Israelis. While they go on with their daily lives, refusing to give in to the fear of terrorism, they do what they can to protect themselves. I feel safe with these warriors protecting me.

We continue marching. This time Nimrod calls out the marching chant. The dawn chill disappears and the air grows warmer, a hint the sun will be up soon. The longer we march, the more the landscape looks like a barren desert. Mountains and rocks are our only scenery, and the uneven pebbly ground meets our shoes.

Some kids at school have asked me what's so special about Israel. It's not like there's a fun amusement park to go to or specific "wonders of the world" like the pyramids in Egypt. Israel is special just by being here—if you've never been to Israel, you can't fully "get it." You can tell you're in Israel because of the people. Israeli citizens are determined and strong. They're harsh, but have a heart. They refuse to let terrorism or fear disrupt their daily lives—maybe it's because of the Holocaust and maybe it's because they've lived in a war zone for so long. Whatever it is, their determination to live life to the fullest, without fear, is contagious.

The land of Israel mimics the citizens of its country. The harsh landscape of the Negev desert makes you wonder why people settled here, until you reach the historical sites and are awed by the rich history of the land. Where my cousins live, in the Golan Heights, you wonder why anyone would live so far from civilization until you step to the edge of the mountain—the Sea of Galilee shines at you and confirms your belief in God all over again.

I'm not feeling the mystical effect of Israel right now, though, because I haven't had enough sleep to appreciate the Jewish homeland. Just when I'm about to complain about rocks in my high-tops, we're ordered to stop and take another five-minute rest.

I'm talking to Jessica and Miranda when Nathan walks up to us. "I feel like Moses wandering in the desert for forty years," he says.

"Why do you think they brought us here?" Miranda asks as she wipes her sweaty face with her sleeve.

Jess shrugs. "Beats me. I'm hot and crabby. Amy, go ask Avi why we're here."

"No."

"Why not?" Nathan asks. "He's your *soulmate*, right? Isn't that what you called him last week when I asked why you were saving yourself for that big oaf?"

"Um, uh, I hate to break the bad news, but that big oaf is standing right behind you," Jess informs him.

Nathan looks at Miranda. "Tell me she's lying," he groans.

Miranda's answer is a rapid shake of her head.

Avi shoves a shovel the length of his arm at Nathan.

"What's this for, to dig my own grave?" Nathan asks as he takes the shovel out of Avi's grip.

"I'm not that lucky," Avi says. "Follow me."

Everyone else is assembling next to a soldier from Sayeret Tzefa. In all, there are five groups of eight people, each with a small shovel. Avi's team consists of me, Jessica, Miranda, Tori, Nathan, and three other American guys named David, Eli, and Ethan.

"This is a contest," Nimrod says. His group stands next to ours, and Avi is stoic as he watches Nimrod explain. "You have to dig a ditch two meters long and one hundred centimeters deep. The winning group gets a ride back to base camp."

Oh, we are SO winning this since Avi is on our team. I clap my hands excitedly and pat my boyfriend's back.

"Don't be too excited. Team leaders can't help."

Huh? Without his help, there's no way we can win. We've got Tori on our team, and after spending a day with her, I know she's going to be a pain in the butt. Nathan's got this testosterone fight going on with Avi so his focus isn't on the prize. We've got Miranda, but she's still panting and sweating from the hike. If pushed more, she might just pass out. David, Eli, and Ethan are all from big cities and are staring at the shovel as if it's a foreign object.

We're hopeless.

"Put your canteens down," Avi orders.

He's treating me just like everyone else. It bothers me. I want him to act like my boyfriend and let everyone know we're a couple. Yes, I'm aware it's selfish and immature, but at least I'm willing to admit it.

"Start digging!" Nimrod orders.

We all look to Avi for direction. He's standing with his arms crossed on his chest, watching us, not saying anything.

"He's obviously not going to help us," I inform my group. "You have the shovel, Nathan. Start digging."

Nathan picks a spot on the ground and starts digging. Dirt and rocks are flying in the air behind him as he quickly gets to work.

After ten minutes, he stops. "My fingers are starting to get numb." He hands the shovel to me. "Your turn."

I take the shovel and start where Nathan left off. I think I'm doing pretty well, although my team is totally annoying.

"Dig harder," Ethan urges.

"Faster!" David screams when I feel a fingernail break and stop digging for a fraction of a second to check it.

The problem is, we're not digging in the sand. We're digging up rocks that may have been here for hundreds, if not thousands, of years. Maybe our holy forefathers Abraham, Isaac, and Jacob walked on these rocks we're digging. It's not an easy task, and now the sun has come up and hits me in the face. I wish I had my sunglasses, because now I'm squinting. I'll be able to blame my premature wrinkles on this rock-digging experience.

I feel a tickle on the back of my hand. I need to scratch it, but don't want to stop digging because I want to (1) show Avi that I can be a good ditch-diggin' soldier and (2) I don't want to *small-ya'mean-small* back to the base. I really want a ride.

When the itching bugs me so much I can't ignore it, I hesitate and look down at my hand.

Oh! My! God!

There is a HUGE creepy black spider crawling on me. I throw down the shovel and shake my hand vigorously.

"AAAHHHHHH!" I scream and run, not able to stop the heebie jeebies. I keep shaking my hand just in case the creepy crawler is still on me.

What if it bites me?

What if it's poisonous?

What if it crawls up my sleeve?

What if it already laid creepy spider babies on me!

"What's wrong?" Jess cries out.

"Are you hurt?" Miranda yells over my screams in a concerned voice.

"Did something bite you?" Nathan calls.

I can't stop to explain, because I'm still jumping around and shaking like a madwoman.

I'm barely aware of Avi attempting to subdue me. I flail my arms and slap his hands away because I'm still worried the spider is on me.

But then Avi twirls me around so my back is against his and he wraps his arms around me so tight I can't move.

I'm breathing hard and I'm sweaty and smelly and totally freaked out from spiders and embarrassment because everyone is watching me.

Now I'm in Avi's arms, which are like a vice holding me still.

"Was it a crav?"

"No, not a crab," I gasp. Do crabs even live in the desert?

"I didn't say crab. *Ah'crav* ... a, uh ... " He's searching his brain for the English word so he can translate. "Scorpion?" he finally says.

"No."

"Are you hurt?" he asks. He's so calm I stop struggling against him.

"I don't know. It was ... " I choke out the word. "A spider."

"A *spider*?"

Everyone else laughs hysterically.

"I ... I think it was a black widow. It was really big! And hairy! And it was crawling on my SKIN!"

"Black widows aren't hairy," he says, but instead of making fun of me like everyone else, my boyfriend turns me around, takes my hands in his, and inspects them. "It's gone."

"What if it crawled up my shirt?" I say, squirming. I swear I feel little prickly legs on my back. It could be my imagination, like when you're talking about lice and you start scratching. But it really feels like spiders are crawling all over me.

"Don't panic."

I keep squirming. "I'm afraid it's still on me. Avi, help me. Please," I beg.

Without hesitation, he picks me up like I weigh close to nothing and calls out for Liron to follow us.

He hurries behind a large boulder. "Take your shirt off. Nobody can see you." He turns around, giving me privacy.

I unbutton the shirt as fast as I can while Liron stands next to Avi. Her back is to me, too. I think he called her over because he didn't want to have our entire unit see him take me somewhere alone. He doesn't want us to get in trouble again.

Liron is our chaperone.

I can't believe I need a chaperone when I'm with my boyfriend.

"Okay, it's off. I'm not going back out there in my bra." I mean, Avi's seen me with just a bra on, but not in public.

Avi holds out his hand, his back still to me. "Give it to me."

"My bra?"

He glances back at me, even though we both know one word from Liron to Sergeant B-S about him seeing me with no shirt will probably have him doing pushups again. "No. The shirt."

After I hand it to him, I watch him carefully inspect it from top to bottom. He turns it inside out, making sure it's free of creepy crawlers. He even opens the pockets and inspects those.

He tosses the shirt back to me. "There's nothing on it, or in it. Trust me."

"Thanks," I say. If there's anyone at the top of my trust list, it's Avi. Now that I'm calm, I can't confirm that the spider was hairy. And maybe it wasn't as big as I made it out to be.

Liron shakes her head. "If I didn't see it with my own two eyes, I wouldn't believe it."

"What can't you believe?" I ask her.

"Avi Gefen inspecting a shirt for a spider."

"Why?" My boyfriend is my hero; why shouldn't he help me?

Liron chuckles. "Avi tells everyone else in Sayeret Tzefa to suck it up, whether they're tired, bleeding, or throwing up from exhaustion. But with you ... and a little spider ... " She shakes her head. "I don't get it."

After I have the shirt back on, they both turn around

to face me. Avi points to me as he talks to Liron. "You saw her—she was freaking out."

"And you came to her rescue. She's ruining your reputation."

"She's my girlfriend," Avi says defensively. "What would you want me to do?"

"Treat her like a soldier, like you treat the rest of us. She didn't sign up to be rescued, she signed up to be a trainee."

"This isn't about Amy. It's about us."

Wait. One. Second. Did he just say "us" as in Avi and Liron "us" … not Amy and Avi "us"?

"Oh, shit." Avi rubs his temples as he squeezes his eyes shut. "I didn't mean to say that in English."

Fear, deep and strong, slices through my body. I'm afraid to ask, but can't stop myself more than I can stop myself from breathing.

"What are you saying, Avi? Are you two, like, a couple or something?"

11

---

milk + meat = not kosher
my boyfriend + kissing another girl = not kosher

I turn to Liron for answers.

"Avi, tell her," Liron says.

"Yeah. Tell me." When he hesitates, my entire body goes numb. "It doesn't matter, anyway, because Nathan and I have been dating since February, after you left. I wanted to tell you, but I didn't want to upset you."

Phew. I can't believe I got the lie out without choking.

Crunching stones alerts us that someone is about to join us. It's Nimrod. He looks at Liron, then Avi, then me. "*Hakol Beseder*—everything okay? No more spiders?"

"No spiders," I say. "And everything is just hunky-dory. Right, Avi?"

I lied to Liron and Avi because I didn't know what else

to do. I'm in total shock. Was everything Avi told me back in Chicago about how much he loves me a complete lie? Were all those letters he wrote me lies, too? He knows I have trust issues because my parents never married and I didn't even have a relationship with my father until last year.

No wonder Avi doesn't want me here. He wants to be free to have his relationship with Liron on base and then have me, his American girlfriend, on the side.

Ugh, the thought of it makes me sick.

I storm back to my group, leaving Nimrod with the lovebirds. Okay, Avi and Liron don't look or act like lovebirds, but he's obviously dating her behind my back. And I'm obviously the idiot girlfriend thinking it was worth it to spend time at a military boot camp to see my boyfriend.

Now I'm stuck. I would quit, but I begged my dad to sign me up and there's no turning back now. If I leave with my tail between my legs, I can just imagine what my dad will say. *I told you you're too young to have a serious relationship with Avi. I told you the program wouldn't be easy, and you couldn't handle military life. Next time listen to your father.*

I glare at anyone laughing at me. Every comment, every snicker, is like nails dragging down a chalkboard, making me cringe.

Jess runs up to me. "Amy, are you okay?"

"I'm fine," I snap back, which earns me a weird look from my best friend.

"Did you get bitten?" Miranda asks me.

"No. I don't want to talk about it."

Our team hasn't finished digging the hole yet, although all the other teams have. Nimrod's team is giving themselves high fives, so I assume they're the winners of the challenge.

Liron orders her team into formation without looking my way.

Avi peers down into our pathetic, three-inch-deep hole.

"We lost," Nathan tells him. "Which isn't a big surprise considering we had one less person and no team leader after you guys disappeared."

"We're not going back until our ditch is finished," Avi informs us. "No giving up."

Like he did with our relationship?

Since Avi left Chicago, I haven't thought of anyone else. I haven't been remotely interested in another guy because I know he's The One. He said we were going to be together forever, that he wanted to marry me one day. I believed him, which makes me the dummy.

Listen, I know I have to finish high school, go to college, and get a job. But I also thought my future included Avi, too.

A big army truck comes into sight, kicking up desert dust in its wake. Nimrod and his team hop on and, within a minute, are out of sight.

My team members are still shoveling, per Avi's orders. I'm purposely ignoring anyone with a name that starts with an *A*, has an *I* at the end, and a *V* in the middle. I can feel his eyes boring into my back like Superman's X-ray vision. But my boyfriend isn't Superman, at least not anymore.

And now, to save face, I have to pretend Nathan and I are in love. I'm not sure Nathan will go for the charade. Dare I tell him? He's afraid enough of Avi as it is.

Avi tells the rest of the teams to file out and head back to base while we finish digging. Tori is shoveling, although she's not going fast and I think we might be here for a few days. We're all so hot and sweaty I wonder if skin can actually melt off of our bones.

"Amy..." I hear Avi's voice from behind me.

"Is someone talking to me?" I ask Jess. "Because all I hear is hot air." I tap on my ears with my palms, pretending to clear my ear canals.

Miranda taps me on the shoulder and nudges me to turn around. "Avi's right behind you, Amy. Maybe you really did get bit by that spider and it affected your hearing."

Thanks, Miranda. *Not*. The girl is not too quick on social cues, that's for sure. I love Miranda to death (okay, not to *death*... that's a bit over the top), but she can definitely use lessons in how to not take everything so literally.

I turn to Avi with a cool smile on my face. "Did you want something, O Unfaithful One?"

"Don't say that."

"Why not? It's true, isn't it?"

"You walked away before I could explain, Amy."

"So explain now."

"Not with an audience."

"We have no choice, Avi, do we?" I focus on kicking a large rock. "Did you sleep with her?"

All conversations immediately stop. Everyone waits for Avi to answer. I think the air even stops moving (although I can't say that's a big feat because there wasn't a breeze to begin with).

"No, I didn't sleep with her—"

"Did you kiss her?"

"Can we not do this *now*?"

"No, we're gonna do this right here, right now. Did you kiss her?"

"Yes."

"I can't believe you!" I attempt to shove him away from me, but the guy is like a solid rock of muscle. He grips my wrists and holds them away.

"You kissed Nathan, remember?" he says, his eyes blazing. "And now you say you're dating him. Is that true, Amy?"

"No, it's not!" Nathan calls out.

I narrow my eyes at Nathan. "There's no need to keep us a secret anymore, Nathan. I told Avi about us."

"But—"

Nathan's words are cut short when Jess pushes him into our team's ditch and he falls right onto Tori.

"Where's your honor and integrity, Avi?" I throw back the words he said to me back in January when he found out I'd kissed Nathan.

"You said we shouldn't be exclusive. You said it wasn't realistic to think we wouldn't be attracted to other people."

The thought of him being attracted to Liron is too

much for me to deal with. "I was just *saying* that," I yell at him. "I didn't want you to actually *do* it."

He lets go of my wrists as if they're on fire and he's about to get burned. "Next time, say what you mean."

"Like you meant it when you said you wanted to marry me one day? It was all lies, Avi."

"You know that's not true."

"Cheating boyfriends become cheating husbands."

"I didn't chea—" Avi runs his hand over his grown-out buzz cut. "Just let me know. Are we breaking up?"

"That depends. Did you kiss Liron just once?"

"No."

"Twice?"

"No."

"Three times?"

"Amy ... "

"Answer me, Avi. Three times?"

"I didn't count."

"Maybe you should have. What did you think, that you could just fast for Yom Kippur come September, repent it one day, and God would wipe your sinning slate clean? What, you think God has only one book? I bet he's got *lots* of books, Avi, just filled with names of sinners. Because while God may inscribe you in the Book of Life for another year, he's probably also inscribing you in the Book of Cheaters."

His eyes get darker when he's angry. They're definitely dark now. "Whatever, Amy. I can't talk to you when you're being irrational. If God's got a Book of Irrational People, *you're* at the top of the list." He whips off his backpack and picks up our team shovel from the ground. "Get out," he orders Tori and Nathan, who immediately scramble out of the ditch.

Avi sheds his military vest. We all watch in awe as Avi finishes digging in less than three minutes.

When he's done, we get back in formation and start marching back to base. After a half hour, he gives us a five-minute break and orders us to drink from our canteens. He does this every half hour. When we reach the base, he orders us to drink what's left in our canteen.

I'm too angry to drink.

He steps in front of me. I can feel the heat of the mid-morning sun, but I can also feel the heat of Avi's gaze on me. "Amy, finish the water."

"Maybe I already did."

"I might be just a sheep farmer to you back at the *moshav*, but here I outrank you whether you like it or not. Drink it all, or you'll dump whatever's left in the canteen on your head."

A bee decides to hover between us. I hate bees almost as much as spiders.

"There's a bee about to sting us," I say, hoping to make him flinch, or at least get a reaction to remind me he's human.

No such luck.

"Drink or dump," he orders.

I could drink what's left in my canteen, but my ego is

fragile and rebellious. I'm holding on to the little control I have left.

"Yes, sir!" I say sarcastically, then salute my now ex-boyfriend.

I slowly lift my canteen over my head. Avi is watching intently. I'm pretty sure the odds are 80 percent he'll stop me before a drop of liquid lands on my head, 20 percent he'll let me go through with the water-dumping. He has always come to my rescue in the past. This time, though, he's the one I need rescuing from.

When my canteen is directly over my head, I realize there's a 100 percent chance he won't stop me.

Pouring water on myself means that my straightened hair will end up a random, curly mess. I can't do it.

"Do it."

I clench my teeth and lift my chin in defiance. "No."

Avi grabs my canteen, lifts it over my head, and turns it upside down. Water rushes down my scalp, making the hairs on the back of my neck stick straight up. It drips onto my neck and runs down my back. Little rivers run down my face. I must look ridiculous, and it's all Avi's fault.

"You cooled off yet?" Avi asks.

"Not by a long shot."

He shoves the empty canteen in my hand, then eyes the rest of the team. "When you're finished, hold your canteen above your head and turn it upside down."

A few people quickly drink what's left in their canteen, making sure not to leave a drop. I'm the only one with a mid-morning sprinkle.

I'm trying not to pay attention to Avi, but I can't help it. Against my better judgment, I focus on his lips. They're full and soft to the touch—I know because I've felt them with my fingers and my own lips.

Ugh. I cannot believe Liron had her lips against his. I shudder just thinking about it.

When Avi dismisses us to our *bittan* for cleanup time, I corner Nathan in the courtyard in front of the girls' barracks. I wrap my arms around his neck and kiss him lightly on the lips. "Please play along while Avi's watching," I whisper in his ear.

"You're the devil," he says. "Stay away from me while your boyfriend's around."

"He's not my boyfriend," I assure him as I shoo away another hovering bee. "Not anymore, at least."

"Neither am I, so stop telling everyone I am. I'm trying to get into Tori's pants, you know."

"Eww. Why?"

"She's cute, she's a dancer...I even hear she's double-jointed. I've never been with a double-jointed girl before."

"You're sick, and totally acting like Kyle, the biggest perv in school."

"I'm a *guy*, Amy. What do you expect?"

Up until a few weeks ago, Nathan was still obsessed with his ex-girlfriend Bicky. Not Becky...Bicky. She's a total druggie and has made Nathan's life miserable, which is the main reason he came on the *Sababa* trip. He has to get over Bicky, but replacing one bitch with another is definitely not the answer.

"Just smile and pretend you love me."

He smiles, puts his arm around my shoulders, and leads me to the barracks. "I *do* love you, Amy. As a friend. And as a friend I'm going to tell you that I'd like to keep my ball sacs intact and not piss off your boyfriend or ex-boyfriend or whatever he is. He's got a gun bigger than my entire arm. And isn't that thing attached to the bottom of it a grenade launcher? Geez, Amy, even his gun is pimped."

I spill the beans to Nathan softly, as if nobody else knows yet. "He's been fooling around with Liron. He's probably dating her for all I know."

"I know. Our entire team got the rundown before he finished our ditch, remember?"

"Don't you feel sorry for me?"

"Amy, didn't you tell me during your conversion class that God gives us challenges to test how strong we are? Maybe this is your test." Now two bees are hovering around us. Nathan shoos them away. "Were bees one of the ten plagues back in Moses' time?"

"Nope."

"Well, God is obviously sending them as the eleventh plague. We had a bunch buzzing around our bunks yesterday. It's a miracle we haven't gotten stung."

The talk of plagues and getting stung makes me look for Avi. He's talking to a guy from Sayeret Tzefa, and looks murderous as he stares down Nathan and me. He tries to walk over to us, but the guy he's with pulls him back.

Nathan taps my shoulder. "Talk to him and find out what the deal is, Amy. 'Cause I'm not gonna act like your boyfriend just so you can save face. That's a cop-out, and the Amy Nelson-Barak I know isn't a coward or a cop-out."

"You sound like Rabbi Glassman," I tell him.

Nathan smiles wide, proud to be put in the same category as my awesome rabbi who sponsored my conversion to Judaism. He stands tall and proud, as if he's Abraham Lincoln addressing the United States Senate (without the top hat, of course). "Yes, well I'm smart beyond my seventeen years."

"Yeah, right. You just said you wanted to date Tori because she was double-jointed. You sounded like an idiot then. Don't push that 'smart beyond my seventeen years' crap."

"Yo, Nate, we gotta do cleanup!" Brandon, another guy on the *Sababa* trip, calls out.

Nathan chucks me under the chin. "I gotta go, Amy. While I probably just signed my death warrant by talking to you for so long, I have to go before Susu starts his inspection."

"Girls' inspection in fifteen minutes!" Ronit calls out. "Nathan, you better not drag your feet. You should have been at the guys' barracks five minutes ago!"

Nathan jogs off, his sandy blond, bed-head hair bouncing with each step and his shirt sticking to his back from the heat of the Israeli sun.

12

---

*Bees are God's little reminder not to get too comfortable
in life; something or someone is going to come out and
sting you when you least expect it.*

I walk into the girls' barracks (which is now a sauna because
the stifling air doesn't move in here). I'm surprised my bed
is already made, with perfectly tight hospital corners. Even
my wool blanket is folded neatly at the foot.

Vic, who just finished making her bunk above me,
clues me in. "Jessica did it."

When I turn around, my best friend gives me a big
hug. I haven't told her what's up with Avi, but she obviously
guessed from the conversation we had back at our ditch.

"So I guess that Avi guy isn't your boyfriend anymore,
huh?" Tori says. "That's so … sad. Are you okay?"

I'm holding it together by a thin thread, lucky to have
Jess beside me for support in the face of Tori's fake con-

cern. I don't believe for a minute that she cares about me and Avi. In fact, I catch a glimmer of triumph in her eyes. I wish a bee was around to sting her in the butt. I know that's rude, and Rabbi Glassman would say that wishing someone harm isn't being a righteous Jew. I can't help it.

Girls my age either love me or hate me, and I have no clue why it's so cut-and-dried. Jess says it's because I come across as confident, and even if I have insecurities I cover them up at all costs. So when the haters see a glimpse into my misery, they're all over it.

"It's not a big deal," I tell Tori as I kneel next to my bed and pull my flat iron out. "You can find someone else to worry about 'cause you're wasting your pity on me."

I plug it in (with the 220 voltage converter attached), thankful for (1) the lone outlet in the room and (2) that my trusty flat iron heats up in thirty seconds.

My hair is already dry from the mid-morning heat. I sit on the floor next to the outlet with my travel mirror and brush in hand, ready to make the curls disappear. Balancing the mirror between my knees, I clamp the flat iron and get to work on the frizzy, curly pieces.

"I can't believe you're doing your hair when we're supposed to be cleaning," one of the New York girls says.

Looking up, I explain. "I can't have half my hair curly and half straight. That would look stupid."

"So put it up in a ponytail, like I do. Then it would be out of your face and nobody would notice any imperfections."

"Great idea, but I don't look good with my hair in a ponytail. Right, Miranda?"

Miranda grunts an unintelligible answer. What's up with that? Is happy-go-lucky Miranda actually upset about something? Maybe she's hungry.

"Why do you have to look good all the time?" New York Girl asks.

That's a really tough question. I thought about it once. The thing about my life is that I've never had control over it. I was ... how can I put it nicely ... I was *a mistake*. My mom and dad met in college, got together one night, and oops! My mom was pregnant.

As much as I prayed for them to get married, they never did. It probably shouldn't have affected me as much as it has, but you never know what's going to be the "thing" in your life that defines you (or the thing you should talk to a therapist about at length). I didn't even have a relationship with my dad until a year ago, when he took me to Israel for the first time.

My looks ... my image ... I guess that's the only thing I can control. God knows I haven't been able to control the people in my family. And today just proved that I can't control my boyfriend. Yes, I admit I have control issues.

The New York girl has her hair in such a tight ponytail her eyes look like they're being pinned back. And she actually bought black military steel-toed boots for this trip. The closest thing I have to that are my cherry red high-tops.

She is still waiting patiently for an answer. I should

tell her the truth. But I don't, because little white lies are in that gray area of life I live in. Even if the military doesn't have any gray areas, I still do.

I tell a little white lie. "I want to look good to impress Nathan."

"The blond guy who played the guitar on the bus ride to the base?"

I point excitedly at my nose, as if I'm playing charades. "That's the one!"

"But rumors are going around that you're dating that Israeli commando guy who was your team leader today."

I go back to straightening my hair. "We dated a little, but it was casual."

Now that's *not* a little white lie. That's a big, honkin' lie. My relationship with Avi isn't casual at all!

I used to imagine our wedding. We'd get married on the *moshav* our families live on in the Golan Heights (I'd make sure it was far from the farm animals, so the poop stench wouldn't drive guests away). I'd wear a white, flowing wedding gown and Avi would be in a casual, light-colored suit. We wouldn't be able to take our eyes off each other as the rabbi performed the ceremony, and I'd circle him seven times in the traditional Jewish way. Our love would last forever and ever; we'd share our deepest darkest thoughts, and nothing could break the bond between us.

Yes, it's totally corny. But that's my fantasy.

I even had our kids' names picked out. We'd have four kids and none would be a mistake like I was. We'd have two boys and two girls, of course—remember, this is still my fantasy—and they would be named Micha (after Avi's brother who died, because Jewish people don't name their kids after living people, only dead people, which is weird to me, but whatever), Golan (where Avi was born), Maya (which means "water" and that's something you can't live without), and Abigail (which means "leader of joy"; I didn't grow up with joy and want our children to grow up with it).

Of course, now, my fantasy is totally ruined.

As I'm doing my hair, a bee starts buzzing in my ear and I seriously almost burn myself with my flat iron.

"Go away!" I tell the bee, as if it speaks English and can understand me. It won't leave me and my hair alone. It's as if the nasty little buzzer wants to build a nest in my hair.

No buzzing insect is getting near my hair if I have anything to say about it. "Go away!" I tell it again, swatting at it with my flat iron, hoping to scare it away. No such luck. I'm not thinking, just relying on a self-protective instinct, and I clamp the hot ceramic plates together when the bee gets too close. Eww! I've trapped the bee inside my flat iron.

The good news: the bee will never bother me again. The little buzzer, shall we say, is toast.

The very bad news: I have hot bee guts stuck on my hot flat-iron plates. Yuck! It even smells like burnt bee. I unplug the flat iron so the plates will cool off.

Tori scrunches her face up after seeing the corpse stuck to my flat-iron plates. "That's not very *green* of you, Amy."

"Umm ... for your information, being green means helping the environment." According to my "green" standards, I just saved the other animals from getting stung, thus helping the environment.

"Bees are *part* of the environment, Amy," Tori says with a snotty attitude. "These are just worker bees anyway. Worker bees don't sting."

They don't? I thought *all* bees sting. But Tori sounds really convincing, as if she's a bee expert, like she knows for a fact that these bees are harmless. I feel stupid that I don't know that little fact. I look at my flat iron again, totally grossed out, knowing that I'll have to scrape the bee guts off the thing once it cools off.

And I'm still stuck with my half-curly/half-straight hair.

If anything goes right on this trip, it'll be a miracle. I'm praying for it, because if miracles are going to happen I'd think God would want to start in the Holy Land. Right?

Ronit walks in the room for her inspection and I gather up my stuff and head to my bunk. After shoving everything into my suitcase, and placing the hot flat iron in between the towels in my cubby, I stand in front of my bunk at attention like everyone else.

Ronit, with her hands behind her back, walks up to each bed, nodding or shaking her head. She gives little comments to each of us on how we can improve. She even orders one of the girls to re-make her bed. Afterward, when she has nodded to all the beds (which I guess is the equivalent of giving it her kosher blessing), we head to the courtyard to once again get in formation.

"Amy, step out of formation. It's your turn to guard the *bittan*." She points to a gray metal folding chair in front of our barracks.

I step out of formation. The hot sun beats down on the chair, the one I'm supposed to sit on to guard our valuables. Seriously, who'd be dumb enough to steal stuff on an army base?

I swear there's no shade in this place so we're at the mercy of the blistering sun. I'm so hot that if I had SPF 50 on I'd be tempted to put on my bikini and lay out. How do the Israeli soldiers deal with living here in this heat, forced to wear long sleeves and long pants?

As my unit marches to lunch, I place the chair in the open doorway, out of the sun, thinking about Israeli teens and their mandatory military service. The Israeli teens don't seem to resent being soldiers. I think for some weird reason they look forward to putting on uniforms every day.

Fifteen minutes later, a soldier I've never seen before walks up to me holding a cafeteria tray with food on it. He's medium height with a round face and a friendly smile. Right about now a friendly smile is definitely welcome.

"*Shalom*," I say when he comes closer.

"You can speak English with me. I'm American, born and raised in Colorado. My name's Noah. I already know you're Amy —from Chicago."

Wait. Noah is American? But I thought he was a full-fledged soldier. He's dressed in a full IDF uniform with his last name in Hebrew on the front of his shirt. He also has a badge hanging off his shoulder with the logo of a military unit on one side and his rank on the other. None of the Americans on our *Sababa* trip have their last names sewn on their shirts, let alone a unit badge. Our shirts are totally blank. But he's not on our trip.

The guy is a poser; what's up with that? "I'm sure the soldier whose shirt you're wearing is looking for it."

The guy looks down at the Hebrew on the shirt. "This *is* my shirt." His smile broadens. "Phew. You had me worried there for a second."

"How'd you get them to put your name on it?" I notice he also has his own army boots, just like Avi's. Maybe he won a ditch-digging contest and the prize was his own personalized IDF uniform. "And how'd you get someone to give you their unit badge?"

"They kinda gave me the shirt and badge, along with the boots and inoculations when I enlisted."

"What do you mean by 'enlisted'?"

"I'm an Israeli soldier."

Before he'd opened his mouth and spoken perfect English without an accent, I'd assumed he was an Israeli soldier. He looks like one, and now I notice his rifle, but... "But you're American."

"I'm also Jewish. I came here after high school and volunteered for the IDF. I felt a connection to Israel and wanted to do my part to help my fellow Jews."

Gosh, that's admirable. Before now, I never heard of a Jewish American just coming over here and enlisting in the Israeli military. On purpose.

"Do you know Hebrew?" I ask, getting more curious.

"I know a lot more Hebrew now than when I first came here a year ago. You learn pretty quick when you have to." He hands me the tray of food. "Here, eat. Before it gets cold."

The food on the tray consists of a glass of water (with no ice), chicken (dark-meat legs, once again), mushrooms, and rice. Two bees have decided to hover around my food, which is totally annoying. But now that Tori told me worker bees don't sting, I'm not afraid like I was before.

"Thanks. I'm starving." I'm too hungry to care that I'll be eating greasy dark meat instead of white breast meat. I chew whatever's attached to the chicken bone as if it's my last meal on earth.

Noah sits against the door jamb and watches me eat.

"I thought IDF guys and *Sababa* teens can't be together alone."

"We're not alone," Noah says, pointing to the guard sitting at the entrance to the barracks across the courtyard.

"I'm the official guard," I tell him as I take a drink of warm water to wash down the food. "If you want to steal stuff, my job is to stop you. Although you have a gun and I don't, so feel free to pilfer whatever you want."

"I'm not here to steal stuff." Noah looks embarrassed as he places his rifle over his knees. "Gefen told me to come talk to you."

As I hear my boyfriend's last name, I almost choke on the slippery piece of dark meat or gristle or fat or skin or whatever greasy thing I'm trying to swallow. "Gefen who?"

"Avi Gefen."

"Oh, him." I say, as if Avi isn't on my mind 24/7. "What did he want you to talk to me about?"

"He kinda wanted me to give you a message."

"And he couldn't do that himself because...?"

"Um, yeah. I think he said it had something to do with being afraid you'd break up with him before you hear him out. And maybe you'll listen to what he wants to tell you if it comes from someone else." Noah puts his hand up when I try to respond. "But don't quote me verbatim on that. I may have gotten a few words mixed up in the translation."

I point my half-eaten chicken leg at Noah. "You go tell Avi that we've already broken up, that I'm dating Nathan, and that if he's got something to say to me, be man enough to say it to my face. I don't want to hear things second-hand from a middleman."

"He doesn't believe you're dating whoever this guy Nathan is."

"Is he kidding? Nathan and I are..." I pick up the other uneaten chicken leg and hold it next to my half-eaten one. "Nathan and I are like this. Two chicken legs in a pod."

"Chickens don't come in a pod. Peas do."

"I don't see any peas around here, so I'm improvising. Work with me, Noah." This round-faced American-Israeli soldier would be a perfect match for Miranda. They're kind of the same person, but of the opposite sex.

Noah shrugs. "So you don't want me to relay his message?"

I shake my head.

He sighs. "Well, I hope you guys work it out at some point. Seeing Gefen upset isn't fun, especially during Krav Maga training."

I know a little Krav Maga—the official self defense of the Israeli military—because my dad was a commando when he was in the IDF. A few months ago he decided I was old enough to learn some of the contact combat basics. Essentially, it's to kick the person's ass (or groin, as my dad taught me) until your target is no longer a threat. If you can't get out of a bad situation, you strike hard, strike fast, and know the vulnerable places on your opponent's body.

My dad thought I would suck at it, but I actually did so well that after my first lesson he bought protective training pads. We've made training a weekly event. Krav Maga Night is my dad giving me new techniques on how to kick his ass, which I have to say is more therapeutic than a fifty-minute session with a social worker.

Seriously, what other teenager is lucky enough to say they're encouraged by their dad to punch, kick, and maim him every Wednesday? Although, given that my dad was a commando, he's specially trained to kick some ass himself.

Now that I live with my dad, we've worked out most

of our issues around him not being a permanent fixture in my life growing up. But he's still uncomfortable having a teen daughter when it comes to parental discussions about dating, sex, and drugs. The drug discussions (I'm using the word "discussion" loosely) go like this:

> *My dad: Amy, if you ever take illegal drugs I'll kill the person who gave them to you and then I'll kill you. Got it?*
> *Me: Loud and clear.*

The most recent sex talk (this time I'm using the word "talk" loosely) went along these lines:

> *My dad: Don't have sex until you're married.*
> *Me: What if I do?*
> *My dad: I'll practice Krav Maga on the guy. Without protective padding.*

I didn't mention then that my boyfriend is quickly becoming a Krav Maga legend in his own right on the base.

My dad is awful when it comes to talking about girly issues, as if he doesn't have a single ounce of estrogen in his body. But get him to talk about Krav Maga, or Israeli guy stuff like soccer or basketball, and his eyes light up.

"Thanks for the food!" I call out to Noah as he walks away, leaving me with my chicken bones, my folding chair, and thoughts of Avi—but not his message.

His answer is a wave and another smile.

Just when I finish lunch, I hear Ronit's *small-ya'mean-small* chant getting closer and closer.

"Amy, bring your tray to the eating area," Ronit says. "Miranda, go with her. Vic, you're in charge of guarding the *bittan* now."

I pick up the tray and start walking to the kitchen. Miranda walks with me...although she's actually a few paces behind. I have the feeling she's doing that on purpose.

"You okay?" I ask, glancing back at her.

She shrugs. "Sure."

"Because you're acting like something's wrong. Want to talk about it?"

"Nope."

Could it be that the Israeli army has broken Miranda's sweet-tempered spirit? I'm always crabby, but I thought I could count on Miranda to smile no matter what sucky situation she's in. I glance back again. The girl is definitely not smiling.

Maybe she's constipated. Seriously, talk to a group of teen girls in private and I guarantee they've all got pooping issues. Considering the lack of a decent toilet in this place, I wouldn't blame her.

But what if Miranda isn't constipated? What if she's upset with me? While I couldn't care less if Tori hates me, I do care if somehow I've caused this alienation between me and Miranda.

I wish Jess was ordered to accompany me, too. She'd know what to say to Miranda to make everything okay again.

As we walk into the cafeteria and I scrape the leftover food off my plate and into the big garbage bins, I realize Miranda isn't behind me anymore. She's waiting by the doorway with a pissy look on her face. I place the tray on the moving belt.

"Why aren't you smiling?" I ask her as we head back into the scorching Israeli death-heat.

"Because I don't feel like it. Why do you care, anyway? You hardly ever smile."

"Yeah, because I count on you doing it for me."

Miranda stops and puts her hands on her hips. "Amy, that doesn't even make sense."

"Neither does your pissy attitude. It reminds me of *me* and, to be honest, I wouldn't be able to stand a friend like me for very long."

"Are you saying I shouldn't be friends with you anymore?" She starts walking away, so I jog to catch up with her.

"When you smile, the world smiles with you, you know," I tell her.

I think she's about to laugh, but she doesn't. She starts walking faster. "You got that off of a greeting card or something."

"Well, if I was back home I'd run to Walgreens and get you a real card."

"What would you write in it?" she asks, challenging me to come up with something on the fly.

"I'd write ... I'd write ... *Don't be upset, Miranda. If I did anything to upset you, please forgive me. I know I'm not always a good friend to you. But if you share with me, I can try and fix it. Your friendship is really important to me, which says a lot about you because I can't stand most people. Being friends with you makes me a better person. So please don't give up on me. Love, Amy. P.S. When Nathan buys me another white chocolate Kit Kat, I'll give the entire thing to you."*

I have to give myself kudos. That was a damn good speech if I do say so myself. Any moment now sweet, shy-at-times/bubbly-at-times Miranda will turn back to her old self again. I stop and give her a look that says I know she's about to cave and envelop me in one of her big, embarrassing bear hugs. This time, I'm actually looking forward to it.

"I'll think about it," she says, then tosses her hair to the side and leaves me standing alone as she walks inside the barracks. No smile. No forgiveness. No bear hug.

Whoa. I just got a dose of Miranda the Diva dissing me.

13

There's a point in time when even the strongest person cracks under pressure.

The next morning our unit marches across the large court-yard and doesn't stop until we get to what's obviously an obstacle course. There's no doubt in my mind that this will be a challenge for me.

"We'll be testing your strength and stamina," Sergeant B-S says to us. "This course should be completed in less than three minutes."

I tell myself not to look over at Avi, but as usual I have a serious lack of self-control. My gaze wanders to him and I find him looking straight at me. So now our eyes are locked. My insides are melting, but I'm still angry and hurt. Even though it's scorching hot outside and I can feel the sweat running down my back and in between my boobs, a chill runs down my spine.

Sergeant B-S orders Nimrod and Avi to stand at the start of the obstacle course. Both get ready to race. When the sergeant blows his whistle, they take off faster than Mutt when he spots a new dog at the dog park.

I watch Avi whiz through the course as if he's been doing this his entire life. I can't help but admire the muscles that bulge from his arms as he jumps to the monkey bars and grabs the first bar, then skips two bars at a time until he's done. Then he crosses the balance beam.

When he gets to the high rope, he uses his thigh muscles and arms to pull himself to the top, rings the bell, then grabs a handle that brings him down to the ground. Nimrod is right behind him. At the half wall they're neck and neck.

I'm holding my breath, wondering who will win. They reach the part of the course where you duck low under a set of entwined ropes. Avi gains a little ground as he slithers on the ground, not hesitating one iota.

In the end, Avi is the one who crosses the line first. Nimrod is close behind him. Both are breathing heavily as Sergeant B-S tells us that Avi clocked in at thirty-eight seconds and Nimrod at forty-one.

Liron and Ronit line up next. When Sergeant B-S signals them to go, Liron blows Ronit away as she effortlessly does each obstacle. Ugh, no wonder Avi is attracted to her; not only is she pretty, but she can scale walls and shimmy up ropes. It's probably more impressive than being double-jointed. Liron clocks in at one minute one second while Ronit lags behind, finishing at one minute thirty seconds.

"Get in the same groups you were in yesterday," Sergeant B-S calls out.

I try to act cool as I walk over to Avi. Unfortunately, I'm not paying attention and trip over something or someone. Oops, it's Tori... I've stepped on the back of her foot again and her shoe came off.

"Ouch!" Tori yells out. "That's the second time you've done that, you spaz."

"Well maybe if you walked faster I wouldn't step on you."

Nathan grabs my shoulders. "Stop getting in fights with Tori," he says as he steers me away from her.

"She's rude."

"She's hot."

"So am I," I say as I wipe away another sweat drop that's falling down my forehead.

"I didn't mean hot as in sweaty. I mean hot as in—"

"I know what you meant," I say, cutting him off. Seriously, ever since Nathan finally stopped being obsessed with Bicky, he's been acting like a *Bachelor* reality show contestant. Since our third kiss and his breakup, he's gone out with more girls than I can count on two hands. And it doesn't help that he's been lead singer for Lickity Split, because lately he's been taking his groupies backstage and making out with them. He hasn't gone out with anyone twice yet. It's like he wants to make sure he doesn't get involved so there's no repeat of what he went through with Bicky. I wonder why the change in tactic since he met Tori.

I grab Nathan's hand while we wait for our other team members to assemble. Nathan pulls his hand loose, but I know Avi's watching so I grab his hand again and squeeze my nails into his skin as a warning not to snatch it back.

Avi growls, "Wait here" and walks away to talk to Liron and some of the other Israeli team leaders.

"You're getting me in trouble with Avi," Nathan says through gritted teeth and a fake smile which makes him look like a marionette on Prozac.

"Do you remember when you had me fake-kiss you in front of your ex-bimbo Bicky, to let her know it was over between you guys?"

"Yeah. I seem to remember you biting me."

"Nathan, that was because your tongue crept into my mouth."

"I was making it authentic. Besides, don't deny you were getting into it."

"Because I was fantasizing you were my boyfriend." It's the honest truth: When I started kissing Nathan that last time, in front of Bicky, I was totally imagining he was Avi when we were last together—which was seriously the best night of my life. After fooling around in the car didn't work, Avi and I moved onto the deserted beach. His touches and kisses and caresses were more than OMG!

"He's looking at me like he wants to kill me," Nathan complains.

"Good. Now that he's watching us, kiss me," I whisper softly, moving my lips closer to his for a repeat performance.

Nathan pries his fingers loose and steps away, although we're far enough from our other team members that nobody can hear us. "Are you kidding? First of all, didn't you sign the *Sababa* rule sheet attached to the brochure? It said, specifically, no fornicating. We're in Israel. For all I know fornicating might include kissing."

"No. It said no *going off in private* and fornicating. You really need to read the details more carefully. Anyways, nobody under the age of fifty knows the actual definition of fornicating so it won't hold up in a court of law."

"I told you I'm not doing this, Amy. Well, unless we *pretend* to date, and then after we're done with the Israeli army portion of the trip I *pretend* to break up with you and you *pretend* to be devastated in front of Tori. You can tell Tori after the fake breakup that I'm good at *everything*. You know, make me sound like the stud you know I am. You have to promise to set us up, without her knowing you're setting us up. Then you've got what you want, and I've got what I want. Deal?"

I don't mention that if he was a real stud, he wouldn't need me pretending he's one. I also don't mention that Tori hates me, so the last person she'll listen to is me. But whatever. "Fine."

Before I can think twice about my deal with Nathan, he takes my hand and leads me to the middle of where our group has assembled around Avi. Avi is standing with his arms crossed, waiting impatiently. His jaw is clenched as he watches us walk up.

"No hand holding," he barks.

Nathan gazes at me with love and tenderness, then kisses the back of my hand before letting it go.

Avi explains that we'll be racing against another team, and it's up to us to make sure everyone participates in each obstacle.

"What if I can't scale that wall?" Miranda asks.

"Have one of your teammates help you over it," Avi tells her. "You're a team. Nobody is left behind. Everyone finishes or everyone loses."

I hate races. They cause me too much stress. But Avi is a pro at this, and I'm ready to prove I'm not all talk and drama. I can kick some serious obstacle course butt when it comes right down to it.

I think.

The first heat is our team against Liron's team. I want to beat her team so bad, I can taste victory in my mouth. If only I paid more attention when they explained how to climb up that rope.

Sergeant B-S blows his trusty whistle.

We all run to the balance beam. One after another we walk across it. Next up are the monkey bars. I haven't done them since third grade, when I caught Michael Matthews looking up my pink-and-white plaid skirt. When I fell right on top of that little perv, and my knee connected with his face, I was secretly glad he went crying to Mrs. Feinstein with a bloody nose.

Tori is first. She maneuvers across the monkey bars easily enough, although she skipped the last three bars because she fell. David goes after her, skipping every other one and finishes effortlessly. Miranda's next.

"I can't do this," she tells us.

"Try," I say.

"Why try when I know I can't do it?"

She sounds more and more like me every day—it's scary. Avi said we have to do it, and work as a team, so how can she do it without actually *doing it?* I'm trying to think outside the box. It's a little hard to think when I see that four people from Liron's team have already successfully crossed the bars.

Ah, I've got it!

"What if we get on all fours and you step on our backs?"

Miranda shrugs.

I tell the team my plan. Me, Jess, Nathan, and the rest of the guys kneel down. Miranda walks on our backs while holding onto the bars above. I catch Avi nodding in approval and pointing to us as he talks to the sergeant. Miranda finishes with the bars really quickly, then profusely apologizes to the rest of the group as we each maneuver across the bars and head to the next obstacle.

Okay, so everyone finished the bars easily except for me. I got to the first bar, then slid off because my palms were sweaty and a bee buzzing in my ear freaked me out, even though I knew it was probably a worker bee. In the end, my team had to go down on their hands and knees again. I walked over them while grabbing each bar, just like Miranda.

The next obstacle is a tunnel. We all climb through easily and stop when we get to the rope. It's at least the height of a flagpole, if not higher.

I turn to my group. "I just want everyone to know that I'm afraid of heights."

"Then don't look down," Tori says. She steps on the first knot and starts climbing. "Hold it so it doesn't swing!" she yells at me.

I hold down the rope, even though I'm tempted to jiggle it hard until she falls off. I don't do it, because that would be mean. I might be whiny and a drama queen, but I like to think I'm not viciously mean to people.

David shimmies up the rope right behind Tori.

When they finish, Jess climbs and then the guys hold the rope for Miranda. For a girl who couldn't do the monkey bars, she's pretty impressive on the rope.

Now it's my turn.

Just the thought of going up that high makes me dizzy. I turn to Nathan. "Nathan, I don't think I can do it. I'll get vertigo. I don't want to die."

Nathan surveys the rope and says to me, "Well, nobody said we can't do it together. Go up and I'll follow behind you. You *are* my girlfriend; it's only natural we do it as a couple."

I roll my eyes so only Nathan can see. He kisses me on the nose, putting on the boyfriend act for anyone who cares enough to watch. When Ethan holds the bottom of the rope, I step on the first big knot.

"Go up one," Nathan instructs.

I pull myself up to the next knot, and Nathan steps on the first. His arms are wrapped around my knees, holding me tight. "You okay?"

"So far, so good."

"Go up one more," he says, loosening his hold.

I go up another one. I feel Nathan right behind me, then holding me tight again. "Any vertigo yet?"

"Not yet."

"Go up another one."

"Come on!" Tori yells. "Just do it!"

"I swear if she yells at me again I'm gonna punch her in the face. *If* I get out of this alive," I add.

"Ooh, a girl fight. What a turn-on."

"My foot is close to your nuts, Nathan, and you're suspended on a rope. It's probably not the best time to piss me off."

"You kick me in the nuts, I'm pulling your pants down," he says, following me up another section of rope.

"Avi will kill you if you do that."

"I'll already be dead from the fall so it won't matter. One more, Amy."

I close my eyes as we get higher. I have to admit, when Nathan's arms are around my knees, I feel safe.

Up and up we go. I close my eyes when I get to the top and tentatively ring the bell.

"Grab the handle and ride to the bottom," Nathan says.

"I can't."

"Yes, you can. You've come all this way—you can't stop now."

"We're losing because of you!" Tori yells at me. "What a *spaz*," I hear her say.

That's it. My anger overrides my fear. I grab the handle and shut my eyes tight while my body glides back to earth.

When my feet safely reach the ground, I open my eyes. Tori is laughing at me. Jessica looks ready to murder her, probably because she's my best friend and we always look out for each other. I storm up to the laughing hyena.

"You are seriously the most annoying person," I tell her. "I wonder how anyone can be friends with you."

She pushes me. At another time or place I might have lost my balance and fallen on my butt. But adrenaline rushes through my body, giving me strength beyond my normal capabilities. I push her back, and she goes flying. She lands on her butt.

I stand above her and let it all out. "Stop harassing me, you double-jointed, breast-challenged, designer-knockoff-wearing bully."

Tori's mouth is open wide. "You hit me!"

"No, I didn't. I pushed you."

"It's against the *Sababa* rules to assault another person. I'm telling!"

Oh, no. "You pushed me first, Tori." Geez, and they call *me* a drama queen.

Tori storms up to Avi. "Your girlfriend assaulted me."

"You've got two facts wrong. She's not my girlfriend. And you assaulted her first. Get back to the group and finish the course."

"She *pushed* me."

"This is not a discussion. Get back to the group and finish the course."

"Can't we just give up?" Nathan asks, watching as the other group nears the finish line. "We've obviously lost."

Looking into Avi's eyes, I see strength and determination. He would never give up. He won't let us give up, either. "Let's keep going until we finish," I say to my team.

We walk half-heartedly to the next obstacle.

When it's my turn to go through the swinging tire, I put my hands and feet in first. It's a big mistake, because now I'm stuck. The front half of me is through the tire, but my butt is sticking out the other end. "Push me, Nathan."

"You're giving me permission to touch your ass?"

"Not touch it. Just push it."

"Avi's watching. Should I caress it first to make him jealous?"

"Oh, yeah. What a great idea. Caressing my butt while

it's stuck in a tire is definitely going to make him jealous. *Not.*"

Nathan puts his hand on my butt. "Don't fart." He pushes me hard until I pop out of the tire. We're all sweaty and hot and it's worse because we know we lost.

The cargo net is easy enough to maneuver, although my foot slips a few times and I get rope burn on the back of my legs.

At the half wall, Miranda and I are hopeless. The guys hold Miranda on their shoulders and heave her over, then do the same for me. I swear, the wall is impossible. You have to have major arm strength to pull your body over it. Arm strength that I just don't possess.

After we step through a bunch of tires, we reach the last obstacle: crawling under the net. I look over at Avi watching us and wonder what's going through his head. There's hardly any room under the net. I kneel on the ground and duck my head. The ground is muddy, so I'm definitely getting dirty. I can't even crawl; I have to wiggle on my belly in order to go under this thing.

I use my fingernails to dig into the ground and my toes to help me slither forward like a snake. Seriously, how can Avi do the entire course in just over a half a minute?

"Push off my hands," Nathan says from behind me. He pushes me forward. I feel the time ticking away as I slide through... all the while my boobs are squished into the ground. My big C/D-cup boobs can probably fit into a training bra now.

I climb out and we all jog to the finish line. I feel victorious, although I must look like a complete mess. And we are in fact the big losers.

Avi has us sit on the ground while the other teams take their turns competing on the course. Tori grudgingly mumbles something about her uncle who's a lawyer and about what it did and did not say regarding assault in that infamous *Sababa* brochure.

Our group doesn't get to compete in the final heat because we came in last. When I look up, Avi is standing over me.

"Amy, can I talk to you for a minute?"

"Whatever you want to say to me, you can say in front of Nathan," I tell Avi. "We have no secrets between us."

Avi takes a deep breath, says, "Forget it," then walks away to stand by himself.

"He's brooding, Amy," Nathan informs me.

"I know."

I did tell Noah that whatever Avi wanted to say, he should say it to my face. Well, I guess it's time for me to hear it firsthand. I shouldn't delay the inevitable, dreaded conversation.

"Nathan, I'm going over to him."

"Want me to go with you?"

"That's probably not the safest idea. I think I can handle it." I stand, ready to face Avi and whatever news he's about to tell me. "I'll be right back."

"Good luck. You'll need it."

"What do you want to talk to me about?" I ask Avi,

who's standing close enough to our team to be seen but far enough away not to be heard.

"You didn't even try on the obstacle course, Amy."

"Are you kidding? I tried. Sorry if I'm not all buff and perfect like Liron."

"Yeah, not many girls can compete with her."

"Thanks. Next time you could give your team some pointers along the way. You *are* our team leader, you know."

"And as team leader, I knew your team could do it on your own. Amy, admit you're lying about dating Nathan."

"No."

"Then why'd you make me take you somewhere private that first day and let me kiss you?"

"I had a brain fart."

"No, you're having a brain fart right now by pretending you and Nathan are a couple. God is definitely inscribing you in the Book of Liars."

My blood is way past boiling now. "How dare you! I'll have you know that Nathan's kisses are the best I've ever had. By far. You could take lessons from him."

He opens his mouth to respond, then snaps it shut when someone walks by. We can't have a conversation in true private and Avi hates dishing his dirt in public. "When are you gonna stop playing games, Amy?"

"Never. I like games. It makes life interesting. You should try it sometime, you know."

"I don't have time for games." He looks behind me to Nathan, who's chatting with Miranda and Jessica. "So this is how you want to end it?"

"Don't you?"

"No. Didn't you talk to Noah?"

"Not about us. Listen, Avi, you and I both know it's not working."

"I'm not good at relationships, Amy."

"Well, that's one more obstacle we'd have to get through if we were dating. You'd have to deal with my games, and with your girlfriend being an obstacle-course flunkee. I'd have to deal with your commitment phobia and the fact that you don't really want a full-time girlfriend you have to answer to. We were doomed from the start."

He lets out a slow breath. "Please don't make more out of this than it is. I've been trying to be who you want me to be, Amy."

"I just want you to be *yourself.* I've never once asked you to be someone else. It may not seem like it now, but I'm actually doing you a favor. Now you can have Liron or any other girl all to yourself, with a clear conscience."

Nathan slides up beside me and puts his arm around my shoulders. "Sorry, Avi," he says. "You win some, you lose some."

Liron comes up out of nowhere and stands next to Avi. She nudges him. "So you told her?"

He nods.

"I'm so sorry, Amy," Liron says so sincerely I want to rip those blond streaks right out of her head. "But I'm glad you know. Now I won't feel so weird around you anymore."

Great. That makes one of us.

Avi puts his arm around Liron. I want to swat it off her, but as Nathan said, you win some, you lose some.

I just wish I wasn't the one who'd lost.

14

Second place is the first loser.
Last place is the biggest loser.

At night, I'm so shaken up by the finality of our break-up that I skip my normal facial cleansing routine and just climb into bed. Avi and I have broken up before, but this time it's for real. I try sleeping, but with the squeaky springs above me (Vic's indentation getting more and more pronounced), along with the fact that I can't get the awful conversation Avi and I had at the obstacle course out of my mind, sleeping is impossible. Listen, deep down I know I should have come clean to Avi about my non-relationship with Nathan. But I couldn't.

Avi uses a rifle, Krav Maga, and non-communication for self-defense. I use games, attitude, and manipulation.

No matter what I've thought in the past, we might just be too different.

In the morning, our team gets assigned kitchen duty, (thanks to Tori and her tirade yesterday on the obstacle course). It's not bathroom-cleaning duty, so I'm okay with it. Again, they wake us up at the crack of dawn. Actually, it's before the crack of dawn, because it's still pitch black outside. My team is held back while everyone else does an activity. Ronit leads us to the kitchen, and even though I don't want to see Avi, I can't help scanning the base looking for him. He's nowhere in sight.

Noah, the American IDF soldier from Colorado, is in the kitchen waiting for us.

"Hey, Noah," I groan, my eyes still at half-mast.

"Hey. I'm going to give you assignments." He points to a humongous pot half the size of me. "Two of you need to set baskets of bread on the tables. Two of you need to put water in that pot. When it boils, put three hundred eggs inside and let them sit in the boiling water for fifteen minutes. Two of you need to put jam in the bowls. And two of you need to make coffee."

We divvy up the jobs.

As soon as Miranda and I start pulling jars of jam from the huge refrigerator, bees swarm around us.

"Noah, the bees are bothering us," I tell him.

Noah waves some of the bees away. "Yeah, that's kind of a hazard of working here. Living with bees becomes part of your daily life."

"I hate bees," Miranda tells him.

"You also hate me," I blurt out.

"I can't believe you just said that."

"Why not? It's true."

Miranda huffs and walks over to talk about me or complain about me to Jessica. I just want Miranda to tell me what I did to piss her off so much. If I don't know what it is, I can't fix it any more than I can fix what went wrong with Avi.

Noah helps me pull more jars of jam out of the fridge. "What's her problem?"

"I wish I knew."

Noah shakes his head. "I keep my expectations low, so nobody disappoints me."

"Yeah, well, I have high expectations." I look toward Miranda. "I guess my friends do, too."

"Expectations make people miserable, so whatever yours are, lower them. You'll definitely be happier." Noah waves his hand around, gesturing to the entire kitchen. "You think I wanted to be assigned kitchen duties? Nope. But to be honest, at least it's quiet and the biggest pests I have to deal with here are the bees. Besides, I'm only here for three months and then I'm getting transferred to another base to get trained as an instructor. It's all good."

"You're a better person than me."

Listen, I know who I am and what my strengths are. And my strengths do not include having little or no expectations. I guess I shouldn't be surprised, then, when people let me down.

After Noah leaves me alone for a minute with instructions about how to ladle spoonfuls of jam into the plastic bowls, I'm having trouble fending off the four bees hovering around me. You'd think dropping globs of the jam would be easy, but it's not. It's sticky and messy and two of the bees just got stuck in the jam.

"Umm ... Noah ... I think there's a problem."

Noah is at my side. Miranda is right behind him, so I guess he was able to coax her back over here. "What's the jam?" he asks, then laughs. "Get it. What's the *jam*? You're scooping the *jam*."

You gotta love it when someone laughs at their own jokes.

"Yeah, I don't know how to break the news to you, but a few bees are stuck in the jam," I tell him.

"Just pick 'em out before you set the bowls on the tables," he says, as if it happens every day. He doesn't even peer in the bowls to see the annoying stinging creatures struggling for their lives. That's what they get for hovering around the jam, I guess.

Noah leaves Miranda and me to fish out the bees while he helps Eli and David with the eggs.

I look down into the first bowl of jam. I can do this. I'm trying to think about the consequences of an IDF soldier, jam on his bread, biting into a little bee corpse as a bonus treat. At least they're not those fuzzy bees, because having a mouthful of that fuzz would definitely not go over well.

I spot a bee in the next bowl. With shaky hands, I slowly

fish it out with a spoon and flick it into the garbage can. "This is so gross," I say to nobody in particular, since my partner Miranda is pretty much ignoring me and everyone else is doing other tasks.

Within five minutes I've inspected and de-bee'd eleven bowls. I look into the twelfth bowl and find the next bee. Seriously, don't bees have eyes and see their cousins and brothers drowning in the sticky stuff? You'd think they'd be smart enough to stay away, but no. Their little bee brains aren't equipped with street smarts.

I slowly fish out another bee and head for the garbage can. The bee is still alive—I can see it walking in the jam on my spoon. Eww. I suppress a gag. If it crawls anywhere near my hand, I'm dropping the spoon and running out of here.

I'm almost to the garbage can when I feel a sharp pain on my butt. "Ahhhh!" I scream, whipping myself around to see what or who was the cause. But instead of it being an insect like I suspected, it's Nathan. With his thumb and pointer finger in a pinching position. My fake boyfriend just pinched my ass.

"How's my sweetie?" he asks, raising and lowering his eyebrows at me. Tori is beside him, giving me the evil eye.

Speaking of sweet mixed with evil, I examine the jam/bee on the spoon in my hand.

Oh. No.

The jam isn't there. Neither is the bee. I quickly scan the floor, but it's not there. I frantically scan my shirt. Sure enough, there's a big glob of jam on my sleeve. The bee is stuck in it, creepily walking in the jam. "Get it off! Get it off! Eww!"

Nathan takes my elbow, looks up at me and says in a sexy voice, "Let me get that for you." He checks to make sure Tori is watching him be my hero. I expect him to flick it off me, but instead his tongue snakes out as he leans close to the jam … and the bee.

I quickly realize he thinks he's only licking jam off my sleeve.

"Nathan, don't … "

"I'm here for you, babycakes." Before I can pull away, he licks off the jam and struggling bee with the tip of his tongue.

My hand flies over my mouth. "Oh, my God. Nathan— you just ate a bee!"

Nathan's face contorts in shock, and I realize I didn't have to tell him he ate a bee. He figured it out all by himself. "Ow! What the fu—"

He runs to the garbage can faster than I've ever seen him move and spits jam and the bee out of his mouth.

"Nathan, are you allergic to bees?" Miranda cries out over the commotion.

"No."

There's a sigh of relief that Nathan isn't going to die. I've never heard so many swear words come out of his mouth at one time since I've known him.

I rub his back as he rinses his tongue in the big metal kitchen sink. "I'm so sorry. I tried to warn you—"

"It sthung my tung. Thit," he swears. He sticks his tongue out and points. "Take de sthinger outh."

"Okay." I examine his tongue. "What should I be looking for?"

"The sthinger!"

Is it white? Red? Black? I've never taken out a stinger before. I'm frantic with worry.

"His tongue is swollen," Miranda says. "I think he needs to go to the infirmary."

"Miranda's right," I cry out. "Nathan, I'm so sorry."

"You're thorry? Amy, thath's the lasth thime I'm pinthing your assth."

"Stop talking, Nathan. Your throat might swell up so bad it'll stop the oxygen."

Nathan opens his mouth wide and breathes in and out, proving his throat is letting enough air through.

"Close your mouth, Nathan," Tori says. "You look like a damn fish gasping for air, you dork."

"Uthually I'm thexy," Nathan tells her, then nudges me to intervene.

"The *sexiest*," I agree, but I don't think Tori is buying it.

Noah leads Nathan, who's now screaming unintelligible obscenities, all the way to the infirmary. Great. Now I've ruined my fake boyfriend's reputation, too.

Tori finishes the task of piling plastic coffee mugs on a tray.

"Hey, Tori. I thought you said these were worker bees that don't sting," I say to her.

"I didn't say they won't sting if you *eat* them," she

responds, then walks back out into the dining area with the tray of coffee mugs.

I follow her with a tray of jam-filled bowls. "It's too bad my boyfriend won't be able to kiss me because of his bee sting."

"Your problem, not mine," she says, attitude dripping from each word.

I set two bowls on each table, wondering how I'm going to make her go out with Nathan after we "break up" and I'm supposedly devastated. "Who do you like?"

"As if I'm gonna tell you."

Seriously, this girl is so one-dimensional you'd think when she turns sideways she'd be as flat as a piece of paper. She belongs on another planet. "You know, it wouldn't hurt if you acted a little nicer."

"Why should I? Acting nice didn't get me anywhere. It sure didn't keep my parents together, that's for sure."

"Are they divorced?"

"That's none of your business. Just leave me alone."

I'm shocked. Tori actually opened up to me. The good part is that I now know what her deal is. She's not mad at me, per se. Okay, so I'm sure I annoy her 10 percent of the time. But the real issue behind her pissy face and bitchy attitude is a daughter who wants her parents to get together and doesn't see it happening any time soon.

"Not that you care, but I know how you feel," I tell her.

"I doubt it. Are *your* parents divorced?"

"No, worse. My parents were never married. How

would you like growing up knowing you were the result of a one-night stand? That's my reality. And no matter how much attitude I have, that will never change."

"But you have friends. I have nobody."

"If you'd act a little nicer maybe we could be friends. If you stop calling me a spaz every two minutes, that might be a start."

"What makes you think even if I wanted a friend, I'd pick you? Besides, you *are* a spaz." Tori tosses her hair with a flick of her wrist, showing me a flash of dark hair underneath her blond locks, and stomps back to the kitchen.

She ignores me the rest of the time as she busies herself with one task or another. I guess now is not the time to become buddy-buddy with her, especially when she's in charge of the hot coffee. It's not a level playing field.

Avi walks in the door and I almost drop a bowl of jam. I wish I could forget the long talks we'd have on the phone when he was on military leave. Or that his hands are strong enough to dig ditches in record time and gentle enough to caress my skin and make me beg for more.

"Where's Noah?" he asks in a businesslike tone, as if I'm someone he just met.

"He took Nathan to the infirmary," I answer back, just as businesslike.

"Why?"

"Nathan kind of ate a live bee."

"Kind of? How does someone *kind of* eat a bee?"

"It's a long story," I say, not wanting to get into it.

Tori appears by Avi's side. "He licked it off her. You know, with his tongue." As if Avi can't get the visual, Tori sticks her tongue out and wiggles it up and down.

So much for the conversation staying businesslike. I have a vindictive urge to pull her tongue until it comes out of her mouth.

Avi looks as if he's about to be ill. "I get the picture. No need to demonstrate."

Avi and I meet up again at the tray full of bread baskets. I figure I need to explain, so I tap him on the arm. When his dark gaze meets mine, I step back. I can't think straight when I'm looking directly into his eyes.

"Um, yeah. The way Tori told you what happened isn't really how it went down."

"I don't need details."

"But I want to explain." I pretend to be busy picking up baskets of bread to set on the tables as I talk, sparing myself from looking directly at him. "So, um, there were bees stuck in the jam. And when Nathan pinched my butt *by accident*, I twirled around and jam landed on my sleeve. He licked it off, not knowing there was a bee stuck in it."

"He didn't do anything by accident, Amy. Tell Nathan to keep his hands off your *tachat*. And while he's at it, tell him to keep his tongue away from you, too."

"You jealous?"

"Why should I be? I have Liron, right?"

"Right. And I have Nathan, right?"

He shrugs. "I don't know, you tell me. You've obviously had his tongue down your throat multiple times."

Oh, that was low. How dare he turn this around and make me the bad person, when he's probably been playing "battling tongues" with Liron! "Yeah, well, he might be tongue-challenged at the moment, but normally he's *the best.*" I emphasize the last two words for effect. If Avi's tight, white knuckles are any indication, I think I've accomplished my goal.

"Amy?" He says, his voice laced with frustration.

I cross my arms on my chest (actually under my chest, because my boobs are so big). "What?" I know we're about to have it out, right here in the middle of the IDF cafeteria.

The door between the kitchen and dining area opens. It's Jess and Ethan, bringing out the baskets of bread. Both stop in their tracks, obviously sensing the massive amount of tension in the room.

"Everything okay in here?" Jess asks.

I narrow my eyes at Avi. "It's all peachy. Avi and I were just discussing the art of a good kiss."

"While that might be fascinating at another time, we have baskets of bread we need to put out. Help us," Jess says.

I see something, out of the corner of my eye, on one of the pieces of bread in the basket Jess is holding. "There are a couple of ants crawling on the bread."

Jess shrugs. "Noah said to consider them spices."

15

Insects, whether they're bees or ants,
should not be eaten alive.

Breakfast is half over when Nathan reappears.

"How's your tongue?" Miranda asks once he reaches our table.

Nathan shrugs. Noah is standing behind him. "He says it hurts to talk. The nurse told him the swelling should go down in a few hours."

"That's what you get for pinching my butt. God was punishing you."

He gives me the finger as he takes a seat beside me.

"God's gonna punish you for that, too."

Across the table, Miranda slams down her cup of milk. It splashes all over her uniform, but I don't think she notices.

"Amy, leave him alone. Don't you think he's dealing with enough without you making him feel worse?"

"I was just kidding, Miranda."

"Yeah, well ... " Miranda looks around, realizing she's causing a scene. Miranda's not used to creating drama. Her voice shakes as she says, "Maybe Nathan doesn't know you're kidding."

"Nathan and I joke around all the time. We always do."

Nathan puts his arm around me, nods, and smiles.

"Oh," Miranda says, slowly sitting back down. She doesn't look up until we're done eating and dismissed from breakfast.

On the way back to the barracks, I catch up to Miranda. "I know why you're pissed with me. You have the hots for Nathan."

She glances sideways at me. "So?"

Wow, I'm right. I mean, I got the idea when she went all ballistic on me, milk splattered on her face during breakfast. But I still can't believe it.

"I'm not really dating him, you know."

Miranda stops and turns to me. "Then who are you dating, Amy? Because you seem to be dating guys you hate, and hating guys you date, and hating girls who like the guys you date, or hate, and—"

My brain is on overload. "You lost me. I'm confused."

"That makes two of us." She stomps away from me.

I hurry to catch up. "What do you want me to do? I hate you being mad at me."

"I don't know. I have no claim to Nathan. He doesn't even like me."

"Are you double-jointed?"

"What?"

"Are you double-jointed?"

"No. In case you haven't noticed, I'm fat and had to step on people's backs in order to complete the monkey bars at the obstacle course."

"So did I. And you're not fat, Miranda."

She picks up her shirt and grabs her bulging stomach. "What do you call this?" To be honest, I've seen people way bigger.

Umm... Umm... "I call it 'extra.'"

"Extra what?"

Oh, I hate being put in a corner I can't get out of gracefully. "Just 'extra'."

She pulls her shirt down. "Well, I call it *fat*. Nathan isn't going to like me. Did you see his last girlfriend, Bicky? She was rail thin."

"Miranda, she was a druggie. That kind of thin is *not* attractive."

"Neither is this extra thirty pounds I carry around. And no matter how much I try to get rid of it, I can't. Because I crave sweets, and once I start eating I can't stop. Do you know what it's like not to be able to stop doing something you know isn't good for you?"

"Sure I do."

She puts her hand on her hip, totally unconvinced.

"Well, I know I do and say things that hurt other people," I tell her. "I can't stop it sometimes. It's a protective thing. You know, so I hurt people before they have a chance to hurt me. Don't let anyone else know, but I've got issues."

"Everybody has issues, Amy." She sighs.

I guess she's right. Tori has issues from her parents' divorce, Miranda has weight/image issues, I have emotional protection/ego issues, Jess has hypochondriac issues...

Is anyone human actually normal?

I'm beginning to think being normal is actually *abnormal.*

16

Zits are God's way of making sure we know we're only
human and far from perfect.
I'd just like him to remind me a little less often.

Looking at my face in the bathroom mirror the next morning, I'm horrified. I stare at the small zit I noticed last night
after I took a shower. The small red bump appeared above
my left eyebrow. It's not small anymore.

Jessica is brushing her teeth at the sink next to me.
"Don't touch it," she says as she wipes her mouth with
a towel and places her toothbrush in a plastic tube she
brought from home. "If you do, it'll just get worse and
take longer to go away. Use cover-up and forget about it.
Give it two or three days, and it'll be gone."

She walks out of the bathroom and I take another look
in the mirror. Two or three days? Ugh. I tentatively touch
it. It hurts. And it's so big it deserves its own name.

George the Zit.

George is being stubborn. Well, I'm stubborn too. I don't listen to Jess and I try and get rid of George myself by squeezing him away. But now George looks worse and has started to throb. It looks like a bright red radish has imbedded itself on my forehead.

If I had bangs, I could hide George from the rest of the world. But I don't. I head to the barracks with my hand over George and sneak past Jess. Lifting my makeup case, I pull out my trusty cover-up. But as I pat it on and examine it in my small travel mirror, the cover-up looks like caked-on silly putty. Besides, when I sweat the stuff is going to come right off. So I do the next best thing: I pull out my travel first-aid kit and cover George up with one of those round Band-Aids. When George is hidden from the world, I head to the courtyard to wait for Ronit to order us into formation.

Nathan is outside, his tongue fully recovered from the bee incident.

"What the hell happened to your forehead?" Nathan asks with a grimace. I swear he says it so loud everyone within a mile can hear him.

"Nothing," I say, hoping against all hope he'll drop the subject.

"I've got two theories," he says. "Either you cut yourself shaving your monobrow, or you're covering up a huge zit."

"Shut up or I'll make you eat another bee."

"Hi, Nathan," Miranda says.

"Let me guess what's for breakfast," Jessica says as she walks up to us. "Ant-encrusted toast, hard-boiled eggs, and delicious bee-jam." Her voice trails off after a glance at my forehead. I'm trying to look the other way, but she grabs my arm. "Amy, please tell me you didn't touch it."

"I didn't touch it," I say roughly. I'm not lying. I didn't touch it, I *mutilated* it.

Nathan pretends to cough, but I know he's laughing. "She's got a big zit she's covering up but is too embarrassed to admit it. Come on, Amy, fess up," he says, then reaches over to pull the Band-Aid off.

I slap his hand away.

"How big *is* it?" Miranda asks.

"I told you to leave it alone," Jess scolds.

"Okay, okay everyone!" I yell, then pull the Band-Aid off and point to my forehead. "Everyone, meet George."

Nathan pretends to gag. "That looks so *nasty*, Amy. What the *hell* did you do to it?"

"You named your zit?" Miranda asks.

"I figured since George and I are going to be together for a while, he might as well have a name," I tell her, ignoring Nathan. Jess is still staring at my forehead as if she's not quite sure how I managed to turn tiny George into big, red, angry George.

Nathan is laughing again.

"Does it look really bad?" I ask my friends.

Nathan gives me a resounding "Yes!"

Miranda shrugs and nods at the same time.

Jess says, "They might make you go to the infirmary for fear it's something contagious."

I slap my hand over my forehead and run back to the barracks. Unfortunately, Tori is still in the room.

"We're supposed to be outside in less than a minute," Tori says.

"So leave." I pull out my mirror and look up at Tori. "Do you mind? I need some privacy."

"For what?"

"It's a long story that has to do with a big zit I named George."

I examine George in the mirror. Unfortunately, Tori sees him too. Her lips curl up in disgust. "Eww."

"I know. You want to call me a spaz again because I have a zit?"

"No. But you better go out there before you get in trouble for being late."

George looks nastier than before. "What am I gonna do?"

Tori shrugs. "Put on a hat."

"I don't even know where mine is. Besides, George might get infected from rubbing against the material."

"I could cut you some bangs, if you want," Tori says. "My mom's a hairdresser."

"Really?"

"Really. Your face structure would actually look good with bangs."

"You'd really cut me bangs?"

"Anything to get you to stop looking at yourself in the mirror." She pulls out scissors from her duffle and slides my hair through her fingers. "Trust me."

She has no clue how hard that is for me, but Rabbi Glassman says that sometimes it helps to make people feel needed. "I trust you," I tell her.

"Thanks for sharing your story about your parents when we had kitchen duty," she says as she snips away. "I see you with all the stuff you have, and I think you have the perfect life."

"It's my parents' way of making up for their shortcomings."

"There. I'm done." She puts the scissors down and holds up the mirror so I can inspect my new *do*.

I never really wanted bangs. I was six years old the last time I had bangs, and they feel weird brushing up against my forehead. I have to admit they don't look half bad.

Outside, sure enough, everyone is in formation. Tori and I come sauntering out. Sergeant B-S isn't here, thank goodness. But Avi is.

All eyes turn to Avi.

"Why are you late?" he asks us.

"It's my fault, not Tori's," I tell him. "It was a medical issue."

"Are you sick?" he asks, his voice laced with concern that makes my knees weak. He cocks his head and inspects me, looking for a wound or weakness.

"Not exactly."

"Do you have a fever?"

To my horror, he picks his hand up and is about to feel my forehead. I jump back, afraid he'll find George. "No!"

"Amy, my patience is wearing thin. Fast."

I can tell. "It's not a fever. Tori was cutting my hair."

"Since when is cutting hair a medical issue?"

"It just is."

Avi looks up to the sky, probably asking God for the strength to deal with me. I don't blame him. Truth is, I *am* a spaz.

"Tori, get back in formation. Amy, give me twenty push-ups."

"Can I do girlie ones?"

"No."

"I can't do guy's ones. I don't have enough upper arm strength."

"Yes, you do." He points to the ground. "Stop stalling."

I stretch out on the ground. Thankfully we're on a paved sidewalk so I don't have little pebbles sticking into my palms.

With my hands on either side of my shoulders and the tips of my toes on the pavement, I straighten my arms.

I look up, and stare straight into Avi's eyes. He's squatting right in front of me. For him, pushups are no big deal. For me, on the other hand...

"Stop thinking and just do them," he says softly so no one else can hear. "Pretend your body is a piece of wood and your elbows are hinges." He gets in position and demonstrates it for me.

I bend my elbows a tiny bit and straighten them.

"That's not a pushup, Amy."

"It is for me."

"Go down farther." He demonstrates it again, reminding me of when I did them in front of Sergeant B-S my first night here.

I look into his eyes, which have determination written all over them.

"I wouldn't ask you to do something you couldn't do," he says. "Push yourself."

The thing is, I want to make Avi proud of me. And if he says I can do it, maybe I can.

I bend my elbows again, all the while trying to keep the rest of my body straight. My boobs are almost touching the ground when I straighten.

"That's it. Nineteen more," Avi says, doing them right along with me.

I do two more, my arms shaking and struggling each time. Going down isn't the problem; it's the pushing up part.

"Seventeen more."

I take a deep breath. My arms are tired. I'm not mad at Avi for punishing me. It's my own fault for being so vain. I look up, wishing everyone wasn't watching.

"I have faith in you," Avi says softly. "No matter what, I always have."

Now I want to cry, because he probably has more faith in me than I have in myself. As I lower my body again, Avi's determination makes me do more pushups. Every time I think I'm going to collapse, I look up into his beautiful milk-chocolate eyes for strength.

Sweat is dripping off my forehead. My shirt is wet from sweat and I probably smell, but I finish my twenty pushups and stand up.

"You'd be a great soldier if you didn't complain all the time."

I shrug. "And you'd be a great boyfriend if you didn't kiss other girls."

17

---

*Running should be saved for times
when you're being chased.*

After we sit through another classroom session on rifle safety and have dinner, we're informed that we'll be going on a night run.

"Like a Taco Bell run?" I ask. "Fun." Although I've never seen a Taco Bell in Israel, I've seen a few McDonald's. I had a McKebab at one last summer, with *cheeps* on the side (which is really just French fries).

Ronit and Liron look at each other in confusion. "What's a Taco Bell run?"

"You know ... a food run."

Liron laughs. "We weren't talking about a food run. We mean *night run* literally."

"Where you run at night," Ronit adds, just in case I don't get it.

"Oh."

If I'm to be completely honest, the last thing I want to do at nine p.m. is run. In fact, the last thing I ever want to do is run, period. I'd hate running if it was at nine at night or nine in the morning (or three in the afternoon, for that matter).

At nine on the dot, just when the sun has almost left us, we congregate in a big, open area right outside the base. I spot Nathan and pull him aside. "Nathan, don't you think Miranda's awesome?"

"Uh, yeah. Why?"

"I was just wondering if you, you know, would ever consider her as more than a friend. You know, like girl-friend material."

"No. She's too serious. And too nice."

"Nice is a good trait, Nathan."

"Yeah, *in a friend*. I like Miranda *as a friend*. Get it? I need a raunchy and inappropriate girl... you know, some-one I consider a challenge."

"I got it." Tori's the one.

Nathan shrugs. "Truth is, I know Miranda's had a crush on me for months. I tried thinking of her that way, but it didn't work. The yin/yang thing just isn't there. I feel bad about it, if that makes you feel any better."

I sigh, knowing that pairing my two friends isn't going to work. "Well, as long as you feel bad about it, I guess you're off the hook."

"What are you wearing on your head?" Sergeant B-S asks me, cutting my conversation with Nathan short.

I reach up and feel the hot-pink headlight my mom bought me for the trip. At the time I thought it was lame to wear a flashlight strapped to your forehead, but when I got ready for the night run that has nothing to do with food or Taco Bell, I put it on. "A flashlight."

"Who told you to put it on?"

"Nobody. I thought of it all by myself. It'll help me see where I'm going."

Sergeant B-S takes the flashlight off my head. "A flashlight in a real military operation would give away your location."

"This isn't a real military operation," I say, stating the obvious.

"We're simulating one. No flashlights. Use the moon as your light." He hands my flashlight back to me and faces the rest of the unit. "In a real operation, troops move at night. Since there are only a few hours of darkness, you have to move fast so the enemy is taken by surprise."

Four guys are chosen to carry a stretcher while they run, with four more guys as backup stretcher-holders. Nathan is one of the backups. Two other guys are assigned to carry what they call "jerry cans," which are water-filled jugs, on their backs.

The rest of us wait to be led on our run. I don't know what to do with my headlight, so I strap it on my head and turn the light off. Yes, I'm aware it looks ridiculous, but at least it covers up George.

Sergeant B-S points to the front of the line. "Stretcher people, move up front. People with jerry cans are next. Then slow runners and then good runners."

"Why are good runners last?" I question.

"So they can help the runners who aren't so fast," Liron informs us. "We're only as good as our slowest runner."

"I need a volunteer," Sergeant B-S barks out.

Yeah, right. As *if.* Jess and I look at each other knowingly. We've been warned not to volunteer. Especially when we don't even know what we're volunteering for. Plus, I'm dreading running at night as it is … the last thing I need to do is carry something as well. I have my big boobs to carry, which is more than enough for one person to handle.

Since nobody raises their hand, Sergeant B-S walks among us to pick the unlucky person for the mysterious task. I learned a long time ago that you lessen your chances of being picked if you don't make eye contact with the picker. I concentrate on my fingernails instead, as if I find my cuticles the most interesting things I've ever laid my eyes on.

Out of the corner of my eye I see Sergeant B-S moving in front of me. I hold my breath and pray he passes me.

He does. Phew.

But he stops right in front of Jessica. "You," he says.

Oh, no. Poor Jess.

"Me?" Jess chokes out.

"Move to the front of the line. You'll be carried on the stretcher, as the pretend-wounded."

Jess's eyes light up. "So I don't have to run?"

"No."

"Cool!" Jess gives me an excited look before taking her place on the stretcher. I watch in envy as the stretcher-carriers lift her up.

The line starts moving, and already I feel like I'm in the Chicago Marathon. I sure hope we won't be running 26.2 miles. We start out at a slow jog on the paved road, but then the front of the line gains momentum and speed just as we're led up some rocky areas.

Jess is lying down, enjoying a ride on a stretcher, while I'm running with a dorky unlit headlight strapped to my head. Avi is bringing up the rear with Nimrod. They're both in full military gear again, with vests, rifles, and everything, which is probably heavier than the jerry cans.

The area gets steeper and steeper. We're running up a mountain. I wonder if, when I get to the top, I can just roll down. Soon I'm struggling to keep up. Miranda has fallen behind, and I hear Nimrod urging her on.

I try to drink from my canteen, but it all spills down my neck and the front of my shirt because it's not easy to drink and run at the same time.

I'm not a fast runner, and when the good runners catch up to me, I get frustrated. Especially because I see Jess in the distance, lying on the stretcher like Cleopatra being carried by her manservants.

When I'm sweating and panting and think I can't run anymore, Avi's words from earlier echo in my head. *Push yourself. I have faith in you.*

I run faster, the mantra helping me along. I feel victorious when I catch up to the guys running with the jerry cans.

Avi's right. I can do this. My arms are moving fast, my legs are moving fast, and I'm ignoring the fact that my canteen is banging against my side with every stride. I think of all the soldiers who have it worse, like everyone in the Sayeret Tzefa unit. They have to carry a big rifle, wear a heavy vest, and still run.

I'm a machine now, running fast without thinking about how much I hate it or want to go to sleep. I'm not thinking about Avi, or George the Zit, or Nathan, or Tori, or Miranda, or even Jess aka Cleopatra ... I am one with the earth.

Except ...

My toe hits what must be a rock, stopping my momentum. I'm gonna fall. I try to get my hands out to break the impact, but my reflexes aren't as fast as my feet.

I slam to the ground. I'm not lucky enough to fall on pavement or grass—just gravel and stones. My hips get slammed against sharp rocks. Pebbles slice into my forearms as I slide over them. As my chin scrapes the ground like a plane landing on a runway, my headlight slides off George and crashes onto the bridge of my nose, blocking my view.

Damn. That. Hurt.

My body is paralyzed from shock and pain. I'm afraid to move. My forearms are burning like someone has lit a match, and the flames are licking my skin.

Some people have passed me, but others have stopped. There's commotion. At least I haven't fainted, which is a good thing.

"Are you okay?" someone asks.

"She totally wiped out," someone else adds.

"Amy!" It's Avi's voice. He doesn't sound like a military commando anymore. He sounds concerned. His concern, along with the burning in my arms and knees and chin, makes me emotional. As I swallow back tears, a warm, comforting hand pulls off my headlight and pushes the hair out of my face. "Amy, can you move?"

I dread the thought of moving. I'd rather stay here for a while because I fear the additional injuries I've gotten and don't know about yet. "I think so," I say, wincing as I attempt, and fail, to sit up. "Oh, God, I'm *so* embarrassed."

Avi orders the gawkers to keep going. Nimrod urges the unit forward and leaves Avi to tend to my injuries.

"Everyone's gone. It's just us."

"Aren't we going to get in trouble if we're alone?" I sniff a couple of times, then wipe my nose with my sleeve. I'm giving up preserving my ego. In fact, my ego is non-existent now... I think I left it back in Chicago.

"It's fine. I'm trained in first aid."

I swipe away the tears running down my cheeks as Avi slowly helps me sit up.

"I'm fine," I say, sniffing again. "I need to get up so I can finish the run."

"You're not doing anything until I know the extent of your injuries."

I push his hands away as he pulls up my now shredded sleeves. "Stop."

"Don't be stubborn, Amy." I try to stand, but Avi pushes me back down. He swears when he bends my elbow and sees the damage. "You're hurt. There's blood all over your arms."

"It doesn't matter. If you got your arm shot off, you'd jump right up and finish the run because you're superhuman."

"I'm not superhuman."

"Sure you are. Liron is, too."

He stops his examination and looks at me. "Huh?"

"She's the female version of you. If she fell, she'd jump up and finish this stupid running exercise on these stupid rocks that jut out of the stupid ground without warning."

"That's a lot of stupids," he says.

"Yeah, well, that's how I feel right now. Like everything is stupid." I feel my hot, stupid tears streaming down my dirty, dusty face.

"I need to clean out your stupid wounds with some stupid water. Okay?" He pours water from his canteen on my arms.

I suck in my breath. "Ow. Ow. Ow. Ow."

"Sorry. Just hang in there." He unzips a pocket on his vest and takes out what I guess is first aid stuff. He rips open a packet and pulls out a little white antiseptic pad.

I jerk my arm away in anticipation of the antiseptic on my open wounds. "Ouch!" I say before he even touches me with it. "It's gonna sting."

"Only for a second. It'll help numb it, too. Trust me."

I give him a "yeah, right" look.

"Trust me," he says, so tenderly it rocks my insides.

He takes one arm and gently wipes the cloth over my wound. When I wince, he softly blows on the cut, easing the sting. I close my eyes and try to focus on the pain instead of his breath and his fingers touching my skin.

Feeling his soft breath makes me think about when we were under the blanket on the couch at my condo. His kisses started at my lips, trailed over my skin, and then his breath followed those kisses ... and then his tongue followed that same path, giving me goose bumps. When he stopped, I begged him to do it again and again. And he did.

"The last thing I want is a female version of me," he says as he's busy pulling out another antiseptic pad. He takes my other arm and cleans it, blowing on it gently like before. It feels so good I never want him to stop. My anger at him weakens with each touch of his hand and each whisper of his breath on my skin. I hope he doesn't notice.

He bandages both my forearms with gauze. "It's only a temporary fix until I get you to the infirmary, but it'll have to do. What else hurts?"

"Everything. My hips are burning, my knees are burning. My chin feels raw." Even my heart hurts—being this close to him and knowing that our relationship is over stabs like a knife. I moan.

"Does anything feel like it's broken?" he asks, his arm supporting my back.

"No." Nothing besides my heart, but that had nothing to do with my fall.

He pushes up my pants leg, and his fingers run over my knee checking the damage. He makes me bend and straighten my leg a couple of times. "No cuts or broken bones, but you're gonna have some nasty bruises tomorrow."

I take a deep breath, gulping back tears. My breath comes out in little spurts. I hate showing this much weakness, especially in front of someone who protects his own at all costs. "Thanks for helping me, Avi."

He rubs my chin with another pad. He cups my cheeks in his hands and swipes my tears away with his thumbs. "I'm your team leader. You're my responsibility."

Duh! I should've known he wasn't being this nice because he still cared about me. I hold back a response. Time stops, though, as being this close brings back a flood of emotions. Avi leans forward, and I wonder whether, if I lean in, we'll kiss. I turn away before I'm tempted to try it. What if he turns away and my lips connect with his cheek? I'd die from embarrassment.

He packs up the unused gauze and the open packets. "I'm taking you back to the base now," he says, lifting me up and carrying me in his strong, protective arms.

While it's so tempting to lean my head into his neck and let him take care of me, his words from this morning are still echoing in my head.

"Avi, I want to finish the run." I swear I can almost hear my bruised body scream "*no!*" But I want to push myself. I want to prove to myself, to Avi, and to my entire unit that I'm a warrior woman. Back when we were digging ditches, Liron accused Avi of taking it easy on me. And as much as I feel happy and safe in Avi's arms, and would love to be carried down the mountain because my body is protesting every movement I make, I don't want to give up.

He slowly puts me down. "You don't have to."

"I know. But you told me this morning to push myself."

He shakes his head and points to my torn pants and shirt. "Not while you're bleeding and hurt."

I show him my gauze-covered arms. "Would you run even if you were bleeding?"

"Probably."

"Would Liron do it?"

"Probably. But she's been training alongside us Sayeret Tzefa trainees."

"Yeah, well, if she can do it, so can I." I strap on my canteen and slide my hot-pink headlight onto my head. I must look ridiculous with torn clothes, a scraped-up chin, and a hot-pink light that I'm not allowed to turn on, but I've got determination on my side. "I'm a kick-ass Jewish warrior woman and don't you forget it."

"I won't," he says, smiling as we start at a slow jog up

the mountain to try and catch up with everyone else. "I'm looking forward to seeing how a kick-ass Jewish warrior woman does at live-fire rifle shooting tomorrow."

Huh? "Live fire?"

"What? You didn't think you were learning M16 rifle safety in the classroom for nothing, did you?"

Umm...

18

Sometimes I'm a kick-ass Jewish warrior woman...
and sometimes I'm not.

Everyone is totally surprised when Avi and I catch up to them on the night run. There's a big bonfire, and everyone is sitting around it. Sergeant B-S walks up to Avi and me and says something in Hebrew, which is obviously about me because Avi gestures to my torn uniform and scraped-up chin when he answers.

"You don't want to go back to the base?" Sergeant B-S asks.

"No." I have to admit I'm still in some pain, but whatever numbing stuff was on that pad Avi used on my arms has taken the edge off.

Sergeant B-S nods approvingly. "Gefen, make sure she gets checked when we get back."

Avi salutes the sergeant.

The bonfire lights up the area and spreads warmth into the cool desert air. I could point out to Sergeant B-S that if my headlight could alert the enemy to our location, a big bonfire would most likely ensure our immediate demise. But whatever. I'm trying to go with the flow here.

"You don't have to sit with me," I tell Avi as he hesitates at my side. He's probably desperate to get away from me and go to his girlfriend. While he was super nice to me when we were alone, it was obviously out of duty. Now that Liron is in sight, he's surely waiting for me to let him off the hook. "You should talk to Liron," I say. "There's an empty spot next to her. She's probably saving it for you."

He looks surprised, but he nods his head and shrugs. "You sure?"

"Yep. I'll be fine. Go." Ugh. My stomach is tied in knots as he walks away from me. I wish I hadn't pushed him to go to her, but it's better than asking him to sit with me and have him reject me ... or worse, have him sit next to me but long to be with Liron.

I find a spot next to Tori.

"You look like crap," she tells me.

"Thanks. I'm sure I couldn't have figured that out on my own."

"Your bangs look good, though, thanks to me. Although the only way to hide the nasty cuts on your chin would be to grow a beard. I don't think it'll be too hard for you."

I stand up. "If I wanted to be insulted, I would have sat next to Nathan. Nice talking to you. Bye."

"Wait!" she says, reaching out to grab the side of my pants. "I was just kidding."

"Do you even know how to be nice?"

I can see Tori perfectly in the light of the fire. Her blond hair shines like a halo, and her darker hair underneath looks like a protective shield. She looks up at me and says honestly, "I used to."

So now I feel sorry for her. Her little sincere comments make her vulnerable, which is something we have in common. I sit back down and stare into the fire.

"My parents thought I'd get over my anger about their divorce if I spent time with kids my own age and my own religion." She shakes her head in disgust. "Parents have no clue what their kids need."

Ha. "You think that's bad? I came on this trip to spend time with Avi. Look where that's gotten me." I gesture to Avi, sitting next to Liron.

"You think that's bad? My dad has a new girlfriend," Tori blurts out. "He says he wasn't dating her before they got divorced, but I'm not stupid."

"That's nothing. My mom dated a new guy every month before my stepfather. She totally had dating ADD. Then she got married and pregnant all in a year. I'm afraid she'll get parent ADD and not want the kid ... or Marc."

"As long as we're playing *Whose Life Sucks More?*, I can one-up you yet again. My parents just got divorced and my dad already cancels the weekends he's supposed to have me. My mom hopes he moves away and never comes back so she doesn't have to deal with him. But that's not what I want. I just wish … I just wish things could go back to the way they were."

I gaze longingly at Avi. "I do, too." I sigh, resigned to living in the real world.

Jess groans as she sits down next to us.

"Where have you been, Cleo?" I ask my best friend.

"Cleo? Wait, what happened to your chin? Did George the Zit spread?"

"No. While you were being carried like Cleopatra on the stretcher, the real wounded—me—finished the run bandaged up like Frankenstein."

"Yeah, well *I* just puked my guts out. Did you ever realize how much vertigo you can get lying on a stretcher bouncing up and down like a frickin' basketball? I had a death grip on the sides the entire time. I seriously thought I was gonna bounce right off."

Miranda, who I just notice is sitting on the other side of Tori, leans forward. "I'm sick of hearing you guys be all negative. I want each of you to say something positive."

Positive? I point to my gauzed-up forearms, gesture to my bloody chin and then to Avi talking to Liron, and then, as the cherry on top of my miserable life, I lift up my bangs to show off George the Zit.

"Say something, Amy," Miranda insists. "Something positive. I'm sure it'll make you feel better."

"Okay, Miranda. I've got it." I motion the girls to lean in close to hear my positive words. "At least I'm not dead."

How's that for positivity?

I have to admit it does make me feel better.

19

Physical strength is needed for obstacle courses,
but mental strength is needed when being close
to your ex-boyfriend.

Tori plops herself down on my cot during a fifteen-minute break the next day. "I hear we're sleeping in the desert at some point."

"Why would we do that when we live in such luxury right here?" I gesture at the bulging springs above me.

"Maybe they want to toughen us up."

"Oh, please. I'm tough enough. Any tougher and I'll grow balls and a hairy chest."

As if the thought of sleeping in the desert at night isn't scary enough, Ronit is leading us to the activity Avi warned me about.

Shooting an M16 rifle.

So now we're all standing in line, waiting to be issued a big rifle.

"I'm afraid of guns," I say, but nobody seems to be listening to me. They're all too excited. I guess it wouldn't hurt to hold the thing.

I have to sign for it and check that the serial number of the issued weapon, written next to my name, matches the actual number on the rifle. I can almost feel testicles growing between my legs as it's handed to me (I'm kidding, of course... about the testicles growing between my legs, not about being handed my very own weapon).

"Do you have any colors besides black?" I ask the guy handing out the guns.

"Are you kidding?"

"Of course I'm kidding. Although I wouldn't mind a pink one to match my luggage." The guy shakes his head and I think he mumbles something like *American princess*, but I can't be sure.

You should see the American boys in our unit as they're given their weapons. By the GI Joe expressions on their faces, you'd think they were just handed a Man Badge.

"I'll show you mine if you show me yours," Nathan jokes when we're standing under a canopy at the range, waiting for further instructions.

"Don't annoy me, Nathan. I have a gun." Of course it's big and bulky and warm from the summer sun. I sling it over my shoulder, feeling every bit of a soldier now. I definitely look the part.

"It's not loaded," Nathan responds dryly.

After handing us safety goggles and earmuffs, Sergeant B-S brings out a big box full of metal "magazines" and shows us how to insert the empty magazine into the bottom of the rifle. We've learned about the parts of the M16 and the different types of bullets in the classroom. Weapons safety has been drilled into my head.

Rules of gun safety in a non-combat environment:

1. Never point the weapon at a person, and always point it in a safe direction
2. Don't put your finger on the trigger until you're ready to shoot the weapon
3. Keep the weapon unloaded until you're ready to use it

After loading their magazines with bullets and shoving them into their weapons, Avi and Liron lie on their stomachs in front of canvas sandbags, with one leg straight and the other leg bent for support. With their rifles resting on the sandbags, they aim for the paper target in front of them and…bang!

When they get up and we're ordered into position on the range for dry firing—shooting without bullets, that is—I raise my hand.

Nimrod comes over to help. "Amy, what's the problem?"

"I'm not sure I can do this. I'm not really a gun person."

He laughs. "That's a good joke. Hey, Gefen! Come here!"

Avi jogs over to us. "What's going on?"

"Amy here says she's not a *gun person*."

"You'll be shooting a target, Amy. Not people," Avi says.

"Yeah, I get that, but… I'm afraid of the kickback, or sidekick or whatever you call it, and the noise. I have sensitive ears."

"It's called recoil." Nimrod rolls his eyes. "Gefen, you deal with your girlfriend."

"We're not dating anymore!" I call after Nimrod as he hurries off to help someone else.

Avi lifts the earmuffs off my ears. "No need to shout. Can we be friends today?"

"Sure," I say, putting the earmuffs back in place. *"Friends."*

Avi crouches. "Lie down."

I lie on the ground and rest the rifle on the sandbag. Avi checks the weapon, making sure the bullet chamber thingy is empty.

"There's no recoil in dry firing," he assures me. "Now move the lever from *safe* to *semi*. Make sure it's never on *auto* or you'll empty that magazine with one trigger pull."

I move the toggle to *semi*. Then I double and triple check it to make sure I didn't accidentally move it to *auto*. That would not be fun.

"Now settle the hand guard of the weapon into the V between your thumb and forefinger on your non-firing hand." He gently takes my knee and slides it up so it's bent. "Bending one knee gives you more support. Aim at your target through the sight guide. When you're ready, put your finger on the trigger."

"Avi?"

"Yeah?"

I look up at him. "I'm embarrassed to say this, because I really am against killing and guns. But I'm kind of getting a rush from this. I feel powerful with a gun this big in my hands."

"Wait to say that until after you sleep with it tonight."

"Huh?"

"Soldiers sleep with their gun every night they're on base or on duty. Come on, stop stalling. Aim at your target, control your breathing, and squeeze the trigger after you exhale."

I look through the sight thingy, aim at my paper target, and pull the trigger.

"Good. Do it again."

I keep dry firing until Sergeant B-S comes around and tells us all to put the rifles on *safe* mode.

We're told to fill our magazines with ten bullets and push the magazine into the rifle. "When you're ready, switch to the *semi* position and fire one at a time until your magazine is empty," Sergeant B-S instructs us.

I get back in position and line up the sights with my target, but I'm too nervous to shoot. I hear everyone else firing their guns on either side of me. Listen, disasters happen to me wherever I go, and I can't keep random thoughts from running through my head. What if the M16 misfires? What if the shell of the bullet hits me when it's ejected and burns my scalp as it lands on my head? What if the recoil dislocates my shoulder?

"I can tell you're thinking too much," Avi says, appearing beside me again.

He lies on the ground, his body next to mine. I have to remind myself not to think about Avi and focus on the gun.

"I'm afraid of the *recoil*."

"You're lying down, so you won't feel so much of it. Line up your target," he tells me.

I line up the paper that seems way too far away for me to hit with a bullet less than the width of my pinky finger. "Done."

He places his fingers over mine. They're strong and soft and I wish my body wouldn't tingle with excitement from him being near me. I'm so afraid that I'll never be able to fully get over him.

"Ready?"

I squeeze my eyes shut and control my breathing. Unfortunately, my pulse is racing. But that's because Avi's body is pressed up against mine. His strong hands on mine remind me of the times he touched me intimately. I try and put those thoughts out of my mind as I say, "Ready."

"Exhale. Hold it . . . " His finger presses on mine and the rifle fires. The recoil definitely pushes my shoulder back, but not as hard or as bad as I feared.

"You okay?"

I pick up my head, now just a few inches away from Avi's. "Oh. My. God. That was *awesome*!"

"Just a few minutes ago you said you weren't a gun person."

"I'm not. You know, when they're used for aggression or war. But just shooting a target is so cool."

Avi scratches his temple as if he isn't quite sure how to say what he's about to say. "Umm... I hate to break the news to you, but you didn't actually hit *your* target. You hit Jessica's. Her bullet went left of her target and ended up in the haystacks."

I lean back and watch as Jessica brags about hitting her target. She analyzes her precision with the range binoculars as if she's a sharpshooter.

"Oh. Maybe this time I shouldn't shut my eyes when I pull the trigger."

"That'd probably help your aim." I can see him trying to hide his laugh with a cough.

Avi watches as I aim again. I control my breathing and shoot.

"Did I hit it?"

He smiles at me. "No. It went low. You overcompensated for the recoil too much by lowering the barrel. Try again."

I keep firing until my magazine is empty. I hit the target a bunch of times. I still think guns are dangerous and scary. But in a controlled environment like this, it's not so bad.

After we shoot two more magazines full of live ammunition, and I've finally learned to hit the target consistently, we're taught how to clean and care for our weapon. Because we're just trainees and not real, full-time Israeli soldiers, we have to hand in our magazines. Unless we're on the range, our issued rifles won't be anywhere near live ammo.

"Keep your rifle in your possession at all times unless instructed otherwise," Ronit tells us. "And watch your weapon closely. Liron or I might sneak up on you and take it in the middle of the night. If you don't wake up and we end up with your weapon, you'll have to do pushups come morning. Whether you keep it under your pillow or next to you in bed is up to you."

I grip my M16. I feel the smooth barrel and ridged handgrip. Not my first choice in sleeping partners, that's for sure. But since I have to sleep with it, I might as well give it a name.

George II.

"You shoot that rifle like a warrior woman, Amy," Nathan says. "I think Avi has rubbed off on you."

I don't feel like a warrior woman in the evening, after showers and I'm sitting on my bed wondering how I'm going to sleep with George II. The cold, hard black metal with traces of grease doesn't match my pink pillow.

Checking out how the other girls are sleeping with their guns, I notice most of them are placing them under their pillows. If I want a crick in my neck in the morning, putting the rifle under my pillow would be a great idea.

I don't want a sore neck in the morning.

Since I slide my arm under my pillow to sleep every night (it's hereditary; my dad does it, too), I figure George II will be better off if I sleep hugging him. I pull the covers up and lie on my pillow. Pulling George II closer, I hug him tight.

If Avi could see me now, hugging a black rifle tight enough so that Liron or Ronit can't steal it away from me in the middle of the night, he'd probably be proud.

I just wish it was Avi I was hugging instead of a big piece of metal. If only I could hug Avi tight enough so no girl could steal him away from me, I'd be happy.

Unfortunately, life doesn't work that way.

20

When your mom told you life isn't fair,
she wasn't kidding.

The next day we're off to the obstacle course again. Avi isn't
with us, so we're without a team leader. Liron said Sergeant
B-S called him into his office, and nobody has seen him
since.

Determined to master the monkey bars, I take a deep
breath when it's my turn and swing my body from one bar
to the next. My team cheers me on ... even Tori, who has
lost a tiny bit of her edge. We've fallen behind because of
me, but when I finish the monkey bars without help and
everyone claps for me, I catch a genuine smile on Tori's
face as she congratulates me.

We still lose the race to Liron's team, but not by much. I
think our team has finally become a cohesive unit, bolstered

and strengthened by each other. When we all give high fives to each other, I catch sight of Avi standing next to Sergeant B-S. They both have very serious expressions on their faces.

Avi tells us we did a good job, then pulls me aside.

"If you're gonna tell me I should have gone up that rope by myself, I just couldn't," I tell him. "Next time I'll try. I promise."

"It's not about the rope, Amy."

He's definitely concerned about something. "What's wrong?"

"It's your *safta*."

My grandma? I swallow hard, thinking the worst. She has cancer, but I thought she was doing okay. Was I wrong? "Is ... is she okay?" I hardly get the words out because there's a lump in my throat.

"Your father called. She was taken to the hospital last night and he thinks you should go there. Just in case."

"Just in case of *what*?"

He shrugs. "I don't know."

"What *exactly* did he say?"

"Sergeant Ben-Shimon gave me a forty-eight hour leave and use of a car. Come on, we can talk about it on the way."

I say my goodbyes to everyone in my unit. Even though Avi and I are abandoning them, Sergeant B-S says he'll take over as team leader for the next forty-eight hours until Avi comes back. My farewell is filled with tears, because I'm not coming back. And while I hated being here, I loved it too.

It takes me less than a half hour to pack up. Avi accompanies me to the *bittan* and doesn't leave my side the entire time. In the car, we're finally alone—without military restrictions or rules.

"So what did my dad say?" I ask.

"He said not to panic until they know more. He just wanted you with the family in case it's something serious."

"What if she's dying?"

"Don't start thinking the worst."

"That's like telling my dog Mutt not to smell crotches."

He looks sideways at me as he drives. "Is that why you think the worst of me?"

"You kissed Liron *more than once*. I didn't make it up."

"I admitted to kissing Liron. When you kissed Nathan, I heard you out and we got past it. Why won't you hear me out?"

I might as well tell him the truth. "Because I'm afraid."

"Of the truth?"

Of course. The truth hurts most of the time. I have a history of pushing people away in an effort to avoid the truth. "Yeah," I tell him. "I'm afraid of the truth. I think of you being attracted to someone else, and I feel sick. And when I visualize you kissing someone else, the pain is just too great. I thought you, of all people, would never disappoint me."

I look out the window, trying to avoid looking right at Avi. Admitting how much his betrayal has affected me makes me vulnerable.

"I've been waiting for some hint that you want to fight for us."

"I'm done fighting," I say.

"I'm not."

"It's an occupational hazard for you. You're a soldier, trained to fight."

"So what do you want, Amy? You want to be enemies? Friends?"

"Friends sounds good. You know, what we are without the dating part. That way, I have no expectations." Maybe Noah has it right... no expectations means you don't get hurt.

Avi takes a deep breath. "If just being friends is what you want, I'll give you that. But when you're ready to fight for more, let me know. Because nothing is as intense as when we're together. Admit it."

"I admit it. But who says intense is best?"

"Me. And you, if you'd just open your eyes long enough to realize we might not be the most perfect couple, but we're better together than apart. Truth is, I'm afraid of losing you," he blurts out. "I know this probably isn't the best time to bring it up, but we don't have many chances to be alone. Nathan isn't the one—you know that. Sure, he talks a lot. Each word out of me is a struggle sometimes. But you and I... Amy..." He hesitates, and I can just feel him trying to get the right words out to express his feelings. For a guy who hardly ever talks in public, expressing emotion out loud is harder than shooting a flea a hundred meters away. "We're just *right*."

The problem is, I don't think my heart can handle another Avi breakup. I'm programmed to be emotional; I can't help it. For better or worse, my attitude and "drama queen-ness" defines who I am. Avi, on the other hand, is emotionally and drama-challenged. And although I came on this boot camp program in order to see him, maybe it was God's way of hinting that we're just too different.

"I'm always going to be afraid a smarter girl or a prettier girl is going to lure you away from me. Listen, I don't blame you for being attracted to Liron. She's beautiful, she can scale walls, climb ropes, and she carries a rifle. If I liked girls, I'd go for her too."

"Just hear me out, okay?"

My resolve is weakening fast. I have the childish urge to cover my ears with my palms and sing *la, la, la, la, la, la* so I don't hear what happened between Avi and Liron. But I guess I can't hide from the truth forever.

"Okay, Avi. Tell me why you kissed Liron."

21

Sometimes the truth hurts...
but you can't let it consume your life.

Everyone can take lessons in life from the Israelis.

We're driving north toward Tiberias. Every time I look out the window, I see Israelis doing the same things we do back home. I see kids playing on playgrounds, teens playing soccer, and people eating at restaurants. I wonder why Israelis don't act like they're living in a war zone. How can they be so strong-willed? How can they know the truth —that some of the countries surrounding them would like nothing better than to destroy their country—and still live carefree lives?

I brace myself for the truth of what happened between Avi and Liron. Listen, I'm half Israeli myself. I can act like an Israeli and tackle any obstacle that comes my way. At least I think I can.

"Now probably isn't the best time to talk about it, with

your *safta* in the hospital, but we might not get another chance."

"At least it'll get my mind off of wondering what's wrong with her. Go ahead, Avi. I need to know."

"Survival training was a total mind game," he tells me. "Lack of sleep, being blindfolded and finding out what it was like to be captured by terrorists, watching actual footage of Jews being brutally murdered just because they were Jewish or Israeli. Some of the bodies were so mutilated you wondered if they were killed by humans or beasts. You question your faith in God, because why would He let those things happen? You end up puking your guts out. You get so sad that every guy, no matter how tough, breaks down and cries like a baby. Then anger and a craving for revenge replaces the sorrow. Fury seeps from every pore of your body. I was so exhausted there were times I had no clue if my thoughts were my own, and at times I was so enraged I wanted to rush out and kill every terrorist single-handedly."

I watch as he shakes his head and lets out a slow breath. I'm not sure if it's because it hurts to recall that week of training or if it's because he desperately wants his country to live in peace but doesn't see how that's possible. Either way, I'm stunned by the rush of words and emotion.

"Afterward, I needed you, Amy," he continues. "I needed you so damn bad. I wanted to hold you in my arms again, feel your warm sweet body against mine to remind me that there's something good out there, that this world isn't only full of hatred and evil. Liron felt the same way. Her boyfriend was stationed on another base and you were in the States. I remember what you said about it being okay if we saw other people. Being with Liron until I started feeling human again seemed like a great solution at the time." He gives a short, cynical laugh. "But it sucked, because she wasn't you." His swipes his eyes with the back of his hand, getting emotional. "She wasn't you," he chokes out.

I'm starting to cry now too. "It's not fair, Avi. We found each other but live in two different countries. Just when I feel the closest to you, we're ripped apart. It's not fair."

"Amy, tell me anyone else can make your heart pound like it does when you're with me," he says. "Tell me you think anything or anyone can compare with it, and I'll give up on us."

Oh, God. I want us to get back together, because nobody can make me feel like he does. I want him so bad. I can't deny it any longer, to myself or him.

"No, Avi. Don't give up on us." The Israeli side of me bursts forward with a vengeance, and I think my fighting spirit has finally come out. Boot camp has changed me. I put my hand over his. "I forgive you. I can't forget what you did with Liron just as much as you probably can't forget I kissed Nathan. But I can definitely forgive."

He lifts my hand to his lips and kisses it. We're both at peace with everything that happened, except there's one thing I probably should tell him. Making up feels so good and carefree. But … "Umm, Avi, I kind of lied to you back on base."

"About what?"

I clear my throat. As long as Avi told the truth, I might as well spill the beans. "Nathan and I have never been a couple. I kind of coerced him into pretending we were dating."

Avi winks at me. "I knew that."

22

Forgiveness takes a lot less energy than holding grudges.

Three hours after leaving boot camp, we reach the hospital. Avi takes my hand after we pass through hospital security and steers me down the front corridor. The closer I get to seeing *Safta*, the more scared I get. What if she looks different? What if she looks weaker than she did last year? I hate cancer. It's as dangerous and deadly as a terrorist.

Avi asks the lobby receptionist something in Hebrew. She points to the elevator bank. The inside of the Baruch Padeh Medical Center hospital in Tiberias looks just like hospitals back home, with stark white walls and the scent of purified air bursting through the air conditioning vents.

"You okay?" Avi asks as we're riding up the elevator.

"Yeah. Why?"

"Your nails are digging into my palm." He loosens my hand and shows me the nail indentations in his skin.

"Sorry. Truth is, I'm freaking out."

He puts his arm around me, holds me tight to him, and lightly kisses the top of my head. "I'm here for you. Always. You know that, even if you don't always want to believe it."

Whenever I've needed Avi for my minor but frequent emergencies in my life, he's been there for me. Whether it was on the base or on the phone or in person, he's always around when I'm desperate for someone to keep my spirits high and lift me up...even physically.

He slows his pace when we get closer to the room. "Remember, it's okay to cry." He shrugs when I glance up at him. "My mom told me that after my brother died."

"And *did* you cry, Avi?"

He bites his bottom lip and nods. "Yeah...I did." He clears his throat and lifts his head high. "Come on," he says, nudging me forward into the room.

I take a deep breath and peek my head inside. *Safta* has an oxygen mask over her nose and mouth. Her eyes are closed and it looks like she's sleeping peacefully in the hospital bed, her pale complexion making her look like an angel. My dad is sitting next to the bed. He rushes from the chair and opens his arms to hug me, but when he takes a closer look his eyes go wide with shock.

"Amy. *Mah carah*? What happened to you?" He gestures to my arms and chin as he inspects my scratched face.

"Oh, that. Umm . . . I kinda fell on rocks. Well, I guess *skidded* is more like it."

"You look like you've been in battle."

"That's kind of how I felt. But it's better today. I've turned into a warrior woman." Sort of.

Back when I begged my dad to let me go on this trip, he warned me not to complain no matter how hard boot camp turned out to be. Either I could stay at my aunt and uncle's house with him on the *moshav* all summer (with possibly no chance of seeing Avi), or I could go on the army portion of the *Sababa* trip with my friends (and possibly see Avi). But if I chose boot camp, I'd better suck it up.

I'd like you to know that this is me sucking it up. Pre-army Amy would definitely be whining *Aba, they make us get up before the sun is up, and run in the dark, and pee and poop in stinky holes, and sleep with our guns, and eat jam with bees in it, and do boy pushups, and march in straight lines, and scale walls, and sleep in beds with springs missing above our heads, and dig holes with big, hairy spiders in them . . .*

. . . but I don't.

"Is *Safta* going to be okay?" I ask, because that's the only concern that I have at this moment. I can't lose my only living grandparent. God *can't* let that happen.

Although what really scares me is that God *can* let that happen. Rabbi Glassman says that death is a part of life. We don't have a choice to live, and we don't have a choice as to when we'll naturally die.

"They'll be taking her for a CAT scan in the morning. We'll know more after the scan and when we get the results of her blood test. When she woke up she was in pain and disoriented, so they gave her a sedative. I don't expect her to wake up until the morning, so you might as well go back to the *moshav* and get some rest." He inspects me again. "Wait, you look different, and it's not just the scratches. Did you get a *haircut* on the base?"

"Yeah. It's a long story; don't ask."

"Okay, I won't." He knows better than to ask for details, because he's well aware of my special ability to get into trouble wherever I go. He shakes hands with Avi. "Thanks for bringing Amy here."

"*Ayn b'yah*—no problem. They gave me a forty-eight-hour leave."

I stand next to my *safta*, bow my head, and pray silently to God to take care of her—just in case He's listening and just in case He wants to answer my prayer.

I don't know what I'll do if I lose her. I didn't even know I had a grandmother until a year ago, and now here she is in a hospital. I feel like she's slipping away from my life already. She never let me tell her how much she's helped me spiritually. During my Jewish conversion classes, whenever I thought about the Jewish matriarchs, I always imagined they would look and act exactly like my *safta*. I read that Abraham's wife Sarah gave birth at the age of ninety and died at the ripe old age of 127. I wish my *safta* could be like Sarah (obviously not the giving birth at ninety part…just the living until 127 part).

"Amy, I'm gonna step out so you and your *aba* can talk alone. I'll be right outside the door if you need me," Avi says.

My dad stands beside me and strokes my back as we both look down at the sweetest woman I've ever known. "I came home from school when I was six and told her an eight-year-old named Ido had pushed me," he tells me. "Can you guess what she did?"

"Went to school and threatened Ido if he didn't leave you alone?"

"No."

"Called Ido's mother and told her that her kid was a bully?"

"No. She told me to handle it myself. She said I'd have to deal with bullies all my life—so I might as well figure out how to deal with them at the age of six."

I try to picture my grandma as a young woman, strong and full of energy.

"Did you know she was in a war?" my dad asks me.

"What war?" I know all Israelis have to serve in the military. The country has been through their share of wars since they were recognized by the UN in 1948, but I can't imagine my grandmother wearing an army uniform or carrying a gun.

"She was in the Sinai War of '56. You should ask her about it. They wouldn't let women on the front lines back then, so she dressed as a boy."

"Whoa. I can't believe my grandmother was in a war.

I can't wait to tell Roxanne back at school, who brags that her great-grandmother was one of the first women pilots." *Pilot, shmilot.* My grandmother was on the *front lines.* I guess I'm not the only kick-ass warrior woman in the family. "So what happened with you and Ido? Did you tell him to stop pushing you?"

"Oh, I told him. Right after that, he pushed me again."

"What'd you do?"

"Well, the next day I came to school with a gift for Ido."

"Like a fist-in-your-face kind of gift?"

"No. Like a new basketball my aunt gave me after she visited the States."

Let me get this straight. "Ido pushed you, and you gave him a gift?"

"Since my mom wouldn't intervene, and there was no way I could fight a big kid two years older than me, I figured trying to be friends with him was my best option."

"So you became friends with the bully?"

He nods.

"That's a sellout. You shouldn't have to give the bully something. That's just *wrong* on so many levels."

"I had to sacrifice a little in order to get what I wanted. We ended up being friends."

I guess we all sacrifice at some time or another. I just hate having to do it so often.

"*Aba,* is she going to die?"

"Eventually."

"You know what I mean. Is this *it*? Is this the start of the end?"

"She had her final chemo treatment last week. They suspect her white blood cell count is low."

"But what if it's more than that?" I cry.

He puts his arm around me. "Let's not worry about that until the morning, when we know more. Let Avi take you back to the *moshav*."

"I don't want to leave *Safta*," I say, watching the oxygen mask fog up when she exhales.

"I know. But you can't do anything for her tonight. You can come back as soon as you wake up in the morning. Now go."

I hug him tight, wondering how I could have ever been distant from my father. I'm so grateful God brought him back into my life. I don't know what I'd do without him, especially now, with my mom and Marc starting a new family.

I don't know if I'll fit in. Will they still have time for me *and* a new baby? But one look at my dad and I know he'll never be out of my life again, no matter if I try to push him away or not. (Believe me, I've tried it. Especially when Avi was in town and my dad was grilling him, having the "Don't Do It" sex talk with both of us multiple times, and acting as an overprotective chaperone the entire time.)

After taking me for a quick dinner, Avi parks the car in front of my aunt and uncle's house on the *moshav*. It's on top of a big mountain overlooking the Kineret lake.

It's rustic and dusty and total farmland, but it feels like home.

Poor Avi had to listen to me cry and sniff and blow my nose every two seconds all the way from the hospital, although he didn't seem to mind. He held my hand the entire time (except when I was being gross and blowing my nose, and when we stopped for dinner). Seriously, just having him here with me gives me strength.

Avi lives a few houses down on the opposite side of the very narrow gravel road, but he doesn't just drop me off.

My cousin Osnat (pronounced O'snot – and yes, it's a very popular Israeli name) is the first person to see me. She's sitting on the sofa, watching television with my aunt (*Doda* Yucky), my Uncle Chaim (I call him Uncle Chime, because I can't do that back-throat-noise Hebrew-pronunciation thing), and my little toddler cousin Matan (who is not naked, for once).

They all wrap me and Avi in big hugs. Even Osnat, and she's not the most warm and fuzzy person I've ever met—although we definitely get along way better now than we used to. I can tell she's been crying, too, because her eyes are all bloodshot.

"Amy, what happened to your chin? And your arms?" *Doda* Yucky looks at Avi accusingly.

He holds his hands up. "Don't look at me. She managed to do that all on her own."

"You beat yourself up?" Osnat says. "In the morning you'll have to tell us how you managed to do that."

I know she's just joking. Normally I'd have some witty comeback, but I'm too upset and exhausted to think of one.

"Are you hungry?" *Doda* Yucky asks. "Let me fix you both something. You've had such a long day."

"I took her to Marinado by Kibbutz Ein Gev," Avi tells them. "I couldn't resist stopping there for one of their burgers."

I sit with my aunt, uncle, and cousins in their small living room as we catch up on the past year. Even though we talk every week, it's not the same as actually spending time with them. Uncle Chime laughs when I tell him about my experiences on the army base, and even tells me a funny story about digging ditches when he was in the army. I guess digging ditches is a rite of passage for Israeli soldiers. *Doda* Yucky shares her own stories about being an instructor on one of the bases. Matan climbs on her lap and dangles off her knees while she's talking. *Doda* Yucky has always been sweet to me. She never stops smiling, and she loves everyone she comes in contact with.

Then the conversation turns to *Safta's* health. *Doda* Yucky tells me how she found her unconscious. The somber mood returns as they tell me to pray for the best.

A yawn escapes my mouth.

"You need sleep," Uncle Chime tells me. "You look exhausted."

"I am." Although I don't know if I *can* sleep. Too many thoughts are running through my head, but I'm so overtired, hopefully my eyes will close as soon as I hit my pillow.

After Avi helps bring my suitcases in from the car, Osnat drags her pillow and blanket out of her room. "Amy can sleep in my room. I'll sleep in *Safta's* room tonight," she says.

I peer inside Osnat's room. Just like I remembered, it has two twin beds situated across the room from each other. "I don't want to kick you out of your room. You've got two beds. We can share."

"It's not a problem. Really. I'd rather sleep in *Safta's* bed. I'd feel closer to her somehow. Besides, you snore."

I give a huff. "That's *so* not true."

"You're asleep, so how would you know? Seriously, last summer I needed earplugs when you slept in my room."

I look up at Avi. "I do *not* snore."

"I believe you," he says. "But right now I need to go across the street to let my parents know I'm here."

My heart starts racing in panic. I grab a fistful of his shirt and hold on tight. "But you're coming back tonight, right?"

"If you want me to."

"I don't want you to leave for a second."

"You need to get ready for bed, Amy. I can't exactly be with you then, unless you want your uncle and dad to threaten to give me a second circumcision." He kisses me lightly on the lips. "Take a hot shower and enjoy it. You haven't had one in a while. I'll be back after I say hi to my parents and wash up. I promise."

Famous last words.

I stand in the foyer pouting like my dog Mutt when he watches me put my jacket on. If I *was* a real dog, I would whimper just like Mutt, too. But I'm not a dog and I have to suck it up and stay positive.

I can do positive.

Taking a deep breath, I grab my PJs and head for the one bathroom. There's still an open keyhole/peephole in the door for anyone inclined to look at someone peeing or taking a dump. I undress quickly, unwrap the gauze from my arms, and turn the water on, hoping none of my Israeli family members open the door without knocking.

When the water turns hot, it's like the Almighty Lord has sent a miracle down to earth just for me. Being super gentle while soaping the still-raw cuts on my arms, I lather up, scrub, rinse, and repeat a few times before letting the water just run down my body. Ahh, this feels great.

I hear the door open.

"Helloooo, I'm in here," I say loudly, then stick my head out of the curtain to see who's barged in on me.

It's little Matan, with his corkscrew hair and Power Ranger pajamas on. "*Shalom*, Ami," he says, smiling wide. He says my name Ah-mee instead of Amy.

"*Shalom*. Do you mind? I'm in the shower here." I know the kid doesn't understand English, but you'd think he'd get the hint. No such luck.

My little toddler cousin pulls down his pants and starts peeing in the toilet next to the shower. Does he not care that I'm in here, totally naked behind the curtain? To top it off, he starts scratching his butt while he's peeing. Eww. Please don't tell me every guy does this.

When he's done, he gives his thingie a little shake, pulls up his pants, and waves to me with a big happy-go-lucky smile on his face. I'll never get over the fact that guys don't wipe their wee-wees after they pee. It just seems so *unsanitary.* It also seems unsanitary that Matan is going out of the bathroom without washing his hands. Totally *not* acceptable.

"Yo, Matan!" I call after him.

"*Ken?*" Yes?

I'm still naked, in the shower with shampoo in my hair and soap running down my body, with my head the only thing peeking out from the curtain. "Wash your hands, little buddy."

"*Lo meda'bear Angleet,* Ami." He doesn't understand English, and he's waiting for me to translate what I just said.

How the hell am I supposed to know what *wash your germy hands* is in Hebrew? I let go of the curtain and rub my hands together using the universal hand-washing motion, then point to the sink. "Wash your hands," I tell him again, hoping he understands this time.

Matan points to my now exposed boobs and says, "*Tzee-tzeem g'doleem!*"

I know that *gadol* means "big," and I can just imagine that *tzee-tzeem* means "boobs" by the direction of his pointing finger. Would he think it polite of me to point to his wee-wee and announce *"Pee-pee katan!"*—Hebrew for his ding-a-ling is tiny?

I quickly pull the shower curtain back over my body. Keeping one hand on the curtain, I point to the sink again. "Wash, Matan, or I swear I'm telling your mom you don't clean your hands after peeing." Yes, I'm aware he doesn't know what my threat means, but it makes me feel better saying it.

Doda Yucky knocks on the door. "Amy, is Matan in there?"

"Yep. He sure is."

She opens the door, apologizes, and helps him quickly wash his hands before shooing him out. "I'm so sorry. I'll make sure he doesn't do that again."

Matan points in the general direction of my boob area hiding behind the curtain and says to his mother, *"L'Amy yesh tzee-tzeem g'doleem!"*

Doda Yucky looks embarrassed as she says, "He doesn't mean anything by that."

"Uh huh." I'll just file that into the folder of embarrassing/humiliating moments in my life.

After my shower, I change into PJs and feel like a new person. At least a new person with scratched-up arms and a chin with racer marks on it.

"Is Avi back yet?" I ask Osnat. She's sitting on our *safta's* bed, looking at a photo album.

"No." Osnat, who's my age and will be in the Israeli army in a year, looks vulnerable and lost. "*Safta* always looked forward to your Saturday calls, you know."

"She never seemed tired of hearing about what was going on in my life." There aren't many people who like to hear the sound of your voice and are happy to listen to you, no matter what you're saying. *Safta* is one of those people. Some kids hate talking to their elderly grandparents on the phone, but I can't wait until I wake up Saturday morning and can call my family in Israel.

"Here's a picture of us when we went to the *Kotel*, the Western Wall," she tells me. I move closer and look at the picture. It shows my aunt, my uncle, *Safta*, and my two cousins pushing tiny pieces of paper into the cracks in the Wall.

I've read about the Wall, the only standing structure from the ancient Jewish Temple. It's also called the Wailing Wall because Jews mourn the destruction of the Temple and grieve while praying there. "What are you doing in this picture?" I ask her.

"Putting prayers into the cracks. It's customary to do that. People think God is closer there than other places, and will answer your prayers."

Oh, great. Why hadn't I known this sooner? I definitely think a trip to the Western Wall is in order. The only problem is that it's in Jerusalem, a few hours from the *moshav*. In another picture, Matan is kissing the Wall while standing next to *Safta*.

I sit on the edge of *Safta's* bed, thinking how lucky Osnat is. Our grandma has lived with her since she was born. I know some teens would hate sharing their home with their grandparent, but I would have loved it. Especially *my* grandma, because she's sweet and kind and has definitely given me good advice *when I asked for it* (unlike my mother, who's a master at giving me unsolicited opinions, suggestions, and critiques).

"What is *Safta* really like?"

Osnat looks up and smiles. "Seriously, with *Safta* what you see is it. When I was younger we used to go out in the middle of the night when we both couldn't sleep and we'd sit on the edge of the mountain and talk…about nothing and everything."

"That's so cool."

"It was. And there's this area about a mile away where eagles fly over a ravine. We'd sit there for hours, talking about Israel and freedom and history." She wipes tears away. "I guess you kinda missed out by living in America. I always think you have it so easy, and I guess I get jealous of your material stuff." Osnat closes the album and sits up. "What's with you and Avi?"

"What's with you and O'dead?" I ask her, quickly changing the subject to her boyfriend. Israelis are not overly gushy or lovey-dovey types, and I'm afraid she'll make fun of me if I open up and really tell her how I feel about Avi. "Are you guys still dating?"

"O'dead and I broke up. He's dating Ofra."

"Wait. Isn't Ofra dating Doo-Doo?"

"She dumped him."

Wait a minute. "Your best friend stole your boyfriend?"

"Kind of. But I'm over it."

I guess when Jessica started dating Mitch, Mitch and I were still technically a couple even though I'd already met Avi.

Teenage dating is definitely complicated. Before Avi and I met, my friends and I used to joke that marrying your high school sweetheart was an urban myth. No teen relationships I know of have lasted.

"You never answered about you and Avi."

"We had some issues. But everything's great now."

"Really?"

I think about Avi, and how I can't imagine him out of my life. I'm glad I decided to give us another chance, because I don't want to be an urban myth. I want us to be real. And being real means dealing with real issues (and drama, because my name is Amy Nelson-Barak and I can't avoid it).

I stand by the doorway to see if Avi is in the hallway. Nobody on the *moshav* locks their doors. Everyone is like family, so they just walk into each other's houses as if they live there. I can't imagine me just prancing into Mr. Obermeyer's condo in our building without knocking. If he owned a gun, he'd shoot first and ask questions later.

"*Shalom*! Earth to Amy." I look over at my cousin, who's waving her hand at me. "Are you daydreaming about Avi again? Listen, since I'm not dating anyone, maybe next summer before my military service I'll come visit you in America to meet American boys. I'm sick of Israeli guys."

I hear the front door open and my heart leaps when I see Avi. He's wearing black sweats and a T-shirt. When he smiles at me, a warm calmness spreads over my body. I think God definitely had something to do with bringing us together. Life *is* too short not to be with the person you love the most, even if you have to work through both of your emotional baggage while you're together. Who better to deal with your issues than a person who loves you?

"Hey," he says. "You okay?"

"I am now that you're here," I answer back as I hug his waist and bury my head into his chest.

Osnat pretends to gag. "Ugh, please get out of here before I catch whatever love disease you have."

"Come on," I say, leading Avi to Osnat's room.

He watches from the guest bed while I blow-dry my hair. Afterward, I sit next to him while he takes the extra gauze the nurse on the base gave me and carefully rewraps my forearms.

"I hope one day I can take care of you," I tell him.

"You already do. You're a constant reminder that life is not one-dimensional. I forget that sometimes."

I lean my back against his chest and hold his arms around me. I feel so safe and protected wrapped in his arms.

"I've got to report back to the base in two days," he says quietly. "We might not get to see each other after that. I assume you're not going back to the base."

There's so much I want to tell him right here, right

now. I turn around and sit on my knees, facing him. "I need to say some stuff, Avi. And I need to say it before I lose my nerve, so don't interrupt me." I take a deep breath, hold his hands in mine, and look into the depths of his eyes. I can get lost in those chocolate depths so easily. "I admire you so much ... the way you lead by example ... the incredible drive you have to succeed at whatever you're doing ... the way you know how to lead our group with authority, but you can also follow directions like you do with Sergeant Ben-Shimon ... I admire the skills you possess in so many different areas ... I love the way you protect the ones you love ... I love the passion you have for your country and your willingness and dedication to protect it at all costs ..."

I cup Avi's cheek in my hand. "I think God had something to do with us getting together, because we're so different. But I seriously think we were meant to be together."

He swipes away tears falling down my cheeks. "God definitely had something to do with it. Amy?"

"Yeah?"

"I think we can do it. You know, just date each other. Nobody else."

"You do?"

He nods.

"Me, too." One by one, my worries and fears and insecurities start melting away.

I lay my head in Avi's lap and he runs his fingers through my hair.

"I should leave," he says after a while.

I wrap my arms around him, holding tight. I know that if he leaves I'll be more of a mess than I already am. Avi makes me stronger. "No. Please don't go. Not yet." I look up at him, this boy/man who challenges me to be a better, stronger person. According to Liron's assessment, I've ruined his Israeli warrior reputation and he's still unconditionally by my side. I don't know if anyone else in this universe could handle me except a guy like Avi.

I hear the front door open. I'm too weak to sit up. My dad cracks the door to my room a minute later. "Amy, you up?"

"Yeah. Just so you know, Avi's with me."

"Oh." If it was any other time, my dad would order Avi out. And maybe even threaten his life. But he sees Avi comforting me and his face softens. "Just ... keep the door open. Okay? And no touching ... things ... things, um, things you're not supposed to be touching."

Yeah, that's how comfortable my dad is talking about sex. He stutters and hesitates and then asks me to talk to my mom. Unfortunately for him, my mom is back in the United States.

My dad is about to give us privacy when Avi calls out, "Ron?"

My dad stops and asks, *"Mah?"* which means "what" in Hebrew.

"Todah rabah." Thank you very much.

My dad's response is a nod.

Avi slides his body behind me on the bed and holds me tight the entire night. I think he stayed up all night. When I woke up and cried against his chest, he caressed my hair and wiped the tears from my face. When I whispered my fears about *Safta* dying an hour later, he listened, gave support, and rubbed my back until I fell back asleep. And when I open my eyes in the morning, he's watching me sleep.

"You must be exhausted," I say, my body curling into the warmth of his body heat. It feels so good in his arms, it almost lulls me back to sleep. But thoughts of *Safta* bring me back to reality.

After a quick breakfast, Avi drives me and my dad to the hospital a half hour away. My uncle and Osnat follow in their car. While my dad and Uncle Chime talk to the doctors and nurses about the next test to determine what's wrong with *Safta*, and Osnat goes to the cafeteria to get coffee, I sit next to *Safta's* bed. Avi leans against the window sill off to the side, giving me privacy.

My grandmother slowly opens her eyes. It takes her a minute to adjust to her surroundings, but when her eyes focus on me she has an apologetic look on her face. She pulls off the oxygen mask. "Amy, *motek*, what are you doing here? You're supposed to be at boot camp."

"I came to make sure you're okay. And to be with you."

"I don't want . . . you to see me like this. It's no fun in a hospital watching some tired old lady sleep."

"You're not just some old lady," I tell her while I give her a gentle hug. "You're my *safta*. How are you feeling?"

"Like an old lady." Her wrinkled, frail hand reaches out and fingers the tiny Jewish star diamond pendant around my neck. She gave it to me last summer during my visit. "I'm so happy you're wearing it."

"I wear it every day. It reminds me of you."

She smiles that sweet grandma smile that makes me feel like everything in my life will be okay. "Are you having a nice vacation?"

"Well, being on the army base hasn't been much of a vacation. Avi's my unit leader," I say, gesturing to Avi over by the window.

"Avi, come closer. I can't see you all the way over there," *Safta* says, waving him over. "My eyes aren't what they used to be."

Avi kisses my *safta* on the cheek. He's known her since he was born. Last night he told me she's like a second grandmother to him. "*Mah nishmah?*—How are you?"

"*Beseder*—I'm fine. I got a little dizzy. I wish my children wouldn't declare it a national emergency."

"*Ima,* stop talking nonsense," my dad interrupts her as he comes into the room. "You were unconscious when Yucky found you. Don't brush it off as if nothing happened."

She shoos my dad away. "Go eat something in the cafeteria, Ron, and leave me alone with the young teenagers here." My dad starts to protest, but gives up when she raises her eyebrows and makes another "go away" hand gesture.

Ooh, I can just imagine her staring at him with raised eyebrows when he was a kid. My dad is a total guys' guy —muscular, masculine, and full of testosterone. Knowing that his frail old mom can make him back off with a raised eyebrow and a hand gesture amuses me to no end.

Once my dad is out of sight, *Safta* turns to Avi. "Is my granddaughter a good soldier?"

Yeah, umm… no need to let my sweet, old, sick grandmother know I suck at being a soldier. I mean, seriously, the woman dressed as a boy to fight on the front lines. Knowing that her own flesh and blood can't even scale a wall or aim a gun without having a few stray bullets hit other people's targets could *kill* her. I take *Safta's* hand and pat it. "Why don't we talk about something else?" Preferably a topic that doesn't have to do with what a spaz I really am.

"She's definitely challenging herself," Avi says to *Safta*. "Right, Amy?"

"I shot an M16," I say, but don't tell her I hit other people's targets more often than my own.

"I did the obstacle course," I continue, but don't tell her I had to be escorted up the rope and had to step on people's backs during my first attempt on the monkey bars.

"I even picked bees out of the jam when I had kitchen duty." I don't mention the whole bee/Nathan/tongue incident, either.

She fingers the bandages on my arms. "What happened to you?"

"Yeah, that. I went on a night run up a mountain. The mountain and I kinda got into a fight. The mountain won."

"That's not true," Avi tells her. "Amy won. She took a hard fall, but kept going."

I guess he's right. I'm still new at looking at things in a positive light.

Safta rubs her fingers over my fingernails, which are totally trashed from boot camp. "I'm so proud of you, Amy."

"Me, too," Avi adds.

"Avi needs to be back at the base tomorrow," I tell her. "He only got a forty-eight-hour leave."

"Aren't you still supposed to be there?"

"Yeah, but I'm not going back. I want to be here with you."

"For what?" my *safta* asks.

I don't want to say it. I can't talk about death with the person I'm afraid is dying. "For you. What if, you know, you're *really* sick?"

"I'm not going to die so quickly, *motek*—sweetheart. But even if I did, I'd die happier knowing you're doing what you're supposed to do—live—instead of watching an old lady die." *Safta*, who seemed so weak a second ago, points her small finger at me. Her face gets stern and spunky, and it's another glimpse into her life as a woman ready to fight for something she believes in. "You're Amy Nelson-Barak. Do you know what Barak means in Hebrew?"

I shake my head.

"It means 'lightning.' Amy, you're a true Barak, inside and out. You have a fighting spirit. No Barak is a quitter, you hear me? Now, make me proud and go back to finish boot camp ... and be a Barak."

I think my *safta* can give Sergeant B-S a run for his money.

23

---

*Who knew the best times of your life
can come out of the worst situations?*

We stay at the hospital all day, waiting for test results. Her white blood cell counts were low, but rose as the day wore on. Tomorrow, her doctor plans to do full scans to make sure her cancer hasn't spread, but my dad assures me her life isn't in immediate danger.

After we get back to the *moshav* and *Doda* Yucky makes dinner for us, I make the final decision to go back and complete boot camp. Soon I'm saying my goodbyes to my family while Avi says his goodbyes to his. Before my own family has time to miss me, I'll have graduated boot camp and be back on the *moshav*. Avi's family isn't so lucky. After my *Sababa* group graduates, Avi and the rest of the Sayeret Tzefa trainees are going to intense training at the Counter

Terror School. The time with the *Sababa* group was supposed to be a relaxing break for them between parachuting and Counter Terror School. Unfortunately for Avi, I don't think being with my unit has been relaxing.

"Be good," my dad says, bending down into the passenger side window to hug me as Avi climbs behind the wheel. "Avi, keep her safe."

"I will."

I know it's going to be a long drive, because the base is south of the Dead Sea. The sun is setting when we reach Haifa, and we still have more than a few hours to go.

I talk to Avi about Miranda liking Nathan, but Nathan liking Tori … and Tori not liking anyone. When I ask about Noah, Avi tells me that he's a good guy who really doesn't mind doing any of the jobs the army assigns him.

"I've never seen Noah upset. Not even once," he tells me.

"When I first met Noah, I thought he'd be a good match for Miranda," I say. "Or maybe Nimrod would."

"Miranda isn't Nimrod's type."

I tsk. "What's that supposed to mean? Just because she has a little extra padding doesn't mean—"

"Nimrod's gay."

"Gay? As in … "

"He's got a boyfriend."

"Does he know that *you* know?"

"Everyone knows. He doesn't exactly keep it a secret. This is Israel. While we might not be the most tolerant people in the world, being gay here isn't a big deal. Even in the military. Nimrod's a damn good soldier, and we're lucky he's on our squad. He's practically fearless and makes me a better soldier."

"*You* make *me* a better soldier, Avi," I tell him. "I just wish I was a better friend to Miranda. I want her to be happy. Do you think setting her up with Noah would work?"

Avi takes my hand in his and kisses my palm. "Trying to make the world perfect again?"

"I'm good at doing it for other people. I seem to screw up my own life pretty good most of the time. I guess we all have our talents, don't we?"

He nods.

"Speaking of making life perfect, Avi. Umm ... do you remember last summer when we pulled off to the side of the road?"

"Yeah. How could I forget?"

"Okay, so I know I'm a girl and shouldn't be asking this, but you only live once and life is short. Can we pull off the road? We're in the middle of a deserted road in the middle of nowhere, Israel."

Avi flashes me a shocked expression. "I thought you didn't want to have sex until we were married."

"I'm not talking about sex. I'm talking about kissing, and maybe a little body exploration ... " But as my voice trails off, I wonder what Avi has in mind. "Why? Do *you* want to have sex?"

He nods. "I'm a guy, Amy. Of course I want to have sex with my girlfriend."

"You do?"

"Oh, yeah," he says, his voice deep and sexy.

My eyes graze over him, and now I know why being alone together brings us closer to dangerous territory. These are the times my dad and mom have warned me about, when my commitment to staying a virgin until I'm married is compromised by my raging teenage hormones.

"Don't look at me like that, Amy."

"Like what?"

"Like you're ready to be mischievous."

"What if I am?"

Avi rakes his hand over his head and moans. "I'm seriously one minute away from begging you to be mischievous with me."

"Well, now that my *safta's* okay, I want to think about you and me. And since you don't have to report back to base until tomorrow, and it's already late, maybe we can spend some alone time tonight. At a hotel."

"Really?"

"Let me weigh the options. Option 1: Go back to the base, not have a second of private time with you, get up at the crack of dawn, or Option 2: Private time alone with you. It's a no-brainer, Avi. I pick private time alone with you."

I think of Avi and me together ... all night ... in a hotel room. The word "perfection" doesn't do the fantasy justice.

"You're not still feeling super mischievous, are you?" he asks. "Because if you are, this probably *isn't* the best idea."

I can't wait to spend all night, alone, with my boyfriend. "Trust me, Avi. It's a *great* idea. Seriously, when are we going to have the chance to be alone again?"

He picks up his cell, makes a reservation at a hotel, and starts driving. Soon we arrive at a hotel on a kibbutz near Ein Gedi.

Avi pays for the room, signs papers, and gets a key from the girl at the front desk. I stand beside him, trying to act like getting a hotel room with my boyfriend is no biggie.

When in reality...

It *is* a biggie. A *real* big biggie.

Avi takes our bags and I follow him to our room. It's at the end of an adorable little one-story brick building with bright purple and yellow flowers outlining the front sidewalk. Avi opens the door and we walk inside.

When the door clicks shut, the reality of being alone with Avi hits me. I'm with my boyfriend without any parental supervision. I'm almost a senior in high school, almost an adult... in a year I'll be living on some college campus by myself, making decisions on my own.

I would never have put myself in the position of being alone with a boy in a hotel room if I didn't 100 percent trust him. I know Avi won't force me to do anything I don't want to do. The problem lies with me: I don't know if I trust myself. I admit, when I look at Avi I want him; I want him to kiss me until I can't breathe and touch me until my body melts under his touch, and I want to feel every inch of him. Will I be able to stop myself?

There are two single beds on either side of the room. They're just simple foam-filled mattresses on wooden frames that don't look very comfortable (which my parents would probably think is a good thing).

"You seem nervous," he says as he puts our bags down by the little desk. There's a chill in the air, so Avi turns off the air conditioner.

"Why do you think I'm nervous?" I look at him and remember our talk in the car about him wanting to have sex with me.

"Because you haven't said anything since we arrived."

I take a deep breath and watch intently as Avi steps closer to me. His boyish expression gives me a hint that he's just as nervous and insecure as I am.

"I'm not nervous. Really. I'm not," I say.

One side of his mouth quirks up into a smile. He doesn't believe me at all. "You want to go change in the bathroom?"

Change? As in getting in PJs?

"Sure," I say. Normally this wouldn't be a problem. This isn't the first time Avi's seen me in PJs, but this isn't just any normal ordinary night. I don't want to wear a big ol' T-shirt to bed. But I don't want to go all sexy, wearing a skimpy tank top to tease him. Okay, I admit I kinda do, so I can see how much I can affect him, but I realize that's totally selfish and manipulative.

Oh, the problems of a teenage girl are endless.

I pull out a PJ set my mom got me for the trip. It's a light blue T-shirt and matching mini-shorts. It covers enough so

I'm not showing too much cleave, but when I take my bra off in the bathroom I'm aware that the chill in the desert air is making me nippy. Over the sink there's a mirror, so I pull up my bangs to inspect George I. He's almost gone—yeah!

When I leave the bathroom, I'm holding the clothes I've worn all day clutched in front of my nippyness. Avi is sitting on one of the beds. He looks up and his breath hitches.

"You're beautiful," he says, staring at me as if I'm a goddess.

A shy smile bursts out of me. "Thanks." I look back at the bathroom. "Don't you want to, uh, wash up?"

"Yeah." But I notice he doesn't bring any PJs with him into the bathroom. I quickly toss my dirty clothes on top of my suitcase, pull out my pink satin pillow, and hop onto one of the beds. Pulling the thin sheet and blanket above my nippy parts, I wonder what Avi will sleep in. When he comes out of the bathroom, I finally know.

My mouth drops open and I swear I have to stop myself from drooling. Avi is wearing black boxer briefs. That's it. His military-ripped bod should be outlawed. He's got a serious six-pack and has muscles in places I didn't even know existed. And when my eyes wander to the bulge in his briefs, I can't help the blush that creeps into my face.

And I was worried about teasing *him*. Believe me, I'm not the teaser in this room. "You are seriously trying to tempt me, aren't you?"

He nods.

I reluctantly tear my gaze away. "Well, good night," I say, patting my pillow and pulling the covers over me. "Turn out the light before you go to sleep, will ya?"

That'll teach him to try and tease me.

But a minute after I pretend to go to sleep, I pop one eye open. He's still standing by the bathroom door looking every bit a hard-core male model with a body to die for...or at least to lose your virginity over. Knowing the guy inside the body is my one true love makes this situation almost unbearable.

"Can I at least push the beds together?" he asks sheepishly.

"I thought you were going to do it while I was in the bathroom. And then I thought since you didn't, maybe you wanted to sleep separately."

"I didn't want to push the beds together without asking you first. And then you came out here in that sexy outfit and I forgot all about it."

"It's not sexy," I tell him. "It's just a top and shorts."

"Amy, that's just about the sexiest thing I've ever seen on anyone. Maybe it's because it matches your eyes. Maybe it's because it's got lace around the edges. Or maybe it's just because you're wearing it." He looks down, embarrassed, as he pushes the beds together.

Since the frames are made of wood, there's a huge wooden gap between the mattresses. Avi folds one of the sheets into the groove and puts a blanket over it so it won't be too uncomfortable.

"What's this?" I ask, fingering the three-inch-long, olive green pouch hanging from a string around his neck.

He opens the pouch and reveals a silver metal rectangle stamped with words in Hebrew and a long number. "My ID tag. We cover it so the metal doesn't burn our skin in the heat."

There's a gold metal medallion hanging next to the ID tag. "What's that?"

He fingers the medallion. "All Sayeret Tzefa trainees get it. It has the words *Respect*, *Strength*, and *Honor* on it. Respect for your country, your enemies, and your comrades. Strength in body and mind. Honor to your country, your comrades, and the ones who served before you." He says it like he's had to rehearse the words for some test.

"Does everyone wear it?"

"If you're caught without it, you have to sing this stupid song to the entire squad. It's a new tradition. I think it was copied from some American Marines that did training here a few years back."

While I lie back on my pillow, Avi turns off the light.

A few seconds later I feel him sliding into bed next to me. His leg brushes mine and I hear his slow breathing. A sliver of light is shining through the window of the room, so I can make out his silhouette in the darkness. My heart is beating furiously with anticipation, especially when he turns toward me.

"Amy?"

"Yeah."

He leans on his elbow and stares down at me. "I didn't tell you this before, but I think you've been a great leader on the base."

"You're just saying that because you love me."

"I do love you. But that's not why I said it. People listen to you."

"Me? Yeah, right. It's a wonder I haven't been kicked out of the program."

"You sell yourself short. Every time your team is standing around looking for some direction, you come up with a strategy. Like suggesting taking turns with the ditch digging. And suggesting people kneel on the ground during the monkey bars on the obstacle course. Whether you believe it or not, you're a born leader."

I guess I never thought about that before. I reach up and cup his cheek. "How come you can see the good parts of me I don't even see in myself?"

"Because you're too busy focusing on negative stuff. You should stop doing that."

"I've been trying. It's kinda hard for me." I lean forward, put my hand on his bare chest, and kiss him. "I'm what you call a work in progress."

"That makes two of us." He puts his arms around me. We kiss. And kiss again. His lips are soft on mine. When he deepens the kiss and his tongue reaches for mine, the tingling sensation zings right down to my toes and back up again. I could kiss this boy forever. His kisses make me as hot as my flat iron, and I toss the covers away. My fingers trail paths around his body and his do the same. All the while, our breathing is getting faster and my pulse is racing in excitement. Our legs are intertwined, skin against skin.

I feel Avi's pulse racing too, as my palm explores his chest and abs.

Being close to Avi, his body against mine, is the best feeling in the world. It's better than eating spicy tuna sushi rolls with little pieces of crunchy tempura inside, better than drinking hot chocolate with loads of whipped cream, better than winning a tennis match.

"What are you thinking about?" he asks as I moan under his touch.

"Sushi, hot chocolate, and tennis."

"You're thinking about food? And tennis?"

He pulls away, but I take his hand in mine and weave my fingers through his. "No. I'm thinking about how being with you is *better* than sushi, hot chocolate, and tennis. What were you thinking about?"

A short laugh escapes from his mouth. "It sure wasn't hummus, falafel, and soccer."

I open my fingers so we're palm against palm. "Avi, what if we get carried away tonight?"

"We won't."

"But what if I want to? My mom bought me protection before I left, just in case. It's in one of my suitcases."

Avi takes a deep breath and leans away from me, the cool air rushing to the open space between us. I want to pull him back so his body heats mine again. Instead, I grab the covers and pull them over us. I don't know if I'm shivering from nervousness or the chilly night air.

"I'm not gonna lie to you," he says seriously. "I'm ready. Like *right now*, I'm ready."

"I think I am, too."

"Your body might be, but I know in the morning you'll regret it. And then I'll feel like crap because I knew you'd regret it." He rubs his hands over his head and moans in frustration. "You said a while back that you wanted to wait until we got married. I promised to respect that."

"I changed my mind."

"What?"

"You heard me. I changed my mind."

"Amy, you hated that you were an illegitimate child. It eats at you every day, and I think sometimes it fuels this insecurity you have. What if it happens to us? You'll never forgive yourself. Or me."

"Can you not be logical now, Avi? You're kind of ruining the mood." I sit up, thinking how right Avi is and how wrong I am. How can I let my overactive hormones rule my life? Though I must say it's kind of easy when Avi's expert fingers are strumming my body like a guitar. "Avi?"

"Yeah?"

"I'm not tired anymore. Are you?"

He shakes his head.

"We can still kiss and do other things, can't we? Remember at my house on the sofa, when my dad was working late? Can we try that again?"

Seriously, it's not like Avi and I haven't fooled around. We have. In fact, I've gone farther with Avi than with any other boy I've dated.

Avi's hands circle my waist and he guides me on top of him. My long hair shields his face as I look down at him. *"Ani ohevet o'tach,"* I tell him.

"You just said *I love you* to a girl. *Oat'cha* is for a boy."

"*Ani ohevet oat'cha.*"

"*Ani ohevet o'tach.* I love you, Amy Nelson-Barak."

We kiss, and I start to move against him. My pulse is racing, and Avi's heart is pounding against my skin ... and the earth is shattering into two pieces.

No, seriously.

The earth is shattering.

And we're falling.

I realize pretty quickly, through my haze of teenage sexual lust, that the earth isn't moving. Our beds are. They're moving apart and Avi and I are falling in between them. Before I know it, Avi falls to the hard cement tile floor. I'm straddling him, so lucky for me his body breaks my fall.

"Ouch," Avi says, his head banging on the tile. "I think I just got a splinter from the bed frame."

"Do you think this was a sign from God?" I ask. We *are* in the Holy Land. God can't be far away.

"More like a sign from your dad," Avi says, helping me up. "He always warns me not to touch your *parts.*"

Whether it's God or my dad or some other divine intervention, Avi and I decide it's late and we should probably get as much sleep as we can before we have to head back to the base. Instead of sleeping with our beds pushed together and having another mini-disaster, Avi sleeps on his bed and I sleep on mine.

We bridge the gap between our beds by holding hands until we both fall asleep.

24

If you don't know where you've come from,
it's hard to know where you're going.

"Have you ever been to the Western Wall?" I ask Avi in the morning when we wake up.

"Many times. I got my Bible during my army induction ceremony there."

"What's it like? Rabbi Glassman told me it's super mystical and spiritual."

Avi sits up, and I think how unfair it is that someone can look so good in the morning. Of course he doesn't have to worry about bed-head because his hair is so short.

He rubs his chin pensively.

"Well?" I say, urging him to respond.

He puts up a finger. "Yeah, um, it *is* spiritual. I'm not

orthodox, but I definitely feel closer to God when I'm there."

I narrow my eyes. "So what's all the chin-rubbing about? Don't you think I'll be spiritually moved there?"

"Definitely. But…"

"But, what?"

Avi scratches his head. "But it's got a *mechitza*. You know, a partition, separating the men from the women."

"I'm okay with that. Rabbi Glassman said it's tradition in more religious synagogues to separate men and women so they can concentrate on praying and not each other. If you're with me, I'll definitely be distracted."

"And you're okay with it even if the men's side is four times the size of the women's?"

Think positive, Amy. "Um, sure."

"And women aren't supposed to pray out loud."

"And men…"

"…pray out loud," he says, wincing in anticipation of my reaction.

Truth is, I'm okay with it. I'm going with the flow. Even if I don't observe all of the Jewish rules and traditions, I respect the people who do.

"We have time this morning, if you want me to take you there. We'll be backtracking a bit, but it's okay."

"Really?"

"Sure."

"What time does it open?"

"It's always open, Amy. Come on, let's get ready so

we can get back to the base on time. Make sure you wear something that covers your knees and shoulders. No tanks or shorts."

It doesn't take long before we're showered, dressed, and heading back toward Jerusalem.

We park a few blocks from the Western Wall. The scenery mixes the old with the new. When we come up to the Wall, the big ancient stones stacked one on top of another reach out to the sky.

I breathe in slowly as I take in the scene. There's a big area farther from the Wall where people can walk, but if you want to go closer, there's a partition.

Directly in front of the Wall, people are praying. The men bob up and down, deep in prayer, facing the Wall. Women, on the right side of the partition, pray just as fervently (albeit more quietly) on their side.

"Jerusalem was destroyed nine times," Avi explains as he covers his head with a small, round *kippah*. "But through it all, the *Kotel* survived."

Kind of like the Water Tower that survived the Great Chicago Fire, which started when Mrs. O'Leary's cow kicked over a lantern (although that historical fact has been hotly debated by the descendants of Mrs. O'Leary). Nobody debates the fact that this wall has been here for three thousand years.

"They say God is here, right?" I ask Avi. Because I'm feeling the enormity of the Wall and the attachment my Jewish ancestors have to it.

"It's the holiest of holy places for us. That's why, even when you're in America, Jews pray facing east—toward the Wall. Even in Israel, no matter where we are, we pray facing Jerusalem and the Wall. Open up and pour your heart out to God here, Amy." Avi hands me a small piece of paper and pen.

I tell Avi to go to the men's side while I head to the women's. I look up at the Wall, its chalky yellow boulders neatly stacked one on top of one another. Each boulder is as tall as my chest. The closer I get, the more I see little pieces of paper wedged in between the cracks of the stones.

Don't ask me why tears come to my eyes when I'm a few inches away from the Wall. I feel my faith getting stronger here, especially when I think about the Jews being forbidden here as recently as 1948, when Jews could only view the Wall through barbed wire. In the Six Day War, Israeli soldiers fought and died for this wall.

It makes me feel privileged just being here.

Reaching out, I touch the Wall. The ancient stones are cold, even though it's hot outside. For thousands of years, my ancestors prayed here. In the future, I hope my children come to Israel and feel this wall, considered "the gate to God."

I scribble my prayers on the paper, words to be shared only between me and God. In my head, I say the *Shéma*, the holiest Jewish prayer. *Shéma Yisrael! Adonai Eloheinu! Adonai Echad! Hear O Israel! The Lord is our God! The Lord is One!* and squeeze my paper inside a crack between the boulders.

I look over to the men's side and spot Avi. He's in his military uniform, touching the Wall with his hand and forehead, deep in prayer. The scene touches my heart.

God, take care of him, I pray silently. *Because he's my past, and my future.*

25

There's no shame in admitting
you're an American Princess.

"How's your *safta*?" Jess asks me in the late afternoon when I join the rest of our unit in the barracks after Avi and I arrive back on base.

I organize my cubby and slide my suitcases under my bed. "She's okay. Her white blood cell counts are low, but they've stabilized her. She told me to go back and finish the program... something about Baraks not being quitters."

"Well, I'm glad you're back."

"Me, too. By the way, Avi and I are back together."

"I knew it was just a matter of time. You guys are meant for each other."

I look at the gun resting on her lap. Guns are used as a means to help Israelis protect their land and their people.

I'm sure these guns mean something totally different to the Palestinians. "Jess, what do you think will happen between you and Tarik in the future?"

I've never asked her this before, because I know she loves him and doesn't want to think about life without him. But if it's not going to work out, why torture yourself by falling more in love with a guy you know you can't have a future with?

"I don't know," Jess says. "I don't think about it."

I think about my future all the time, and always imagine Avi in it. "Have you ever gotten in a fight and thought of breaking up?"

Jess chuckles. "Sure, but I can't stop dating Tarik any more than you can stop dating Avi. When the time comes to talk about the serious stuff, maybe we'll decide it won't work. Until then, I'm not stressing about it. Don't tell me you and Avi talk about the future."

I smile at her. "Yeah, we do."

Her mouth opens wide. "Wow. Please tell me you're not gonna get married at eighteen and skip college."

"I'm not getting married or skipping college. But I hope one day … " My voice trails off, thinking about what our life might be like in the future.

" … you'll have little Amys and Avis running around the house," Jess finishes for me.

"Maybe. But we won't name them Amy and Avi—you know most Jewish people don't name their kids after a living relative." Rabbi Glassman told me it's because of an old superstition that the Angel of Death will accidentally take the baby instead of the older relative of the same name. As if the Angel of Death would be confused. Maybe I don't believe it, but I'm not taking any chances. There won't be an Amy Jr. or Avi Jr. in my house. Naming zits is another story.

"So when did you and Avi have this discussion?"

"Last night. We stayed at a hotel in Ein Gedi."

"Just the two of you?"

"Yeah." I pull out my suitcase and pretend to rearrange my stuff.

"So? Come on, Amy. Don't keep me in suspense."

I look around to make sure nobody is eavesdropping. "We didn't have sex, if that's what you're getting at," I whisper. "I mean, I wanted to. And he wanted to."

Jess hasn't been a virgin for years, ever since she and Michael Greenberg did it sophomore year. But Jess isn't the result of two people getting together one night out of lust and nothing else; I am.

Jess waves her hand in a "come on, spill the beans" gesture. We seriously have less than five minutes before the next activity. I can't possibly describe how amazing it is that Avi and I reconnected. My body is still humming from the touch of his hands and the sound of his voice whispering sexy things in my ear, making me shiver with excitement. I'm definitely applying to colleges in Israel so we can be together whenever possible. I can't wait until our next boot camp activity just so I can see him again ... even if we can't be "with" each other. As long as we can see each other, I'm totally psyched.

Ronit comes into the barracks with Liron and they tell us to line up outside. I actually smile at Liron and don't fear that she's my rival. I pick up George II and head outside. The guys are waiting for us. I know we're going to the shooting range to practice, but I don't see anyone from Avi's unit besides Liron here.

Liron taps me on the shoulder. "Avi's not here. He wanted me to let you know that he was sorry he couldn't say goodbye."

What? Avi's not here? For how long? "Will he be back tomorrow?"

Liron shakes her head. "The Sayeret Tzefa trainees have been taken off base for intensive combat training exercises before they head to Counter Terror School. It was a surprise for everyone. Since I'm an operations specialist, I can stay on base until your unit graduates."

The thought of not seeing Avi for the rest of my trip to Israel is terrible, especially after last night. But Avi would want me to stay strong and positive.

"You okay?" Liron asks me.

Blinking back the tears about to spill out, I force a brave smile. "Yeah. I'm okay."

We're introduced to our new team leaders. There are two Israeli girls assigned as new team leaders, and three guys.

As one of the new team leaders steps in front of us, I

notice she's wearing sunglasses suspiciously similar to the $235 ones I dropped in the poop hole my first day here.

My mouth drops open. They *are* my sunglasses. I look over at Jessica, who I know also noticed because she's got the same open-mouthed, shocked expression I do.

"She fished them out," I whisper to Jess.

Jess shakes her head. "I'm speechless, Amy. What are you gonna do? Ask for them back?"

"Absolutely not!" If a girl wants those glasses so bad she'll fish in poop to get them, she can be my guest and keep them forever.

Noah got reassigned, and is also now a team leader for our unit. I wish Noah had another message from Avi, but he doesn't. I also wish I had Noah's outlook on life … no expectations, and then you won't be disappointed.

When we get to the shooting range, I walk up to Nathan as we're waiting for our turn to shoot. "Just so you know, I'm breaking up with you."

Nathan shakes his head vigorously. "Nuh uh. You can't do that. *I'm* supposed to break up with you first. That was our deal."

"So break up with me. I'm back with Avi."

"Well, you can't tell Tori. You promised to pretend to be devastated about our breakup." Nathan pouts. "How's it gonna look to Tori when she sees you broke up with me to go out with that … that beast?" He puts his arm around me and says, "Come on, Amy. You're my best friend. What's a girl best friend worth if she won't help you get laid?"

I push him away from me. "Eww. You're so gross."

"I'm a guy, I was born gross. Now go tell Tori we broke up. And that you're devastated. I want to see some tears. And don't forget to tell her I'm good in bed."

"I'm not telling her that."

"Why not?"

"Because what if it's not true? I don't want my credibility questioned."

"Are you insinuating what I think you're insinuating?"

I hold my hands up. "Don't blame me. Listen, Nathan. Ever since you broke up with Becky—"

"Bicky."

"What*ever* her name is. You don't have to act like a player. I'm only gonna say this once so you don't get a big head. You're cute, with that streaked-blond messy-haired garage-band-guy look you've got goin' on." I gesture to his hair and cute boyish face. "You're cool . . . when you're not eating my white chocolate Kit Kats. And you're funny . . . in an entertaining, Muppety sort of way. I'm not setting you up with Tori just so you can get into her pants. I'll set you up with Tori because you're a great guy."

"You think I'm a great guy?"

I roll my eyes. "When you're not being an idiot you are. But I've got to warn you, Tori's got issues."

"I do, too." Considering he doesn't have parents around and lives with his aunt and uncle, who aren't deliriously happy to be fostering their nephew, I'm well aware of Nathan's issues.

"There's just one more problem," I tell him, as Sergeant B-S calls us to take our places on the range.

"What?"

"Nothing I can't handle." I don't tell Nathan that while I'm trying to get Tori to fall *in* love with him, I have to get Miranda to fall *out* of love with him. Nathan may rock Miranda's world, but he doesn't feel the same way about her. That's not to say that it will never happen ... it just won't happen now. As much as I hate to admit it, Nathan and Tori have potential. They've both got *chutzpah* ... a lot of attitude and nerve. Both of them could use a person to challenge them.

"Just don't tell Tori anything that'll ruin my reputation as a stud," Nathan says as he releases the magazine to his M16.

"Don't worry, Nathan. You can do that all on your own."

The sergeant passes out bullets and tells us to load our magazines. I look down at George II. I don't have Avi to help me this time. Noah is walking behind us, making sure everyone knows what they're doing. I look over at Miranda, fitting her bullets in the magazine chamber just like everyone else. I raise my hand and wave Noah over to me.

"Hey, Amy!" he says with a big smile. "How's it goin'?"

"Good."

He kneels next to me. "Need help?"

"Not me. My friend Miranda over there ... you met her in the kitchen when we had the bee incident. She says she knows how to shoot, but that's just a cover-up. She needs help. She's just too shy to ask for it."

Noah pats me on the shoulder. "I got it. I'll go over there and *not* help her, if you know what I mean." He walks toward Miranda and kneels next to her. When she says she's okay, he stays with her and chats while she loads and aims the rifle. I think I hear her laugh at something he says right before she shoots.

I might just open my own matchmaking service when I get back to Chicago. I set up my dad and Marla this winter. Seriously, it might be hereditary ... maybe my great-great-great-grandmother was a matchmaker in some little village in Russia or Germany.

As I load George II with ammunition and get in position to shoot, I think back to my first time on the range, when Avi was lying next to me, placing my fingers into the correct position and relaxing me with his voice.

I imagine he's here with me now, acting as my support and guide. With the butt of the rifle against my shoulder, I put the rifle into the V in my left hand to steady the barrel. I settle my fingers into position, pretending Avi's hands are patiently guiding mine. As I aim at the target ahead of me and put my finger on the trigger, I take a breath and hold it while I fire.

I hit the target. Yeah!

I fire again. Another hit!

And again.

"*Avodah tovah*—nice job," I hear Sergeant B-S's voice from behind me.

I look back at his approving nod. "Thanks, sir," I say.

For the rest of the day, I remember that "nice job" and the approving nod from Sergeant B-S and it gives me strength. Until right after dinner, when Ronit gives us the news.

"Yes, the rumors are true. We're going on a night hike and sleeping in the desert tonight."

Like Noah, I force myself to have low expectations and keep a positive attitude. I can't help thinking about what *Safta* said: *You're a Barak. No Barak is a quitter.* But I also can't help thinking about desert scorpions, snakes, and hairy spiders. I'm thinking about other comforts of home as I raise my hand.

"Amy, do you have a question?"

"Yeah," I say. "Umm ... is there a bathroom where we're headed?"

"Absolutely." She comes back and holds up a small shovel. "The entire place is one big bathroom. Just dig a hole and relieve yourself."

26

Being a leader sometimes means taking one for the team.

We line up with our rifles strapped to our backs and our canteens freshly filled with water. We've been told that sleeping bags will be issued at our final destination, but it might just be a rumor. What isn't a rumor is that we're sleeping in our fatigues—talk about roughing it.

The girls are freaking out about the toilet situation, so we've all come up with a plan to bring Jess's biodegradable wipies in our pockets. As a last-minute grab, I snatch my pink satin pillow off my mattress. I won't be able to sleep without it.

"What's that?" Sergeant B-S asks me in the courtyard, before we're ordered to march out. He's pointing at my pillow, which I'm clutching to my chest.

"My special pillow. I can't sleep without it."

He shakes his head. "No. *Zis* is not *beseder*—not okay. Put it back."

Well, it was worth a try. Luckily he can't see the wipies hidden in our fatigue pockets. I set my pillow back on my mattress and hurry back to Sergeant B-S and the rest of my unit.

I'm not risking another fall like I had on the night of our run, so I find myself in a slow jog next to Miranda. "Are we friends again?"

She glances at me as we jog side by side. "Yeah. I was always your friend, Amy. I just got upset for a stupid reason."

"Because Nathan was pretending to be my boyfriend? I'm sorry, Miranda. I know you like Nathan as more than a friend. It was insensitive of me to think you wouldn't care that I made a deal with him to get Avi jealous."

"It's okay. I know Nathan likes Tori. Girls like me never get a guy. Seriously, I tried to hit on Nimrod a few nights ago and he didn't even notice."

That's not a shocker, considering he's gay. "I hear he's already dating someone," I say. "What about Noah?"

"Colorado Noah?"

"Yeah," I say, feeling her out. "He's such a teddy bear, isn't he?"

"You mean chubby."

"I mean nice. Like you."

"Yeah, he's nice."

I nudge Miranda and smile. "Give up on Nathan,

Miranda. Now don't get mad at me for saying this, but I think you've been crushing on Nathan for so long because you're afraid to like someone who might actually like you back. You're stalling."

"You're acting like a therapist, Amy."

"I've been to enough of them to know what I'm talking about. Open your eyes to new people." I point to Noah, who's up ahead giving encouragement to our unit, telling us to keep going even though we're tired.

"He helped me on the range today," she tells me.

I give myself an inner high five for instigating that little moment. We jog slowly beside each other, neither of us saying anything for a while. It could be because we're panting from the jog...or it could be because my words are sinking in.

"Thanks, Amy," Miranda says eventually.

"You're welcome."

We finally get to our destination, which is a makeshift campground in the middle of the Negev desert. I can just sense the Israeli scorpions and snakes waiting for a taste of American blood. It's dark already, but the billions of stars in the sky brighten the night. I look up, wondering if Avi is looking at those same stars. I miss him so much I ache inside, but I'm trying to stay positive and strong. I've got to admit it's tough to be running and setting other people up when the love of my life, the guy who makes me want to be a better person, isn't with me.

Ronit tells us to sit in a big circle. She passes out cans of what looks like fancy dog food.

"What is this?" I ask her as I lift off the top.

"Dinner."

"Dinner?"

"It's called Loof."

Oh, no! Loof! I remember the bathroom wall with the words *Beware of the Loof!* "Don't we have pita? Or hummus?" I ask her. Listen, those are Israeli staples.

"No. It's Loof or nothing tonight. This is what the soldiers eat on missions and in desert training. Remember, this isn't a spa."

I examine the muddy brown substance. "Do you eat it with a fork or a spoon?"

"Whichever you want," Ronit tells me.

I look at my friends, all sniffing their own processed chunk of food/meat passing as a meal. I have to admit it smells like pasteurized liver, if there is such a thing. I admit I've never eaten liver before, even the chopped liver my dad made a couple of times. But it's Israel, so at least I know it's kosher and has been blessed by a rabbi.

"Plug your nose and eat the Loof," Noah suggests. "Then it's not so bad." I watch as he scoops out a chunk of the stuff and chows down.

My friends are looking at me for direction. Should we follow in Mr. Positive/No Expectations' footsteps or starve?

I could reveal that I brought my own provisions—*Kif-Kafs*—in the pockets of my pants. They've probably melted, but melted *Kif-Kafs* are probably better than Loof any day of the week.

But we're soldiers now. And Israeli soldiers eat Loof, no matter how bad it is. I plug my nose with my fingers, scoop out a chunk, and eat it. "Mmm. Yummy."

"Really?" Jess asks.

"No, not really. It's absolutely disgusting. But we're Jewish warrior women, right?"

Jess nods. Miranda nods. Even Tori nods. "Right!" they say in unison.

We look at Nathan. "Don't look at me. I'm no warrior woman. I'm not eating it."

Tori takes a tester bite from her little can. Miranda and Jess do, too. We all eat the Loof as if it's a rite of passage.

"Nathan, don't be a loser. Eat it," Tori says, tossing him a fork.

Not wanting at provoke Tori's wrath, even Nathan chows down. He's a warrior too, after all.

A truck with a pile of sleeping bags in the back is waiting for us. We're instructed to grab one and find a spot on the ground to sleep. Tori, who I haven't had a chance to talk to in a while, comes up to me.

"So how's your grandma?" she asks.

"Alive. I think she's okay, at least for now." I see a bandage on her neck that wasn't there when I left the base two days ago. "What happened?" I ask, pointing to it.

"You promise you won't laugh?"

"I promise."

Tori says, "I got stung. By a worker bee."

I suppress a laugh. "I thought you said they don't sting."

"Obviously I got my facts wrong. Subject over."

Time to start a new subject. I crane my head, looking for Nathan. Ronit is handing him a small shovel. Gross—he's about to dig himself a hole to poop in. He's probably about to Poop the Loof. I shudder thinking about it. "Listen," I tell Tori. "Nathan broke up with me."

"It probably had something to do with you staring at that guy Avi all the time," she says.

"No. It had something to do with you."

She looks at me like I'm crazy. "Me?"

"Yeah. Nathan likes you. He thinks you're pretty and fun ... when you're not glaring, sneering, or insulting everyone."

Tori places her sleeping bag on the ground next to mine. "Nathan isn't my type," she says.

"Why not? Sure, he's a pain in the ass most of the time. But he's funny. And smart. And cute. And, to be honest, he's the best guy friend a girl could ever ask for. He's just about perfect."

Tori looks over at Nathan, coming back with the poop shovel. "Not interested."

I wave Nathan over to us. He tries to act cool as he says, "Hey. What's up? Mind if I sleep with you guys? I mean, uh, sleep *next* to you guys."

As he lays down his sleeping bag, head-to-head with Tori's with hope in his eyes, I tell him the truth. "Tori says you're not her type."

Tori nods to Nathan, emphasizing my statement.

"Did you tell her I was good in bed?" he asks.

I. Can't. Believe. He. Said. That.

Tori's eyebrows go up. "You guys had *sex*?" she asks me, just as Jessica lays her sleeping bag alongside ours.

Oh, man. I'm the one who's gonna need the poop shovel now for the flying bullshit about to come out of my mouth. I say a silent prayer for God to forgive me for lying. "Yeah. Nathan is better than…better than…better than eating a black olive without the pit."

Nathan looks at me as if I'm a total mashed potato. Jess shakes her head in disbelief. I couldn't think of anything else to say. I hate olives in general, so having sex with Nathan has got to be better than eating olives, with or without the pits.

Tori gives him one of her sneers. "I think I'll take a pass," she says tartly.

"Give me a chance," Nathan responds quickly.

"Why should I?"

Nathan kneels next to her and a sincere look washes over his face. "Because for some reason I've been itching to put a smile on your face since I met you."

"Nobody can do that."

"Won't you let me try?"

I see Tori's face softening. "You can try, but I guarantee it won't work."

"Ooh, I love a challenge." Nathan slides into his sleeping bag and rests his chin on his fists, facing Tori.

"Are you gonna watch me sleep?" she asks, trying to

sound annoyed. I notice she's not sneering, which is a good sign.

"Yeah. Watching you helps me think up lyrics to my next song. After boot camp, I'll take out my guitar and sing it to you."

Tori wipes at her eyes. Obviously nobody's ever done anything like that for her. She needs Nathan, whether she believes it or not. And he needs her.

I look around for Miranda. She's usually with us, but we're all settled and she's nowhere to be seen. I finally see her in a deep conversation with someone a few yards away—Noah. He's smiling at her. And laughing.

I slide into my own sleeping bag (after opening it and checking for snakes and scorpions) and bring George II inside it with me. George is cold on my unshaved legs, the hard metal of the barrel reminding me where we are and why we're here. Once again I think of Avi, and what military exercises he's been pulled off base to do.

"Are you wearing your bra?" Jess whispers.

"Yeah. Aren't you?"

"The wire was poking into my side, so I took it off and shoved it to the bottom of the sleeping bag. Remind me to reach down and get it in the morning."

My bra isn't at all comfortable to sleep in, but I'm keeping it on. I put a sports bra on before we left, which I'm perfectly aware makes me look like I have a monoboob shelf in front of me. But it does the job of smashing my boobs down and together so they're not bobbing up and down like a buoy in Lake Michigan when we run. Bouncing boobs is not an option.

Of course, squished boobs are not the most comfortable way to sleep. But whatever. I'm smelly from not showering, I don't have my favorite pillow, the sweat between my squished boobs is itchy, and I've got a metal rifle named George II in the sleeping bag with me. The old Amy would whine and complain. The new and improved Amy sucks it up.

As I lie here sucking it up, trying to sleep but with my eyes wide open, I glance over at Tori. I see her hand sneak out to tentatively touch Nathan's. He weaves his fingers through hers without saying a word and they fall asleep holding hands.

Which only reminds me of last night, when Avi and I fell asleep holding hands.

Argh. I can't sleep. All I can think about as I look up at the twinkling stars above me is Avi.

"I can count every single rock under me," Jess whispers. "How do they expect us to sleep?"

Now that Jess mentions it, I can feel every rock *and pebble* under my own body. "Maybe if we clear out the big ones it won't be as bad," I say, reaching under my sleeping bag for the big rock sticking into my backside.

Jess whimpers as she shuffles her body around. "Ouch. Remind me never to complain about my life back in Chicago."

"And remind me to appreciate my dad more. He probably had to sleep like this all the time when he was an Israeli commando," I say. "But the stars are so cool. Why don't we see as many stars back home?"

"Probably because we live near civilization," Jess says.

We both stare up into the sky. Seriously, there must be billions of stars above us. After a minute, a streak shoots through the sky. It's there and gone before I know it, making me wonder if I've even seen it at all.

"Was that what I thought it was?" Jess asks.

"I saw it, too. I've never seen a shooting star before."

"Me, either. Should we make a wish?"

I wish ... (I can't tell you, because then it might not come true. But I bet you can guess.)

As we're whispering, I have the sudden urge to pee. "I've got to go to the bathroom. Come with me."

"No way," Jess murmurs. "I'm not risking getting bitten by a night creature. Wait until morning."

I try to settle back in my sleeping bag. But since I'm not able to sleep, and I hear people snoring (Nathan is like his own little symphony), I take George II and decide to wander away from camp to find a perfect spot to squat. I need to find a place far enough away that I can take my panties and pants off, so I don't make them grosser than they already are.

Eventually I find a large, flat rock jutting out from the ground. Thankful for the little light the billions of stars offer and for the fact I don't have to dig a hole in order to pee, I situate half of my butt on the rock and the other half, well, you get the idea.

As I relieve myself, I hear little pop-pop-pops in the distance. Like gunfire. We're in Israel, on the grounds where the military does its training operations ... can Avi be just a few hundred yards away? In the past, gunfire would freak me out, but now it's getting to be a familiar sound. I'm getting desensitized to it. Freaky, I know.

I must look ridiculous naked, from the waist down, sitting with half my butt on a rock and the other half hanging off—with an M16 strapped to my back while I'm intently listening to gunfire. If Avi could see me now (not that I'd let him see me pee, *ever*), he'd be proud that I'm roughing it without complaining.

If the Sayeret Tzefa trainees are on some sort of outdoor firing range doing night exercises, maybe I can say a quick goodbye to him. I'm aware it might not be the best idea, but I'm thinking positively. As I put my pants back on, I take a few steps toward the popping sounds.

When I hear more popping sounds, I hurry closer. Live ammo this close to the army base means training exercises, not war.

I've been walking for over ten minutes, praying that a snake or desert creature doesn't think I'm their midnight snack. I wish I had my headlight with me so I could see better. Despite the stars, the desert has too many scary shadows. I don't know if my eyes are playing tricks on me or if the rocks are really moving snakes and coyotes.

I climb up and over a steep hill. I think the firing range must be close, because the gunfire is getting louder.

As I maneuver around a big boulder blocking my path, a large, strong hand clamps over my mouth.

I try to scream as loud as I can, but the hand around my mouth tightens and my attempts at screaming are useless. I'm spun around with the force of a tornado.

27

Brilliance and stupidity are probably as closely related as love and hate.

As I'm twirled around so fast it makes my head spin, I'm face to face with an Israeli soldier. Even with his black mask and black clothes, I know it's Avi. I can see his eyes shining through the holes in his mask. I'd know those sexy eyes anywhere.

"Amy?" he whispers.

My panic starts to subside, but my pulse is still racing frantically. "Hi," I say sheepishly. "We were sleeping in the desert somewhere over there." I point in the approximate direction of our campsite. "And I heard gunfire so I thought you might be over here doing night range shooting. I know I smell because I didn't shower today. And I have sweaty cleave from my monoboob. And my underwear is full of rock dust that chafed my buttcheeks when I sat on the rock and peed. But I wanted to see you one last time before I went back to Chicago."

"First of all, *never* go toward the sound of gunfire. *Ever.* You hear me?" he says sternly.

"I hear you."

"And second—" He doesn't finish his sentence. He does curse a few times, though. Some of the words are in English, and I know some are curses in Hebrew because I've heard my dad say them on rare occasions when he's royally pissed.

I watch as Avi pushes a small button on a headset I didn't realize he was wearing. He says something in Hebrew. I can't hear the response, because the receiver must be some kind of earpiece in his ear.

"So I guess you're not doing range exercises, huh?"

He shakes his head.

"Running exercises?"

He shakes his head. "Amy, I hate to break the news to you but you've just entered military war games."

"War games? With real guns?"

"With real *paintball* guns." He picks up his rifle and shows me the gadget attached to it, which turned the gun into a paintball gun. "It's dangerous. I'm taking you back."

"I'm sorry. I just wanted to say goodbye to you. It was an innocent mistake."

"All of your mistakes are innocent, and yet they still get you in loads of trouble. Come on," he orders. He talks into his headset again as he leads me back up the mountain. He groans into the microphone, then turns to me. "I just got word from Nimrod that Ori got captured. He did manage to hide his weapon right before they got him."

"What does that mean?"

He winces, obviously pissed at this new predicament. "It means I can't take you back, not now."

"I'll go back myself, then."

"When the other team sees you walking up the mountain, it'll give away my location. I can't let you do that. It could jeopardize my team." After making me put on his vest for protection, he motions for me to follow him.

"When will this exercise be over?" I whisper.

He gives a short laugh. "When one team wins and the opposing team members are either dead or captured. Dead meaning paintball dead... not real dead."

"Oh," I say, grateful for the elaboration.

Avi leads me over the rough terrain. I slip every once in a while because my high tops aren't exactly made for mountain climbing... or war games, for that matter. Avi is moving quickly, holding my hand so I don't fall on my ass.

"Get down," he mouths, motioning for me to lay on the ground next to him and stay silent. "Stay here." He crawls away, and is back in less than a minute. He takes my M16 away and hands me another one. "This is Ori's. It's loaded with paintballs. They're dangerous, so don't shoot at close range and don't shoot unless fired upon."

"Don't worry." I might be a Jewish warrior woman,

but I'm not about to shoot this thing without Avi telling me to.

I move right next to him as he pulls small binoculars out of his pocket and surveys the area. He pushes that button again on the headset he's wearing and talks softly into the microphone in Hebrew.

"We'll stay here and wait for instructions from the team leader."

"Who's the team leader?"

"Nimrod."

"Why not you?"

"Because Nimrod doesn't have a civilian tagging along on the mission who also happens to be someone he's romantically involved with."

Wait. Does that mean ... "Avi, were you the team leader ten minutes ago?"

"It doesn't matter."

Oh, no. It's bad enough I've been dragged into military war games because of my own curiosity and stupidity. But Avi being stripped of his team leader status because of me is awful. "Let me be captured so you can be team leader again."

He shakes his head. "Not happening."

"Why not?"

"Because this is real, Amy. Even though this isn't real war, we're supposed to act like it is. It's not capture the flag in gym class. In a real situation, I'd give my life up to protect yours. I know it and my entire squad knows it. That makes both of us liabilities."

I'm quiet as this new news sinks in. "You'd die for me, Avi?"

He pulls the mask off his face. His soul is reflected in the depths of his pupils. "I'd do just about anything for you."

Heart-melting time. I'd do anything for Avi, even die for him. I'm not sure he's convinced I'm tough enough to deal with the war games scenario. One thing I know for sure, though, is that I've single-handedly ruined my boyfriend's reputation. He got demoted because of me. How am I supposed to fix it?

Avi, oblivious to the fact that I'm ruining his military career, talks to his squad and waits. Then he talks again, getting information from Nimrod and passing back information from our end. "Doron got hit." He lets out a breath and shakes his head. "This isn't good."

"Where's Nimrod?"

"Near the other team's headquarters, where Ori is being held. Come on," he says. "Crawl on your stomach to the big rock over there. Stay low."

I follow Avi to the big rock, my knees scraping the desert floor and my monoboob pressed to the ground. I don't complain, but look on the bright side of being caught in the middle of war games: I'm with Avi.

I wished on the shooting star, and my wish came true. Next time I should specify for it not to be while he's in the middle of war games, but whatever. Being *with* Avi is better than the alternative, any day.

Avi is listening to instructions from Nimrod. He motions

me forward, so we're side by side. "Udi is covering Nimrod so he can rescue the hostage. I told them they needed a second cover man, but Nimrod ordered me to stay put."

"You think they can do it?"

"Yeah. But it's risky with us being outnumbered." Avi pulls out his binoculars and surveys the situation.

"Can you see them?"

"No. They're out of sight range."

"What happens if they're caught?"

He looks at me and shrugs. "Then it's just us."

I hear the pop-pop-pop of gunfire. Avi curses again. "Nimrod's down. Udi's captured. The other team ambushed them. Nimrod and Udi got two down before getting hit. It's just you and me," he says. "I probably don't have to tell you the odds aren't in our favor."

I'm to blame for Avi's team dying and/or being captured, one by one, as soon as I arrived. "Are you giving up?" I ask him.

"No."

"Because I have a plan."

"I do, too. It involves me opening fire when they start shooting at us. The other team knows me, and they know I'm not going down without a fight."

"I have a better plan. One that might give us the advantage."

"Let's hear it," he says, gesturing for me to share my idea.

"You'll really listen to my suggestion?"

"Of course. My girlfriend might be an American princess, and gets herself into ridiculous situations all the time ... but she's no dummy."

I straighten my back and hold my head high, ready to reveal my perfect plan. "Avi, take off your clothes."

28

With an M16 retrofitted paintball machine gun in my hand and Avi's clothes on my body, I head into enemy territory. The mask is too big, the shirt is flimsy except in the boob area, and the pants are about to fall off, but I manage to look enough like Avi maneuvering through the rocks.

My heart is racing wildly, because I know it's just a matter of time until they realize I've got boobs and not muscular pecs. While my boyfriend is slinking around the other side in his undies, with black paint on his body (my artwork, thanks to the small container of face paint he had in his vest) and his own paintball gun, I'm the decoy.

Avi gave me specific instructions to surrender so I don't get hit. They won't fire unless fired upon. Although I know and they know that Avi would never go down without a fight.

I run from one rock to another just like Avi told me to. (Imagine one of those ducks going back and forth in a carnival shooting game.) I'm still a bit shocked he agreed to my plan, but it just goes to show that a great leader like Avi knows how to listen as well as lead. I admit it took a little coaxing from me. At first he wasn't into letting me become the target. But when I assured him I'd be okay, and that we were in this together, he finally relented.

He said to count to ten and then hold my hands over my head to surrender. But as two of the opposing team members move closer to me, cornering me on both sides, I start to panic. They're too far away to make out that it's me, but I desperately want Avi to have time to rescue the hostages from his squad and fix this botched exercise. I have to help him, even if it means opening fire to kill the enemy. I wouldn't shoot anyone in real life, because even after all of this training, I'm still totally for peace and happiness and rainbows and sushi.

But this is paintball. And I'm taking no prisoners.

I turn my gun on *auto* and shoot.

Pop! Pop! Pop! Pop!

Little paint balls are flying ferociously out of my gun. Since it's dark, I have no clue what I'm shooting, and hope I'm hitting at least some part of the enemy squad. I'm Rambo and GI Jane all wrapped into one.

Something hard whacks my back and thigh. "Ouch!" I scream. "That hurt!"

I look down at my thigh and realize I've been hit.
By a paintball.
I'm officially dead. I think.

29

I'll have you know I took down two guys before I was
paintballed to death. My idea actually worked. During the
shootout, Avi was able to rescue Udi and Ori. They captured
the last guy on the other team and we were victorious.

That's the good news.

The bad news (besides the paintball-sized welts I have
on my thigh and stomach) is that I'm waiting in a large military tent, with Avi sitting on the chair next to me, about
to be debriefed on how I got into the war games in the first
place. At least they let us change back into our own clothes.

The guy who's in charge of the war games isn't Sergeant B-S. It's this other guy, with a bunch of stripes on
the side of his sleeve, who happens to be sitting at a table

opposite us in the tent. He's dark-skinned, bald, and does not look happy.

I don't know his rank, but he's high up there.

Considering I'm zero rank, I can't be demoted. But Avi can. And even though he personally had nothing to do with me wandering into the war games, he ended up being an accomplice.

When Sergeant B-S files into the tent, his stern eyes focus on me. This is not good. It's the same look my dad gave me when he found out I'd taken his credit card and signed him up for an online Jewish dating service.

"How did you get here?" he asks me. The bald guy with the high rank stands next to him.

I clear my throat and will myself to stay strong and positive. With Avi beside me, I get an inner strength. "I kind of wandered away from our campsite to find a place to relieve myself."

I know that telling them the entire truth—that I also wanted to say goodbye to Avi—wouldn't go over too well. I decide to play the confused American girl. I know, I know, I'm not doing my country any favors by playing dumb. But my friend Kayleigh from Georgia totally uses her southern accent to get what she wants. And this girl Renee at my school—she's super-smart and super-blond—plays the dumb blond so that guys give her attention and come to her rescue even if she doesn't need rescuing.

Who says I can't play the game for my and Avi's benefit? They don't call it war *games* for nothing.

"I got lost," I lie. "So I followed noises, hoping it would lead me back to the campsite."

Sergeant B-S huffs at my explanation and definitely looks skeptical. "Gefen," he says, staring solidly at Avi. "Why did she have a paintball gun in her possession?"

Avi quickly glances at me, then looks at the sergeant and the bald guy. "After I found her wandering on the rocks, and realized I couldn't take her back without revealing my location to the enemy when we were already down by two men, I recruited her."

"*Recruited* her? Instead of *protected* her? She's a civilian. That was bad judgment, Gefen," the bald guy pipes in. "What right did you have to *recruit* her?"

"I was team leader. I made the decision based on my professional opinion of her abilities."

The bald guy crosses his arms over his chest. "You've got to be kidding me."

I raise my hand tentatively.

"What?" he barks at me, just as the rest of Avi's squad enters the tent.

"Sir, I might not be Israeli, but my father is. He was a commando. And my boyfriend is a Sayeret Tzefa trainee. I'm trained in Krav Maga and I've just spent time in boot camp."

"She's a good soldier," Nimrod says from behind Sergeant B-S. "If it weren't for her being a decoy, our squad would have lost. Avi made the right decision."

"*Ze nachon*—it's true," Ori says.

Nimrod shrugs. "It was quick thinking on Avi's part. And Amy's, too. Protecting someone unarmed would have put him at a further disadvantage, so he gave her the means to protect herself."

Sergeant B-S turns to Avi's current superior. "Commander, what's your assessment?"

The bald commander stares at Avi and me. "I think Gefen should be reprimanded for not following procedure. And commended for his quick thinking."

"Does that mean he's not in trouble?" I ask hopefully.

"That means he gets the pleasure of running extra kilometers every day for the next week," the commander says.

"Don't think *you're* free and clear of this mess, Ms. Nelson-Barak," Sergeant B-S tells me. "I'm thinking of assigning you permanent kitchen duty until you leave."

Ugh. Not again. Picking bees out of jam, brushing ants off bread. *Amy, look on the bright side,* I tell myself. Well, at least I'm not going to be eating any more Loof. Next to Loof, the food back on base is an absolute delicacy. How's that for positivity?

"Move out, everyone," Sergeant B-S calls out. "You've got a few hours to sleep before wakeup." He then tells me that Liron is waiting for us in a military jeep to drive us back to the campsite.

I look over at Avi, and a wave of sadness washes over me. What if I don't see him for another year?

"I'll give you five minutes, Gefen." Sergeant B-S points to Nimrod. "Stay here as chaperone."

Nimrod nods, then when everyone leaves the tent besides the three of us, Nimrod turns around and gives us what little privacy he can.

Avi takes me in his arms and holds me close.

A lump forms in my throat and tears well in my eyes. I can't keep the first tear from falling. Avi holds my face in his hands and swipes the tear away.

"Tell her you love her already," Nimrod says, his back still to us.

"She already knows I do," Avi says.

"Girls like to be told."

"How would you know?" Avi shoots back.

Nimrod shrugs. "I don't. I'm guessing."

Avi leans down and kisses me, his lips warm and gentle. I pull him closer, not wanting to let him go.

When Nimrod coughs out a one-minute warning, Avi pulls back. We're both breathless. "Be good and stay out of trouble," he tells me.

"It's me you're talking to, Avi."

He smiles. "Yeah, I know. Forget what I said. Be spontaneous. It's what makes you special. I love that about you."

"I have a new motto in life. Wanna know what it is?"

"Yeah."

"Everything in the end is going to be *sababa*. You and me, my mom's new baby, my dad and Marla ... even Jessica and Tarik."

"You want to know my new motto, Amy?"

"Yeah."

"Gefen, I hate to break up this *sababa* party," Nimrod says. "But time's up. Your girlfriend's got to go." He puts his hands up in mock surrender. "Sergeant's orders."

"Go," Avi whispers in my ear. "Before I'm tempted to go with you."

"Wait," I say, as Sergeant B-S bellows my name and orders me out of the tent. "What's your motto?"

Avi winks at me. "Look in your pockets when you get back tonight."

I hop in the back of the jeep Liron is driving. Sergeant B-S is sitting in the front seat next to her. I'm frantically searching for whatever Avi left for me in one of my pockets. I reach in and pull out a piece of crumpled paper. When I open it, Avi's Sayeret Tzefa medallion drops into my hand. I remember the words he said were etched on it: *Respect, Strength,* and *Honor.*

Back at the campground, I take my headlight under my sleeping bag and examine the medallion. The paper the medallion was wrapped in has handwritten words on it: it's a note from Avi. Tears come to my eyes as I read the words over and over…

> *You'll always hold a part of me, Amy, whether we're together or not. Love, Avi*

When I fall asleep that night, with the medallion in one hand and George II in the other, I know that even if Avi and I aren't together physically, nothing can keep us apart ever again. Well, except my dad … especially after he finds out Avi and I stayed at a hotel alone. Dodging that bullet will prove harder than dodging those paintballs.

This adventure called my life is never dull, that's for sure!

About the Author

Simone Elkeles was born and raised in the Chicago area. She has a bachelor's degree in psychology from the University of Illinois and a master's degree in Industrial Relations from Loyola University–Chicago. She was president and CEO of her own manufacturing company before selling it in 1999 to stay home with her children. Simone started writing young adult and historical fiction novels while raising her kids and has earned numerous writing awards for her work. She strives to write emotional stories that touch the lives of her readers.

Simone loves to hear from her readers! Contact her through her website at www.simoneelkeles.com.

Also by

SIMONE ELKELES

Leaving Paradise   *Return to Paradise*

Now available from